PRESIDENTS
IMAGINARY MOMENTS IN THE
LIVES OF AMERICA'S GREAT

PRESIDENTS
IMAGINARY MOMENTS IN THE
LIVES OF AMERICA'S GREAT

THEODORE ROSCOE

PRIMARY ILLUSTRATORS
SAMUEL CAHAN
MARSHALL FRANZ

COVER BY
V. E. PYLES

POPULAR PUBLICATIONS · 2025

TABLE OF CONTENTS

THE MAN WHO WOULDN'T BE KING

Perhaps you didn't know that George Washington was offered a crown, that he could have been as unqualifiedly ruler of the United States as George III was of Great Britain. But he refused. No one knows how he made the decision, but it might have gone something like this...

1

DID YOU EVER hear about that fiasco in the Caribbean called the "War of Jenkins' Ear?" Do you know who was our wealthiest President? Do you know which President's birthday is celebrated eleven days after he was born; which President accepted no salary while in office; which President was dead for five days before Congress learned about it; which President got into a lot of trouble with the authorities up in Harlem; and the President whose false teeth were exhibited at the Chicago Fair?

Well, the answers to those questions do not concern this story except to illustrate the difference between a historical fact and a story that is apocryphal.

There *was* a War of Jenkins' Ear. Probably you missed it in your schoolbooks, but it happened. 1739 to 1741.

This Jenkins was a sea captain; ran a commercial sailing vessel between Jamaica and other Caribbean islands. England and Spain were squabbling over colonial rights, and one day Jenkins turned up in England with his ear in his hand. Literally.

It was dried and brown as a fig and, dangling from his fingers instead of jutting from his head, it couldn't hear a thing. The British Parliament heard some things, though. Jenkins waved his ear in front of the House of Commons and told them a Spanish sea captain had cut it off over there in the West Indies. If Chamberlain had been prime minis-

ter probably Jenkins would have been given an ear-trumpet and told to make the best of it; but Walpole declared war.

An expedition was recruited in the American Colonies and sent to beat up the Spanish at Cartagena down near Panama.

That's historical fact. So is the fact that Lawrence Washington was a leader of the American-recruited expedition. So is the fact that the Spaniards retired to a fortress at the top of a cliff, and leaned their elbows on the parapets and grinned down at the little American fleet in the bay and waited for the American expeditionary force to die of fever. So is the fact that most of the Americans did.

That Jenkins had really lost his ear in a fight in a British prison, and that the British politicians thought to use the ear as anti-Spanish propaganda, is a story, believed by many historians. But it has never been authenticated, never been proved. It is apocryphal.

Now Lawrence Washington had a younger half-brother who wanted to go on the expedition. Had he gone, he might have died of fever with the others. Then he wouldn't have been our wealthiest president. He wouldn't have worked at the hardest job in America for nothing. He wouldn't have been dead five days before the news reached Congress.

His birthday wouldn't have been celebrated, because he wouldn't have lived long enough to be celebrated. His false teeth wouldn't have been on exhibition at the Chicago Fair, and very possibly there wouldn't have been a Chicago to hold a Fair.

No, had the boy gone down there to help punish the Spaniards for cutting off Jenkins' ear, it is highly probable that his life might have been cut off by yellow fever. Then there wouldn't have been any stories about him, apocryphal or otherwise.

His name was George.

THERE IS A story around that when he was a nipper his father had a cherry tree, and—but you know it by heart. You heard it at a party on the twenty-second of February when you were a small boy—a party where you ate ice cream and waved a cardboard hatchet. It is a nice story, written by a benevolent old gentleman named Parson Weems, but there is reason to suspect that the parson's enthusiasm for Truth, and his desire to emphasize a Moral for the Young, led him to stretch the subject just a little; therefore, the story is apocryphal.

There is another story that Washington threw a dollar across the Delaware. But there is considerable doubt about that, because Washington was always pretty careful of his accounts, and who'd he be throwing a dollar to, anyway? That is apocryphal, too.

Now then, somebody will say this is an effort to belittle a great national hero. Don't you believe it!

The people who need tin gods for heroes are people who never quite got over their childhood. They don't wish to think of men like Washington and Lincoln as humans like themselves. That would give them inferiority complexes. They'd begin to ask themselves why they, themselves, didn't amount to something important.

No, it's better to think, of all great men as more or less gods. You can worship a tin god, but you' aren't expected to be one. Of course to be a tin god a man has to be perfect, and when someone is perfect, you don't have to compete because *you* are only human. That lets you out nicely.

Let George do it.

But George Washington wasn't any tin god. He was a human being who had trouble with his dentist, and chilblains at Valley Forge, and arguments with the gardener, and insulting letters from politicians. As a general he lost his share of battles; as a gentleman he liked a good glass of wine and was apt to preen a little in a new suit of clothes; and if there'd been scandal-mongers on the radio in those days, they'd probably have gossiped about him.

It was just this element of humanity that made him the greater man—a tin god doesn't have to rise above a toothache and win debates in Congress when he'd rather sit down on account of his corns—you can't tempt a tin god.

Besides, we're only trying to establish the difference between historical fact and a story that's apocryphal. Washington fought a losing Revolutionary battle against the British in Harlem—that's fact. But the following story is apocryphal....

2

GEORGE WASHINGTON WAS pretty tired (a lot more tired than a tin god could ever be) and he was weary and disgusted, too. He'd just had a long ride back to Mount Vernon, and the roads had been bad with wet snow; and his new suit was soaked; and his boots were muddy; and his feet, which had never quite forgotten Valley Forge, were hurting; and he had a lot of things on his mind.

He was hungry, too, and he remembered, as he galloped up to the house, that for some reason or other there was to be a late dinner tonight.

He was a little gruff with the stable boy, and as he stamped into the hall and flung off his wet cape, he wouldn't let Black Tom take the leather saddlebag out of his hand, and sent the rascal off for a bottle of Madiera.

This wet snow might give him a touch of the malaria he'd picked up as a lad in Barbadoes—why the devil had he gone there, anyway?—or anywhere? Times like tonight he wished he had spent his life right here in this pleasant plantation house in Virginia. Man ought to have enough sense to stay home.

Martha came in from the music room, looking beautiful as always; he kissed her rather austerely and said he was glad to be back. But he was in a hurry to get upstairs to his

room, and expressed the hope that there wouldn't be any
guests for dinner.

Martha Washington gave him a frowny little smile, and
asked him if he had forgotten what day it was.

"Day? Day? Eh—why, Tuesday, of course. Six days from
Philadelphia, and on my word; the foulest weather since
the New Jersey campaign. Dinner at ten, didn't you say in
your letter? I will be in my room, then. Please instruct the
servants I do not wish to be disturbed."

She watched him up the white staircase, smiling and
sighing and shaking her head. Ha! what a man. So many
duties to weary him; so much to distract him on his mind.
She wondered what important documents of state he had
stuffed in that saddlebag, and she hoped he'd have time
for a nap before the dinner—such a delight of Southern
cooking—was to be served.

"Tuesday, indeed!" said Martha Washington to herself;
then gave a little laugh, and hurried into the dining room
to count the plates.

George Washington stamped into his room and tossed
off his tricorne hat, discarded his damp wig, flung the
saddlebag onto his writing table and dropped into a chair
before the fireplace, grunting.

He stared a while at the crackling backlog, thinking of
next to nothing, hardly aware that Tom had come in with
the wine and yanked off his painful boots.

Presently he was bathed and shaved and comfortable in
slippers and fresh linen drawers and dressing gown. Tom
went out, softly closing the door, and then George Washington took out his false teeth made of rhinoceros bone,
they were, and they hurt like Goshen, and that scoun-

drelly French dentist in New York had charged an infernal fortune—General Washington took out his teeth and dropped them in a glass of water, and puckered his mouth, and drank a draught of Madeira, and felt better.

In the chair before the fireplace, he closed his eyes and tried to relax. But when he closed his eyes he could see the road unwinding on the underside of his eyelids.

By heaven, he knew every mile of that Philadelphia turnpike—in wet snow, it was vicious—he hoped he'd never have to ride it again. His head was achy and his joints felt stiff, and it was just good to sit there in front of the fire and be home.

No, he wasn't as young as he'd been when he could stand up to his belt in a creek of ice-water, out surveyin'. Nothing like the athlete who'd let the colonials in the French and Indian War (that fool General Braddock!) or the horsemen

And the Father of His Country
gaped helplessly at that parade
of phantoms in the snow

who'd sat in saddle days at a time, riding all over Hell'an gone trying to find the British.

He stretched his hands to the fire, wiggling a stiff thumb. The wine warmed his stomach, and the fire was a blessing.

It was a charming room of white panels and candle-light—snow fell in white curtains at the window-glass—there was a fragrance of furniture polish and pine cones burning on the hearth. The fourposter bed with its patch-work quilts and eiderdown pillow was like a corner of heaven.

The general shook his head at the bed. It wouldn't do to lie down. Never wake up in time to dress for dinner. Too much to think about, meantime. He consulted the great silver watch he'd left with his teeth on the dresser. Seven-fifteen, and dinner would be, for some reason he couldn't imagine, at ten.

Just two hours and forty-five minutes to think some-thing out. Two hours and forty-five minutes to make the hardest decision in his life. Two hours and forty-five minutes—he eyed the saddlebag pensively—to decide American History.

HE DIDN'T FEEL like deciding American History, either. As a matter of fact, he was sick and tired of American History. For the last twenty years he'd been up to his neck in the subject, and it seemed as if all the tough decisions had been left up to him.

Not that he minded making decisions. He could take responsibility as well as the next man, and a whole lot better than most. All his life he'd had to make decisions. Some-times he made them, snap!—sometimes he'd pondered a little too long, as that time when Howe almost trapped him in Harlem and he escaped with the army to White Plains only by the skin of his teeth (that had been pretty close, remembering he didn't have any teeth). Generally he decided right; and when he made up his mind, he stuck to his guns.

Yes, all his life they'd said, "Let George do it." And he'd done it. Willingly. For his country. Yet, the minute he'd done it, they'd begun to criticize.

Take the army. They'd asked him to be General-in-chief. John Adams had asked him personally. They'd given him a vote of confidence. The Continental Congress had commissioned him.

Minute he accepted the command, they'd started to jump on him. The New Englanders wanted him to defend Boston. The Virginians wanted him to bring the troops to Virginia. Maybe he'd made a mistake about the strategic importance of the Hudson River—he knew, now, he should've had more cavalry and less artillery—he shouldn't have wasted a lot of time trying to defend New York City—but hindsight was always easier than foresight, and he'd had to fight the British somewhere.

He'd fought 'em, too. Beat 'em, finally. But he could've done it a lot quicker, maybe, if there hadn't been too many cooks with their spoons in the broth.

Take the government. They'd elected him President by unanimous vote. "Let George do it," they'd said again. And now it was worse than the army had been—they asked him to make the decisions, and when he made them, he was in hotter water than ever.

John Adams was jealous of him, and Jefferson tried to scotch half the things he did. He appointed a cabinet, and five hundred people wrote to tell him the appointments were wrong.

Hamilton couldn't get along with Jefferson, Henry Knox sided with Hamilton, Randolph sided with Jefferson—a cabinet meeting became an endless wrangle—Congress argued like a bunch of sparrows—the public carped, whichever side won; and whatever happened, he was going to get the blame.

He didn't mind blame—it was part of the responsibility—he had to expect it, the same as he had to take snubs from his old friend George Mason, and those scurrilous writings of Thomas Paine who wrote that open letter that said the administration was deceitful and perfidious, practically accused the President of fraud.

And there was that whipper-snapper grandson of Ben Franklin's who wrote those editorials calling him treacherous and inefficient. And that pamphlet by William Duane—he could see it in his mind's eye now—claiming that if Braddock had promoted him during the French and Indian War, he, Washington, would have fought with the British instead of against them in 1776.

WHY THE DEVIL did people elect a man President, and then, as soon as he took office, begin to slander him? Why, if he wanted to pin down these slanderers, he'd be in the law courts for the next two thousand years.

They accused him of manipulating the bank, of grafting in real estate, of double-dealing in trade. Even his personal life was under fire from their miserable tongues. They said he maltreated his slaves—that he'd married money—that he was parsimonious with his poor old mother.

This vicious campaign of whispering was worse than the

British propaganda at the start of the War when the Tories forged those love letters calculated to ruin his reputation.

George Washington got all worked up, thinking about the slanders he'd been subjected to. (This story is fiction, but those slanders are historical fact). But the main thing that bothered him was that he couldn't get things done. They'd said, "Let George do it." They'd elected him President to do it. But now, they seemed determined not to let him do anything. They asked him to make the decisions. All right. He decided.

Then nothing was done.

And so many things in this big, new, sprawling, turbulent, unformed, wilderness-bordered country needed doing. The roads had to be fixed, new turnpikes built. The frontier needed forts. The Indians had to be handled. There ought to be a good sound banking system, and a regular army, and a system for distributing the mails.

The courts ought to be better established; there ought to be a sounder enforcement of Law; the States should quit bickering and get together; some kind of tariff should protect American goods. Taxes had to be collected regularly and levied with fairness, so there couldn't be any more Whisky Rebellions like the row in Pennsylvania.

The veterans had to be decently compensated to keep quiet such rascals as that malcontent Shays, up in Boston. There was the merchant marine to be built up; there ought to be a navy to do something about those pirates in the West Indies and Mediterranean; foresighted men should plan inland canals.

The European situation was ticklish as anything, and American dangerously located what with the colonies of France, Spain and England surrounding the Thirteen States on all sides. The Dutch and French loans had to be somehow paid back. Somebody had to do something about these highwaymen roaming the American roads; about building a new capitol, preferably on the Potomac; about the politics of Rhode Island; about cementing the people into a solid country, a real nation. And sooner or later someone would have to settle the tragic problem of the slaves.

AND CONGRESS BICKERED. Congress haggled. Congress debated and sidestepped and stalled. All these things that needed doing were urgent as the devil, and Congress sat around that draughty hall in Philadelphia and argued and harangued and fiddled as if there was all the time in creation.

There wasn't any time to lose. On the frontier the Indians were raising hob. Foreign creditors were pressing for payments. America was on the verge of bankruptcy. The international situation was a powder keg. The new little Union was as shaky as an eaglet in a nest on the edge of a cliff, and just at a time when all good Americans should be pulling together, the government was at sixes and sevens.

You tried to push through a bill to stabilize the currency, and it was blocked by some shortsighted fellow like James Madison. You asked for a canal in Pennsylvania, and the delegates from Massachusetts voted it down because they wanted a canal there first.

Important bills were shelved by pettifogging argufiers. Issues were lost under clouds of rancorous words.

Each politician had his own axe to grind; personal passions ran riot over things that should have been accomplished for the general good; the people cried for this and that in a million demanding voices—everybody in America wanted something in a hurry—and everywhere there were cross-purposes, quarrels, delays.

George Washington muttered an oath, glaring at the fire.

It wasn't that all those fellows were grafters or selfish demagogues, either. Nobody could say Jefferson and Madison and Adams weren't sincere. Nobody could doubt their honesty and patriotism. Congress was an honor roll of patriots—hardly a man who hadn't risked his life and fortune in defiance of British rule. Why, some day those men would be named in history books as the heroes of the American Revolution. Their signatures were on the Declaration of Independence; they had framed the Constitution.

And now?

And now, having licked the British, they were fighting among themselves. Having freed American from tyranny, they didn't know what to do with it; they couldn't get together on how to run it; each wanted the nation built to his own specifications. They were like a thousand carpenters working desperately to erect a house on a thousand different plans—knocking each other off the scaffolds—squabbling about the foundations—stopping to argue on the ladders.

Some wanted a house of brick; others demanded lumber and plaster. One wall was made of pine, another of limestone; the roof hung unsupported; workmen ran about in all different directions; the voices rose like those about the Tower of Babel—and like the Tower of Babel, the edifice threatened to tumble down.

"A house," George Washington thought grimly, "divided against itself cannot stand."

They'd elected him foreman—made him overseer—but they wouldn't agree to his plans. America, Land of Liberty—this fine new house!—it ought to be built of granite, instead of jerrybuilt on sand.

George Washington told himself he was sick to death of all the argufying, wrangling and delays. He wanted to see America built; wanted to get things done. Think of what would've happened to his plantation if he'd run it as these muddlers and inefficient fiddlers were running the Union. Think of what would've happened during the War, if every move he made had been argued over, delayed and shelved.

General Washington stood stiffly to his feet. He had an hour and a half to make up his mind. It was probably the biggest decision he'd ever had to make. Stalking to his writing desk, he opened the weather-stained saddle-bag; fished out a letter.

General—the letter said—*We want you to wear this. You Know Who.*

Washington tightened his lips. That colonel in the veteran's Society of the Cincinnati was a reckless chap, but—

"There's no harm in looking at it, by gad!"

George Washington reached into the saddlebag and took out a parcel wrapped up like six pounds of sausage. He looked hastily around his room; made sure the door was latched.

Then he unwrapped the parcel and held up in the candlelight something that flashed and shone and glittered in his hands like a chunk cut out of the sun. It was a crown—a golden, gem-encrusted crown!

3

WELL, YOU CAN'T blame George Washington for indulging in a gasp of admiration. He liked fine things, and that crown was a beauty. It was as big and round as a Christmas pudding, and as heavy as lead; the golden brim shone like fresh butter; it was lined with fine blue velvet, and the top was all sprinkled over with emeralds, pearls, rubies and diamonds thick as candies in a cake.

In the candlelight the gems sparkled and twinkled and blazed in George Washington's eyes. My, what a flare! At the peak of the crown there was a Maltese cross like the decoration on the dome of a palace—a gadget of blazing jewels that took George Washington's breath away.

The General's hands began to tremble just as yours or mine would tremble at holding such a fabulous present. Maybe a little more, for if you or I were presented with a crown, we'd know it was a dream, but George Washington knew that crown in his hands was real.

There'd been considerable talk of it in certain quarters. At the Inauguration in New York City a number of people had called him "Highness", and it was not uncommon for countryfolk and backwoodsmen and people at roadside inns to address him as "Your Majesty."

Those facts ran through George Washington's mind (they really happened, although this story didn't) as he stood there blinking at the marvelous treasure he had unwrapped.

You can see him turning that crown from side to side; perhaps counting the jewels (for he was always a careful man); weighing the thing in his hand.

As he turned it in his fingers, the gems flashed and sparkled and sent sprinkles of colored light around the charming colonial bedroom. There were two or three dozen rubies, and a couple of hundred pearls, and forty-eight emeralds, and eighty-six diamonds in that bauble on the peak. George Washington guessed it weighed about sixty pounds, which was thirty pounds up on the crown of the Czar of Russia; and he judged its value on the jewel market at about a quarter of a million dollars.

He forgot that his gums were aching and the plaguey crick in his thumb; and he said "Ha!" and "Ah!", as what man wouldn't?

Sixty pounds in gold and a quarter million dollars in gems was a lot of money, and all Americans had a hankering for money (ask any European), even George Washington. He was fond of good clothes and expensive adornment, and that crown was the most expensive piece of adornment that had ever been in the States. In fact, there'd never been anything like it in America before.

Next thing he knew, the General had that crown on his head. That's nothing—you do the same when somebody gives you a new hat. Try it on. George Washington wasn't so much different from us ordinary Americans. He wanted to see if that thing fit his head.

And it fit him fine.

It might have been made at the goldsmith's to his

measure. It was comfortable, too. The gems shimmered in all the colors of the rainbow, and the gold filigree blazed like a bonfire. Standing before the mirror of his dressing table, George Washington had to admit it was macaroni. That doesn't mean Italian macaroni; it's early American slang from the days of *Yankee Doodle*, and it means pretty swell.

George Washington couldn't help thinking that that crown on his head looked pretty swell.

No sir, he just had to preen a little. That dazzling, velvet-lined caubeen of gold and flashing gems was a mighty fine article of headgear. Even in his bathrobe and linen drawers, and with his teeth out, George Washington cut a figure. He was six-foot-two in his stocking feet—chin high above the crowd at any time—and that bonanza on his head set him up tremendously.

"By Gad, sir, that is a crown!"

You bet it was. The General struck an attitude, and that headpiece made him seem about ten feet tall.

He wheeled sideways to get a focus on himself in profile. Then he worked up one of the postures that Gilbert Stuart had liked to paint him in—hand in bosom—features thoughtfully stern—and with that crown aloft, his portrait in the mirror was devilish important and impressive.

It looked even better when he snapped in his spring-hinged teeth and pinned on a fresh linen jabot and thrust his hand under the jabot.

Wheeling and posing before the mirror, he caught his picture at all angles, and the more he saw of himself in that crown, the better he fancied the picture. He tried it at a slant; he tried it square on his head with the brim down about his ears; he adjusted it this way and that, giving it a jaunty tap the way a modern Brummel taps his topper. No matter how he wore it, it looked macaroni.

He thought of the other headpieces he had worn—the coonskin cap when he'd been a surveyor—the flatbrim he'd worn when he courted Martha Custis—the General's hat with its red-white-and-blue cockade—the sweat-stained tricorne he wore as President. This crown was certainly an advance in headgear. He wondered what the boys in his lodge would think if he walked in wearing it. If the men of his old regiment could see him now! Jehu, what Gilbert Stuart couldn't do with a blazer like this!

And Jefferson. John Adams. Madison. He could just imagine their eyes.

He couldn't accept it, of course....

Still, they were offering it to him; there were those who wanted him to wear it. All those veteran officers in the Society of the Cincinnati who wanted to establish a nobility, and that camarilla that felt a monarchy was the only way to get things done.

YOU CAN SEE George Washington weighing that crown in his mind. It's hard to know exactly what he thought, but you can bet that under the circumstances he began to think about that dilatory, long-winded batch of bickerers in Congress. About the endless wrangles between Jefferson and Hamilton in his cabinet. About the stupidity and general incompetence of the voting public. About the country's crying-need for action, and the government all at sevens and sixes; all the urgent things that ought to be done quickly and weren't being done at all.

He began to wonder about Democracy.

Do you think George Washington didn't have his doubts about Democracy? Remember, it had never been really tried before; it was a brand new formula for running a country, and from the first there'd been plenty of patriots who thought it wouldn't work.

Nobody in Europe believed it was going to pan out, and all the monarchies sat around sneering behind their hands, waiting for the little Republic to collapse, ready to jump on America like a pack of hungry wolves. George Washington wanted his country to be free of Europe. But to be free you had to be strong. To be strong you had to have a unified nation, a strong government.

But how strong should the government be; how much freedom should the people have? Could you ever have a government when men sat around bickering under the Liberty Bell all day long and never got anything done?

George Washington's thoughts probably went like that, and you can see him beginning to pace.

It was a tough problem, this problem of Democracy— men's minds had been struggling with it for five thousand years. George Washington had to decide it in an hour, and you can see the muscles wrestling on his forehead. Did the people know enough to run a Republic? Would they have ever enough education? Would politicians ever bury their personal axes for the common good? Certainly Congress wasn't getting anywhere.

Gad! all a monarch had to do was flourish a scepter, and the job was under way.

Think of all the roads you could build, the canals you could dig, the forts you could put up, the treaties you could order drawn? Wouldn't it put an end to delays, arguments, shilly-shallying? A king didn't have to take back-talk. You ordered the currency stabilized, and it was stabilized. If you wanted to fire your Secretary of State, you merely said, "You're fired!"

Congress would jump when you spoke from a throne. Everybody would jump. These sovereigns in Europe got action. Ha! and wouldn't those triple-tongued diplomats and sly ambassadors look up! How the public would look up, too! By heaven! it would put an end to those slander-ous editorials and scurrilous politicians' lies. It would put an end to crooked elections and the dangers of being ruled by a rabble.

Think of the efficiency! Think of the advantages, the absolute law and order! Think of what you could accom-plish! An autocratic state—that was the way to get action in a country. And Martha—!

WHY, MARTHA WOULD be a queen! Those society gadabouts like Mrs. Bingham would have to take a back seat, then. Imagine Martha on the throne at his side in a robe of ermine with a diamond coronet! And he would be king—first ruler of America!—founder of a dynasty!—monarch of all he had surveyed! A *king*, by heaven! One of the great, historical figures of the world's history!

Talk about the chance of a lifetime! Well, without quite knowing how he did it, there was George Washington standing in front of that mirror with a satin bed quilt wrapped around him for a robe, a silver candlestick for a scepter in his hand, and that great crown blazing on his head—sovereign for the history books—a monarch for America—a king if you ever saw one!

And in just another tick the whole history of our country

might have been different—for when George Washington made a decision, he made a decision—if something hadn't happened; something that isn't in your history book, either.

There was George posed for portrait of a king in front of that mirror. There was Martha downstairs, perhaps making candy. The whole house was quiet with that hush of a stately mansion enveloped in a flaky snowstorm. And then, clear and penetrating, from the night outside and right under the bedroom window, there sounded a low, eerie whistle.

4

THERE WAS SOMETHING furtive about that whistle—
something signally and furtive, like a redskin imitating a
birdcall—and George Washington, who hadn't forgotten
his woodsmanship, got over to that window in a hurry.

He snuffed out the candles on the way, and he ducked up
to the sill and pulled aside the curtains an inch, and peeped
out and down, his body pulled back from the window
frame so anyone on the ground below couldn't see him.

There was someone down there, too.

What with the darkness and the drifty snowfall, it was
hard to see, but a haze of yellow candlelight came from the
windows of the dining room down below, and there was a
blurred, snow-powdered figure moving along the side of
the house like a shadow. As the General glared down, the
figure turned and beckoned toward someone following
from around near the front veranda.

Again there sounded that furtive, signally whistle-call.

George Washington said, "By God!" He didn't often
permit himself to swear, but that prowler down there
under his bedroom window took him back to his old Indi-
an-fighting days.

He reached to the table behind him and found his
silver-handled horsepistol, and gritted his teeth while he
drew a bead on the shadowy figure down beneath. There

hadn't been any redskin raiders in this part of Virginia for a hundred years, but you never could tell about those savages.

That skulker down there was an Indian, certainly. Its blanket was pulled up over its head, and it was sneaking along in a way to curl your periwig. There were others behind it, too. Somewhere out on the road.

George Washington could hear a ghostly stomping of horses; a muted murmur of voices muffled by night and snow.

Tensely the General took aim; the creeping figure was almost under the window; George Washington's finger tightened on the trigger. And then, as that prowler down below sneaked into the wash of light which came mellow from the dining room, George Washington froze.

"Well, I'll be damned!"

It wasn't an Indian. Listen! Just as that footpad came into the patch of windowlight it paused to lower the blanket and peer around; and George Washington found himself looking down at a man's bald head.

The only bald-headed Indians he'd ever seen before were scalped Indians, and that man down there in the snow was not a redskin. What George Washington had mistaken for a blanket was a robe—a robe as white as a bedsheet. The General's face went even whiter, for he recognized the style of that robe, and it wasn't a bedsheet, either, but a Roman toga!

Yes, sir, that figure down there at the side of the house wore a Roman toga. And that wasn't all.

It made a step forward, and George Washington caught a glimpse of what looked like Latin sandals. There was a wreath of laurel leaves circling that bald head. Up there in his bedroom George Washington like to've fallen down. That figure down below pulled the toga up over its head to shield its bald-spot from the snow; covered its face with an arm, and went sneaking off into the darkness toward the mansion's rear.

As it passed out of sight, there was a cry of wind under the eaves, and that wintry breath seemed to come through the upper window and go right through George Washington. Following that, retreating figure with his eyes, George Washington had seen the dark crimson blood-stain on its back. Whew! that toga was splashed all with red between the shoulder-blades. George Washington didn't have to consult his schoolbooks to remember who that figure was!

"Great Caesar's ghost!"

THE GENERAL DARN near swallowed his teeth as he gulped that out. Julius Caesar! Surely he must've been dreaming. Nobody was going to tell him he'd seen an emperor from ancient Rome down there under his bedroom window. Julius Caesar, who was assassinated in 44 B.C.! Julius Caesar in Mount Vernon, Virginia, prowling around an American colonial mansion at ten o'clock at night in a snowstorm!

George Washington steadied himself at the window frame and passed a hand across his forehead. It must have been the wine. The room was too warm, and he'd had a spot too much of Madeira.

That had to be it.

But just as he'd satisfied himself about that, he glimpsed another figure coming. It was moving up from around the front veranda, skirting the snow-wigged shrubs and scouting along the side of the house in the tracks of that first apparition.

George Washington froze behind the curtains, and the horse pistol shook in his hand.

Another spook. A great, fat-bellied one that came thefting along on tiptoe, holding up the skirts of its robe to keep clear of the drifts. Another Roman! Snow gusted around the creature's head, and George Washington only had a glimpse of the face.

But he knew that painted, distorted countenance with its high-bridged nose and flabby red lips. The thing was carrying a violin, too—an old fiddle clutched undergone elbow. Gripped in one fist was a big crimson butcher-knife—the knife with which the monster had slashed his own throat.

George Washington gasped, "*Nero!*"

He couldn't believe his eyes. The creature melted off in the darkness and snowflakes, there and gone like an evil thought. George Washington grabbed himself by the forehead; and wondered if he were having hallucinations. The ghosts of Julius Caesar and Nero wandering around Virginia?

The General yanked aside the curtains of his bedroom window, scrubbed away a little patch of frost from the pane, and glared down at the snowy ground dim-lit by the glow from the dining-room. Ghosts? By heaven! there was no one down there now. The General knew he had imagined those phantoms. George Washington was a modern American, and he didn't believe in ghosts.

"Great Scott—!"

Even as he scorned the previous specters, why, there was a third. Coming along the side of the house, catfoot like the first two. A great, rangy shadow wrapped in animal skins—at first, the General thought it was a wild beast walking upright—a horrible apparition with a tangled yellow beard and a great blowing mane of yellow hair. It carried a long spear, and fended the snow from its face with a bearskin shield; around its waist there dangled a circlet of human skulls.

"Attila!" George Washington groaned, recalling a woodcut in a schoolbook. *"Attila the Hun!"*

You can wager the General thought he was seeing things when he saw that medieval barbarian pass through the faint haze of light that bathed through the frosty panes of the dining-room. Attila melted off in the snow gusts on the heels of Nero and Julius Caesar, and the wintry wind whistled across the sills of the bedroom window, and George Washington had a chill worse than anything at Valley Forge.

"I've got a fever!" he told himself. "I'm having delusions from the chills and fever!"

HE OPENED HIS mouth to call Marsha, and then he closed it with a snap. His teeth were clattering so hard he had to hold them in his jaws with one hand and grip the window-sill to support his legs with the other. Down there in that lighted patch where Attila had been, there was standing a knight in armor! Word of honor! a dark figure in chain mail. It carried a battle-axe in the crook of its-elbow the way a dandy might carry a walking stick. Its helmet was weighted with snow, and the visor was pulled down, but George Washington thought he could identify the device emblazoned in the warrior's cape.

"God save me! *William, the Conqueror!*"

He wanted to yell down at that phantom below and tell it to return to Hell, but he couldn't utter a sound out of his choking throat.

He could hear, though. The night was so still he could hear the patter of snowflakes soft as feathers against the window, and he could've sworn he heard the Conqueror's chain mail jingle as he beckoned at someone out by the road, then vanished off in the snowy dark at the mansion's rear.

The goose pimples were out on the General's skin by this time; he was sure he had gone mad and was suffering mental delusions. The Conqueror, Attila the Hun, Nero and Julius Caesar. Why, it was just as impossible as if you looked out of your bedroom window some wintry night and saw, prowling down there in the snow, George Washington.

The General rushed across his darkened bedroom to his cabinet—stubbing his toe as he did so, and saying words quite off the Presidential record, you may well believe—and pored himself a good stiff jigger of whiskey. Then he was back at the window like a shot, because he knew that corn, distilled at his own supervision, was the sort of vanilla that cleaned the cobwebs right out of your belfry.

"Ye gods and little fishes!"

Instead of clearing his head, that jolt seemed to have made it worse. There were two wraiths down there under the window now. Advancing out of shadow, arm and arm into the faint, frosted candlelight, hobnobbing together like a pair of bosom friends. They moved on through the snowflakes, and George Washington could have fallen out over that upper sill.

"Rufus the Red and Richard the Second!"

There was no mistaking the pair. That rascally, red-faced devil who had misruled England and so got himself murdered in the Year 1100. And that weakly, pompous young Richard who had betrayed the Irish and was assassinated in Pontefract Castle in 1400 A.D.

They paced by slowly, bright birds in their gaudy velvet robes, royal plumes hanging bedraggled on their heavy-bowed heads. George Washington could even hear the murmur of their voices, but he couldn't catch what they were saying, and they had faded off into the night before he could yell down at them to ask.

And then, like the snow, the others came thick and fast. The Henrys, the Edwards, King John. They crept by under the window in the snow-flurries, and melted off into the dark like shades.

As if from the Netherworld they came with their scepters, their coronets, their tarnished coats-of-arms. That wicked Henry who had blinded his brother with hot irons. Henry VI, whose machinations plunged England into a dozen wars, the blood of murder on his cruel face. Edward II, stooped and hobbling, his crown tilted drunkenly, frame crippled by imprisonment and the rack, his breast stained scarlet by the assassin's knife. Charles I, opinionated, arbitrary—that scheming Charles who lost his head in 1649 to the Regicides.

There was James III of Scotland, another murder victim, followed by his unhappy descendant James V. After that George Washington couldn't say how many there were or who.

They kept on coming, blurred phantoms in the snowfall.

He recognized the bloated, besotted, benighted behemoth Henry VIII, swaggering in his court dress, with the blood of his beheaded wives making red gloves of his hands. That murderer King of Denmark was there, and Juan of Portugal, and one of the Philips of Spain, and Ivan the Terrible, clad in red and black, and along toward the last Mad Czar Paul, drooling and grimacing with the strangler's cord still about his neck.

They came around from the dark of the front veranda and stole along the side of the house and melted out of sight at the rear, a gorgeous-robed, gem-bedecked line of phantoms—as if, on this night, all the haunts of history were passing in review before George Washington.

ALL OF THEM were there—all the red-handed conquerors and iron-heeled tyrants—the instigators of persecution; the oppressors of the people—the dissolute, depraved, degenerate, decapitated monarchs and sovereigns and kings and warlords who had misruled Europe and held their countries in bondage and misery for the past thousand years, and so been forced to abdicate, or had been poisoned, stabbed or beheaded for their wickedness.

Had George Washington seen that review today there might have been added some interesting specimens to that processional—a little Frenchman in cutaway and cavalry boots with his hand thrust into his bosom—a Czar whose beard made him look kindlier than he was—an emperor with fierce moustachios and a German eagle on his knob.

And had he seen that review tomorrow, he might have beheld a couple more—if you've read the papers lately, you can guess who.

But this story took place about a hundred and fifty years

ago—it was a miserable enough review as it was—those figures passed under George Washington's eyes like the dreads and warnings of conscience, and they made George Washington sick.

And the last ghost he saw on that wintry night was a mincing-little figure all in velvet, lace and silk—a horrid, soul-curdling specter not so long-dead as the others, and it was carrying its head under its arm. At least, that was how it appeared to George Washington, looking down from his upper window. Maybe the collar of its princely greatcoat was pulled up high to hide face and ears. Maybe what looked like a headless neck was a wig covered with snow. But it didn't seem to have any noggin save the one it carried under its arm like a cabbage—George Washington could glimpse the face on the wretched thing—a sulky, hooked-nose face, doll-like with its shawl of feminine curls—the General knew whose head *that* was. Why, only a few months ago he'd read about it going to the guillotine.

"Louis the Sixteenth!"

That was too much for the General. Louis XVI creeping around the house with his head under his arm! Those other apparitions had chilled him to the marrow, but the scepter of this miserable king whose decapitation was still featured in the news from Europe sent the temperature to zero in George Washington's soul.

His heart was thumping like a giblet in an icebox. His pores were faucets gushing hot and cold running water. He had the megrims. He doubted every one of his senses.

That parade under his window had been a nightmare—a fevered imagination—an illusion of shadows and window-light and blowing snow. Yet he could have sworn those phantoms had had body and voice; he might have imagined one or two of them; but his brain could not have conjured a wicked score.

Hallucinations? Ghosts? There was only one way of finding out, and always the General was a man of action. There has never been a doubt as to George Washington's bravery; surely he proved his courage *that* night.

With one leap he reached his famous sword, and with another he reached the door. The house was as quiet as anything—the servants and Martha must have all been in the kitchen—his bedroom slippers flying down the staircase didn't make a sound.

The grandfather clock ticked loud in the stillness of the hall, and the General went out of the front door like a gust of wind. He crossed the dark veranda in two bounds. In the icy blackness of the road he couldn't see a thing, and he dived through the snowy shrubbery and raced around the corner of the mansion, his breath puffing clouds of white vapor like steam from one of James Watts' inventions.

5

OUT THERE IN the night and wind he was half blinded;
the snow swirled around him in white flurries; the wet
flakes clung to his lashes; the cold went through him like
the breath of Norway.

The sword was freezing in his right hand as the pistol
had frozen in his left; at the same time he was sweating like
a horse. As he stole along the side of the house, his eye on
that haze of candle-glow drifting from the dining-room
window, he was scared as he'd never been in his life.

That's when you're brave—when you go out in the dark
after something, in spite of being scared half to death—
George Washington had to call on every ounce of his courage to get himself along the side of that house.

All the scepters from Tophet seemed to be there at
Mount Vernon, Virginia. He'd seen them out there in the
snow flurries and wind howl; the night came around him
like an icy menace; but George Washington was the kind
of man who didn't believe anything until he'd had proof,
and he went out scouting for proof of those ghosts just
as he determinedly as if they'd been nothing more than
savage Indians.

He went straight toward that lighted area where he'd
seen them. And all the time George Washington knew
there couldn't have been any such thing, because it was

the Age of Reason, and ghosts and spooks and haunts had been banished along with superstition and witchcraft and all that other stuff by the Age of Reason.

Why, that was part of the Revolution—the effort to free men's minds from the bondage of that sort of rubbish.

And then George Washington got probably the worst shock a man ever had. He'd just screwed up the last of his courage with logic and reason when he arrived under that lighted window. Then all the terrors of the world's dark past came down *bang!*

There were the tracks!

Yes, sir, there before him, clearly revealed by the mellow light from the dining-room, were the footprints. Plain as anything in the snow. Tracks of sandals, princely slippers and square-toed Cavalier boots. Iron heels and courtier shoes.

The General knew foot-tracks when he saw them, and those prints left deep in the snow weren't any hallucination. The eyes just about jumped out of George Washington's head. It wasn't any time to argue logic and reason.

A black wind moaned around the house, bringing a whirl of spookish flakes, and the General turned about and ran. It wasn't the first time he'd had to do some running, but that time he'd pulled out ahead of Lord Howe in Brooklyn, and some of those races he'd run in New Jersey were nothing to the dash he made that night in Mount Vernon to get back into the house.

You can't call it cowardice, either.

You'd have run yourself if you thought Caesar's Ghost was on your heels. Add Nero and Attila the Hun and William the Conqueror and Ivan the Terrible and Henry the VIII and Mad Czar Paul and all those other hoodoos with Louis XVI with his head under his arm bringing up the rear, and you'd have probably beat George Washington.

He was back inside the house in nothing flat, and he slammed the door after him, *bang!* and bolted it, too. As he flew across the hall, he yelled, "Martha! Martha!" but his throat only let out a squeak.

YOU MANY THINK it funny—George Washington racing upstairs to his room like that—but before you feel too superior (you who live in a day of electric lights and radio and gasoline and talking pictures) just remember all the superstitions still alive today.

George Washington blew into his room like a blizzard, and he threw fifteen pieces of wood on the fire, and had all the candles lighted before you could say Jack Sprat. The room was fairly ablaze with lights when he heard a step in the doorway behind him, and he spun with a gasp, clutching saber and pistol, expecting to face heaven knew what.

But it was only Martha Washington in her ribbon-laced-cap—Martha, pink-cheeked and smiling in a charming party dress, quaint and pretty as a picture. She blinked in the light-blaze for an uncomprehending minute; then her eyes on her husband widened, startled; she stepped in quickly and closed the door.

"George Washington," she demanded, "what in the world is going on? Why, you're covered with snow—wet from head to foot! You've been out of the house! And in your bedroom slippers! You take off those wet things this minute, George Washington! Look at you—pale as if you'd seen a ghost."

"Madam," said the General, and he was shaking so he

could hardly talk, "Madam, I have seen a ghost! A whole parade of ghosts. On my word of honor! Right there under our bedroom window, and they left their footprints in the snow!"

"Footprints in the snow? From ghosts?" Martha Washington raised her hands as in despair. "I declare, George Washington, if I didn't hear this from you, I would never believe—"

"Nor did I!" he panted desperately. "Not till I saw their tracks! Imagination doesn't leave tracks in the snow, I tell you, and the prints are there. I saw them, Martha! All of them! Julius Caesar! Nero! Attila! William the Conqueror! Rufus the Red was with them, and Edward the Second, and Charles the First, and Henry the Eighth. Yes, and that mad Czar of Russia who was strangled with a cord, and a lot of others, and poor wretched Louis of France with his head under his arm was last—I swear it, Martha!—Louis the Sixteenth!—carrying his head—under his arm—!"

He broke off for air, and Martha Washington looked at him in unbelief.

"George Washington," she said, "I do think sometimes there never was such a man! Caesar's ghost! The phantom of Czar Paul! Louis Sixteenth with his head under his arm! Why, those weren't ghosts, you silly goose. They're friends of yours.

"Just friends dressed up in masquerade—Aleck Hamilton and Sam Adams and Tobias Lear and some of the others—and that Louis you saw was only Doctor Craik, and that head was the false-face for his costume. That's who you saw, only your friends made up in costume, and they came here for the party."

"Party?" George Washington blurted. "What party?"

Martha's eyes were blinking as if she wanted to cry. "Your party, George—not a political party! A masquerade ball, and I so much wanted to surprise you! I told them all to leave their carriages at a place down the road, and asked them to enter quietly by the back door!" And as he still appeared baffled and in confusion, she clamped her hands in dismay. "Heavens to Betsy! George, haven't you yet remembered? Have you still forgotten the day?"

"Day? Day?" the General muttered, just as he had when she'd asked the question early in the evening. "Why, it's the twenty-second of February, but—

"It's your *birthday!*" Martha cried. "Are all the matters of State so heavy on your mind, poor man, that you can't even remember your own birthday?"

THE GENERAL SHOOK his head mournfully, and allowed he'd quite forgotten. It was that New Style calendar, he said—that Gregorian calendar that England had adopted in 1752. He was always getting fuddled about dates, he admitted, and he'd never quite got used to the change in calendars. Always thought of his birthday as February the eleventh, as it had been in the Old Style calendar.

Well, that explained to Martha why George Washington had forgotten his birthday, but in consequence there was another look of startlement on Martha's face.

"But if you've forgotten it was your birthday," she cried, "what are *you* doing, all made-up as for masquerade? What"—she pointed—"is that thing you're wearing on your head?"

George Washington looked at himself in the mirror, and pulled a gasp.

There he was, still wrapped up in that satin bed-quilt with that dazzling crown a-topper, only he didn't look very regal now. The bed-quilt was soaked and muddy, and the crown was askew about his ears with the brim slanted over one eye. To George Washington, right then, it didn't look at all macaroni.

"Madam," he faced his wife, for he couldn't begin to tell a lie at this age, "Madam, it's a kind of crown. Some of the boys in the Cincinnati sent it over, and I—well, there was no harm in trying it on."

"You take it right off," Martha ordered, "and you put on some good dry American clothes and come downstairs."

She was frowning and shaking her head in exasperation as she backed from the room, and as she closed the door the General heard her murmuring there was no accounting for men's whims.

And that's about all there is to this story.

Some say that George Washington took that crown and threw it out of the window into a snowbank, and it sank into the mud in the Spring thaw and was buried in the good earth of Mount Vernon.

Another version has it that the General flung it into the fireplace and watched it melt. The fire was mighty hot from all the wood he'd put on, and that crown, melted like it was made of butter. Even the gems dissolved, and the General felt a little cynical. They might have done better than glass diamonds and so much gilded lead.

At any rate, that crown was never seen on George Washington's head.

It didn't suit the head of an American, and the General had had his history lesson on crowns.

Pausing at his bedroom window he looked down at the foot-tracked snow. What a scare those historical figures had given him. "Sweet Land of Liberty!" he exclaimed.

Then he adjusted his starched linen jabot, and went down to his birthday party.

OF COURSE ALL that is apocryphal, which means it's fiction and never happened. Not that it's impossible.

The calendar *was* changed in Washington's time. The people in those days *were* fond of costume balls. And it wouldn't have been beyond the humors of some of Washington's friends to dress up as a batch of misguided monarchs. The patriots of those days loved to lampoon the tyrants of the past; they cherished their Liberty, those early Americans.

We know Washington had his doubts, and we know he rejected them—perhaps he did remember all those rulers who, when given absolute power, had degenerated into tyrants.

At any rate, he was offered the crown, and he refused. He had his chance to be king. And he turned it down so that this government of the people, by the people and for the people might not perish from the earth.

THEN PLACID JOHN ADAMS

He was our second president, and he wasn't so placid at the outset. Here's the merry account of his lively journey toward serenity, as well as the possible explanation of what the fiery little statesman was up to when he dropped out of sight for three months....

1

BACK WHEN SCHOOLBOYS used to recite their lessons instead of dodge them, the classrooms chanted a poem that went something like this:

> *Washington first of the presidents stands,*
> *Then placid John Adams the country commands—*

Then Jefferson something on the "glorious score" and masterful Madison "comes number four," and so on down the famous list in fine chronological order, its purpose calculated to make young Americans remember their Presidents.

It is a stirring epic, and its patriotic theme might well be learned in these forgetful times, but it seems the author was more poet than historian. What in the world did he mean by "placid John Adams?"

Placid John Adams?

I'd like to know that poet's conception of temperamental. John Adams was just about as placid as the boiling water that brewed the Boston Tea Party, and if he didn't boil outwardly a lot of the time, he boiled inwardly, and it wasn't any tempest in a teapot, either.

Certainly he wasn't placid in those pre-Revolutionary years when he and his cousin Sam worked their heads off to

cook up resis-
tance against
England. Why,
it was John who
wrote most of
the Declaration
of Indepen-
dence. It was
John who got
Washington
appointed head
of the army. It
was John who
rushed over to
France to raise
war loans and write treaties, and when he couldn't borrow
money in Paris, he borrowed it from the Dutch—and no
placid man ever borrowed any money from the Dutch.

Then after the War he was our first ambassador to
England—no placid job, in a country still smarting from
defeat. He came back to be our first Vice-president, and
he wasn't placid then, no matter how you look at it. There
was a cantankerous streak in John Adams all wool and a
yard wide—he was too plain honest to be suave or tactful
or serene. He didn't like playing second fiddle to anybody,
even Washington, and he sulked about Washington's
popularity, crabbing most of the time.

Politics isn't likely to bring out the smoother side of a
man, and John Adams was only human. Even when elected
our second President, he was miffed at being second. He

thought the country had slighted him, electing him President as a compromise in the Federalist Party.

The government was in Philadelphia—they were just building the new capitol down on the Potomac—and he wrote letters complaining to his wife, Abigail, that he didn't like Philadelphia. He had no patience with Congress; he wrangled with his advisers; he mistrusted his cabinet.

He didn't get along with Jefferson, his Vice-president, and he didn't approve of Ben Franklin's morals.

Then he got into a violent quarrel with Hamilton (both men flinging insults in a way which did credit to neither); fired most of his cabinet officers; broke with the Federalists who'd elected him; exploded the X-Y-Z Affair, and split the country wide open politically.

Now don't think this is an attempt to belittle John Adams. He was a great patriot, a great statesman, and a great American. No man in the little Republic was better fitted to be Chief Executive. He came to the Presidency at a time of desperate need, and he steered the Ship of State through the treacherous international shoals as no man before and few since.

But he wasn't placid. Never!

He was proud and stubborn, and full of explosive emotions like all our early forefathers. Why, it's historical fact—maybe you never heard it—that John Adams got so mad at the way things were going one time when he was President that he walked right out of his office and let the nation run itself without him for three months!

Yes sir, John Adams walked out of his office, mad, and for three months he didn't come back. Can you imagine a President doing such a thing today? There hasn't been a temper to equal his in American History. Maybe you don't believe it, but you can find it in your history books. But what did he do during those three months absence when he let the nation go hang?

Did he go fishing in Maine or did he go on a spree? Did he rage off by himself in some cabin in the woods? If you care to make the research, you can probably find that out, too; so far, I haven't been able to find out (I haven't made the research) but I've been wondering.

Suppose he stayed there in town, in angry disguise. Suppose, disgusted with everything, he took a packet back to Europe. Suppose he crossed the Appalachians to hibernate with sensible Indians.

Or suppose—

JOHN ADAMS SLAMMED the door behind him, and snatched his old tricorne from the hatrack in the hall, and stamped out of the building. He didn't see the guard who raised his musket in salute. He saw red.

Crossing a crowded square, he looked neither left nor right; his chin was thrust like a cobblestone block; his shoulders were puffed like a cat's; his lips were clamped as hard as galvanized iron.

John Adams had never been so mad.

He pretended not to hear the Negro who had run after him from the historic building—an old trusted messenger of the government who waved an important paper in his hand and called, "Mr. Adams! Mr. Adams!" He only quickened his stride, and the old Negro was lost in the shuffle.

John Adams walked blindly on. He was almost run down by a bucket brigade racing to a fire somewhere. Cartwheels missed his toes. Pedestrians jostled him. Nobody paid any

attention to him—everyone was running to the fire—and
that increased his dudgeon, despite the fact he didn't want
to talk to anyone. Outraged, he walked faster than ever.

In fact, he walked right out of town.

He followed the main thoroughfare, and he walked right
out of Philadelphia. He took the first turnpike he came to,
and he walked along that. The pike was lively with horsemen, drays, coaches and ox-carts, and he swerved up a side
road to avoid them. A teamster driving a dozen hogs to
Trenton offered him a lift, but John Adams only snorted
a splenetic, "Nah!" and the teamster went on, muttering,
"Godfrey, what a crosspatch!"

Crosspatch was a strong term in those days, but it hardly
did justice to the feelings of John Adams.

Besides being mad, he was aggrieved. He felt annoyed,
infuriated, bitter and grossly insulted. Altogether he was in

And then began such a riot as
few had ever seen, with John
Adams right in the thick of it

a fit of spleen. When had a man ever suffered such ingrat-
itude? When had a man been as unappreciated? He'd
devoted his whole career to his country, and what had he
got? Peanuts!

They'd elected him President, but at the inauguration the
applause had been for Washington. Everyone else got the
honors; all he got was the work. And what a job!

National affairs in a muddle. The international situation
a powder keg. A cabinet full of fools. All the headaches left
over by Washington's administration. The Union appeared
ready to fall to pieces at any minute, and nobody seemed
willing to cooperate—Jefferson wanting this; Pinckney
wanting that; that confounded Hamilton making trouble
at every turn—surely President of the United States was
the toughest job in all the world.

Not that he'd expected gratitude—the public was inca-
pable of it!—the job was thankless, and he could have
put up with that. He could have stood the hours of office
work, mental strain, awful responsibility. Even the slanders of political opponents, the editorial jibes, the blame
and criticism for everything that went wrong—all that he
could stand.

Yes, he could even stand the intrigues and backbiting
of Hamilton, who wanted to run the country. But when
they paid you a measly twenty-five thousand a year and
expected you to entertain in regal splendor—! When
you were supposed to run a household like the Czar of
Russia on such a pittance that you couldn't even afford to
keep your wife in Philadelphia—! And then the Treasury
Department won't give you expense-money for a coach

and four—! Well, that was the straw that broke the camel's back.

No, the stingy Treasury had refused to pay his coach bill, and the ache that came to his legs as he stumped up the country road thinking about it didn't soothe him any. The more he walked, the hotter he got under the collar.

He'd scraped along in meager lodgings. His dining table was frugal. He'd sacrificed family life, leaving wife and comforts in the big wide house up in Braintree, Massachusetts. But when the President of the United States couldn't even afford a coach and four—John Adams was so preoccupied with this outrage, that he walked a lot farther than he intended, for instead of cooling his spleen the hike had only aggravated it, and now he was madder than ever.

BESIDES, THE ROAD had entered a deep, dark woods, and he wasn't quite sure where he was. Twilight was making, and he was hungry. He hurried back the way he'd come, but it didn't seem to get him any nearer Philadelphia—the forest deepened and the twilight darkened—he wasn't sure of his way.

Well, he consulted his great silver watch—half an inch thick, it was, with a chain stout enough to anchor a twenty-gun frigate—it was later than he'd thought. He decided to find an inn and have his supper, but he couldn't find an inn.

No, there didn't seem to be any hostelries by the road, or any farmhouses, or woodcutters' cottages or log cabins, either. Night darkened the forest, and a big yellow moon shouldered up over the trees.

The road was a ribbon of moonlight, but there weren't any road signs to direct him back to town. There was just this brown, moonlit road through the forest, and John Adams had to keep on walking.

Jehu! he felt as if he'd walked a thousand miles.

Well, at last he came to a stile, and he sat down, mighty hungry, thirsty and wornout. His nose was sunburned, the silver buckles hurt on his shoes, the calves of his legs were cramping, and he was lost.

That was a pretty situation, wasn't it? The President of the United States lost in his own country, sitting supperless on a stile!

It seemed to John Adams as if America had always treated him like that, and when he thought of the injustice that had set him out walking in the first place, he was fit to be tied. By heaven! he wouldn't put up much longer with such treatment. For two cents he'd throw over this job of President!

A pang of appetite filled him with such a yearning for a good side of beef and a bottle of porter that he groaned aloud. Memory of his wife's cooking; and the big comfortable house up in Braintree increased his bitterness. Why had he been such a fool as to enter public life? Time and again he'd wanted to get out of it, but he'd persevered for the sake of his country. This was the reward! Lost and hungry on a lonely road. He groaned again.

Then he sat bolt upright. That groan might have been a prayer, from the way it was answered. It was answered by a whiff of bacon—an aroma of frying bacon that wafted out of the forest on a little nocturnal zephyr and circled his nostrils with a teasing insistence that made his head swim.

It was accompanied by a fragrance of coffee that set his

mouth a-water. Jumping up from the stile, he probed the nearer thickets with famished eyes, sniffing furiously.

He was on the point of bellowing to know its source when from the timber at his left the forest's stillness was startled by a song. "The Girl I Left Behind Me!" No nightingale, that, but a good Yankee-nasal tenor, and John Adams, himself a good Yankee, went into the forest on the bound.

He picked up a hickory staff on the way—you never could tell, this singer might be a freebooter, an army deserter, or (perish the thought) a vagrant Federalist, and the President of the United States couldn't be too careful. But the bacon whiffs got the better of him.

In his haste he stumbled over a root. Head over teacup, he went somersaulting down into a glen. There was a brook and a campfire and a big oak tree and a long, lean man with a frying pan in his hand.

And that's how John Adams met a tinker.

2

YES, THE MAN was a tinker, and he and John Adams got along fine. Naturally he wanted to know who John Adams was, and when John Adams said cautiously, "A traveler who's lost his way," he invited John Adams to sit right down and have vittles.

His eyes were as honest blue as John Adams' own, so John Adams knew he wasn't any freebooter or politician. Before you could say Jack Sprat, John Adams consumed five cups of coffee and fifteen slabs of bacon. The banquet was washed down by a jug of dandelion wine, and John Adams reckoned it was the best bang-up meal he'd ever tasted.

Now Yankees aren't liable to say much at first acquaintance, and John Adams said less. The tinker didn't say more. He gave John Adams some of the blackest burleigh you've ever seen, and for the next hour they sat with their backs against the tree, just nodding and smoking and spitting into the fire.

Finally the tinker allowed that his name was Caleb Dingman, and, odd enough, he'd got lost in the forest, too. He pointed at his big canvas tinker's pack under the tree, and declared he'd pretty well traveled all over New England, but this stretch of territory was new to him. He said he was a down-East man.

John Adams warmed to him for that, especially when Caleb said he'd fit in the Battle of Lexington and was the man who'd held Paul Revere's horse.

John Adams owned up that he, himself, was from Boston way. He said his name was Rotundity, wryly using a name that Izard had dubbed him, and he declared that he was a lawyer, which he was, and that he'd missed the Philadelphia turnpike, which he had.

Well, they sat there thinking their own thoughts again, listening to the leaves and the fire. An owl hooted, friendly in the trees, and the night was just right for a camp.

John Adams found himself envying his companion's healthy tan and the easy relaxation of gypsy life. Caleb, sideways, was secretly admiring John Adams' city clothes and gentlemanly air.

"Funny," he said at last, "I missed the Philadelphia turnpike, myself." He allowed to John Adams as how he was on his way to the capitol to see the President.

"The President?" John Adams demanded, suspicious. "What do you want to see the President for?"

Practically everybody wanted to see the President to complain about something or other; but Caleb Dingman just stared off into the trees.

"Jest want to see him, that's all. Like to git one good look at him up close."

"What do you want to see him up close for?" John Adams felt a twinge of alarm. Maybe this fellow wanted to assassinate him.

"Why, I jest want to see him," the tinker's eyes were bright. "I'd jest like to shake his hand. Seems to me bein' President of the United States is about the biggest position in the world

today, take a pretty slick man to win it. This John Adams—
Bonny Johnnie like we call him back home—I reckon he's
a real humdinger. Got about the best job in creation, and I'd
jest like to congratulate him for gettin' it."

"Maybe it's not such a good job," said John Adams, caus-
tic. "Might be a tinker's job is better."

"A TINKER'S—?" CALEB stared. "Say, a tinker does nothin'
but work. Sunup to sundown, and then nowhere to sleep
but under a tree. They say the President sleeps in a big
feather bed, all curtained with American flags."

"Maybe he doesn't get much fresh air," growled John
Adams, "and urgent messengers keep waking him up at
night."

"Well, at least that'd be exciting, signing Declarations
of War and the like of that. 'Tain't boresome like mending
dishpans. No work to it, either. The President jest takes out
his big gold pen an' signs."

"Maybe his hand shakes from the responsibility, Caleb.
Maybe signing Declarations gets on his nerves."

"Not on the President's," Caleb shook his head. "It's
common men like me got nerves. Times hard, an' never
knowin' where my next penny's comin' from. Think of the
President's salary!"

"And think of his expenses," John Adams thought.

"Laborin' with tools gits tiresome," Caleb said.

"But builds healthy muscle," John Adams thought.

"And the President don't git into rows," Caleb said.

"No," John Adams thought, thinking of Alexander
Hamilton.

"He don't git into jams," Caleb pointed out ruefully, "like
the one I got into in a place I'm in recently. I'm mendin' a

spinnin' wheel for a woman, an' she's bendin' over to help me. Parson passes the window, an' goes tells her husband he seen me give her a kiss. I hear he's comin' with a gun, I do, an' I have to git. Fixin' clocks an' pumps an' dishpans, you git into jams. President wouldn't never git into such a scandal."

"Never," John Adams thought grimly, thinking of scurrilous mud-slinging political campaigns.

"Nobody'd dare take a shot at the President," the tinker went on in an awed tone. "Biggest job in creation, takes a mighty big man to hold it down. They say he's seven or eight feet tall at least, magnificent to behold. All covered over with glitterin' medals an' decorations like to make the kings of England and France look like tramps. I've heard he wears a long blue coat an' a weskit all spangled with stars, an' red and white striped pants.

"They say he lives in a palace all full of gold eagles, an' the band plays marches all the time, an' most of the day he jest sets around readin' the Constitution an' tellin' 'bassadors from Europe where to head in. They say he goes out in an imperial satin-lined coach pulled by thirteen horses for the Thirteen States. It sure must be splendid"—Caleb's eyes were shining—"and I'd sure like to see him."

"So would I," said John Adams, choking on that "coach" and "thirteen horses" as if he'd swallowed a chicken bone. "So that's what they say about the President of the United States."

"Heard it from a sojer who said he'd seed him," Caleb nodded. "Wisht I had all those fine clothes an' wages an' eddication an' gentlemanly ways. Sell out my tinker's trade to be President any time."

Well, you know what John Adams was thinking as well
as I do, and it didn't take him long to make up his mind.
He was thinking how nice it must be to travel around the
country doing odd jobs for pretty housewives. How easy to
retire at sunset and not be kicked out of bed by diplomatic
nightmares. This forest was luxury compared to the noise
of Philadelphia; the *tonk* of a tinker's hammer would be
music compared to the yells of Congress.

Right then John Adams made one of the most decisive
decisions of his life. "Caleb, did you mean that, that you'd
sell your tinker's outfit?"

"'Most give it, I would, to the first customer as would
buy."

"How much?" John Adams poked a finger at the tinker's
pack.

"Thirty dollars," said Caleb, recovering from surprise.

"Twenty," John Adams offered. "Sound American
money."

"Twenty-nine an' she's yours," said the tinker, eyes bulg-
ing at John Adams' pocketbook.

Well, they bargained and bickered as Yankees will; in the
end John Adams bought the tinker's kit for twenty-three
dollars with his silver shoe buckles thrown in. Both went
to sleep, each sure he had the best of the bargain.

In the morning John Adams shook the tinker's horny
hand, and the tinker shook John Adams' official one; wishing
each other God speed, they set out on separate ways—Caleb
well pleased with the unexpected wealth that was going to
make him a gentleman and take him to Philadelphia to see
the President—John Adams right contented because at last
(he'd always wanted to do it) he'd got out of public life.

3

SO JOHN ADAMS went tinkering around the country, and for the first couple of weeks he had a wonderful time. Fresh air and sunshine did him a lot of good, and he reflected there was nothing like the gypsy life. It was fun to stop at some farmhouse or cabin and fix up the cookpots and churns. By heaven! it was easier than mending Foreign Relations and fixing up Bills and Acts.

It was good to turn in at night and not have some secretary banging on his door. Or not have his breakfast ruined by the latest European crisis. What a relief not to have to face Congress in the afternoon or have to deal with that knave, Alexander Hamilton. No grafting diplomats—no nagging politicians—it seemed to John Adams he was free since the first time he'd fought for Liberty.

He grinned, wondering what they'd said when he hadn't come back; and he hadn't grinned in so long that it cracked the corners of his mouth.

Those lumpheaded statesmen would be in a panic. He could just imagine the furore his absence would make. The idea amused John Adams—couriers running their legs off—politicians hunting him—dispatch riders riding posthaste—maybe they'd toll the Liberty Bell. Yes, they'd read proclamations. Call out the army. Summon all the big men of the nation. Oh, plenty of those big men had said they didn't want him. Maybe they'd appreciate him, now he wasn't there.

He didn't worry about his wife worrying about him. Word of his absence wouldn't reach Braintree for days—the postal service was slow—there wouldn't be headlines in the Boston papers, because newspapers didn't have headlines in those days, and without telephones, telegraphs or radios they didn't have much news.

He figured he could walk to Braintree before the news got there, and he aimed his steps in that general direction. He just didn't worry about anything; it was great not to have any worries. All his life he'd worried about the country, but now, so far as he was concerned, they could go fly Ben Franklin's kite.

At first he was on the lookout for scouts who might be hunting him, but nobody bothered him at all. The road was little traveled. The farmers and woodcutters he encountered were simple folk who wouldn't have been able to recognize him from such pictures as were in circulation. That tinker's pack was enough for a disguise.

He reflected how easy it was to lead a quiet, everyday life, and he wondered why the devil he'd wanted to be President in the first place.

But then he ran into rain.

The open road turned into a slough. He couldn't sleep at night in soggy woods, and stopping at inns cost too much money. He fell into a bog and couldn't get dry—fires were hard to start with flint and tinder—he began to wonder about the gypsy life. And when he burned his fingers on the soldering iron and cut his thumb on the tinshears, he began to wonder about tinkering.

It seemed there were some angles to it he hadn't suspected. A tinker was a man who did most everything in general, and John Adams walked into a neighborhood where his predecessor, Caleb, had done some pretty general tinkering. He might've been warned by Caleb's singing "The Girl I Left Behind Me", but he'd forgotten the story about the pretty wife and the spinning wheel.

Pack on back, he trudged into this pleasant hamlet, and next thing he knew, it wasn't so pleasant. A flintlock banged. Hot lead whistled over his head. Turning, John Adams saw a big red-whiskered man charging at him with a musket. It didn't take him long to recognize an outraged husband.

THIS WORTHY, IN turn, recognized the tinker's pack even if he didn't recognize the tinker. Perhaps he was out to exterminate the profession. Bullets began to fly like the Battle of Bunker Hill, and John Adams shed his pack and considerable of his dignity in a retreat that isn't in the history books.

He lost his tricorne hat in the race, and he lost his desire to tinker. When friend husband caught him on a covered bridge at hamlet's edge, John Adams might have lost his life, too, if he hadn't been a first class diplomat.

Arguing out of that triangle took a masterpiece of diplomacy—talk about the X-Y-Z Affair! But to show you what a super-diplomat John Adams was, he not only saved his skin, but ended up by selling his tinker's pack to the husband and wangling a dinner invitation besides. He sold the kit for two dollars more than he'd paid for it; the wife in the case patched the bullet hole in his pocket, and

John Adams went on, a little relieved to be through with tinkering.

Well, he fell in with a cooper.

Walking into New Jersey—he knew it was New Jersey from the mosquitoes—he reckoned he'd buy a horse. He'd raised a corn, and mosquitoes heckled him almost as much as Congressmen, and Massachusetts was still a long way off. But horses at the time were scarce—the older generation had been killed off by the Revolutionary War—a good horse cost about the price of a car today, and John Adams didn't want some old nag.

In Morristown there was a horse fair with some pretty good buys, but John Adams found out they wouldn't take his money. He got a lesson in finance there in Jersey.

American banks were in an uproar in those days—in some states paper money wasn't worth a Continental—others issued their own currency—the money he'd got in Pennsylvania wasn't any good in Morristown. Hamilton had been monkeying with the Treasury again; instead of a coach and four, John Adams couldn't even buy a nag.

That made him hopping mad, and hopping hurt his corn. He could've written to Philadelphia for his back salary, but that meant declaring his whereabouts, and he was as stubborn a man as was ever elected to the Presidency. Thought they could make him walk, did they? Well, he'd raised his last corn in America, declared John Adams.

Across the street from the horse fair was a cooper's shop, and John Adams made a deal with the cooper. He said he could learn the craft in half an hour, and he offered to make barrels for a penny a barrel. You must make a heap of barrels to earn enough to buy a horse, but work never fazed John Adams. He was mad enough to trade his kingdom for a horse, and he told himself that whatever he did would be an easier job than President.

So John Adams tried his hand at coopering.

He was quick with his head, John Adams, and he mastered easily the tricks with jointer, truss hoops, krisset stove and champering knife. All the other tools of that honorable and ancient craft came likely to his hand, and I warrant there wasn't such a cooper anywhere in America at the time: You can bet he made the shavings fly!

Yes sir, for three weeks he made barrels just as fast as his boss could hand him the staves, for every time he pounded a nail-head he pretended it was Alexander Hamilton's. He made flour barrels and potato barrels, molasses barrels and cracker barrels; but mostly he made cider barrels, the season being ripe for Jersey Lightning.

Only rolling out the barrel wasn't necessarily a barrel of fun, as John Adams found out. The day started at five and ended at ten—at night. Seventeen hours wasn't extraordinary in those days, except it didn't allow much time for recreation. The shop was hot and dark, and there weren't any inspectors to check up on ventilation. Union wages were unheard of. So was workmen's compensation. The boss was a mean man full of cuss words and applejack, and in half a week's time John Adams wanted to strike.

He scorched his hands on the krisset, pinched his fingers in the hoops, hammered his sore thumb, and wanted to strike his employer on the nose. Holding his temper choked him half to death. But at the end of three weeks he had his money for a horse, and it didn't take him long to get out of Morristown.

HE WAS HAPPIER to be through with coopering than he had been with tinkering, and he figured he'd clip up to Boston and try his hand at something else. Then he hadn't gone far before he found out *he'd* been clipped. That poet who called him placid should've seen his face when he topped a hill in the Orange Mountains and the engine went dead.

Did that make John Adams mad! If your engine goes dead in the Orange Mountains today you can call up a service station and put in a fresh sparkplug, but back in the 1790s there weren't any service stations, and you can't put a fresh sparkplug in a dead horse.

Bonny Johnnie had a conniption. It almost killed him to think how hard he'd worked to pay for that dead horse. He wanted to go back and have that horse-trader arrested for treason against the President of the United States under the Alien and Sedition Act. Then he remembered he couldn't invoke the Act under the circumstances, and he called that chiseling horse-trader all the names he'd been saving up for Hamilton.

It was a conspiracy, that's what it was. As if the whole country was trying to make him walk! You can see John Adams vowing not to walk another foot; he set his jaw like granite, and he sat down at the side of that mountain road like a statue. That wasn't liable to get you very far on the mountain roads of Jersey in those days. A couple of horsemen went by, and a pretty milkmaid on an ox, then for the next thirty hours John Adams saw nothing but rabbits. Likely his bones would be sitting there yet, if it hadn't been for the doctor.

Just at dusk of the third day John Adams sighted a

wagon toiling uphill—a most extraordinary wagon. It was pulled by a team of brown mules wearing straw hats like a pair of old ladies on their way to church; tethered to one side lumbered a cinnamon bear; the roof was decked with flags and bunting. Signs proclaimed, *Usnea For Asthma!* and bold lettering over the driver's seat announced, *The Wizard of Physic!*

In case you might misunderstand, this introduced a physician, and the physician in this case was a great, jovial fat man, big as a lard tub, dressed in buckskin and Indian feathers, for all the world Humpty Dumpty in the guise of a Choctaw chief. Such an equipage on a road today would send a hitch-hiker running for his reason, but John Adams stubbornly stood his ground with cocked thumb, and the physician roared at him to know his trouble.

"Is it rickets or quinzy that stands you there, sir—water of the brain or knee? Name your ailment, stranger; I've the answer at once, for there's nothing I can't cure with my vast store of medical wonders."

John Adams pointed at his horse; the Wizard had to confess that death was the one thing he couldn't cure. "But I've a remedy for corns," he boomed, moving over on the driver's seat. "The best in the world—a compound of mules and wagon-wheels. So climb aboard, sir, and mind the bear! Join a master of medicine on his way to the relief of a suffering mankind!"

4

JOHN ADAMS ACCEPTED the invitation with alacrity. The doctor needed an assistant, and he accepted the job with alacrity, too. It seemed the physician's assistant had died on the road the night before, and the Wizard assured J.A. he could learn all there was to know about medicine in an hour.

Perhaps this was true. Those days, there wasn't much known about medicine. Doctoring was somewhat a matter of luck—salts and bleeding were in general favor, while other prescriptions depended largely on the doctor's imagination and the signs of the Zodiac—the patient who survived such treatment could know himself Fortune's darling.

The Wizard admitted medicine was in its experimental stage, but neglected to tell John Adams that his late assistant had died in one of the experiments, and that portions of the hapless medical student were at that moment under the driver's seat in bottles—while other portions accompanied the party in the digestive tracts of the bear.

Unaware of these hazards, John Adams went in for medicine with all his heart. He'd always wanted to relieve suffering mankind; medicine, he reflected, was far more to the point than politics; while the fees made a President's salary look sick. Fifteen dollars just for sawing off a leg!

"And everybody," the Wizard assured him, "has two legs!"

Well, he got along with the doctor fine. The Wizard taught him the latest cures, and the Wizard had them all. He showed John Adams beozar stones for the headache and mummy-dust for the plague. He revealed the healing formula of the Abacadabra.

Salves, plasters, leeches for bleeding, cat's blood to cure nightmares—the Wizard's stock was enormous. He was gay as well as learned, was the Wizard; he chuckled and poked John Adams in the ribs, winking and beaming and nodding his headdress of Indian feathers as he talked.

It was a lot more interesting than tinkering or coopering; certainly it was a higher-minded service than being President; John Adams wondered why he hadn't gone into medicine before.

John Adams wasn't long in passing his medical course. He learned the influence of the stars on one's health; how to use Doctor Perkins' tractors for the "jolly nose"; where to bag a corpse that could furnish usnea.

Doctor Perkins' tractors? One of the medical wonders of the period—a pair of silver tweezers charged with electricity, guaranteed to cure that common complaint "jolly nose" which is just as common today, but known as "rum blossom" and treated somewhat differently. As for usnea, that was moss scraped from the skull of a dead criminal; the standard Pharmacopeia and our forefathers recommended it for asthma—John Adams, himself, smeared it on his chest—if you don't believe it, look it up in the Encyclopedia Britannica.

And before you go jeering at our forefathers, remember the present market in patent medicine.

Anyway, John and the Wizard did a thriving business dispensing nostrums. After all, healing is largely a matter of faith. They sold quantities of usnea in the Jersey villages, and the Wizard had no trouble getting testimonials.

Villages in those days didn't have drug stores. Few of them had doctors. Your average villager dosed his own ailment while his wife advised the parson to keep Friday open for the funeral. The average person died early in early America, which gives you an idea of how stubborn John Adams was.

He died when he was ninety.

ENTERING A VILLAGE, the Wizard would park his wagon in the market place. The bear danced. John Adams distributed cures through the crowd while the Wizard spieled. It was a paying business. There was something the matter with nearly everybody. For example, nearly all of our forefathers were pitted with smallpox. The Wizard sold a salve guaranteed to erase the pits.

Sometimes surgery was called for, and John Adams assisted at some unusual operations. In one town, there was a man with a terrific pain in his left side. The Wizard advised salts, a mustard plaster, sulphur and molasses and a hot bath. When the patient worsened he was bled. John Adams' duty was to tie the raving man to the bedpost, and afterward inform the wife she was a widow.

Quite as colorful was a leg amputation in which the patient—a village blacksmith—refused to lie still while the Wizard sawed. Ten men were required to hold the unruly smith. A fiddler, brought in as an anaesthetic (music being the forerunner of ether), was himself knocked cold. The Wizard received a black eye for his pains, and in the scuffle John Adams almost lost his own leg.

But they came off, triumphant, with the blacksmith's limb; if the patient died afterward, at least the operation was a partial success.

In the main, John Adams preferred medicaments. He enjoyed mixing emulsions, stewing herbs, cooking up simples and brewing the Wizard's remedies. Not far from Newark Village they found a dead criminal in a crossroads gallows. They barbered this cadaver of its skull-moss, and with a new supply of asthma-cure they set out for New York.

Now the city toward which our physicians were traveling was the New York of the 1790s, not the New York of 1939. Manhattan began down by the Battery, which was an island, and petered out somewhere near the Woolworth Building, then an elm tree. Little sailing ships hugged the riverfront docks. The streets were paved with cobblestones. Horsemen cantered in the lanes, and dandies smoked clay pipes in Fraunce's Tavern or exercised on Bowling Green.

Sanitation consisted of a file of slaves which trotted through the mists of early morning with buckets on black shoulders. Ladies went calling in sedan chairs, handkerchiefs to noses. New York danced the minuet and took snuff and resembled a cluster of those toy cardboard houses you used to play with as a child. It was little and quaint, and the houses were full of candlesticks and early American antiques.

But in some respects the city was same as today. Tough and shrewd and cosmopolitan, it thought itself ultramod-

ern. Then as now, its New Yorkers regarded the world with
a wise, hard, slightly cynical eye.

OUR MAN, ADAMS, was aware of this eye. He was aware
of it when the medicine show opened up in Maiden Lane.
First night audiences are always hard to play to, and John
Adams had seen that eye before from a platform during
an election campaign.

He tried to warn the Wizard with a signal, but the
Wizard refused to notice it. Trouble came from that glib
word "guaranteed." If you can find that on a patent medicine today, you can sue the maker for a trip to Europe on
the *Normandy*—our modern medicine wizards are mighty
careful about guaranteeing anything. But the Wizard of
Physic was not as circumspect. With the naive faith of the
spellbinder, convinced by his own verbosity, he offered his
cures as sure-fire.

"Usnea for asthma! And I guarantee, good people of
New York, it will cure you of almost anything—!"

Which would have been all right, if the Wizard, himself,
had not been at the time asthmatic. Unfortunately there
were a lot of horses around, and the Wizard was allergic to
horses. Just at the line, "My assistant will now pass among
you with the bottles!" he emitted a terrific wheeze.

You could pull a wheeze in Jersey, then as now, but you
couldn't and can't get away with that stuff in New York.

Some skeptic hollered, "Fraud!" There were cries of,
"Quack!", "Knave!", "Villain!", "Rogue!" and "Rascal!" A
voice roared, "Make him take his own medicine!"

The wagon was overturned, crashing. Someone cut loose
the bear. The uproar was worse than the fight in Congress

over the Alien and Sedition Act. A faint disillusionment in doctoring came to John Adams.

He opened his mouth to call out the Army; then remembered he couldn't call out the Army. It was a tough situation, with fists, clubs and bear-claws flying about his head. Let someone knock him flat and find out he was President! The President of the United States in a New York Street brawl! What Franklin's journals couldn't do with that!

Well, there was nothing for it but to cut and run, so John Adams cut and ran. Fifty strong boys were pinning the Wizard to the cobbles, pouring salts, nostrums and panaceas down his gagging throat—you'd have run, yourself, to escape that.

The bear joined the chase, but after an hour's sprinting John Adams discouraged his pursuers, and, breathless, somewhat disconsolate, made his way to Fraunce's Tavern.

Now a less stubborn man might have thrown up the sponge, but a less stubborn man wouldn't have chucked the Presidency to begin with.

Alone in a corner of the tap room, John Adams told himself he wasn't going to give up like some weakling. If doctoring was too strenuous, he could do something else, but whatever, he did, by Godfrey! it was better than being President.

That no one in New York recognized him hardened his resolve. Nobody talked about him, either. There was a gilt-framed chromo of George Washington on the tavern wall, and plenty of gossip in the pipesmoke, all of which ignored John Adams.

He saw what had happened. The government wasn't going to let the public know he'd gone A.W.O.L. There was a Depression on after the Revolutionary War, and the leaders were afraid the news would start a panic.

Jefferson was keeping it a secret. Hamilton was probably gloating. Well, they couldn't do that to John Adams. He'd show them!

He got himself a job as a journeyman printer, figuring if Franklin could make a fortune at it, so could he. He smudged his hands, and the ink-smell made him sick, and he didn't have the temperament for typesetting.

The end came when he had to set up an editorial pamphlet accusing him—John Adams!—of being a monarchist, a grafter, a charlatan politician and a danger to the country. John Adams blew up with a bang that completely wrecked the printer's shop. Like this. *Bang!*

He tore up the copy and flung sticks of type. Kicked over the press, punched the editor in the nose, broke a window. Once more he found himself leading a mob, and the race he'd run to escape the purge was nothing to that dash through the forests of Central Park. "An Adams man! An Adams!" They came baying after him like bloodhounds. Some of his pursuers he recognized as members of the Essex Junto, part of Hamilton's machine—if he ever got back into politics how he'd pay those scoundrels off!

Only he wasn't going back into politics, by Godfrey! not if he had to retire in Canada. They might have chased him that far, too, if a circuit rider hadn't saved him up near Harlem Heights.

You know, of course, what a circuit rider was. Well, this was one of those big, black-bearded preachers with a Bible in one hand and a whisky jug in the other, and when he saw John Adams come haring up the trail hard-pressed, he offered him the rumble seat on his nag.

5

IT WOULD TAKE too long to go into John Adams' decision to enter the ministry; possibly you see the connection. Circuit riders ranged the country far and wide; the Reverend Joshua Gunn was en route to Boston; John Adams went along as assistant pastor.

Two men on a horse, they trotted through the forest discussing rye and Deuteronomy. The Reverend Gunn was an authority on the one hand, whereas John Adams knew considerable Deuteronomy. Those were the days when people quoted reams of Scripture, and John Adams was no mean student of theology. The Reverend Gunn was delighted to meet up with so scholarly a theologian, and John Adams thought at last he'd found his calling.

Life was pleasant, idling up the Post Road on horseback, taking nips of whisky and religion as they went along. Everything went well until Sunday. Then, in a maple-shadowed, sleepy New England village, the circuit rider asked his assistant pastor to preach.

Well, it was an idyllic setting. Sunlight sprinkling down through arched foliage. Villagers standing bareheaded in Sabbath array. John Adams prepared his sermon in two shakes of a lamb's tail, and he made a mighty impressive-looking preacher.

"Today's text is, Brethren and Sistern—'A prophet is without honor in his own country.'"

Amen. The congregation droning politely. The Reverend Gunn beaming benevolently, retiring with worshipful jug behind shady tree. John Adams' great voice rolling on, "There is much in the Gospel, Brethren and Sistern, that applies to us today. Galilee was not so different from America, even if its people did wear cloaks and sandals, like us, those people yearned for Liberty. Like us they strove for Freedom from oppression—!"

Amen, again, except this sounded more like politics than religion.

"Then a great leader came among them—a man who wasn't appreciated—a lowly carpenter—"

What was that? Behind the tree, the Reverend Gunn pricked up uneasy ears.

"Yes, he was a carpenter, Brethren and Sistern, and people didn't appreciate his ideas. For instance, he wanted to drive the money-changers from the temple. He just didn't think that money and godliness could mix. I tell you, there are those in his country today who could learn that lesson. There's high men in our government—one in particular—who ought to read the Good Book. Finance seems to've become more important than Liberty, but this carpenter didn't approve of amassing wealth. He thought wisdom was better than rubies. He said it was harder for a rich man to get into Heaven than for a camel to get through a needle's eye—!"

Rich men? Camels? The Reverend Joshua Gunn dropped his whisky jug and emerged from retirement with open mouth. A voice from the congregation shrilled, "Stick to religion, Preacher; it's a sermon we want, not this every-day talk!" On the crowd's fringe an old gaffer hailed, "Aye, preach to us on Heaven and Hell!"

"And it's Heaven and Hell I'm preaching," John Adams retorted, flushed. "You think the Bible just applies to the Afterworld? It's for everyday life, I warrant, and the Hell it refers to is a condition right here on earth, not some mythical Perdition in the Hereafter!"

WELL, THAT WAS too much for the Reverend Gunn, same as it was too much for New England. Religion was a touchy subject in those days—then as now, the question of riches embarrassed the pious who had money. Too, there was a strong strain of Puritanism in New England, and they believed in their Hades, hook, line and sinker. But they preferred to think of it as in the Hereafter, for the obvious reason that if there's a Hell right here on earth you may catch it any day, but if it comes in the Hereafter, you can always change your mind the last minute and get out under the wire.

First thing John Adams knew, he had a red hot religious argument on his hands. Someone yelled he wasn't orthodox, and he allowed he wasn't or wanted to be.

"If you don't believe in Hell in the Hereafter," shrilled the banker who'd challenged him first, "where do you expect to go when you die?"

"Me?" John Adams reared up like an equestrian monument. "I'm never going to die!"

That raised Cain! You bet it did! The now thoroughly aroused circuit rider ordered his assistant pastor down from the pulpit. There were cries, "Heretic!" "Freethinker!" "Agnostic!"

John Adams flung back, "Pharisees!" and "Hypocrites!" Dogs barked. Swains swore. Farmers, shook upraised fists. The Reverend Joshua Gunn went off with a bang, shattering the Sunday calm with, "Atheist!"

"Tar an' feather him!" someone roared. "Ride him outa town!"

Well, Bonny Johnnie blew up like a bombshell. Nobody was going to dunk him in hot tar. He'd always believed in the separation of Church and State, and it looked like the time to separate had arrived. Yes, sir, he abandoned the clergy a whole lot faster than he'd joined it; once more he found himself leading a howling mob.

Now you can read his free-thinking opinions in his diary, and some of the entries might have been made after that ministry episode.

Only Providence saved him that time. Providence, Rhode Island. In the city that had rescued Roger Williams from intolerance, he escaped down an alley; pawned his watch for the fare and fled on the first sailing packet for Boston.

Boston, 1790s was a lot like Little Old New York— full of stout Yankee Independence and sound American conviction. Those were the days when it had a pretty good library, and its streets were thronged with seafaring men and Unitarians.

The story goes that John Adams landed on the wharf at midnight, pretty blue and dusty and down-at-heel. The city wasn't far from Braintree, and memory of the big wide house and Abigail filled him with nostalgia.

He'd go there and write, that's what he'd do! Write books on politics and keep his diary; sit by the fireside like any normal citizen, in quiet family life with his wife and his son, John Quincy.

Tears came to his eyes as he looked out over the harbor where he'd seen the famous Tea Party. Ah, there was the Common! And yonder, the court house where he'd defended the Englishman, Prescott, from a Yankee lynching—as fair an exhibition of justice as any in American history.

Massachusetts appreciated him, by Godfrey! and sniffing cod and Abigail's beans, John Adams set out for home. Never dreaming, as be walked up that wharfside, of a trip to Martinique with the *Blonde of the Sea*.

MARTINIQUE? WHY, THAT'S an island way down in the Caribbean—a little French colony colorful with Creoles, palm trees and Negroes and, in those days, the flags of King Louis' frigates keeping watch for the Union Jack. And what would a man like John Adams be doing with a blonde?

Especially the toughest blonde to ever visit Boston Harbor in fiction or out of it—a tramp of the first water with an eye out for men.

Well, the *Blonde of the Sea* was a slaver—fat-beamed with four masts—a hell-pack in her foc'sle—the Devil himself on her quarterdeck. John Adams didn't join up with her willing, either. Stiff as a fence post, he went aboard, smuggled by five sailors with belaying pins snaredrumming on his head.

Then imagine John Adams' feelings when he woke up three days later on the Gulf Stream. Shanghaied! Impressed on a British vessel engaged in illicit slave traffic. What a story for the school books if they ever got hold of that!

John Adams slammed up to that *Blonde's* quarter deck, and what he told that skipper then was a caution. They say his roars echoed clear to Portugal; that whales, deafened, fled for Davy Jones' Locker; the bottom fell out of every ship's glass on the Atlantic, and there was a tidal wave in Japan.

That's probably exaggerated, but it's no exaggeration to say that if John Adams ever found himself shanghaied there would've been a storm at sea. But the *Blonde's* skipper laughed at storms. He had a peg leg, but you ought to have seen the shark that did it!—and he squalled at John Adams like to blow the man down.

"Avast, an' swab the decks, you Yankee lubber! Pipe down! Belay! I wouldn't care if you was the President of the United States, you'll work aboard this ship, or it's all hands to give you a flogging!"

So it was all hands to give Bonny Johnnie a flogging, and a flogging in those days was something to remember. John Adams got a taste of the cat that would have killed an ordinary man. Only John Adams wasn't ordinary.

When they knocked him down, he bounced right up again like one of those equilibrial toys. They pounded him with belaying pins, and he wouldn't stay belayed. Hanging him by the thumbs from a yard-arm didn't calm him, and when salt in his cat-stripes didn't tame him, they keel-hauled him for a spell.

It was all part of the British method of impressing American seamen, but instead of being impressed, John Adams kept on telling that skipper what he thought of him. He said some day the British would pay for it, and he'd bet it would be soon. All the way down the Gulf

Stream he kept up his one-man mutiny. There was hell and highwater aboard that *Blonde of the Sea!*

No matter, the peg-legged skipper wouldn't come about and return John Adams to Boston; the incorrigible mutineer continued on his Caribbean cruise. It is the fashion, I know, to sigh over the good old days of the sailing ships, but the life aboard was brutal as the cat-o'-nine-tails, and even so indestructible a man as our Adams had a hard time trying to survive.

One day they were beating down through the West Indies, towing John Adams off the taffrail at his rope's end, when the *Blonde* ran into a rival. Meet *My Lady of the Boudoir,* French and fast, barkentine out of Cherbourg with twenty-one guns. She took an instant dislike for the *Blonde of the Sea,* and you know what happens when a brunette dislikes a blonde.

France and England were squabbling over the slave trade, and *My Lady* and the *Blonde* flew at each other, no holds barred. Cannon balls screaming. Musketoons flashing. They caught each other with grappling hooks, and the battle was on.

Get an idea of John Adams' predicament, then—floundering astern on a tow-line!—especially when *My Lady* bounced a ten-pounder through the slaver's midriff and the *Blonde* decided the best thing to do was sink.

Just in time they fished him out, as ferocious a catch as was ever hauled from the Caribbean. And that's how John Adams got to Martinique. One look at him, and the French vessel's captain knew he'd caught a Russian spy; and even Rafael Sabatini couldn't have saved him, for he refused to tell the Governor of Martinique his name.

They'd have shot him sure as shooting, if it hadn't been for the French Revolution. Yes, his back was against the wall and he was just refusing a bandage for his eyes when the French Revolution reached Martinique.

"Free?" he whispered at the young lieutenant who had dashed up with the reprieve. Convinced as he was of his immortality, he'd been none the less reluctant to test the theory, and his knees, in spite of him, were shaking.

"*Oui!* Congratulations, *monsieur! Liberté, egalité, fraternité!* King Louis has lost his head for the last time. *Vive la Révolution!*"

"I always knew the French people were all right," said John Adams huskily. "*Vive la Révolution!*"

"And now that *monsieur's* troubles are over," the officer smiled, "where would *monsieur* like to go?"

"Philadelphia!" said John Adams.

6

AND THAT'S ABOUT all there is to this story. Except this. John Adams walked up the dock at Philadelphia, and looked around at the red brick houses, and emitted a sigh that sounded a whole lot like a sigh of relief.

Three months he'd been away—Sweet Land of Liberty! it seemed like three years. And it seemed to John Adams as if every time he'd opened his mouth in those three months a mob had got after him. Two New York mobs had chased him, one in Connecticut, and an outraged husband. Tinkering, coopering, doctoring—all had their tougher aspects, it appeared.

Why, a man couldn't even preach a sermon without getting into trouble. If there's a moral to this tale, I think John Adams, himself, suspected it. Something about the grass on the other side of the fence always looking greener.

Well, it was certainly nice to saunter for a change; and what pleased him even more was the sight of a large crowd moving toward him as he strolled into Fauneil Square. So his hiatus had been justified! A welcoming committee! They appreciated him, after all!

Halting by a horse-block to await this demonstration, he struck a statuesque pose; couldn't help thrusting his chest a little. Then he almost turned to granite in astonishment. Why, there was the tinker! Right there in the forefront of the crowd! And the cooper from Morristown, full of apple-jack! By George! the Wizard of Physic was with them, a lot thinner than he'd been before the purge, but recognizable in his Indian hat. There, too, was that scoundrelly New York printer! And the Reverend Joshua Gunn! And the captain of the Providence packet! And the sailors who'd shanghaied him on Boston Common!

Not only that, the whole United States Army seemed to be escorting them, each accompanied by a cockade-hatted trooper armed with musket, bayonet fixed. Drums were rolling somewhere, and the Liberty Bell began to toll. John Adams stood like statuary. Misty-eyed. Emotion-choked. Never had he been received by such a reception!

A bristling colonel stepped forward and placed his hand on John Adams' shoulder. For a moment neither man could speak. You can see them standing there regarding each other like figures in a historic painting; well, it was the colonel who spoke first.

"In the name of the Government of the United States, I arrest you on a charge of murder!"

"Murder?" John Adams broke that statue-pose as a monument is animated by a bomb. "Me?" voice shriller than an off-key fife. "You're arresting me for *murder?*"

"It's him, all right," came the tinker's nasal twang. "I'd reckonize th' critter in any disguise. Him as traded th' silver buckles off'n his shoes."

"Sure, it's him," from the cooper. "Know him anywhere! I thought he seemed mighty nervous an' careful never to tell me his full name."

"Never give me no name any time," cried the Wizard of Physic. "Look! He's still wearin' the same coat!"

The printer roared, "He's a maniac, I tell you!"

"Dangerous atheist!" cried the Reverend Gunn.

"Same one as pawned the watch for a ticket to Boston!"

"Yah, that's 'im we shanghaied, ain't it, Peter? G'ory! A bleedin' murderer!"

At that, the foul yell of "Murder!" loosened half the bricks of Philadelphia, and John Adams' answering roar sent twenty chimneys toppling.

"And who am I accused of murdering?" he thundered at the colonel of the guard. "Who am I supposed to have murdered, hey?"

"The President of the United States!" roared the colonel. "There's a rumor afoot he hasn't been seen for the last three months, and my private opinion was he'd been assassinated. So I sent scouts out to search for the body.

"They didn't find the corpse, by heaven, but they found this tinker wearing the President's shoe buckles! We've been trailing you ever since, my man! The tinker says you gave him those silver buckles—you pawned the President's watch!—I'm a liar if that's not his coat you're wearing now! Assassin," roared the colonel, "I accuse you of murdering John Adams!"

"But *I* am John Adams!" John Adams squalled. "Don't you know me when you see me, you infernal idiot! I'm the President of the United States!"

"Ha ha!" That colonel was convulsed. "Listen to that, will you? Look who says he's the President of the United States!"

THE CROWD LOOKED and laughed, and John Adams looked, too, but he didn't laugh. He caught his reflection in the watering-trough beside the horseblock, and he pulled a green breath of horror. His clothes hung his frame in fragments. His linen resembled that of a scarecrow. He was wearing wooden sabots which the French officer in Martinique had loaned him; his face was sun-fried, brine-cooked, frizzled; his hair hung wild about his ears, and he had a lousy, gray beard.

Well, the crowd was screaming, "Lynch him!" and John Adams didn't even bother to argue. He sailed over that horse-block like a wild man taking off for Borneo. He went through that crowd and across that square like a shot. Shots were pretty swift in those days, too, but the ones that came after him didn't overtake J. Adams.

There he was leading a mob, again, and this time across Philadelphia, but he'd had some mighty fine practice at mob-leading, and they say it isn't in the history books because John Adams went so fast that no historians saw him. He didn't let any grass grow under his feet that time. Even the grass that looked greener on the other side of the fence.

I don't have to tell you where he went, either.

Right! Straight back to that very brick building he'd walked out of three months before. Yes sir, and he was so darned glad to be back there in that building that he locked himself in his room so he couldn't get out.

Some say he bathed, shaved and changed into fresh linen in three minutes, and some say he did it in two. At any rate, he was there at his desk in State garments with the Constitution in front of him when Alex Hamilton banged on the door. He opened it, even for Alex Hamilton.

"Good morning, Mister President. I hear you've been away. I didn't notice it."

"I am almost glad to see you, Hamilton."

Thomas Jefferson rushed in. "Great Scott! Mister President, you've kept the cabinet waiting for three months! Congress is wild! There's a row over the Alien and Sedition Act! You've got to sign this Finance Bill! Hamilton, here wants to be appointed General-in-Chief of the Army! That Liquor Tax needs revision! You must settle the X-Y-Z Affair! The Ambassador from Spain wants an appointment! Here's a report from Jay on England! Can you receive a delegation from Virginia? What about the Navy? That Italian Count is here demanding an audience! My God! we're on the verge of a war with France! And there's a great crowd out in front—it seems there's a rumor you've been assassinated—would you mind stepping out on the balcony and making a speech to the American people—"

John Adams beamed.

How good it was to be back at his Presidential desk. What a luxury to be able to relax. Restful, that's what it was. Serene. He smiled quietly at the mass of documents to be signed; calmly told Hamilton he wouldn't get the Army appointment; assured Jefferson he would veto any war with France. As he strolled out to the balcony amid a storm of protests and cheers, he told himself that for the first time in his life he felt—and the word came to him as a balm—placid.

ALL THAT, OF course, is supposing. Which means it isn't a true story. But there's some truth in it, just the same. Adams did walk out on the government, as previously stated, and he was hardly noted for placidity. As a matter of fact, too, he was once lost in the woods—with his wife while they were on their way from Baltimore to Washington where they were to be the first occupants of the White House.

Stubbornly resisting political pressure, he kept America out of war with France. Disliking Britannia's method of ruling the wave, he ordered a fleet to challenge that misrule, and was the father of the American Navy.

As for his quarrel with Hamilton, his free-thinking agnosticism, his scrappy temper, all those are a matter of record. He even quarreled with Thomas Jefferson, and was so resentful of his Vice-president's consequent election to the Presidency that he left Washington in a blue huff with wire wheels, refusing to attend his successor's inauguration ceremonies.

Years later, he and Jefferson were reconciled. They wrote long letters to each other, discussing politics, philosophy and religion. After sixty years of study, John Adams wrote to his friend, he thought religion could be summed up in four simple words. "Be just and good."

It is true he declared to some New Englanders he was never going to die, and in all likelihood his short-lived hearers misunderstood him.

The Fourth of July—Independence Day, 1826—old John Adams, frosty-haired, dim-eyed, lay semi-conscious in his sick bed. Told his old friend Jefferson was ailing in Monticello, he whispered, "But Jefferson still lives!" and died.

But his old friend and political rival had beat him on the record—for Thomas Jefferson had died two hours before. What a painting for the history books—the fireworks down below, and the zenith bright with dawn-stripes and late stars—the two great patriots meeting on that final highroad, taking leave of America on Independence Day!

And perhaps John Adams was right, and both will forever live. Certainly Jefferson has been timeless, and who can say John Adams is not immortal? Scrappy he may have been. Temperamental and full of spleen. But he hated tyranny and oppression; worshipped Democracy and Freedom. His sense of Justice was as even as the very scales, bearing out Jefferson's appraisal—"Disinterested as the Being who made him."

That sort of man can never die.

THREE MEN AND A TUB

1

Bathtub for Sale: Twenty-Gallon Capacity—Cast Iron—All Modern Conveniences Including Installed Chair and Charcoal Stove at Foot—Short Size, but Truly Fit for a King—Ye Interested Parties Seeking Magnificent Bargain Please Communicate This Department New Orleans Times-Picayune—1803.

HAD YOU LIVED in New Orleans in 1803, you might have read such an advertisement in your morning copy of the *Times-Picayune*—had there been an 1803 edition of the *Times-Picayune*.

You didn't live there at that date, and there was no such edition of the *Times-Picayune,* but there was (and still is) such a bathtub. You may see it any time you care to in the old Cabildo Museum down below Canal Street—as fantastic a household appliance as any concocted in that early era of bathing and the machine age.

In shape, the tub resembles a great shoe. The prospective bather would sit himself in this shoe, his chin thrust over the rim, while slaves filled the vessel with hot water. A charcoal stove in the boot-toe serves to keep the water warm while the bather, ensconced like Mother Goose's Old Woman, may relax and soak in comfort. At the same time, if he cares to do so, he may modestly converse with

the ladies and gentlemen in his court. You might say it isn't
strictly Kohler.

Pardon me! and doesn't this seem like a remarkable
introduction for a story about Thomas Jefferson?

But there were many remarkable things about Thomas
Jefferson. Idolized by all Democrats today as the father
of Jeffersonian Democracy, he was elected to the Presidency (1801–1809) by the Republican Party. He gave us
our American money system of dimes and dollars, and in
his last years went privately bankrupt. A firm believer in
temperance, his wine bill in the White House ran over ten
thousand dollars. Devoutly religious, he believed Chris-
tianity could be condensed to the Sermon on the Mount,
and he was publicly howled down as an atheist by the Pres-

Like a fury Madame X charged through the door,
knocking Talleyrand head over heels

ident of Harvard University. Great humanist, he thought
the people were fools.

Did you know he was an architect? An inventor? A
writer? Philosopher? Scholar? Accomplished musician?
As well as an orator? Lawyer? Political leader? Patriot?
Diplomat? Founder of our American Republic and third
President of the United States?

Go to Monticello and see the amazing and beautiful

thirty-three-room house that took him thirty-two years to build. See his own designs for the building. The music he composed. His extraordinary "elevating bed." His fine drawings and handwriting. His set of razors named for every day in the week except Thursday.

If he didn't have time to shave on Thursday, it's no wonder. Expert linguist, he studied and spoke Greek, Latin, Spanish, Italian, German and French as well as English. He wrote three volumes on politics and eighty volumes of letters. Meantime, he ran a plantation, raised a beautiful daughter, planned the University of Virginia, and in his spare moments dabbled in everything from surgery to astronomy.

Lay aside such lofty historical titles as The Sage of Monticello, and imagine the man! Scholarly, yet possessed with the energy of a dynamo. Aristocratic, yet all for the common people. A polished, gallant Southern gentleman, yet entirely unassuming.

If there were paradoxes to Jefferson, they came from his amazing versatility—many-sided, he could see many sides. He was a pacifist, but he approved of Shays's Rebellion against the government as something to keep the people on their toes—the people would only appreciate Democracy when they had to fight for it. "The Tree of Liberty," he said, "must be watered with human blood."

He wanted peace; argued against a large standing Army or Navy. Then he was forced to arm to the teeth and vote for a stout-fisted battle fleet. It doesn't do to shake your fist at a man like Thomas Jefferson.

And the bully who did shake a fist at Jefferson—and incidentally the rest of our United States—was a little man, a scowling pint-sized Corsican, a onetime corporal, squatting in one of those iron shoes with a charcoal stove in the toe over there in a back room of the Tuileries Palace in Paris. If we introduce this fellow clad only in his skin and be-medaled with soap bubbles, it is only because that was one of his favorite uniforms.

From here on this isn't strictly history (although the background is authentic) but here's the story—

NAPOLEON DROPPED THE soap and glared over the rim of his tub at Josephine and Talleyrand. Sitting in a mist of steam, he might have been some sort of pagan idol.

"Talleyrand, have you forced that treaty from Spain as I ordered?"

"Spain is at your feet, Sire."

"Has Marshal Victor conquered all of Austria as I commanded?"

"Practically all Europe is conquered, Sire."

"Magnifique! Then get out of here, all of you! A new conquest must be planned at once. Leave me my map!"

This is doubtless a pretty free translation from the French, but you can read its equivalent in the pages of world history. Napoleon was taking one of his historic hot baths. It is the fashion of dictators to be eccentric, and the Little Corporal set the fashion. His specialty was the hot bath.

Relaxed, then, in his unique tub, he wiped steam from his eyes and consulted the map.

Oui, Talleyrand was right. All Europe, with the exception of Russia, had been conquered. Moscow, of course, was the usual question mark, and he didn't want to bother with it yet. England, too, was waiting her turn, but England could wait. What he needed just now was an easy victim. Conquerors, as any one knows, must keep on conquering— nothing like a conquest to keep a dictator on his throne.

But with Europe laid out neatly in pelts, the season had been slow. All dressed up with no place to go, the armies were getting restless. The Treasury needed money. *Sacré bleu!* something had to be conquered and conquered quick, or the public might rebel because of the taxes.

Such were the Little Corporal's thoughts while he sat a-tubbing and a-mapping. Then his eye glinted brightly as it fell on one corner of the map—a corner of the map he'd been saving for just this sort of doldrum. The map in his hands was not the map that hangs on your study wall today. Europe and the Atlantic Ocean had much the same outline, but the country west of the Atlantic was different.

All over the north sprawled Canada. Florida belonged to Spain. There was a strip of coastline marked the United States, but it didn't extend much westward of the Appalachian Mountains; the miles and miles of blank territory beyond belonged to Spain, too. That was the Territory of Louisiana. New Orleans at the bottom, and miles up the Mississippi.

OF COURSE, IT didn't really belong to Spain. La Salle had claimed it first in the name of France. The Spaniards had taken it later. But now that the Little Corporal had taken the Spaniards, the territory, to all intents and purposes, belonged to him. To all intents and purposes! Well, so far he hadn't had any use for it, but now Napoleon Bonaparte, First Consul, there in his Paris bathtub, saw a use for it.

"Talleyrand!"

"I am coming, Sire."

"Talleyrand, you rascal, do you see that stretch of Louisiana Territory over there on the American Continent?"

"But, name of a blue pig! Louisiana belongs to Spain. Spain, so to speak, belongs to us. Surely there is no need for us to conquer Louisiana."

"Who said anything about conquering Louisiana? I propose to *buy* Louisiana!"

"Buy it? But you already own it!"

"Not openly, thick-head! The King of Spain is my puppet, but outwardly he appears to rule. I intend to do this legally, all very open and above-board. I shall send my brother, Lucien, to close the deal. The Spaniards won't want to do it, but we shall convince them.

"For payment we shall offer those nincompoops the Kingdom of Etruria—what loss to us, since it belongs to the Duke of Tuscany?—and we will promise the Spanish king to keep Louisiana forever in his name. And now that we have bought Louisiana"—Napoleon grinned, for when he made up his mind, a matter was already settled—"we will land our invincible army in New Orleans."

"But, Sire, I do not understand!"

"You are only my foreign minister; foreign ministers are not supposed to understand. Nevertheless, I will try to explain. Look there in the Caribbean. Do you see our island of Haiti?"

"Our troops are already fighting in Haiti, *oui*."

"We will send more troops to Haiti. Thousands of troops. From there they will be carried to New Orleans. I will have such an army in New Orleans as the world has never seen. My veteran grenadiers. My *grognons*. Fifty thousand cavalry. As many cannon!"

"But your conquest, Sire! Name of a name! Why move a vast army into New Orleans if you have bought Louisiana legally and there is nothing over there to conquer?"

Napoleon's quick eyes glittered. "Look at the map, you fool. Who said nothing over there to conquer?"

Talleyrand stared. Then a slow, crooked smile cracked the lower part of his face. Napoleon, tracing a certain outline with a soapy finger, chuckled. Presently he began to laugh. Marshal Victor looked in, let loose a guffaw. Josephine, entering with towels, broke into peals of mirth. Napoleon's brothers joined the scene to howl. Two minutes later the whole imperial bathroom was doubled up and roaring.

You can see Napoleon lifting a sudden, wet arm for silence. Gripping his foreign minister by the elbow.

"Have you ever failed in a diplomatic trick, my Talley-rand?"

"No, Sire."

"Has our Madame X ever failed?"

"Invariably she gets her man."

"Have I ever lost a conquest."

"You are Napoleon. Invincible!"

"Very well, Jefferson's new ambassador is due here within the month. We will work on this yokel as soon as he arrives. Meantime, the armies will be secretly mobilized. The fleet is to stand prepared. Personally, I think I am going to enjoy the American climate. And by the way, order the imperial iron-works at Marseille to ship that new bathtub they are making for me to New Orleans!"

2

THOMAS JEFFERSON, PRESIDENT of the United States, sorted his morning's mail. A letter from the Butchers Guild of Philadelphia—hoping the prize, slaughtered calf had reached him in good condition and that he would enjoy choice cuts from same. (Too bad the meat had spoiled in the four days journey to Washington; he must thank the worthy butchers in the name of the Republic.)

A letter from a Boston clergyman accusing him of heresy, anti-Christian activities and atheism "that will endanger the virtue of our citizens to the extent that the flower of our womanhood will not dare set foot in the streets." (Hypocrites! Bigoted, narrow-minded, blue-nose hypocrites!)

A letter from a New York banker advising Thomas Jefferson that his latest speech, favoring the farmer and workingman, would reduce the country to a state of anarchy. (These plutocrats would substitute money rule for monarchy; make riches the measure of a man; evolve an aristocracy of dollars!)

A letter from the Dey of Algiers declaring that he, the Dey, was not quite satisfied with the yearly tribute of twenty-one thousand dollars paid by American seamen for the privilege of sailing through Gibraltar unmolested, and would appreciate an extra forty thousand. (Well, those scoundrelly Barbary pirates! If John Paul Jones had only lived to deal with them! A time is coming, Mr. Dey, when you and your blackmailing Arab Corsairs are going to be blown off the map!)

A letter from a certain agent in France, postmarked Paris—

"What's this? What's this?" Thomas Jefferson sat bolt upright in his swivel chair.

He read the letter once, twice, again! It was a missive in code—a piece of information that made the threatening piracy of the Algerian Dey look like small-time racketeering in comparison. A cold, steely light came to Thomas Jefferson's eye. As he re-read the letter, his jaws set like iron. That fellow now! Sweet Land of Liberty! Of all the villainies! Well, the miserable old Dey would have to wait. America had a bigger fish—the biggest shark of all, by heaven!—to fry.

"And he's already sent over his new bathtub!"

Thomas Jefferson reared, quivering, to his feet. Six-foot-two he stood, tall and straight as George Washington, but even quicker than Washington would have been to see the implications of this villainous scheme. Subtle Jefferson knew subtlety when he saw it. The danger to the United States—its Army disbanded; its Navy miniscule—was appalling.

The little republic was like an eaglet, wobbly, scarcely feathered, overshadowed by a gigantic, carnivorous, cruel-beaked hawk. Seas would mean nothing to this menace, whose talons were already fastened on New Orleans. At the moment its hungry grip was clutched on the island of Haiti. The Haitian slaves were struggling for freedom, but the tiny army of Toussaint L'Ouverture could never dispossess this devouring gargoyle, for all the black general's amazing genius.

What a trick! The revolt of those poor Haitian slaves was giving Napoleon just the excuse he wanted for transporting his army to the Western Hemisphere. He had forced the wretched Spaniards to give him New Orleans. A blind man could see he didn't want that outpost to plant pineapples on.

THE SHORT HAIRS bristled on Jefferson's neck. Napoleon! Where could unprepared America, menaced by such a giant, find an ally? England might help with her navy, but England was uncertain; the British people favored American Democracy, but could you trust the British ruling class?

Spain, Rome, Prussia—their despot rulers under the thumb of a greater tyrant—all would be glad to see the United States assailed. Since the inception of diplomacy it has been the practice of European powers, imperiled by some war lord, to throw the little fellow to the lions. Appeasement is not a new diplomatic device. Thomas Jefferson realized in a second that the U.S.A., the fledgling eaglet, had been selected for the sacrifice.

That made Thomas Jefferson mad. As with men who don't anger easily, it made him mighty mad. Always he'd been willing to arbitrate and listen sympathetically to the other fellow's point of view. At heart he was a pacifist, for he knew full well the agony of warfare from his experience in the American Revolution. As President he'd voted for disarmament, and he'd stood, with George Washington, against entanglement with foreign military alliances.

And this was what America got for it! It was singled out as an easy mark by the first bully that came down the pike.

The old Dey of Algiers had been getting under Jefferson's collar, but he'd been holding his temper, advising patience. This new pirate was too much.

Thomas Jefferson did a clicking right-about-face from pacifism. He sprang to his desk and prepared an order calling for eighty thousand volunteers.

But arming would take time, and that conqueror across the Atlantic had his barkentines and bayonets ready to go. At present the American Navy amounted to four frigates, some row-boats and a sloop. It was hardly possible that our volunteers, tough as they were, would be a match for the veteran grenadiers and cannons of the Little Corporal.

So, on second thought, Jefferson did another about-face. Summoning Madison, his Secretary of State, he proposed an alliance with England by which the British were immediately to "capture" New Orleans in case of an American-Napoleonic War. He even suggested that the British should, for the time being, hold Louisiana, in preference to Napoleon and his well-known real-estate agents. He wrote a famous line that has come down through history: "From the moment that France takes possession of New Orleans… we must marry ourselves to the British fleet and nation."

But Jefferson didn't want that kind of shotgun marriage; the United States wanted a friend, but it hadn't thought of matrimony. Having proposed, Jefferson knew he must do everything in his power to stall off the ceremony. Suppose, once settled in New Orleans, the Red Coats refused to withdraw? No, if Napoleon was a dangerous neighbor, J. Bull was equally dangerous.

UNDER ANY CIRCUMSTANCE, war was impossible.

Napoleon must be stopped in some other way. How? His baleful genius didn't stop at military craft; as a statesman he put Machiavelli in the shade. His mouth-piece, Talleyrand, tore up treaties into scraps of paper, made promises only to shatter them forty ways. Diplomats visiting the French court were gulled, tricked, beaten down, bought up and hoodwinked like bumpkins in the parlor of a card-sharp.

Jefferson, who had to send a green ambassador into this spider's-web, stared in desperation at the secret letter.

Now there's no historic confirmation for this agent's letter (this is fiction, remember) but the situation is historically authentic. We had our agents in Europe at the time; such a letter is highly possible.

It warned Jefferson of the Louisiana danger. Napoleon, it went on to say, was diplomatically about as trustworthy as a crocodile. Invariably an envoy sent to deal with him came away in utter defeat. Always his methods were the same. First the envoy would be threatened, denounced, terrorized, browbeaten. Failing intimidation, the next step, operated by Talleyrand, was bribery. Should the envoy survive these two generally fatal operations, he was subjected to a final pressure—a certain Madame X whose methods, so far as our espionage department had been able to determine, had never been resistible.

"War," the letter went on to say, "is the alternative. That, with Napoleon, is always fatal. Yet diplomacy seems equally fatal, for no diplomat in Europe has so far been able to withstand the threats, the bribery, or the guile of Madame X."

3

THOMAS JEFFERSON WALKED the floor. America had never been in a tougher spot, and he knew it. No time to consult Congress. No time for politics and long-winded Senatorial harangues. He had to stop the Little Corporal, and stop him fast.

What had brought Napoleon to draw a bead on the United States? He needed a conquest, of course. What would a conqueror, greedy, lustful for power possibly want more than a conquest? Napoleon seemed to have everything in the world one man could need. Was it just barely possible there was something he needed besides a conquest, something he didn't have?

"I might find a way out," Jefferson thought, "if I could just think of something Napoleon needs more than a conquest."

Well, he put on his thinking cap, and Jefferson's thinking cap was no mean article of headgear. When he gathered his wits that day to tackle that problem, he had plenty of wits to gather. He dismissed his secretary and paced alone. He thought and thought and thought. But there wasn't any easy answer. He wrestled with that problem until the perspiration sprinkled out on his forehead, and still he didn't have his answer.

Going to the cabinet—not his political cabinet, but

the one in the corner of the room—he took out his violin. Music always eased him at a time of strain; he fingered the instrument lovingly, and played a quiet little composition he had written the day before.

As if some devil possessed his fingers, the tune strayed into martial chords—an air he recognized as the *Marseillaise!* Good heavens! he couldn't fiddle while that American Foreign Policy burned. Tucking the tactless instrument back into its case, he picked up his long clay pipe and forced himself into a chair.

But he'd never liked tobacco, and he wasn't the sort of man who could sit idle. Seizing a pencil, he began to sketch on a pad—a design for window curtains he wanted for his house at Monticello. Interior decorating was one of his hobbies; instead of doodling like an ordinary man distraught, he sketched valences, bannisters, ceiling decorations or floor patterns for the mansion he was planning. But today it didn't work. He threw down the pencil. Instead of window curtains, he'd been drawing French flags!

Maybe a look at the sky would clear his head. Afternoon was waning, and there were early stars. Jefferson loved the stars. They were in the American flag. He unwrapped his telescope—astronomy was his special hobby, and he prided himself on being one of the first Americans to calculate an eclipse—and he took up his position at a window.

The sun had westered, and the sky over Washington was evening blue. Ah, there was Arcturus, shining like Ohio which was just coming into the Union. There was old Alpha, gleaming new as Tennessee. But there was Venus, bold as—as Madame X? And Sirius, the elusive dog-star. And—and Mars!

Yes, Mars—low and red in the sky like a burning coal—
or a war-like, menacing eye! And in the east a great pile
of rumbling, smoky clouds—clouds that blackened and
gathered as they moved in off the Atlantic toward America. Baleful lightning played behind the storm-heads. There
was a nearing echo of thunder. Hastily, Thomas Jefferson
closed the window.

His jaw was grim. That sky was an omen, and he was
getting nowhere. He kicked into his carpet slippers and
put on his old brown house-jacket. Every fiber in him was
a fiddle-string. His mind must be elastic. He must relax.
Pacing across the floor, he picked up a volume on finance.
A little easy reading. Hamilton said the money system was
imperfect; maybe he could tinker up a new coin. A five-
cent piece! That might do the trick. What this country
needed was a good five-cent piece. Everybody would like
it. Everybody needed money.

"Everybody!"

Thinking aloud, Thomas Jefferson broke off with a stifled
shout. His fist came down on the finance book with a crash.
By George! he had it. How to deal with Napoleon. It was a
chance. A mighty risky chance! Everything would depend
on the ambassador. Sweet Land of Liberty! Somehow,
somewhere, he must find the right man. A man who could
withstand the threats of Napoleon, the bribery of Talleyrand, and the *coup de grace* of Madame X!

THAT WAS NO small order—to find a man who could beat
that triple threat—and Jefferson clutched his forehead. It
was like some terrible algebra; having solved one brain-
crusher, he was up against another.

The smartest statesmen in Europe, the cagiest diplomats,

the toughest kings had crumbled before Napoleon like
so much clay. Americans were new at this game of international diplomacy; an inexperienced player would have
about as much chance in Napoleon's court as a hayseed in
a New York gaming house.

The man who went to France must have the courage of
Richard the Lion Heart; the integrity of George Washington; the invincibility of Sir Galahad! Such men don't grow
on trees, even in the United States of America.

Jefferson went down the list. He would've gone himself
but he couldn't leave the presidential chair. He couldn't
send trustworthy Madison, and his friend, James Monroe,
was away on state business. John Adams would oppose
him in the matter of policy, and his temper was too uncertain for delicate foreign relations. Pinckney, Hamilton,
Aaron Burr—all the old hands he might have counted held
governmental posts from which they couldn't be removed.
If George Washington and Ben Franklin were only alive!
Where now could he find an unbeatable ambassador?

So he was up against another poser, harder than the first.
He forgot that he'd missed his lunch and dinner. Forgot the
reception that evening for the British ambassador—that
pompous little man! Once more pacing the floor, he went
over every available American he could think of, analyz-
ing character, examining their records. This one? That one?
Which one to send. One fell down here; another there and
every minute counted. He had to decide on his ambassador with no time to decide in, and the whole history of the
United States would depend on that decision.

Jefferson's heart sank. But he didn't give up the search.
He took off his coat and rolled up his linen sleeves, and

went over the records again. The clock ticked like a metro-
nome, and his head began to ache. Time out for a glass of
wine; he must pull his thoughts together; keep cool.

It was like a world-shaking chess game—his move—
everything depending on his choice of piece. Too much
hinged on this decision. He was white with tension, and
his hand on the Madeira bottle was trembling.

He pulled himself up. None of that, now! He'd been in
sore need before, and always pulled himself out. Necessity
was the mother of invention.

Ah, that was a way to sharpen his wits. Going to his desk,
he sat in the swivel chair he'd invented, took a reassuring
spin, and rummaged in a gadget-littered drawer. There was
the pedometer that had been such a problem—the little
machine that measured the mileage one walked. Perhaps
some day he would attach the thing on a wagon. And
there was his little model of a semaphore signal by which
he could wigwag messages from his house to neighbors
on surrounding hills. There was the design of his famous
plow, and here was the working model of a dumb-waiter
he was going to install in the dining room of his house,
and another little model of his famous folding doors, and
a new-style weathervane.

He ranged these thingumbobs on his desk and tried to
relax, tinkering with his inventions. But the pedometer
reminded him of marching feet. The semaphore of military signals. The weathervane of War Clouds in the sky.
Glumly he pushed the inventions aside; returned to the
unrevealing records.

He must find a man who wouldn't fear Napoleon, yet
keep cool while the Corsican shouted. A man with a level

head. A diplomat. But diplomacy was Talleyrand's department—Talleyrand, the coiled snake. How many men could resist that sort of poison? And then Madame X! Those that weren't hotheaded were liable to be hot-blooded. Jefferson, the psychologist, knew he must find one man in a million.

THE CAPITOL WAS asleep that night, but the President wasn't. Amidst guttering candles and hundreds of written records, he was hunting an ambassador. Midnight, he bolstered himself with coffee, and for relaxation he wrote some notes on surgery, how to set a broken leg. But surgery reminded him of battlefields—the bloody harvests in America if he didn't find that man.

Desperately he returned to the search. One after another he rejected possible names. He couldn't take a chance; he had to be certain. Three a.m., hair tousled, neck-linen askew, aquiline features lined with fatigue, he was on the point of exhaustion.

He was concentrating too hard. For a moment's recess, he penned a memorandum on the right way to bake brick and manufacture nails. Nails! He ought to be thinking of a way to manufacture bullets. Deliberately he turned to his drawings of a wall he planned for the future University of Virginia—a serpentine wall, one brick in width, of such cunning engineering it would one day be considered an architectural marvel. Dear heaven! if he could only build a similar wall around America.

He braced his elbow on the desk, leaned his forehead on the heel of his palm. His lips hardened in self-scorn. Ha! They called him the Sage of Monticello! The great thinker. The great inventor. The great architect.

Well, he couldn't even think of a workable way to beat

Napoleon. Inventor, bah!—he struck his models aside—if he could only invent a robot to go to France, that would be something. As for architecture—his restless, brilliant eye swept scornfully across the plans for his house at Monticello; the dining room with its dumb waiter, the second story concealed from the outside, the ballroom with its parquet floor where guests would dance and play pretty charades; the bedroom with its elevating bed and servant's compartment hidden in the wall—as for architecture—!

"Hidden compartment! Charades!"

Thomas Jefferson spun up out of his swivel chair. He grabbed up the plans of his house. Fatigue vanished from his features. His eyes shone. By Old Glory! he hadn't found his man tonight—but he'd invented a way to find him!

4

—

HE DIDN'T DILLYDALLY, then. Not for an instant. Crack of dawn, he had his Secretary of State on the job and the machinery of government turning. First thing was to make that play for England's help; then let Napoleon know he was angling for such an alliance.

Next thing was to start Army recruiting and propose a Big-Navy Bill. Nappy was to learn about that, too—the news to be conveyed through secret channels so the Little Corporal would think it was a leak. They had their way of doing such things in those days, same as today, and you can read about all that in the history books.

Then Jefferson set to work a machine that isn't in the history books. It isn't in the history books because it was all very secret—a fiction secret—and even the historians can't find out about a fiction secret. But this story has it that thirteen secret messages were sent post-haste from Washington that dawn. Thirteen secret messages to thirteen different men.

The story doesn't say who those thirteen men were (save the last) for that is a fiction secret, too. Some of them fell by the wayside, as we shall see, and it doesn't do to discredit anyone in fiction.

Anyway, next afternoon they began to arrive. They came to Washington on horseback, spattered and muddy from hard galloping over the early American roads. They came by stage coach and gig, and several afoot. Some came from Virginia, and two from Philadelphia; a couple from New York, and one all the way from Boston in a racing sloop.

From the window of his study Jefferson, busy with his drawing board, watched them come up Pennsylvania Avenue. End of the week, all thirteen were there. On tenter-hooks from the emergency, Jefferson was ready for them.

Instructions were for them to be in a certain room of the White House at a certain hour on Saturday night; and what happened when they got there is another fiction secret not recorded by historians. They didn't know what they were wanted for—the summons hadn't said. A White House attendant admitted them to this ante-chamber where they sat in thirteen chairs named for the first Thirteen States.

Cheroots and brandy were at hand. Snuff for those so disposed, and fried chicken legs from Maryland, walnuts from Carolina, red apples from Maine. A log fire crackled in the fireplace; music tinkled from a music box. Everything was set as though for a party, save that the curtains were heavily drawn, the walls seemed to be in shadow, and the room had the atmosphere of a seance—clandestine.

You can see those thirteen early Americans sitting down and looking at each other and wondering. Something was up. What? No one of them knew. They cracked nuts and tried the wine, whispering together, exchanging political gossip. But presently they lapsed into silence.

As the time passed, one or two began to fidget. They

adjusted their linen stocks and shifted in their chairs. Coughed and fooled with their garters.

"Demmit!" The Marylander finally displayed his watch. "It's nearly midnight. When is Jefferson coming?"

"What's it all about, anyway?" another exploded, exasperated. "What did the President summon us for? What's in the wind? Why doesn't he come?"

But Thomas Jefferson wasn't coming. He wasn't coming because right at that moment he was watching the room from behind a picture of George Washington on the wall at room's end; watching from the concealment of a compartment built in for just that purpose—such a compartment as he later built over his bed in his bedroom at Monticello.

He was watching the room and studying those thirteen men, wondering which of them were going to pass the test. Test? Listen. Twelve o'clock struck like a curfew. An attendant entered the room and requested those thirteen men to come with him, one at a time, to another chamber. He beckoned the nearest initiate, and the man followed him, wondering what in Uncle Sam was going to happen.

THE ATTENDANT LED him down a dark-lit hall to a dark-lit chamber, bowed him across the threshhold and closed the door behind his back. It was all very hush-footed and creepful. One candle burned in a corner of that room; the walls were curtained with shadows; and at first our visitor thought himself alone. Then he saw a figure standing back, enshadowed.

He'd expected Thomas Jefferson, but it wasn't Thomas Jefferson. No sir, it was a short, stocky figure in dark cutaway, breeches and hose, standing with back to the room, legs splayed, chin down in thought, head bowed in cocked hat. A gasp from the visitor brought that figure wheeling around. The visitor like to've swallowed his Adams' apple.

"Napoleon!"

You know it wasn't Napoleon. It was an actor—the best character actor Thomas Jefferson had been able to locate on the American stage. This story can't divulge the name, but can bet he was the star of his day.

Night and day for a week, at Jefferson's instruction, he'd been rehearsing for that part, and he looked more like Napoleon than Napoleon himself. His orders were to out-Bonaparte Bonaparte, and he put on a piece of character acting never equaled in the American theater.

That counterfeit Napoleon began by declaring that his troops had invaded America. Armies of grenadiers and *grognons* were concealed in the woods surrounding Washington, waiting to seize the capitol. Jefferson and his cabinet had been kidnapped.

Tomorrow the whole country would be conquered. Therefore (roared this spurious Napoleon) he had sent for thirteen prominent Americans to meet him here in the White House and deliver over the nation.

Well, by the time the bogus Bonaparte got through with that speech, our first initiate's teeth were rattling. It all looked very plausible and real. Communication lines were skimpy back around 1802. A fleet could sneak up the Potomac without Boston hearing about it for a week. An army could camp in one valley while the enemy over the hill thought they were five hundred miles away. Even ten years later—to show you how slow information was—the

Americans fought a great battle against the British two weeks after peace had been signed in Europe.

So that gag about the French surrounding Washington didn't seem impossible. It explained Napoleon's presence there in the White House. Back in those days the very name of Napoleon was enough to send children hiding in the china closet; and our unsuspecting visitor thought sure he was on the mat before the Little Corporal.

Then that actor let loose the works. He stormed and raved and shouted in a marvelous imitation of Napoleonic wrath. He scowled and struck postures, waved his fists and howled. He threatened to smash America to bits and that man in front of him with it. Ten minutes of that terrific tirade, and that poor visitor's knees were clapping.

Thomas Jefferson, watching, from concealment, sadly crossed off a name. He pulled a bell-rope, and the attendant removed the first tryout. Tight-lipped, in an anguish of suspense, Jefferson waited as the second was introduced.

HE DIDN'T BLAME the four who failed in that first initiation. That actor was good. Once, at a party given by Dolly Madison, he had put on a charade that had scared Jefferson into an indigo funk. That but four out of thirteen failed was sheer tribute to the bravery of the nine who came through that ordeal. Jefferson wondered if he, himself, could have out-faced that actor.

Nine came through the test with colors flying. And one in particular Jefferson had noticed. In the antechamber he had sat off by himself and spoken little; in front of that histrionic Napoleon Bonaparte, he had sat like a rock, immobile, unflinching, granite-lipped, unshaken by that roaring verbal bombardment, never batting an eye.

But if that first test was tough, the second was tougher. Jefferson in his hidden cubicle mopped perspiration from his forehead. He, too, was on trial—on trial for having subjected his fellow Americans to such a test.

Conceive those nine strong men coming out of that conference with that spurious Napoleon, only to be closeted with Talleyrand. Of course it wasn't Talleyrand, but you get the idea. Another actor made up and coached for the part, waiting in a furitive backroom with bags of stage-money gold.

Those nine who believed they had outfaced Napoleon Bonaparte found themselves led from the frying pan to the fire. One after another they were conducted to that conference with Talleyrand, and that actor was so convincing that Talleyrand's own mother wouldn't have guessed the difference.

Well, that actor playing Talleyrand was every bit as good as his colleague who'd played Napoleon. He leered and whispered, put his finger alongside his nose and gave his audience the inscrutable smile, the suggestive nudge, the soft-soaped lie and crooked invitation, exactly as the real Talleyrand would have done.

What, he asked each in turn, was the use of further resistance? Napoleon was ready to wipe America off the map; why stick out your neck and fight? Democracy was a lot of nonsense, anyway. An emperor was a lot more sensible than a president, An emperor could keep a stupid public in line.

You can imagine this imitation Talleyrand whispering and cajoling and sneaking in the old stale arguments against liberty and personal freedom—the same triple-tongued lies you hear all too often today. And in the end,

Talleyrand rattled his moneybags. It would be a whole lot easier, he suggested, for his hearers to sell out than to fight out. Napoleon would pay generously. You can see what a tough test it was for those unsuspecting nine.

It was a mighty tough test. Think of yourself submitted to it. A dark-lit room. Only yourself and a man you believed to be Talleyrand. Nobody listening, you think. The case for your country hopeless, you think. Then that suggestive tinkle of gold. Talleyrand clinkling the gold pieces in smooth, white hands. A yellow gleam in the candlelight. More gold—a whole, glittering bag. Another bag. Another. *Voilà!* half a million dollar! A million dollars! Two million! Three! Four! Five!

It will make you rich for life, my friend. Luxury is yours, security, all the things in the world you could ever want. And no one will ever have to know. No one will ever find out. Just say the word and it's yours. Come, won't you sell out your country for five million dollars?

It took granite-strong Americans to withstand that fabulous, whispered bribery, and there were five men among these citizens who could not, who let themselves be bribed by that bogus Talleyrand. By fool's gold! Yes, five fell down on that test, and Jefferson, watching, must have been pretty desperate. Napoleon and Talleyrand there in the White House were only actors—what would happen when our ambassador came up against the real thing? It was getting close to the end, and Jefferson was sick. Nine names scratched out of a possible thirteen.

But four remained!

Four strong Americans who had withstood the thunderous threats of Napoleon and the bribery of Talleyrand.

Four strong Americans who'd refused to quail at danger or
sell their country out for gold. And one in particular—a
man who, in front of that convincing Talleyrand, had sat
like a rock, immobile, granite-lipped, staring straight ahead
while five million dollars clinkled in bags at his ear, never
batting an eye.

THEN THOSE FOUR remaining Americans who'd survived
the courage test and the bribery test were put through the
final trial. You can see how thorough Jefferson was. He
knew Napoleon was a cunning student of human nature.
Fear, gold and women—those are the three most powerful
influences in the world, and Napoleon took all the diplomatic tricks when he played them as his trump cards.

Jefferson wasn't taking any chances. A man may be brave
as a soldier. He may be brave as a soldier and honorable as
Integrity, itself. But when it comes to women! A man may
withstand one temptation; he may withstand two, but three
in a row are almost too much to ask.

Let's recall our own shortcomings before we criticize the
poor fellows who fell before Madame X. Talk about the
third degree! The lady who waited for those final contestants wasn't the real Madame X, of course, but she was an
A-1 substitute. There's no record of where Jefferson got
her, but there were some pretty high-voltage charmers in
the America of that day—if you don't believe it, read Ben
Franklin—and that lady-in-waiting was a Siren with a
capital S.

She turned the heat on those four survivors, don't think,
she didn't. One after another they were ushered into her
presence and left to her devices, and her devices were as
new as Garbo and as old as Eve. They included subtle

perfume and rare champagne; green Egyptian eyes and
soft blond curls; a beauty-spot on a marble shoulder, and
a gown as revealing as cellophane. Her figure would have
troubled an asbestos saint, and she smoothed the worried
foreheads of those four early Americans with fingers cool
as mint; her voice was emotional as a cello, murmuring
promises in their ears.

Lord knows what those promises were, but you can
doubt that she was talking about the weather. The weather
was pretty sultry around there, too.

You can't blame the three who melted like snow before
that siren. Give them credit for surviving tests one and two.
Courage and honor had been strained to the limit, and
when they staggered into that last unexpected round—
well, the miracle was that any man should have survived.

Jefferson, agonized at the sight of melting snowmen,
gritted his teeth and clutched his forehead. Those last
hopes went down, one, two, three. But one tryout remained.
The door was opening to admit the last possibility. Jefferson pulled his eye from the knothole. He wasn't any Peeping Tom.

At the last, he couldn't stand it; he had to leave his post
and race to his study and play his violin. His fingers were
stiff as if from neuritis, and the fiddle made dismal squeaks.
After an eternity the study door inched open. The lady in
question was there. Her eyes on Jefferson were amused, her
mouth mockingly rueful.

"You can send him to France, Mr. President. I don't
know what he's made of, but whatever it is, it won't melt."

So one still remained!

One incredible American who'd refused to quail at

danger or sell out his country for gold. That one in particular who'd never flinched before Napoleon—never listened
to the bribes of Talleyrand. One amazing man who, with
that siren working all her charms, had sat like a rock,
immobile, granite-lipped, staring straight ahead while she
murmured cello-voiced promises in his ear, never batting
an eye.

Then Thomas Jefferson knew he had found his man.
With the courage of Richard the Lion Heart; the integrity
of George Washington; the invincibility of Sir Galahad—
the one man capable of beating Napoleon's triple threat—
Jefferson rushed out to take him by the hand.

Even then the man stood before him like cold marble.
Convinced by that unassailable expression, Jefferson's heart
soared like the American eagle. He wasted no time in
words, but handed the man written instructions to buy
New Orleans from Napoleon, and gave him the portfolio
of American Ambassador to France!

WOULD IT WORK? Would Napoleon fall by his own
human nature—trump his own ace? Jefferson, the philosopher, in old brown housecoat and worn carpet slippers,
paced the White House floor. Had he guessed aright—that
what a conqueror wanted most was power? That to have
power, the conqueror must have money? That Napoleon,
for all his pomp and panoply, was hard up?

In the end it wasn't New Orleans he had to buy, but
Napoleon. Could Bonaparte be bought? Everything
depended on it—the future, the whole history of America. But of one thing Thomas Jefferson was certain. If the
deal could be closed, the ambassador he had sent was the
one man in America who would close it.

Only then did Jefferson make his last appeal. Not for himself. Not in his own behalf. But for the man he had sent into that spider-web of France.

Fumbling into his pocket, he drew out his Bible—that Bible he had made by clipping out the sayings of the Master from the New Testament and pasting them in a notebook—for which he had been branded a heretic and atheist.

"Lord, grant that he may keep his strength. But if in Thy wisdom Thou shouldst see a lesser destiny for America...."

5

NAPOLEON, PACING THE floor of the Tuileries, was furious. What to do? This scheme to conquer the American continent was turning into a headache. The campaign in Haiti—that miserable Caribbean pest-hole!—was going badly. Everything was in a *brouhaha*. The army and fleet were standing idle, eating him out of house and home. There must be a conquest. His whole career depended on a succession of conquests; the public was clamoring, and to keep them satisfied he must go out quickly and conquer.

But conquests cost huge sums. Bullets were more expensive than bread—muskets worth more than babies. The army was getting ragged and the generals needed new uniforms. Prices everywhere were going up.

Then that fool minister of the treasury, Barbe-Marbois, had to say the banks were almost empty. *Sacré bleu!* something had to be done. And on top of that the English were getting restless. *Sapristi!* perhaps there was something in this mysterious report that the fool Americans were offering the British an alliance.

Napoleon pulled his forelock in rage. An alliance with the British would be fatal to his plans. Maybe that President Jefferson wasn't so stupid. These swaggering, homespun Americans might fight if once aroused. With the

English navy behind them, these miserable squirrel-hunters might be dangerous.

And who was this new American ambassador who sat around the court like a lump of nothing? A farmer, by the looks. Unsociable as a fencepost. A dummy. The man wrote letters and left them around where a one-eyed spy could have found them—letters declaring the Territory of Louisiana was a swamp, a pest-hole, a fever-ridden everglades full of mud and alligators, and flooded twice a month by the Mississippi.

At the same time, he pretended the United States wanted to buy this morass. What was the bumpkin's game?

Alors, the dolt couldn't put anything over on Napoleon. Maybe it would be worth while to sell the Americans this swamp. Let them flounder around in this wilderness. Talleyrand was against selling, but Talleyrand was a fool. What did he know about American real-estate?

Besides, the treasury needed the money. Might be enough to start a conquest, right here in Europe. Russia, maybe. Or England. *Voilà!* it was an idea. But why did this stupid Yankee want to buy? What did he know? What secrets did he have up his sleeve; did Jefferson really have eighty thousand volunteers and a treaty of alliance with England?

The man must be made to talk! The secrets must be wrung from this amateur diplomat! This American must be put through the wringer!

A knock at Napoleon's door.

The Little Corporal whirled, roaring. "Who's there!"

"Sire; it is the American ambassador."

"Send him in!"

DO YOU KNOW that line of poetry about Napoleon: "Cannon his name; cannon his voice, he came"? That is the way Napoleon came down the room on our American ambassador.

A booming bombardment of threats and contumely, warnings and bellowing pronouncements, thundering like the Battle of Austerlitz and all its guns. Cornering our lonely ambassador, he roared and bullyragged and stormed. For twenty minutes his shouts rocked the Place de la Concorde, but throughout all that blast our American ambassador only stood there expressionless, hat in hand, like so much cold marble.

Then Napoleon went into high gear. He banged the desk, bringing his fist down crashing. He rattled his saber till it clanged with the noise of Vulcan's Forge. Stamping up and down the room like the Four Horsemen of the Apocalypse, he promised to demolish the United States in three weeks, blow Washington sky-high and level all of America with fire and sword.

He squalled at the American ambassador about the cavalry that would over-run America; the fleet that would sink the American shipping in the seas; the armies that would sweep across our plains; the cannons that would knock our Democracy into a cocked hat.

Still the American ambassador only stood there like granite.

Then Napoleon was fit to be tied. He turned black in the face and howled like a jackal. He raged up and down the room, smashing the bric-a-brac and overturning gilt-legged furniture. Foaming at the mouth, he fell down screaming and bit the carpet.

All the tricks known to dictators since the breed began, he tried. He bulged the veins in his forehead and popped his eyes; swore like a giant; wept in fury; kicked and squalled like a spoiled baby in a tantrum. But he might as well have saved his breath. Screams, curses, and dire warnings made no more impression on that American Ambassador than beebee shot would have made on the fort at Jena.

At the end, the American Ambassador still stood like granite.

Napoleon, mopping his forehead, sent for Talleyrand.

So our American ambassador was set upon by Talleyrand, and the genuine article (if Talleyrand could ever have been called a genuine article) was nine times more dangerous and intriguing than the imitation had been. Past master at skullduggery was Talleyrand, schooled in the ways of the back-hall camarilla and the double deal; grandfather of much of the cynical, doublecrossing diplomacy of today.

Sly? He was sly as a cat and nine times as deceitful. He advanced on our American ambassador like an alley grimalkin stalking an inexperienced sparrow—in comparison to Talleyrand in court dress, you can imagine our homespun ambassador did resemble an unpretentious sparrow.

Talleyrand was the type who would have purred. Here was his dish. He knew Americans. He had journeyed to America in 1794, attempting to clean up a fortune in land speculations. The experience had taught him something. He suspected the true value of the Louisiana Territory, and he thought Napoleon should hang onto it. Also he knew that Americans weren't easily scared. But like most Europeans who judge others by themselves, he thought all Americans would do anything for money.

But the American ambassador to the court of Napoleon was not so easily digestible as our catty Prince Talleyrand had anticipated. The American ambassador, it seemed, was another sort of bird.

TALLEYRAND TALKED. HE talked well. Why, he asked our American ambassador, if New Orleans was a swamp did Jefferson want to buy it? Wouldn't it be better all around if France kept Louisiana?

Surely the Americans weren't suspicious of Napoleon's intentions. In that case they had nothing to fear. The Little Corporal was only teasing. He hadn't meant all those threats. He only meant to send over a few troops to bring civilization to the Indians. *Oui,* at heart he was a missionary. Let France keep Louisiana, and the boundary would never be violated by Napoleon, on Talleyrand's personal oath.

That was a more than convincing speech, and Talleyrand crossed his heart at the end of it. It made about as much impression on our American ambassador as a spatter of raindrops on the Great Stone Face.

Then Talleyrand tried chicanery. Let the American Republic disarm, and Napoleon would disarm, provided, of course, the Americans disarmed first.

Then Talleyrand suggested a treaty—any kind of a treaty so long as the Americans didn't try to buy New Orleans. He was an expert at treaties, Prince Talleyrand. He had held office during the French Revolution, and now he was foreign minister for Napoleon, and later he was going to be minister for the Bourbons. Communist, Fascist and Monarchist in turn, that's how clever he was. He suggested some mighty fine treaties to our American ambassador. Huh! He might as well have been talking to a cigar-store Indian.

Finally he pulled out the moneybags. This time it wasn't stage money, either. It was real gold, ear-marked for just such a job as this, and Talleyrand was an expert at such jobs. Why didn't the American ambassador just go away and forget the whole thing? How about a vacation in Switzerland? An annuity for life. There were two million dollars in those money bags! *Non*, three million. Pardon, *monsieur*, it is four. No answer? All right, then, five!

Five million dollars? For all the response, he might have been offering five million wooden buttons. When he jacked up the pot to ten million, his voice went hoarse as a crow. But Talleyrand's nudges and suggestions our ambassador answered not a word.

You can see the prince shading yellow in consternation. Wiping bilious perspiration from his forehead. Bones of Diogenes! this American was honest. Ah, but nevertheless he was a man. It was time to introduce Madame X!

6

SHE WAS DRAPED in diaphanous cerise. Her little slippers were crimson, her fan was scarlet, her lips behind the fan were luscious cherries. But her eyes peeping over the fan were blue ponds of innocent wonder, wide as stars under a great Aurora of curly, dark-gold hair. She was wondering when she had beheld so uninteresting a man.

In his sober Republican black, he sat at the sofa's end like wood. His face was wood, and his hand was wood, holding a little gilt-edged card.

The American Ambassador Is Politely Requested to Honor France with His Presence in the Blue Salon of the Tuileries for This Afternoon's Reception. Informal. Tea.

He seemed puzzled by the card as well as the salon. Embarrassed by the pictures. His eye had averted hastily from the bathing beauties painted on the wall, although he could not resist an occasional upward glance at the ladies and the swans floating across the ceiling. Most of the time he stared straight ahead, studiously ignoring the champagne, benedictine and absinthe handy at his elbow.

"Ah, *oui*," she repeated an introductory explanation, "the court receptions, they are so dull. When I saw you the other night at Josephine's garden party—standing off by yourself, so aloof, so bored, so handsome—ah, I wanted to give a private reception. Just for you."

If he was flattered he did not show it. Merely sighed and tucked the card into his weskit and gave her a meaningless smile. She lowered the fan archly, making a Cupid's-bow of her lips. His smile remained meaningless.

"Tea?" she extended a glass of absinthe in coy humor.

He looked at the glass; shook his head.

"You are tired, *chéri!*" She was deeply solicitous, patting a lace-fringed pink pillow behind his shoulders. "Now then. Now then. Do make yourself comfortable. I know you must be exhausted from your work in the ministry. With me, *chéri,* you can relax."

He nodded, meaninglessly polite, and shifted his shoulders stiffly; then removed the pillow from the small of his back and placed it beside him with an uncordial nod.

Really… she caught herself on the verge of a frown; gave him a heart-shaped smile. "La!" She tapped his shoulder with her fan. "I, too, am boring you. How thoughtless of me. I know. You would like me to play the harpsichord."

For twenty minutes she went over her repertoire—soft love songs, crooning ballads, a naughty little thing from *La Grande Armée.* And while she sang the American ambassador sat like an unlovely piece of furniture, his face as blank as a sofa cushion.

She paused, pouting. "Come now, *chéri.* Is it that I play and sing so badly? Here." She patted the harpsichord bench. "Come, sit here beside me." But as he made no move or ready response, she rose from the instrument with something close to a flounce.

Hands on hips in a show of mock anger that came close

to being the real thing, she appraised him with cocked head. He met her puzzled frown with steady, disinterested eyes. Truly, this Yankee was a difficult specimen. Was he going to sit all day like a log of wood?

He was scared, that was it. Afraid to open his mouth. Some uncouth frontiersman from the American hinterland, perhaps, frightened wordless by the palatial magnificence of a Paris boudoir; scared to move for fear of knocking over something.

"Ah, you are afraid of me, *mon brave.* Do not be afraid of little me. See, I am not afraid of you. Look how I trust you, you great handsome American."

Crossing to him with a swish of silk, she seated herself at his feet, rested her cheek against the hand on his knee and gazed up at him with eyes calculated to inspire trust in the most reluctant of men. *Brrrrrr!* The creature's hand was without feeling.

SHE SWUNG BACK on her knees like a feline, challenged. So! Here was one of those strong, silent men. *Eh bien,* she had had this type to deal with before. Always they broke down in the end, and in the end they were more violent than the others. She would see about this Puritan. Ha! Seating herself on the sofa beside him, she gave him a look that would have softened the New Year's resolutions of Oliver Cromwell.

"Now, *chéri,* please do not be that way. Let us be friends. Let us be very good friends. I am so lonely since my husband died." Tears glistened in her eyes. "Ah, so very lonely. But my marriage was not happy. *Oui,* I was sixteen and he was old. But all that is in the past. I did not love him, but I miss his companionship. You, here in Paris, you must be lonely, too."

She snuggled against him, and her voice was more than a cello, much more. At the end of that speech it was throbbing like a string quartet. "Is there any reason, *mon ami,* why either of us now should be lonely?"

If there was such a reason, he didn't give it. He sat there in his Republican black like a clam with lockjaw. Stiff-necked. Ramrod-backed. Expressionless. As remote and impersonal as if the lady weren't there.

When she put her head on his shoulder, he made no ordinary response; merely sat like a traveler in the Calais coach, crowded by a stranger. She whispered, purred, made cooing sounds. He examined and picked at a callous on the palm of his had. She skirmished openly, talking in throaty contralto of birds and things—ah, romance, romance in the spring!—slipping an arm behind his back. He stirred uncomfortably; adjusted his cuffs and linen stock; studied a swan on the ceiling.

Then that lady quit skirmishing and got right down to brass tacks. Like her American understudy, she knew all the tricks from Garbo to Eve, but she had some wiles that put her understudy in the shade. Someone will think of Ninon de L'Enclos or Zaza. Madame du Barry or Madame Recamier or Madame Pompadour. Well, Madame X had the lure of all those charmers combined.

Yes sir, she set right out to make history then—the sort of history to be recorded in *The Confessions Of An American Ambassador.* That palace boudoir had been built for just such diplomacy by the wicked Catherine de Medici; some of the most edited *memoirs* in France had come out of that silken room. But they didn't come from our ambassador to the court of Napoleon.

She said, "Come up and see me some time!" and he sat like a basalt carving.

She pulled a bell-cord and from an aperture in the ceiling came the moaning romance of a hundred violins. He stared at the floor.

She knelt at his shoe-buckles, plucking Spanish and Russian love songs from a guitar, songs that would have evaporated the sales resistance of a Trappist monk. He stared at the ceiling.

SHE SANG. DANCED. Posed with a rose in her teeth. A mist of desperation dewed her forehead as she asked him to help her pin her shoulder-strap, and he made no move. Then she tried scorn, challenging him with the French equivalent of, "Boy Scout!" She cried, "This is a fine romance! What is the matter with you Americans?"

Sneers did no good; rage seemed equally futile. A fiery French tongue-lashing evoked no more response than a crossing of the knees. She screamed, "Answer me! Answer me!" and he drew out and looked at his watch.

Tears. Great shuddering sobs. "I did not mean it, *chéri*. Ah, *mon brave,* I would not hurt you for the world. I love strong silent men! I love you, *chéri.* You are so handsome— so silent—so strong! From the moment I saw you, I loved you." She was sitting on his knee; murmuring contralto into his ear like a hundred-piece string orchestra. "You are the only man I ever loved—"

Talk about Circe sitting on her rock!

In the wicked palace of Catherine de Medici, court-iers came up the hall on tiptoe; pages peered from behind marble statuary; a lush, diplomatic quiet pervaded the main hall.

This was shattered by an earthquaking bang! As if blown by a cannon, the boudoir doors burst open, knocking Napoleon and Talleyrand head over heels. Pages and courtiers scattered like sheep before the furious figure that rushed out. Confronting the Little Corporal and his minister, the figure made a sculpture of living hate. The face ice-pale. Eyes sunken, black-circled. Hair torn, in wild despair. Lips wrenched in fury.

"Out of my way!" She aimed a savage finger at the overturned rulers of France. "Am I to be made a fool of? A jest? You, Bonaparte; you, Talleyrand—I thought you were playing a trick on me! I did hot know at first what it was when I entered the boudoir and found that thing waiting for me there.

"It looked like somebody—ah, a good likeness of something human—very good! So I put on my song and dance. It did not move! I sat on its knee. It did not bat an eye! Then I murmured in its ear—such promises—such avowals—such entreaties!

"Mon dieu! I said, 'I love you!'—I, Madame X, who have never before found need to ask the love of any man. Not once did it open its lips! *Non,* it sat there granite-lipped, motionless, immobile!

"So I thought it was a dummy, a waxworks, a mechanical statue! I thought it was a joke you idiotic prank-players were trying on me! Ah, I was raging! I wanted to get even. In turn I thought I would put the joke on you!

"Voilà, I would change into my riding habit and go to the park as if nothing had happened; I would send Jose-

phine back to entertain this dummy. So I changed, but at the point where I was exactly midway between change of costumes, I found out it wasn't a statue. It spoke! That man! Do you hear me? He spoke!"

"What did he say?"

"He said, 'Madame, what do you think of the Mexican situation'!"

The rest is history.

7

YES SIR, IT'S history for a fact; you can read it in the records in any good library. The famous scene in the Tuileries. Napoleon in his bathtub, and the whole court creeping around with the shakes, wondering what the Little Corporal would do now.

A knock at the door.

The valet, Rustin, thrusting in a timid head: "Your brothers are here, Sire."

"Send them in, lump of dirt! Send them in!"

Enter Joseph and Lucien Bonaparte, brothers of the Little Giant whose rise from corporal to conqueror of the World had left them, relatively speaking, down at heel. However, Napoleon had elevated them to jobs of considerable prominence; but working for your big brother is no sinecure, as Joe and Lou continually found out.

"What do you want, you two thickheads! Out with it!"

"Listen, *mon frère,* there is bad trouble. A rumor has it that you are thinking of selling New Orleans to America. The Chamber of Deputies has just sent us here to tell you it is impossible. The French people will not allow you thus to sell the people's territory."

"*Oui,* Napoleon, and what of your plan to conquer the American Continent? You say nothing about your famous plan."

The following is an exact copy of the ensuing conversation, as quoted from Lucien Bonaparte's account.

Napoleon: "Take note, Lucien! I have made up my mind to sell Louisiana to the Americans!"

Lucien: "But it is too unconstitutional!"

Napoleon: "Constitution! Unconstitutional! Republic! National Sovereignty! Great words—fine phrases—but do you think you are still sitting around the Club of St. Maximin? We are past that, you had better believe! *Parbleu!* Unconstitutional! It becomes you well, Sir Knight of the Constitution, to talk that way to me! Go on! Continue, Sir Orator of the Clubs! But at the same time, take note of this, you and Monsieur Joseph, that I shall do just as I please! In fine, I snap my finger's at you and your national representation!"

The above is a precise picture of a dictator behind the scenes, and gives a clue to the people's chances with such a fellow. Reminded of his promise to the King of Spain that he would never sell Louisiana in the first place, Napoleon said the devil fly away with the King of Spain, and it was no time to get fussy over promises.

To quote: "It is certainly worthwhile to sell, when you can, what you are certain to lose. The English, who have seen Louisiana returned to our hands, are aching for a chance to capture it…. Our land forces have fought and will fight victoriously against all Europe. But as to the sea, my dear fellow, there we have to lower the flag…. America perhaps some day—but I'll not talk of that! The English navy is and long will be too dominant; we shall not equal it!"

For those Americans, in turn, who have quibbled about

Jefferson's buying Louisiana without our own constitutional authority, historians point to the emergency indicated by that baleful wish of Napoleon's "America perhaps some day—"Lucky for us we had an acute statesman at the head of our country.

Napoleon was stymied, and he knew it. You can bet he told his precious brothers some things they didn't dare add in their memoirs. Splashing them with oaths and bath-water, he ordered them to fetch Barbe-Marois. To his trembling minister of the treasury he bellowed these historic lines:

"I know the worth of that Territory! I have recovered it on paper through some lines in a treaty—eh?—hardly have I done so when I am about to lose it again! But irresolution and deliberation are no longer in season.

"It is not only New Orleans I will sell, but the whole blasted colony without reservation! I direct you to negotiate this affair this very day. Send for the American ambassador! I will sell him the whole confounded Territory of Louisiana for fifty million francs!"

Summoned to close the bargain deal, our American ambassador never altered a muscle of his face.

All he said was: "Put it in writing."

But perhaps that line is apocryphal, like the following anecdote. Talleyrand, apprised of the real-estate deal, rushed to Napoleon in despair.

"What of our conquest, Sire? What of our plan to conquer America? What of the armies waiting idle—the expeditionary force in Haiti—the fleet we are building—the stored-up cannons? What of that new bathtub you ordered sent to New Orleans?"

But Napoleon couldn't answer. He had soap in his eye.

SO HISTORY TELLS us we bought Louisiana from Napoleon on April 30th, 1803. Arranging that historic transaction, Thomas Jefferson removed such a threat to our country as it has never known before or since.

The ambassador who put over that deal bought a piece of property that ranged from the Gulf of Mexico up the Mississippi to Ohio, and as far west of that as our frontiersmen cared to go squirrel-hunting. The price, all claims included, was sixty million francs. Today we spend about that much on a week of Mardi Gras.

Let's hail that early American ambassador who wouldn't take any graft. And to resume our story, let's conclude with the day when he returned to our shores, beribboned with honors, and Louisiana, so to speak, under his arm.

This story has it that a vast delegation was waiting to meet him on the White House steps. Thomas Jefferson was there; and Madison, our Secretary of State; and James Monroe, who had hurried the money to France; and lots more of our early American forefathers.

As the returning ambassador's carriage came up Pennsylvania Avenue, the whole crowd cheered and roared. The sound was that of all America applauding, but the ambassador never turned his head.

The band broke into *America* as he mounted the White House steps, but the ambassador's features were like carved rock.

Wild shouts of, "Speech! Speech!" rose in tumult as the ambassador handed President Jefferson the deed to Louisiana, but the ambassador took his chair and sat there, granite-lipped, immobile, never batting an eye.

The band became a blare of brass.

A delegate stepped forward, flourishing a scroll.

"To Robert R. Livingston from the people of the United States for his services as ambassador to France, I deliver this speech of congratulations—"

Thomas Jefferson tugged the speaker discreetly by the sleeve. "You can turn off the band. Put the speech in writing."

"Eh? What's that, Mr. President?"

"He can't hear you. He's stone deaf."

AND THAT'S ALL there is to the story; that last scene, of course, being fictional, too. But the truth *is* stranger than fiction, as an examination of the facts included in this tale ought to prove.

Take that marvelous versatility of Jefferson's. That scheme of Napoleon's to conquer North America. That bathroom scene between the Little Corporal and his brothers. The fact that there was a Talleyrand, and that Jefferson had the wit to outwit him; that Napoleon *did* sell Louisiana to our ambassador, Robert R. Livingston; the fact that Livingston *was* stone deaf.

It may be drawing the longbow to suggest that Jefferson sent Livingston to Napoleon for that very reason, but the fact remains that Livingston couldn't hear a word of all the threats, lies, blandishments and false promises which Napoleon's court dished out to him; and since everything had to be put in writings—well, who can tell? A pity we don't have more stone-deafness.

So Napoleon took the money and went to Waterloo.

Livingston retired to his estate up the Hudson to help

Robert Fulton build steamboats, and live in the peace and quiet of a job well done.

Thomas Jefferson served two administrations as President, and twenty-nine more in our Hall of Fame as the Sage of Monticello, the Philosopher of Christian Justice, the Gentleman from Virginia, the Man of the People. On the Fourth of July, 1826, he joined his old friend John Adams in making his American farewell. They say the firecrackers frightened the angels delegated to meet them at the Pearly Gate—but you can't stop a couple of good patriots on Independence Day!

> *Bathtub FOR SALE: Twenty-Gallon Capacity—Cast Iron— All Modern Conveniences Including Installed Chair and Charcoal Stove at Foot—Short Size, but Truly Fit for a King—He Interested Parties Seeking Magnificent Bargain Please Communicate This Department New Orleans Times-Picayune—1803.*

Had you lived in New Orleans 1803, you might have read such an advertisement in your morning copy of the *Times-Picayune*—had there been an 1803 edition of the *Times-Picayune*.

You didn't live there at that date, and there was no such edition of the *Times-Picayune*, but there was (and still is) such a bathtub. You may see it any time you care to in the old Cabildo Museum down below Canal Street where it remains to this day as a warning to the next war lord or world conqueror who might want to come to America and get up to his neck in hot water.

MR. MADISON'S WARS

He was an undermuscled little half-pint, that fourth President of ours; but he'd stood off all comers from cold feet to the Grim Reaper, and thrown them for a loss. Then, when his Britannic Majesty and his Satanic Majesty appeared to join forces, he ran for the first time—but it was a two-way Marathon!

1

NOT SO LONG ago, back in 1815, the postman delivered in the City of Washington one of the wackiest letters ever delivered in the United States in that or any other year.

Get the writer's opening description of himself. Quotes:

> *With the aid and assistance of Divinity, and in the reign of our sovereign, the Asylum of the World, powerful and great monarch, transactor of all good actions, the noblest of men, shadow of God, King of Kings, possessor of Great Forces, emulator of Alexander the Mighty, Emperor of the Earth, to wit: the Sultan of Arabia and Persia, Conqueror son of a Conqueror, Mohammed Khan (may Allah end his life with prosperity while his reign be everlasting and glorious)—I, his humble and obedient servant, actual Sovereign Governor and Dey of Algiers, submitted forever to the orders of Mohammed Khan's noble throne, am Omar Pasha (may my country remain happy and prosperous.)*

Try to brag all that in one breath! Omar, if we're to take his own word for it, has quite a backing (the assistance of Divinity plus the might of Mohammed Khan) and is quite a guy.

We'd like to read his autobiography. Did the possibility of writer's cramp keep him from penning one—imagine his version of *Mein Kampf!*—or was there some other reason?

The letter continues without pausing:

> *To his Majesty, the Emperor of America, its adjacent depen-*
> *dent provinces and coasts and wherever his government may*
> *extend, our noble friend, the support of the Kings of the Nation*
> *of Jesus, pillar of Christian sovereigns, most glorious among the*
> *princes, elected amongst many lords and nobles—the happy, the*
> *great, the amiable James Madison, Emperor of America (may*
> *his reign be delightful and glorious, his life long and prosperous);*
> *wishing him long possession of his blessed throne, long life and*
> *much happiness, Amen.*
>
> *Hoping that your health is good, I inform you that mine is*
> *excellent, thanks to the Supreme Being to whom I constantly*
> *address my humble prayers in your behalf.*

Well, that's certainly nice from the eloquent Omar. Apparently he's mistaken the American system of government for some kind of imperial monarchy, but being an Arab he probably doesn't quite fathom the meaning of "Republic"; whatever he thinks sounds flattering, to say the least.

Letters to our first three Presidents, as a look at their mail will show, were too often addressed in less congenial tones. Remembering the calumnies, criticisms and complaints heaped on the desks of Washington, Adams, and Jefferson—well, James Madison couldn't help warming to this correspondent from far-away North Africa.

Alas, he soon cooled off!

The writer, in true Arab solicitude, discussed the weather.

*Fiery dragons whizzed past him; everything was dust and
panic and noise and confusion. It was like the end of the world*

When he finally finished that topic (doubtless fearing there
wouldn't be room for his historic missive in our American
archives) he got down to business.

He had been, he admitted, very happy to receive our
American ambassador, Stephen Decatur, who'd just arrived
in Algiers with three warships and a treaty. Our ambassador, Omar assured President Madison, was a charming
man. The three warships were pretty.

But the treaty, which said America wasn't going to
pay any more tribute to Algiers, just wouldn't do. Would
Emperor Madison please send over another treaty right
away—a treaty which allowed the Algerians their privi-

lege of kidnaping and ransoming American seamen—in
which case the solid friendship between Algiers and the
U.S.A. would continue.

James Madison

Having come to the point,
Omar signed brusquely off:

> *I hope that with the assistance of God you will answer this
> letter immediately after you have had a perfect knowledge of its
> contents....*
>
> *Requesting only that you will have the goodness to remove your
> Ambassador as soon as possible, assuring you that such removal
> will be very agreeable to me. These are our last words to you, and
> we pray Allah to keep you in his holy guard.*
>
> *Written in the Year of the Hegira 1231, corresponding to April
> 1815, and signed in our well-beloved city of Algiers.*
>
> Omar, Son of Mohammed,
> Conqueror and Great.

YOU DON'T BELIEVE it? You can read it in the American
archives, or Ralph Page's *Dramatic Moments In American
Diplomacy,* wherein the historian recommends it to all
later practitioners in international piracy and blackmail as
a model of its kind.

Hitler and Capone have nothing on old Omar; and as
the historian points out, the letter is a masterpiece because
Omar was a seafaring man. Think of the temptation to use
stormy language!

Why, since the Fifteenth Century the Algerian pirates
had had a free hand in the Mediterranean. The racket was

a winner: the Corsairs merely grabbed whatever vessel came sailing through Gibraltar and snatched the cargo and crew. While the sailors groaned in Algerian dungeons, the Dey wrote nice letters to the governments concerned, demanding ransom.

France, Spain, England, all those European countries paid (fighting among themselves, they didn't have time to wipe up the coast of North Africa) and when American ships started navigating, the United States paid too.

It seems strange to recall that Uncle Sam once put up with such high-handed capers on the part of those Arab hoodlums; but we paid, and through the nose. Up to Madison's time the kick-in was more than seven hundred thousand dollars. Captains cost four thousand dollars. Cabin boys, two hundred dollars.

Visit Algiers and you can still see the holes where many a Yankee sailor starved in chains, waiting for ransom to arrive. If it didn't come he was fed to the sharks. The Dey of Algiers wanted his money in the dot, and more than one poor cabin boy was dunked in that Mediterranean shark-pond when the mailboat was late.

The mailboat was often as not late because our forefathers, swamped with Revolutionary War debts, didn't have the money to pay. They couldn't beat up Algeria, either. Tripoli and Tunis had joined the Dey's mob, and altogether they called themselves the Barbary Pirates.

In 1800 our Navy boasted one first class warship. Our one admiral, who might have done something about it—John Paul Jones—was dead.

The Algerians had dozens of pirate ships and dozens of pirate admirals. Their ships were fast and murderous as barracudas. Their sails clipped over the seas like the fins of man-eaters.

In hiding, they'd lie in wait at the entrance to the Mediterranean (where the German subs and raiders are lying in wait today) and they'd pounce on a merchant ship like sharks on a minnow. In 1793, just for instance, the Algerians kidnaped one hundred and five Americans.

This was a fine state of affairs, and to make it worse the insatiable Algerian Dey wangled a bonus treaty by which he was to get twenty-one thousand dollars extra as a Christmas present annually.

Congress finally woke up out of the fog and authorized the building of three frigates, and the little Navy attacked Tripoli. But Jefferson, fearing a Napoleonic invasion, had to call the Navy home, and Uncle Sam had to keep on paying.

That made the old Dey laugh, and he kept on raising the ante. Our forefathers had to take it.

Anyhow, the old Dey got fatter and fatter, and his Barbary batch had everybody buffaloed. Their knives were sharp and their whiskers fierce, and there was the mystery around them that surrounds all Moslems.

Yes, Omar had become such a first-class bugaboo that Christian mariners jumped overboard merely at the whisper of his name. His racket was going like a house afire. Safe in his pirate's roost, surrounded by his vast Corsair fleet, he was doing a holiday business.

Then figure his astonishment when there arrived in the harbor of Algiers the aforementioned Stephen Decatur, carrying, instead of the annual Christmas gift, a treaty which said the U.S.A. wouldn't pay him another red cent.

That from his favorite Santa Claus. What a nerve! What a gallon of gall! Here was this skinny hayseed Uncle Sam suggesting the racket was over. This Stephen Decatur with his three picayune warships daring to sail right into Algiers harbor and cock a snoot at the Dey!

Who was this James Madison who dared send over such an envoy? By the beard of the Prophet! it was said this Madison weighed less than a hundred pounds and was the shortest man who ever went to Washington.

The Dey puffed himself up to the size of a Barbary bull. Turban and scimitar included, he weighed about five hundred pounds. Uh huh, it was Omar the Conqueror— he with the backing of Divinity plus the mighty Mohammed Khan.

Then and there he wrote to Mr. Madison that beautiful letter requesting the immediate removal of Ambassador Decatur and the prompt continuance of ransom payments and Christmas gifts.

He was right about Madison's jockey-weight size which made him the smallest President of the United States then or since.

But there were a lot of things he didn't know about James Madison. He didn't know James Madison was a shorthand expert and hated long, flowery letters. He didn't know that some day a great avenue in the biggest city in the world would be named after this James Madison. He didn't know that his prospective shake-down victim was called in America "the great little Madison."

And he didn't know (too bad for him) about Mr. Madison's Wars.

WHEN DOLLY TODD was widowed, twenty-six and pretty

as a cameo, she wrote to all her friends, "Who is the man Colonel Burr introduced me to last night?"

Dolly's mother ran a genteel boarding house which entertained the best people, but a girl couldn't be too careful. The answers, however, were reassuring. "That is the great little Madison."

Dolly, so history tells us, took to coming down the front stairs whenever Mr. Madison arrived; and often, although she wasn't a great reader, she wore a studious look on her face and had her finger in the pages of a book.

But, as the gossip columns might have put it, who was this "great little Madison" who so easily sparked the famous belle who was later to win the blue ribbon as the most charming First Lady of American History?

Well, forty-three years before he'd been a little shrimp, no bigger than a minute, not at all the kind of kid whose father assures him. "Son, some day you may be President."

No sir, he was so small the learned doctors didn't think he could survive.

It was no fault of theirs that he did. Medicine, too, was an undersized infant in 1751. Although there were a few able physicians like Dr. Benjamin Rush, who campaigned against yellow fever and later signed the Declaration of Independence, the average family doctor knew little more about medicine than that famous quack, Spot Ward.

Healers like Dr. Perkins, who could cure anything with a pair of magic tweezers, roamed the country. It was the heyday of such grifters as Cagliostro, alchemist, necromancer and palm-reader, whose miraculous powers were the talk of Europe till he landed in jail on a charge of impersonating the Almighty.

Germs raced all over the place undetected, and the public relied on bleeding, prayers and goose-grease.

A modern mother would faint at the doctoring given a 1751 baby. You were either born healthy and you lived (comma), or you were born sickly and you died (period).

The doctors looked down on small Mr. Madison and wagged their powder-wigged heads. In their birth certificates they put a big period. Minute-sized Mr. Madison looked up and saw that period. What? Finished already? James Madison clenched his fists and kicked his heels on the pillow, and opened his mouth and squalled, *"Naaah!"*

So Mr. Madison's first war was against germs. Right from scratch he was fighting and kicking fiercely, determined to beat off the thousand and one deadly enemies that assailed all early Americans.

The colic knocked him out, and the crib tried to smother him, and the Virginia malaria got after him, too. The doctors were as dangerous as anything, and it was an uphill fight all the way; but when he was old enough to toddle he was still alive.

You can bet there was something pretty stubborn in this miniature Mr. Madison.

Well, then he found himself in another war. One day he went exploring down to the road and some boys from the neighboring plantation called him Midget. He didn't know what that meant, but he guessed it was pretty uncomplimentary.

When the boys added, "Sissy!" he charged the enemy. There was a barrage of sticks and stones and persimmons, and Mr. Madison got a beaner. He never told his father where it came from, and that's why there's no record of it in the biographies; but small boys have been picked on since Adam tried to steal his first apple, and you can wager it happened.

All his brothers were bigger than he was, and the skirmishing went right on—families being the same, then as now. Then there were reading, writing and arithmetic, and the professor with the hickory stick behind the chair: tough enemies for any boy.

But James Madison was getting used to enemies; he figured he couldn't compete in athletics, but he could be plenty athletic mentally, and he'd have to do his fighting with his head.

So he began to train his head as a boxer trains his muscles, and he went after the toughest books he could find. A war with books can be a harder fight than an occasional alley scrap, and Madison got in there and slugged.

He flattened the schoolbooks in apple pie order, and went fighting right along.

"WELL, JAMES MADISON, are you quitting your education?" The professor glared one morning through his square-rimmed spectacles. "What do you mean, drawing pictures while I lecture you on English history?"

Mr. Madison, parched on the edge of his chair, held up his slate indignantly. "No sir! These aren't pictures."

"Hieroglyphics! Crude Indian signs! What? Can't you listen without making those bird-like scratchings?"

"Scratchings!" James Madison's turn to glare. "It's a system of writing I've invented. My own device, sir. Quicker than longhand. I've been taking notes on your lecture."

"Notes, indeed. Those indecipherable scribbles are

quicker than handwriting! Perhaps you can read to me these notes. Mr. Madison."

"Yes, sir. You named all the wives of Henry the Eighth. You said all the kings of England, including George Third, ruled by divine right."

"So you can actually read those funny curleycues! Humph! What do those scrawls and dashes at the bottom say?"

"That's my own comment, sir. It says I don't believe that kings rule by divine right. Would the Almighty appoint a wicked monarch like Henry the Eighth? Or was the approval of divinity a story invented by the rulers them selves, to scare the common folk into letting them keep power?"

"Good heavens, James Madison, who put such thoughts in your head?" You can imagine the professor's popeyed stare. "Why, that sounds like the treasonable talk one hears in the ale houses these days. Fie! A boy shouldn't ask such questions!"

Well, that anecdote is apocryphal, which means it isn't in the history books; but young James Madison did invent his own shorthand, and there was plenty of such talk in the American colonies at the time, and you can be sure that James Madison was as full of questions as anybody who has a brain.

He went right on asking questions and knocking the stuffing out of easy answers. He was fighting with his head, you see, and he had the sort of mind that punctures fiddle-faddle as a needle punctures a toy balloon.

Quick and sharp as a rapier his mind was, and his fight to win honors at the College of New Jersey—called Princeton today—is not apocryphal. He almost killed himself battling the books, and the doctors sent him home to die.

That made him mad. He was sick of being told he was going to die. He made an end run around the Grim Reaper that hasn't been equalled by a Princeton quarterback since, and he chalked up a record.

He lived longer than all our Presidents save one, and he didn't go off the field till he was eighty-five.

Beating that college death-sentence gave him confidence, and after that he was ready to tackle anything that came along. The Revolutionary War came along, and you can imagine James Madison being first at the recruiting office, and the recruiting sergeant looking him up and down and saying he didn't need a drummer boy.

Drummer boy! Maybe he was too small for the army, but he could enlist his brains for the fight. And his brains were the kind that made plenty of havoc for the British.

No patriot got farther out in the front line than James Madison; his attacks on tyranny make history to this day. He wrote speeches and documents and protocols enough to swamp any tyrant, and he won himself a seat at the Continental Congress.

Nobody noticed him much, he sat so small in his chair, except Jefferson, who knew a good man when he saw one. Then the other delegates wondered how the devil he wrote things down so fast. No other patriot could write American history with such speed; they marveled at his shorthand, and told him to write the Constitution.

2

THE REVOLUTION WAS over at Yorktown, but our Republic had to be established, and the struggle to found a democracy was tougher than beating Cornwallis on the battlefield. James Madison pitched in like a Trojan.

What battles in Congress! What political wars! Those old Generals Stupidity, Self-interest and Prejudice were the enemies, then, and mascot-sized Mr. Madison went right into the trenches after them.

First, he opposed the establishment of a ruling church like the one in England, voting for religious freedom and independent thinking. Like Adams and Jefferson, he was accused of being an atheist, but he knocked General Prejudice for a loop.

General Stupidity reared his wooden head at the Constitutional Convention, and James Madison slapped him into splinters with brilliant argument, meantime taking down all the records in shorthand. Self-Interest tried to kill the Constitution, and James Madison slapped him down, too.

And meanwhile he found time to write our Constitution, besides.

He had to fight like a tiger to get it ratified. Patrick Henry, for one, didn't think it would work. Madison standing up to answer Patrick Henry was like David sending up to answer Goliath; for everyone knows what a brilliant patriot Henry was, the best orator of his time with a voice like thunder under the sky.

But James Madison answered with verbal slingshots that had great old Pat Henry tonguetied with admiration. Singlehanded, little James Madison stood up and won the battle for our Constitution.

So people slapped him on the back and called him "Father of the Constitution" and "the great little Madison," and those were pretty big titles for a fellow of Madison's weight.

He might've retired with the championship, then, and settled down to run a nice, quiet business, but he didn't.

His private affairs were in bad shape, too. People forget that government salaries were mighty thin for some of those early patriots. The average statesman who doesn't take graft (that's the difference between a politician and a statesman) could earn twice as much in big business.

James Madison didn't get royalties on the Constitution; and neglecting his private business to write it, all he got was behind a financial eight-ball. He had to ask his father to pay his bills, and then enemy politicians said he was a ninny who couldn't manage his own affairs.

Did that floor James Madison? Not a bit! It was just another handicap to overcome. It's true the average man supported by a wealthy parent doesn't amount to a hill of beans. With rotten health to boot, James Madison could have easily become a panty-waist, pill swallowing hypochondriac.

He might've lolled around taking snuff and writing the milksop romantic poetry of the era. Or more likely he could've turned into a society darling, a fox-hunting Virgin a snob.

No sir, he was a fighter! Instead of giving in to such handicaps as a number five shoe and financial trouble, he went straight on looking for new wars to win.

Even when a New York debutante gave him the run-around (did she think he was too small, or his income?) he kept scrapping. He forgot Miss Floyd, as our history books forget her today, and he set out to win the belle of all the town.

He stood at five feet two and weighed a hundred pounds—a colossus of a man!—in 1794 when Colonel Aaron Burr introduced him to beautiful Dolly Todd.

STANDING BY THE punch bowl, he sized up his chances and surveyed the field. There was Aaron Burr, pale, tall and handsome, a little cavalier in his booted perfection, posing with an elbow on the fireplace mantel.

Gilbert Stuart, the famous portrait painter, with the suave air of the connoisseur and successful artist.

Dapper Dr. Greenwood, long notable as the maker of George Washington's false teeth.

Gallatin, the young financial wizard.

Preble, the crisp young officer who had a future in the Navy.

All those others who bowed over Dolly's hand: young officers back from frontier posts in Pennsylvania; smart New Yorkers; rich Boston scions; distinguished, debonaire or celebrated, all of them. Gad! what made him presume he had a chance?

Written the Constitution? What girl in the world would want a beau called the "Father of the Constitution?" What was a seat in Congress compared to fighting Shawnee Indians in the unexplored Northwest?

He thought, "I haven't got a chance!" and when dashing Major Monroe joined the group about Dolly—sporting, handsome Monroe with the glamour of a Revolutionary bullet still in his shoulder—James Madison's heart sank to his boots.

If only he had a constitution instead of having written one! Besides, he was almost forty-three. Lordy, did he dare—

Well, he saw Dolly's mother looking straight at him from a corner of the room, and he began to waver. And then Dolly was moving toward him, her cheeks pink from all the compliments around her, a book in her hand and that look of contemplation on her face.

James Madison's knees were giving out. He had a glimpse of himself in the wall-mirror; perspiration on his forehead, neck linen awry. His cue—confound it, it was the smallest in the room—was sticking straight out at the back of his head.

For the first time in his life he wanted to run, and he thought of beating a retreat around behind the punch bowl.

Then he pulled himself together. Was he going to give up like a coward? Dash it! he'd never run from anything before. He was scared as he'd never been in his life (if you've ever been a bachelor, you'll know) but he squared his shoulders and set his two-ounce jaw and swept off his three-cornered hat, ready to throw it into the competition.

"Evening, Miss Dolly. I mean, Madam. I mean Dolly." (How the devil did one address a beautiful widow?) "I—

would you care to accompany me outdoors for a breath of air?"

"La! The candles do make it warm. I'd be happy to."

Everybody was looking as he offered her his arm, and he felt just like a French royalist on his way to the guillotine. But he kept his chin up, even when he tripped on the carpet near the door and Dolly's mother snorted. His hand fumbled so at the knob he was sure the girl would think he'd had too much punch.

Out on the porch he'd thought it would be easier, but it wasn't. He was hot and cold all over, as if he'd had an attack of malaria. But nobody could say James Madison was afraid.

"Dolly—" It took a heap of nerve just to begin.

"Yes?"

"Dolly, we've only known each other six months, but—"

"But what?"

Well, he'd had tough speeches to make before—standing up in front of the Continental Congress, and that time Patrick Henry—but this time he just couldn't seem to get it out. It stuck in his pocket like something glued. He'd written it down, you understand, knowing he'd never be able to say it but he'd have to read it.

Then it came out of his pocket with a yank that almost sent him off balance over backward.

"Landamercy! James Madison, what funny writing!"

"Funny writing?"

"On that piece of paper. What is it?

"That? Oh, that!" he gulped at the paper. "Why—it's something I just wanted to—to show you. It's—it's shorthand."

"James Madison, is that why you asked me out here—to show me a piece of shorthand?"

"Eh?" And then his whole life seemed to pass before him. He saw himself beating the doctors at the cradle, the bigger kids at the front gate, the professor, that college death-sentence, the Tories of the Revolution, the enemies of democracy.

He straightened himself up to five feet two and he didn't care whether they called him the Father of the Constitution or not; he wasn't going to back out now, no matter the handicaps or whatever the competition.

"No, ma'am! Dolly! I came out here to say—"

"I accept, Jimmy darling. You're so wonderful! I'd just love to be called Dolly Madison!"

NOW IF THIS were a Hollywood story, it would fade out here with a blur of soupy kisses, whereas in real life your average man would have settled down to live happily ever after and grow a paunch.

They swamped James Madison with presents and gave him a seat in the Virginia legislature. The weather was delightful—Dolly made lovely juleps—life was easy as a rocking chair in the cool white mans on at Montpelier. Lord knows, a fellow who's written the Constitution and married Miss America has done enough.

But the rocking chair didn't get James Madison. Not much! James Madison was a fighter, and his latest victory put him in fine fettle, ready for the very next thing that came along. That was long Tom Jefferson, riding over breathless from Monticello in his gig, and the proposition he put up to James Madison was a test for anybody.

"Jim"—he put his hand affectionately on James Madison's shoulder, and looked down, anxious—"I know you've done more'n your share in laying the foundations of this country, but a Republic has to keep going once it's started, and America needs your help."

"What's wrong?" said James Madison, quick, like the fighter he was. "Where?"

Jefferson shook his head. "John Adams says he's going to retire after the Presidency, bitter about politics as he is, and—well, we can't ask George Washington to take the responsibility again, so the boys have asked me to run for President, next election. If I'm elected will you be my Secretary of State?"

"Secretary of State!" said James Madison, giving a gasp.

"It's the devil of a job, Jimmy, most important in the Cabinet," Jefferson admitted. "You'll have the whole confounded international situation on your hands, and the international situation is getting terrible. There's those pirates in the Mediterranean, and there's the British. And Napoleon's going to make trouble as sure as anything."

"The pirates, the British and Napoleon!" James Madison echoed.

"The pirates are kidnaping our sailors, and the British claim they own the Atlantic Ocean, and Napoleon's certain to try and invade us through Louisiana. It all comes under the Secretary of State. Jimmy, and it's a whale of a job and a thankless job," said Jefferson.

"Big and thankless," James Madison echoed.

"Cynics will say you took it because you're ambitious. They won't see that an ambitious man would pass the buck because of the blame; and whatever you do, there'll he a heap of blame," said Jefferson.

"Trouble and blame." James Madison nodded.

"There's nothing in it for you, and you won't have a minute to yourself," said Jefferson. "Napoleon; the British; those pirates—they're cannon balls, red-hot cannon balls!—and you've got to juggle them all at the same time. Drop one of them, and America may be finished. I know you won't want the job," said Thomas Jefferson.

"Who's first?" said James Madison, thinking of the pirates, the British and Napoleon, and rolling up his bantam sleeves. "Wait till I call Dolly and tell her I'm going to be Secretary of State. How soon do we begin?"

That was the fettle he was in, and he tackled that job of Secretary of State just the way he'd tackled everything else. Keeping those red-hot cannon balls in the air would have exhausted many a giant, but it didn't exhaust James Madison.

For eight long years he juggled that international situation—the State Department brought America through in safety—and when he leaned back finally to get his breath, it was like an armistice on a battlefield.

JEFFERSON WAS RIGHT about the job's being tough; the office had been like a hornet's nest. That brush with Napoleon had been close, but Louisiana was now marked "American Territory." The seas weren't closed to American shipping, and Yankee traders still coasted the Mediterranean.

Of course everyone hadn't been satisfied. When Jefferson bought Louisiana instead of fighting for it, politicians had shouted misuse of public funds, and the New England papers had cried havoc, and William Cullen Bryant had written a poem telling Jefferson to resign and go wade in his swamp. Such were the opinions of poets and politicians.

The Britons were still bullying American seamen, threatening the three warships in the United States Navy with their eight hundred. The British people wanted justice even if their rulers didn't: the new Ambassador Erskine was promising adjustment of marine laws and reparation for the attack of the H.M.S. *Leopard* on the U.S.S. *Chesapeake*.

But big business men in Boston favored truckling to London, fearing loss of British contracts. Such were the opinions of Bostonians and big business.

Captain Preble and young Stephen Decatur had distinguished themselves in the Mediterranean by kicking the bottoms out of the pirate fleet of Tripoli—such a daredevil stunt that Lord Nelson, the great British admiral, declared it the bravest naval exploit of the age.

Lord Nelson went on to say, "There is in the handling of those American ships a nucleus of trouble for the navy of Great Britain," and because of that famous quotation, James Madison had summoned the tiny navy home to build it bigger.

Pacifists deplored such naval action, and war-mongers said it hadn't gone far enough. Such were the opinions of preachers and army men.

But you couldn't satisfy everybody, and James Madison knew he'd done a good job. He tore 1808 from the calendar, and was just reaching for his hat to go home to Dolly, when Jefferson burst in to hand him the toughest job of all.

To hand it thus:

"Congratulations, Jimmy Madison! We've just nominated you for our next President!"

3

RIGHT OFF THE bat there was the Creek War. Then the war with the Shawnees and Tecumseh. Then wars on the edge of Florida and Louisiana, in the Northwest Territory, the whole frontier afire with Indian Wars.

Right off the bat there were political wars—sectionalism! The South refusing to aid the West; New England refusing to aid New York; all shouting against each other in Congress, and Massachusetts threatening to break away from the nation.

Right off the bit there was fighting with British frigates at sea; and in Washington, James Madison found himself up against Mr. Copenhagen Jackson.

This Mr. Copenhagen Jackson (never to be confused with our Andy Jackson or Stonewall Jackson) considered himself the biggest figure in America at the time. Priggish, proud and something of a Pimpernel—a cross between a snob and a conspirator—he stepped elegantly off the boat from London to replace the friendly Ambassador Erskine.

His instructions were to undo the good work of the previous British ambassador, to show the Americans a thing or two, and to put James Madison in his place.

He started by writing down his opinions for the historians; Washington was a miserable, one-horse town, and the natives were astonished at his elegant carriage, a Landau barouche.

"Madison," he wrote, "is a plain and rather mean-looking little man of great simplicity of manners." He was amused, he said, by the clumsy social life in America, and he said Dolly Madison must have been good looking when she was a bar maid.

He finished off with, "Our country has been made… the instrument of these people's cunning. I wish to teach them not to presume on my patience in a similar manner."

Such were the writings (you can read them in the records today) of that famous British ambassador, Mr. Copenhagen Jackson; and James Madison must have looked mean, for a fact, when confronted by that snob-nosed cockalorum.

With all those wars on his hands he didn't have time for fancy diplomacy and varnished heels, and it didn't take him long to find out Mr. Copenhagen Jackson was a heel.

Mr. Jackson drove up to the Executive Mansion one night in his wonderful Landau barouche, and requested an interview. All gold braid and furbelows of court dress, he was ready to give James Madison that lesson in presumption, and the interview is historic.

"The British Ambassador to see the President."

"Send him in."

A clack of polished boots—a stir in the doorway—Mr. Copenhagen Jackson bowing from the hips—a polite nod from the little figure in Republican black.

"Ah, there, Mr. President"—you can picture this Jackson's stare climbing James Madison's five-feet-two like a sneer—"my compliments and those of my government. You are looking well this evening."

"I would like to return the compliment, sir. Have a chair?"

"Ah, thank you, thank you"—lounging down with crossed leg; arranging handkerchief in lace cuff. "And now, Mr. President, may I dispense with formality and get straight to the matter in hand?"

"The straighter the better, sir. We Americans have neither the time nor the inclination for much formality."

"Indeed." Mr. Jackson's smile of lofty understanding dusted the map-littered table, the dispatch-cluttered desk, the battered waste basket, threadbare carpet and ink-stained escritoire of the homely office. "I quite understand how busy you must be. The frontier. The Indians. Haw."

"And the high seas," James Madison added. "The high seas."

"THE HIGH SEAS precisely, Mr. President. It is of those seas I wish to speak. It seems our previous British ambassador was a little too previous.

"In giving you the impression that England was going to revoke the rule which gives British warships the right to search American vessels for deserters from the British Navy, my predecessor acted without authority.

"I am empowered by my government to disavow this action. Also, unless America lifts the recent boycott on British goods, there is to be no reparation for the *Chesapeake*."

"But the former British ambassador assured me—"

"He acted without authority of the home government,

Mr. President. England shall continue to search your ships for British deserters."

"Our ships are manned by Americans, sir! If a few deserters from the hard life of the British Navy join up with our merchant marine, it is scarcely the fault of our government. And it is American sailors who are shanghaied into your Navy, instead."

"I shan't argue the point, Mr. President. My navy operates within British marine law. In this respect, may I review the *Leopard-Chesapeake* affair. H.M.S. *Leopard* signaled your ship to stop. The *Chesapeake* refused. Quite legal for the *Leopard* to fire upon your vessel. Some American sailors—a pity, I am sure—were killed, but had your ship obeyed orders this accident would not have occurred."

"American seamen, Mr. Jackson, are not given to obeying British orders. Furthermore, this unwarranted attack took place in American waters. All of which is beside the matter, Mr. Jackson. The point is, the previous British ambassador promised a proper settlement."

"And I repeat he was acting without proper authority."

James Madison held himself in by scratching little dashes and curleycues on a pad. Mustn't lose his temper with this popinjay. The man's attitude was almost as insufferable as that of his government.

"Then, Mr. Jackson, your government now refuses to accredit the promises of its previous ambassador?"

"We do not admit to those promises, Mr. President."

"I am afraid," James Madison said, holding himself in, "that the United States will find this intolerable. Great Britain offers a settlement, and we accept it. Then next week England withdraws the offer."

"I insist our envoy had no right to make such an offer!"

"Your government has no other explanation, then?"

Mr. Copenhagen Jackson was annoyed. Really, this undersized fellow's questioning of the British government was rude. As he wrote afterward in his official report, *Madison is obstinate as a mule, and he takes his stand on our former ambassador's arrangement which he denies our right to disavow. I took it up in a style that brought him in some degree to his senses.*

"Let us not mince words, Mr. President. You know very well that the former British ambassador exceeded his authority. In effect, his offer was a fraud on our home government. Take care we do not think you were a deliberate party to this fraud!"

"Party to a fraud?" said James Madison, scratching shorthand like fury to repress an explosion. "Mr. Jackson, this country does not go in for diplomatic frauds. But we are not unaware of the diplomatic trickery of the present British Government.

"Too often you make promises on Thursday only to break them Friday—make agreements which are later to be disavowed—sign treaties only with the intention of tearing them up should they come to prove embarrassing."

"Really!" Mr. Copenhagen Jackson rose from his chair. "But I think it is the present American Government which lies. I am sure you were well aware that our former ambassador had no right to make full agreements with you. You would hold us deliberately to a fraudulent reparation!"

Rigid-jawed, hard-eyed, an exclamation point of iron, the mean-looking little Mr. Madison was on his feet.

"I will hold you personally to nothing, Mr. Jackson! The

American Government does not accept such insinuations from a foreign ambassador. Any further communications from your government will he accepted only from another envoy. You will remove yourself from Washington immediately, and kindly remove your Landau barouche with you!"

So it's down in history that Copenhagen Jackson removed himself and his Landau barouche, taking time out only to write: "I came prepared to treat with a regular government and have had to do with a mob and mob leaders."

He didn't remove himself far enough for James Madison, though. He removed himself to Boston, Mass., where our history books regretfully recall how he was wined and dined by the pro-British faction and kissed by anti-Madison politicians.

Some weeks later James Madison received a startling piece of news. Mr. Copenhagen Jackson was promising the Boston politicians that if New England broke away from the Union they'd get plenty of British help. Mr. Jackson's agents were making similar suggestions in Louisiana.

"Dolly," James Madison told his wife, "that man Jackson has got to go!" And he wrote a note in shorthand faster than he'd ever written anything before: a note deporting Mr. Jackson and his Landau barouche back to Europe, and warning England that such underhand diplomacy would bring stern reprisals.

Receiving his walking papers, Mr. Copenhagen Jackson lifted his nose. "It will all end in talk only, of which these Americans are mighty fond," said Mr. Copenhagen Jackson.

But the voices that talked were guns. It all ended in the War of 1812.

4

THEY CALLED IT Mr. Madison's War—when it was going badly. When it was going well they called it the War of 1812, or something dignified like the Second War of American Independence.

But mostly it went badly, and along with calling it his war, they called him not "the great little Madison" but "withered little applejohn" and "pore wee Jimmy."

James Madison found himself fighting the hardest war of his career, the strangest, cockeyedest war in American history.

To begin with the war was ridiculous; one clear-thinking English diplomat could have settled the thing with a pen. But Copenhagen Jackson's elevated nose was typical of the English Tory government, too haughty to deal with a homespun Republic.

Pride refused concessions to a smaller country. Great Britain made thundering gestures, biting off her nose to spite her face, you might say; Clay and Calhoun thundered back; then when concessions were made, the mailboat was late, and the war was on. They called it Mr. Madison's War.

Did you know New England almost seceded from the Union? There was James Madison fighting to free the seas, and New England, which did most of the shipping, not caring whether the seas were freed or not.

What, cried the ship-owners, were the losses of a few sailors compared to the business losses they'd suffer in a war!

Ship-owners have never been too solicitous of their crews, as anyone knows who's been a sailor (up to a few years ago a seaman's quarters on a merchant ship were worse than a bed in a flop house) and those New England shippers didn't give a hoot about their seamen.

They refused to buy Liberty Bonds. They sold arms to the British; smuggled supplies to the Redcoats in Canada. Rhode Island, Massachusetts and Connecticut refused to mobilize the militia.

Yes, sir, they called a convention at Hartford and threatened to break away from the United States. They called it Mr. Madison's War.

Along the Great Lakes they called it Mr. Madison's War, too. The British began invading from Canada, and the American army fell back. Transports bogged down; Congress couldn't raise funds; soldiers deserted their posts; undisciplined troops ran away.

The Secretary of War slept in bed till noon and mislaid dispatches. General Wilkinson, commander-in-chief, took so long reporting from New Orleans to Buffalo that Major Monroe declared he must've crawled there on his hands and knees.

While Wilkinson fumbled the ball along Lake Ontario, the British captured Detroit—our Detroit commander was courting a plump widow in Boston—and his second in command promptly handed the British Illinois, Michigan and Wisconsin.

The Indians broke loose from New Orleans to the Ohio.

The Mississippi was bottled up. The American generals didn't know what to do. They called it Mr. Madison's War.

The British laid an Atlantic coast blockade, and sugar sold at twenty-seven dollars a pound in Philadelphia. Coffee vanished from the tables in New York; society ladies went without Paris hats and parasols. Butchers shut their doors. Bakers sold out. Candlestick-makers failed. They called it Mr. Madison's War.

But where the odds were heaviest, our Navy gave a good account of itself. You bet it did. It wasn't any bigger than James Madison's hand, but it grabbed right out to take the British whale by the throat.

U.S.S. *Constitution,* first crack, knocked the stuffing out of H.M.S. *Guerrière.* U.S.S. *Wasp* stung the life out of H.M.S. *Frolic.*

Then U.S. sloop *Essex* shot up H.M.S. *Alert* before *Alert's* crew knew what had hit her, and the Tory Admiralty woke out of that shock just in time to hear that U.S.S. *United States* had massacred H.M.S. *Macedonian,* and the tiny American Navy bid fair to sink all eight hundred warships of Britain's fleet.

THE BRITISH NAVY got mad at that, and sent an Armada that floated like an iron wall around the United States. They stopped our gunboats, but they'd never heard of privateers.

Privateers? Fast little ships of American pine, low-hung, racing-rigged, narrow in the beam. Out of our beleaguered ports they dashed like whippets to attack a herd of Great Danes.

They went through the British blockades with the speed of wind and light, taunting the big frigates with their spray. Armed sometimes with but a single gun, they sailed rings—yes, rings!—around the British warships; dashed out into the Atlantic and laid a counter blockade around England.

Prize after prize fell to these unexpected raiders; great battleships were raked by their wildcat claws; merchantmen were scuttled from China to Cape Horn; British cargoes captured.

They captured Wellington's pay-money for the British troops leaving Waterloo. Gold dust from Africa and rare freight from the West Indies. They captured the British admiral's pants. They called it The Second War of American Independence.

Well, James Madison didn't care what they called it as long as they won it; and he pitched in as if it were all his own war, for a fact. He fought to keep New England in the Union. He fought to get action from Congress. He fought to keep his Cabinet together.

For two years he fought like fury against overwhelming odds, but he couldn't win a war as big as that single-handed. The news got worse every day, and finally came a message that the British had landed an army to attack Washington.

"Dolly"—James Madison drove his small fist into his palm—"we've got to win! America can't go on forever taking orders from European countries. We'll never be a united nation till we stand up on our own. The British must never capture our nation's capital!"

"Jemmy, Jemmy," she patted his arm. "It's almost nine o'clock. Please don't worry. Please come up to bed."

He looked at the flag draped over the trophy case—the

battle-flag taken from the *Macedonian.* "If only the army would fight as well as the navy! Our troops are in terrible condition. The young officers blame the older ones, calling them sluggards, and the old ones call the young ones untrained and insubordinate. I don't know what to do about General Wilkinson. There's a petition to have him removed, and—"

"Jemmy, you can't go on like this, working day and night—"

"Did you ever hear of such a war? It remains for a Quaker militia captain to beat the British along Lake Ontario, and the Governor of Ohio to whip the Indians. If only my whole army were made up of Friends and governors.

"And that wild fellow, Andy Jackson—they call him a frontiersman who's always fighting duels—let him duel the British, I say. I'm going to promote all those men, and every jealous old gaffer in the army will complain—"

"Jemmy, please come to bed. You're worn to skin and bone."

"They've got to forget personal glory, Dolly. They've got to forget sectionalism. We must all stand together and fight for a single cause—the United States of America.

"But New England's selling out to Great Britain. Nobody's supporting the Treasury.

"Ah, these business men and anti-democracy politicians—they'd have me surrender the country tomorrow for five dollars! Surrender the United States? Never!"

"Jemmy, you haven't slept for a week. Are you coming—?"

James Madison paused to set his jaw and roll up his sleeves. There were dark circles under his eyes and he was tired enough to drop, but they called it his war, and he was going to win it.

"In a little while, Dolly, in a little while. Will you put some fresh candles on my desk? And open that window? Lordy, what a hot night, even for August."

"Oh, Jemmy—and I've made you a new nightcap—"

"But I've got to write all those letters, Dolly. And three state papers, and instructions to our ambassador in Russia, and twenty-five army dispatches, and a note thanking Commodore Perry for his victory on Lake Erie, and a speech to the Printer's Guild, and an appeal for volunteers and an address to Congress.

"But I'll hurry. I'll do it in shorthand."

WELL, HE WROTE and wrote and wrote, but he couldn't seem to get anywhere even with shorthand; for every time he answered one dispatch another popped up, and most of the war news was bad.

Midnight, the candles guttered low, and the curtains hung like dish rags in the hot dark of the window. Everybody else in Washington could be abed, but not the President.

Yes, Secretary of War Armstrong was snoring in his four-poster, and Commander-in-Chief Wilkinson was asleep somewhere in a tent, but the British were somewhere near the capital, and James Madison was on the job like a sentry, as he'd been on the job every night since the war began.

He was fagged. Mighty fagged. His little cue hung limp; lack of sleep bleared his eyes. The weight of all America was bowing his shoulders, and despite shorthand his fingers suffered writer's cramp.

But nobody could say James Madison wanted to throw up the sponge. When his eyes bleared and prickled, he thought of George Washington's vigil at Valley Forge. When his fingers ached he thought of Adams and the Declaration of Independence. When his shoulders bent under a world of responsibility, he thought of Jefferson saying. "The Tree of Liberty must be watered with human blood."

No, he couldn't ease up on this war a minute; for he wasn't fighting germs, now, or an inferiority complex, or ill health, or against Greed, Stupidity and Prejudice—he was fighting all those wars put together, and he was fighting for the United States of America. His pen scratched on and on and on, and one candle after another melted away.

Off across the town the night-watch called; some horsemen galloped up Pennsylvania Avenue; a detachment of militia marched past the President's window, all out of step and singing.

Oh say, Bonny Lass, would you live in a barrack—
Would you marry a soldier and carry his wallet?
Oh yes, I will do it and think no more of it—
A soldier I'll marry and carry his wallet—

James Madison listened to the voices fade away; the tramping died out; the capital was quiet—then there was only the scratching of his pen. At last he put it down and looked up wearily.

Go to bed? Why, it was dawn. He walked tiredly to the window for a breath of early morning air; raised his head at a rumble somewhere in the sky. It was going to storm?

"Mr. President! Mr. President!"

He hadn't heard the door burst open behind him, and he spun around dizzily, startled by the man there, thinking, "Too much quinine!" Then he shocked wide awake as he recognized his mud-spattered visitor.

"What is it, General Winder?"

"They've landed in Chesapeake Bay! They've captured Bladensburg! The British are coming! The British are coming!"

NOW ONE VERSION has it that Winder kept right on going, right through Washington and so on out of American history. Another has it that he scrammed only as far as Virginia (he was in charge of the capital's defense, you'll remember) where he blamed it all on Secretary of War Armstrong. As well he might, for after it was all over Major Monroe found Armstrong hiding in a barn, which was pretty thin conduct for our fat Secretary of War.

Never mind those two! We do know about James Madison. First he called for his Cabinet, then he called for his carriage, and he took the Bladensburg Road straight out to the heart of battle, as he'd always charged the enemy since the day he was a mite.

As the carriage swerved and careened up the sandy road through the forest, he could hear the swelling gunfire. His Negro coachman wanted to turn back, but James Madison wasn't that kind.

Someone told him the thunder he'd heard at dawn was the exploding of Chesapeake gunboats blown up by the Americans to keep them from the British.

The battle roar grew louder, and James Madison cried at the coachman to lather the horses. He hadn't been told the

British were that close to Washington. Frantic citizens had been digging trenches for a week, but Armstrong hadn't believed the Redcoats would attack overland.

They were attacking overland, all right: James Madison could hear them coming, and all at once he stood upright, aghast, in his carriage. Figures were bolting across the roadway ahead, throwing down their muskets in flight.

Men came bounding like rabbits through the woods. The ground all around was littered with discarded powder horns, canteens, ramrods, drums and knapsacks and bayonets and cast-off equipment.

James Madison had expected to see Redcoats running; the coats of those fugitives were homespun!

"Good God, sir!" James Madison shouted at his aide who was riding alongside. "That can't be American militia. They're retreating!"

Cannon crashed somewhere ahead; the horses reared; and before the aide could answer, another squad of militiamen came pouring out of the forest, fleeing pellmell past the carriage.

"Stop! Stop!" James Madison cried, beside himself, but his voice was too small to penetrate the din, and the runners went by in high gear.

James Madison, who'd never run from anything, couldn't believe his eyes. He yelled at his driver not to spare the horses, and the carriage went bouncing and careening smack out into the battlefield. Through clouds of dust and gunsmoke it careened until the coachmen pulled up sharp on the slope of a valley where James Madison could see it all.

Across the valley the Redcoats were lined up in martial

array, their ranks moving slowly toward a ragged, gray line of Americans that fired in panic and fell back. Behind the Redcoats, Bladensburg village was burning, sending up a pillar of smoke.

On a hill behind the Americans, a company of brave sailors from the blown-up gunboats held their ground, firing three cannon at the oncoming British parade. Cannon balls whistled across an intervening creek.

Smoke belched from the iron guns. Grapeshot whined. Muskets banged. Bugles rang brazen from the British line, and there was a wild yell as Redcoat skirmishers rushed the creek bridge and American militia fled for dear life.

That yell came from James Madison, standing up at five feet two in his carriage. "Where's Winder? Where's our commander? Those sailors aren't afraid! Why are our soldiers running?"

No one heard him. If anyone did, he didn't have the breath to reply. At valley bottom, five thousand Americans were hollering in panic, and as the Redcoats charged, the panic became a rout.

Captains threw down their swords and dashed for cover. Cavalrymen clutched their mounts about the neck and were gone with the wind. The militia's ragged line broke into five thousand separate pieces.

Only the sailors with their salvaged cannon held their hill; the army went by James Madison in one terror-stricken stampede.

James Madison stared in a daze of horror and anguish, for it wasn't an army breaking up around him, but the United States of America.

"Fly! Fly!" As they rushed by the carriage, the militiamen wheeled and pointed shaky fingers. "They're coming! Fly for your life!"

"But they're only the Redcoats!" James Madison's voice was like a dented toy trumpet trying to defy the crack of Doom. "They're Redcoats, and you're Americans! Stand your ground! Stand and fight!"

He looked around wildly for a sword, a flag, anything to stop the rout. "Fight! Fight!" he wailed. "Fight for your United States of America!" But there wasn't a shred of Old Glory anywhere to be seen, and cries of terror drowned him out; and whether we like to remember it or not, those American soldiers of the War of 1812 went right on running in panic.

BRITISH BULLETS CROONED over James Madison's head, but he wasn't afraid of bullets just then. It was the terror on the faces of those soldiers that appalled him— those men whose fathers had fought the Revolution. Had the spirit of '76 become a ghost? Had the cradle of liberty bred a race of sheep?

It was a bad moment for James Madison when he saw his army running like that; but then he saw something worse. Something that made him think his brain was playing mad pranks with his eyes. He saw why five thousand militiamen were running from the Redcoats as if they were devils unleashed from Tophet; and he wanted to run himself!

Out over the British line arched a streak of green fire—a streak of green fire that whizzed high in the sky and dragged a tail of bright sparks through the sunshine. Zooming and looping like a bat it came, all flame and smoke and a noise such as he'd never heard.

Straight over James Madison's head it whistled, for all the world like Haley's comet; and when it landed in a squad of Marylanders beyond the carriage, they howled and fell on their faces.

Instantly it was followed by another whizzing monster, this time a red one that lashed a long tail of crimson smoke. Then the air was alive with the hissing, whizzing things; they rushed across the valley like a horde of aerial lizards—green, orange, purple, scarlet, blue.

"Meteors!" a soldier screamed at James Madison. "They're firing comets at us! They carry them in their knapsacks! The British are shooting stars!"

Well, it was pretty terrifying, even to James Madison. Grape or cannon balls wouldn't have moved him, but meteors!

The cue stood up on the back of his head. They weren't meteors, either, but more like fiery dragons, and when they landed on the ground they jumped and scuttled around like frenzied snakes.

In the air they made a fizzing, rushy whistle, leaving a wake of staggering fumes. *Whis-whoosh! Whis-whoosh!* you could hear them coming. Some flamed up a mile in the sky, and some zigzagged close to the ground, whip-lashing through grass and underbrush. He saw one chase a soldier across a briar patch like a hoopsnake after a sparrow.

The sweat broke on James Madison's forehead as it would on anybody's when you see something you've never seen before. He turned to ask his aide what it was, but his aide wasn't there to be asked.

"It's the end of the world!" his Negro coachmen wailed. "Yes suh, Mistah President, it's Judgment Day!"

All over the valley the fiendish things were flying. All over the valley the American army was running. It was like that chaos the Seventh Day Adventists said was going to overtake the world, but it seemed worse than Judgment Day to James Madison, for it looked like the end of America.

He saw his Negro driver jump so fast he appeared to vanish in midair, and there was one of those monsters flying straight at the Presidential carriage—a winged dragon with a gushing, fiery tail.

Lucky James Madison was short, for it wasn't in him to duck. Right over his hat it whistled—five feet three, it would've got him!—and swerved like a demon to dive at three militia captains towering behind a split-rail fence. The horse reared and neighed in terror. James Madison pawed and strangled, enveloped in a funnel of nauseous pink smoke. Black Sam caught the reigns to save the carriage from turning turtle, and after that James Madison never quite knew what happened.

HIS EYES WERE full of tears from the fumes. His nose stung with a smell like powder and burnt paper. Everything was dust and panic and noise and confusion; and when he came to his senses, there was his coachman back on the driver's seat whipping the horses—soldiers clinging to the whiffle-tree—two Cabinet members hanging on astern—and the carriage going like hell and maria back to Washington.

Do you think Janus Madison liked that? But the American army was ahead of him, and he couldn't go back and fight the British single-handed—not an army with wizard artillery that fired meteors and winged monsters.

It was touch and go with that barrage behind him, and he reached the capital just in time.

Dolly had set up a meal on such plates as the servants hadn't buried, but there wasn't time to eat it. The militia had fled, and most of the citizenry, and those Redcoats with their infernal bombardment were coming up Pennsylvania Avenue.

"I'll stay!" James Madison swore to Dolly. "Run into the woods with George Washington's picture, and have someone save the Constitution and the Declaration of Independence! I don't care if they've got all the terrors of the zodiac to bombard us with. The stars in our flag are more to me than all the comets in the sky! I'll stay and fight them all!"

Dolly looked at the little man standing there in bitter despair, and then she looked out of the window at the horde of redcoated invaders. They resembled the troops of Mars, and they showered the housetops with those fiery comets as they came.

"You can't stay and be captured!" she cried. "You're the President of the United States—the head of your country! And you've always said one's head was what was important, James Madison, for if one lost that, all was lost!"

She was taking George Washington's picture out of its frame, and James Madison ran to help her. William Morris darted in from somewhere with the Declaration of Independence in his hand. "Mr. President, we've got to run for it!"

Dolly rolled up the portrait and tucked it under her dress, and just in time they got out by the back door. How they reached the woods in the very nick; how James Madison and brave Dolly concealed themselves for three days in a pine-screened hut some seventeen miles from Washington, while Morris hid the Declaration of Independence in a haymow; how the Redcoats entered the capital with such wizardish ammunition as the American militia had never beheld; and how Admiral Cockburn, the British commander, sat down in the Executive Mansion and finished James Madison's supper, then gave orders to burn the town—all that is one of the bitterest and least read chapters in American History.

Yes, our militia ran away and left the President and his wife to save themselves, and the Redcoats took Washington like troops down from Mars, and Cockburn himself set fire to the Executive Mansion—you can find all that in your history books.

But you can't find this. Maybe you can't find it because, as this story has it, all the records were burned in that history-making fire.

BUT YOU DON'T need any record to tell you James Madison's feelings that night out there in the forest, homeless with his wife—his house, his capital and his country in flames behind him.

You can picture him in the doorway of that hut watching the crimson sky, while the tears rolled unchecked down his face.

Over Washington the sky was like a heating stove lid, its crimson flush spreading over the night. The heart of America was in that pyre, and it seemed to James Madison as if his own heart were going to ashes.

Dolly came over from the crude hearth where she'd brewed some tea, but James Madison just couldn't drink it. He could only stand there heartbroken with his face all pinched, while the tears splashed down into the cup.

"I can't drink it," he told Dolly miserably. "I'm sick. I've always been an invalid. I feel that I'm going to die."

"Then go out there and chop some wood, quick!" said Dolly, practical. "You've malaria chills coming over you, and you'll need a log fire. Chop some wood, quick, while I make up a bed."

"I couldn't swing the axe," James Madison groaned. "I'm not strong enough. Look at the size of me. I'm not big enough to cut down a tree."

"Then drink this tea while I do it myself," said Dolly. "Come on, Jemmy! Bundle up in this blanket and drink all of this tea."

"Don't bother over me." James Madison shook his head. "I'm not worth your trouble, Dolly, and I've never been. You're beautiful and wonderful, and you should've married someone else. I'm not good enough to touch your hand."

Well, Dolly Madison stood back at that, never having heard such talk before. "James Madison," she demanded, "what's come over you? You're no more an invalid than you've ever been. As for size, you're the biggest man in America right now! And I won't have my husband telling me I should've married someone else."

James Madison shook his head, small and sad. "Don't you see I've lost the war?" he groaned. "At least I've lost the country's capital, that's the same as losing the war. I've beat germs and books and won elections and debates and all the other fights I've ever had; but this time I've lost, and—and I've never lost a war before."

He sighed deeply.

"No, you've never lost a war before!" said Dolly Madison, squaring back. "And maybe it's just the thing right now you need. Listen to me, James Madison! No man can really call himself a winner until sometime he's been beaten. No fighter can really rise up until he's been once knocked down. All those other victories were easy for you because you'd never lost a contest.

"No man is worth his salt who's never once been licked. It's a licking that shows a man he can really take it," said Dolly Madison. "You've got to lose once before you can learn how to win."

JAMES MADISON SAW the truth in that, and drank his tea—a whole pot of it—shamefaced at his outburst. "I ought to be hanged like Guy Fawkes!"

He jumped up and swung his arms. "There's Washington burning and I sit sniveling—a man my size and fitness with a grand wife and a grand country to fight for. Clear the table, Dolly, and fetch out all those state papers I brought.

"And get yourself some sleep because we're going to be busy tomorrow. You'll be packing up, and I'll be fighting at the head of my army, and I promise you in three days we'll be back in the Capital!"

So he was writing shorthand like anything when Dolly went to sleep with a smile; pawing through his papers and documents and dispatch cases, signing official orders and penning a new call for volunteers.

Frogs chirped outside, and there was the tramp, tramp, tramp of the loyal sentry on guard, and after a while he didn't even hear the random shots of enemy search-parties hunting for him. But all at once he jumped up.

"My notes on the Constitutional Convention! The Bill

of Rights! I've forgotten my notes and the great Bill of Rights!"

He didn't yell it out, but he cried it out in his mind, stunned by the disaster. Yes, he'd left them back there in the capital. The only records of the great convention, and the very bulwark of American democracy—back there in that blazing, burning town.

Why, right now the Redcoats might be throwing them on the bonfire. Right now they might be crumbling into ashes. It seemed to James Madison as if that were the last straw, and he stood there staring at the fire-reddened sky, sick at heart all over again.

Then he stiffened up with a snap. Maybe the looters hadn't found them yet. Maybe they hadn't yet been burned.

"Sweet Land of Liberty! If there's a chance—!"

James Madison looked over at Dolly, smiling in her sleep, and he knew that smile of confidence was for him. It said he wasn't any invalid or a midget, either; it said he was the biggest, toughest, winningest fighter in America.

You can't find this in the history books, because history books don't tell things like this; but this story has it that James Madison grabbed for his hat like a bobcat, and tiptoed out like a panther, and came up behind his scared sentries so swift and silent they thought he was a mountain lion.

He told those loyal sentries to guard Dolly with their last ounce of vigilance, and he slipped off into the woods without saying where he was going. Soon as he was in the timber, he wrapped himself in his cape and ran.

He'd never been an athlete, but his small legs flew like Olympic champions, and they carried him bee-line for

Washington where the night was as red as Hell's doorway and the dreams of American democracy were bellowing in a nightmare of flames.

Well, the nearer he got to the capital, the madder he got. At the Redcoats for setting it afire. At the Americans for abandoning it. At himself for forgetting the records of the Constitutional Convention and the great Bill of Rights.

Pretty soon he could hear the flames. He could smell the smoke of burning buildings and national monuments and flags. He clenched his fists and set his jaw, racing through the forest like a miniature wild man.

6

NOW ALL AROUND him the trees were scarlet. Smoke stung his eyes. The town ahead was like a range of volcanoes, embers and firebrands raining down. He could see the Chesapeake spread out crimson as a bay of blood, and the Navy Yard bellowing like a blast furnace.

The Treasury Building was going like a stove, and the brand new Library and Capitol were erupting great towers of fire.

Every once in a while one of those blazing red dragons would soar up over the housetops to set some roof aflame. James Madison wasn't afraid of them now. Every evil constellation of astrology could have been falling, and he wouldn't have cared a fig.

He ran those seventeen miles to Washington as if in seven league boots instead of number fives, and he reached the edge of town just as smoke started pouring from the upper windows of the Presidential Mansion.

He paused then only because the outskirts were alive with Redcoats who rushed about with guns and torches, shooting glass out of windows and setting matches to everything combustible. In the smoke and flame-light the scene looked hotter than Dante's Inferno, and a lot of that beat came from under James Madison's collar.

He halted to smear his face with dirt and ashes; then

he pulled down his tricorn and rewrapped himself in his tattered cape, and legged it for the Presidential Mansion.

Two Redcoat sentries caught him and let him go, saying, "Blimy, it's only a boy!" That made him madder than anything yet, but it was a lucky mistake. It got him into town and past the fire-lines.

He streaked around by a path he knew and reached the Executive Mansion's back door. Nobody saw him, and if those Redcoats had, they'd never have guessed it was the President.

The back hall was stifling with great sluggish wallows of brown smoke, and the fire was eating its way upstairs with a sound like a thousand hungry demons at a banquet. The flames were chewing up the woodwork in the right wing, too; but the executive office wasn't yet consumed, and James Madison raced along the corridor with his cape over his face.

A crashing gallery almost buried him; it was touch and go under a roaring staircase, and his boots were frying on his feet when he reached the office doorway.

Staggering across the threshhold, he found the Bill of Rights scattered over the floor; but his shout of joy choked to one of despair, for nowhere did he see his notes to the Constitutional Convention.

American History would be nothing without those notes; he had to find them, and he searched the office desperately. Blisters were swelling on the ceiling, and the walls were browning like a cake; his cue was scorching yellow, and he was blinded and suffocating when he finally had to retreat.

Out in the hall, he started blindly for the rear exit. Then

he heard voices at the front of the house—British voices! James Madison turned and deliberately ran that way.

They were in the dining room: the British admiral, all gold lace and braid; the Redcoat officers with their medals, swords and side-whiskers. Pulled back in an ambush of smoke, James Madison peered into the room with stinging eyes.

Staff officers and admiral were arguing in highpitched Oxford accents. On the table, strewn with the remnants of James Madison's supper, was a vast pile of papers. James Madison wanted to cry out when he saw them.

"I tell you," Admiral Cockburn was shouting, "they must be important or they wouldn't have been in that lockbox! But what are they, by Jove! General," he scooped up the papers and handed them to a red-coated general, "what do you make of these documents?"

The general peered, frowning through lorgnettes. "I'll tell you what I make of them, Admiral. Code!"

"Hieroglyphics," exclaimed a colonel, nodding excitedly. "That's what those are. I agree! Written in cipher!"

JAMES MADISON LISTENED in astonishment to the cries of surprise and bafflement from the British staff.

"We can't stay here much longer trying to solve them," the red-coated general cried. "What is your opinion, Admiral Cockburn?"

"Well, I'll tell you," the admiral thundered. "I've been trying all along to remember where I've seen characters like these, and it's just come to me. In the Barbary States, by heaven!"

The general's mouth flopped open like a frog's. "In the Barbary States!"

"Certainly, you fool! This is written in Arabic!"

"Why so it looks!" gasped the general. "Arabic!"

"Of course it's Arabic. Don't you think I'd know Mohammedan writing when I see it? Look at those queer quirks and curleycues! By Heaven, General, we've found something important!"

The admiral shook his fist at the papers. "Look at the volume of those documents. Page after page! And see those official seals? It's a treaty, an alliance of some kind, that's what it is! These Americans have made a secret alliance with the Barbary pirates!"

The general stared. "Good Lord, Cockburn—"

"Exactly! It means all those American privateers will have bases in the Mediterranean. Why, if those Arab pirates join up with the American Navy, we'll never be able to beat them. Maybe right this minute they're setting out to attack England. Maybe they're on their way over here."

The admiral clawed through the papers wildly. "That's what this Arabic writing means! That's the only thing it could mean! I tell you, General, we've got to move, and move fast!"

The general saluted excitedly. "We can't hold Washington!"

"No! We must withdraw from Washington at once and attack the American naval base at Baltimore. If we can destroy the naval forts there we'll break the American sea power at home, and we can meet this new enemy in mid ocean with our fleet. It's our only chance, if they've signed up with those Arabs—"

"Then I'll give orders to attack Baltimore immediately."

"Without delay!" the admiral thundered. "And we'll use

the same ammunition that defeated the American militia today. What a joke on these ignorant clodhoppers! Stampeding them with missiles that couldn't kill a soul! Scaring them to death with—"

Upstairs a roof crashed with the roar of Armageddon, but James Madison heard the admiral's concluding word, and the roaring in his ears then was from the bombshell that word touched off in his heart. It isn't nice to learn that you've been fooled.

But even so, James Madison had the last laugh.

Cockburn and the generals came rushing out of the dining room like madmen. Stumbling over each other to get out of the burning mansion and spread the order for an immediate attack on Baltimore. They never saw the President of the United States crouching there.

Nobody saw him as he sprang into the dining room to pick up the notes of the Constitutional Convention—notes written by James Madison in his own system of shorthand—and nobody heard the last laugh he gave as he dived through the window and off through the night to warn Baltimore and tell the Americans to stand fast in the face of any British bombardment.

ALL THAT *MIGHT* have happened. For the pay-off, you know of course what *did* happen. About the rainstorm that came up that August night and put out the fires in the capital, saving enough of the Presidential Mansion so that later it was rebuilt and painted white to hide the smoke-blackened walls, ever after to be called the White House.

About the British attack on Baltimore, and the heroic defense of the town.

About the all-night bombardment of Fort McHenry

where the Americans stood like rock while the Stars and Stripes floated defiant above the ramparts, and aboard a British frigate an American captive, watching the battle, wrote the words of our national anthem to the tune of an old song—

And the rockets red glare
The bombs bursting in air—

Yes, all that you know. Stubbornly the fort held out. Baltimore wasn't captured. The British fleet sailed away.

Three days after the Capital was burned, James Madison and Dolly were back in their home, rebuilding from the ruins. And not long afterward the British people—the democratic British people who'd lever wanted the war in the first place—were forcing their Tory rulers to sue for peace.

Our Navy (without the Arabs) had beaten Cockburn's fleet all hollow. The peace was signed at Ghent; and two weeks afterward, since the news hadn't yet reached America, that wild man Andy Jackson smashed a British army of eight thousand into two thousand dead men at New Orleans—the Americans losing seven.

Mr. Madison's War was over. People called it the War of 1812, and The Second War of American Independence. James Madison didn't care what it was called as long as it was won.

"And it's won!" he told Dolly, hugging her like a bear. "The Union has been preserved, and America's fount her place in the sun! From now on we'll be best of friends with Britain. At last we can have peace."

He beamed and looked at Dolly and hugged her again.

"Yes, Jemmy," she sighed—and the year was 1815—
"at last we can have peace. I'm giving a ball tonight; the
Monroes are coming, and Mr. Clay and John Calhoun and
Daniel Webster—I do hope they won't argue—and we're
going to have punch and seed cakes and such a grand party.

"Oh, but I forgot to tell you. The postman left a letter
a little while ago—I put it on your desk. It's from away
over in Africa, but it looks just like your shorthand. It's
addressed in such funny writing!"

> *With the aid and assistance of Divinity, and in the reign of our*
> *sovereign, the Asylum of the World, powerful and great monarch,*
> *etc.—*
>
> *To His Majesty, the Emperor of America, its adjacent depen-*
> *dent provinces and coasts and wherever his government may*
> *extend, etc.—*
>
> *Requesting only that you will have the goodness to remove your*
> *Ambassador as soon as possible, assuring you that such removal*
> *will be very agreeable to me.*
>
> *These are our last words to you, and we pray Allah to keep you*
> *in his holy guard. Written in the Year of the Hegira 1231, corre-*
> *sponding to April 1815, and signed in our well-beloved city of*
> *Algiers.*
>
> > *Omar, Son of Mohammed,*
> > *Conqueror and Great.*

FROM JAMES MADISON, President of the United States,
to Stephen Decatur, Commodore U.S.N., American
Embassy, aboard U.S.S. *Washington*, Harbor of Algiers.

(Transcribed in shorthand and not found in history books)—

My dear Commodore Decatur:

I am recipient of a letter from the Dey of Algiers refusing to agree to our treaty which cancels all further ransom payments and tribute to the Barbary Pirates. He asks your removal and threatens war. You will naturally remain where you are and use your own judgment in establishing freedom of the seas.

P.S. If you would panic the Algerian troops who will not be as familiar with such objects as are navy men, try bombarding them with sky-rockets. Do you get me, Steve?

Steve got him, and we got Freedom of the Seas.

MAJOR MONROE
CHOOSES WEAPONS

Long remember, America, this man who
posted the perpetual KEEP OUT *notice to*
European war-lords… Here is the story of one
fateful frightful day, that might have been,
when an old Gypsy had History in his palm

1

IF YOU VISIT Ash Lawn, not far from Monticello, Virginia, you'll come away with memories of a charming little colonial house, a magnificent garden of boxwoods, and a somewhat too statuish statue of James Monroe, Fifth President of the United States and expounder of the famous Monroe Doctrine.

But most of all you may remember a pair of old dueling pistols.

The pistols are cased on a table recessed in the bedroom, and a card over the weapons tells a fascinating yarn in history—an unfinished mystery story.

In 17— James Monroe challenged Alexander Hamilton to a duel. The men had long been political enemies, and in the founding of our Republic the struggle between State and Federal authorities had raised tempers to white heat. The outcome of the engagement between the two patriots is not known—whether the contestants obtained satisfaction on the field of honor, or whether the affair was settled prior to a meeting. Curious as coincidence, it was Aaron Burr who, as James Monroe's second, carried Monroe's challenge to Alexander Hamilton. There is no record of what occurred and the duel remains a mystery, but Fate, or friends intervened, and it was Burr who, years later, killed Hamilton on the bloody heights of Weehawken.

MAJOR MONROE WAS mad. Mad? He was downright savage! His boots scattered gravel as he stamped up the walkway; his spurs jingled fiercely; his knuckles shone white on clenched fists; and his forehead under his tricorn was black.

James Monroe

People got out of the way when they saw the major coming like that.

Yes sir, the major was a gentleman from Virginia, sir, with Virginia mustard and Virginia pepper in his blood. He could be quick-tempered as a Shenandoah bobcat and fierce as a Blue Ridge bear, and when Major Monroe was angry he was a mighty angry man.

Right now he was so enraged that the temperature of his fury heated the Revolutionary bullet in his shoulder so that it burned like a ball of molten lead. That didn't do a thing to soothe him, for it reminded him of Trenton: he'd met his enemy in General Washington's tent at Trenton, and the way he felt about it now, he wished he'd shot at him instead of the Redcoats.

"That blackguard! That cockalorum! That clapperclaw! That cozening, office-seeking, money-juggling piece of macaroni!"

Cuss? Well, Major Monroe was an army man. When the major started cussing, the minister put his fingers in his ears just like the historians did later, because James Monroe was a human being first and a soldier second, even if afterward he was President.

Alexander Hamilton

He could ride and hunt and shoot like a trooper—he enlisted with Washington's army when he was just turned seventeen—and sometimes the legal terminology and diplomatic wordage which he had to learn afterward didn't strike him as being as honest and straight to the point as some of the words in his trooper's vocabulary.

"That huggermugger! Rat-tail! Son of a sea cook...."

Hot and heavy the major was going as he slammed on into the house; he flung his hat atop the newel post and pitched his saber across the hall; and strode into the dining room to wet his scorched throat at the liquor cabinet.

Well, that didn't calm him, either; it just seemed to make his blood boil all the hotter. He was glad his wife, Betty, was away visiting with relatives, because it always calmed him down just to look at her, and this time he didn't want to calm down.

"By heaven, I've taken enough from that fellow. This is the last. Absolutely the last!"

He strode up and down the room, glaring, sizzling, snapping his riding crop at the mellow colonial furniture when it got in his way, working up into a regular passion. This storm inside him had been brewing for a long time, and now he'd reached the limit, sir, of what a man of honor could stand.

He didn't go red in the face like plump John Adams, whose temper exploded into tantrums. Wrath turned him white, like a heated Toledo blade; for although his temper was quick, he generally kept it leashed with steely discipline. Then at the end, after a long time forging, his fury was white hot and blinding, like steel melted into lightning.

"I'll horsewhip the man! He'll learn what it is to cross with James Monroe. This time I'll stop his palaver, I'll horsewhip him out of the government!"

Flinging himself into a chair, the major sat breathing and quivering, hands clenched on the chair-arms, body tense as a panther, his features under the cloud of his forehead as white as a starched sheet. Nothing was going to quiet him down this time. At least he was determined. Too long he'd held his wrath caged. Now it was out.

"I've stood a lot. I've put up with his crossing for years. Now he's gone too far. I'll show him what it means to dare take advantage of James Monroe!"

The more the major thought of it, the hotter and whiter he got. Until, sitting there steely-eyed, his boots—the great cavalry boots with the thirteen Revolutionary stars on their musketeer tops—thrust out before him, his hands clenched on the chair-arms and his shoulder throbbing in agony, he was practically molten.

WITH THE ROARING of inner fires in his ears, he didn't hear the horseman who galloped through the gate. He'd forgotten an expected tea-time call from Aaron Burr. And that was how Burr found him, clenched there in the chair, white and seething with sparks glinting in his eyes and his teeth breathing fire and brimstone.

Well, it didn't take Aaron Burr a second to size up the situation from the doorway—Aaron Burr, tall, dark and handsome, had an eye for situations. He saw the major's sword where it was pitched across the hall. He saw the empty bottle on the liquor cabinet. He saw the major sitting there like a volcano.

Aaron Burr and the doctor stared into the pine-top. Monroe's eyes blurred as he pulled the trigger, so that he couldn't even see the owl

"Ah there, Major Monroe—my dear fellow!—what's happened?"

"Burr!" The major was on his feet. "Come in. Come in. Forgive my lack of hospitality. There's brandy. I'll send to the kitchen at once for tea."

"Let's enjoy some brandy; never mind the tea," said Aaron Burr, sweeping forward in his cape. "God's truth, Major, you're white as bone. I pray it's not malaria."

"Malaria!" thundered James Monroe. "It's worse than malaria. I tell you now, Burr, that what's poisoning me is something far worse than malaria. Alexander Hamilton!"

"Hamilton!" said Aaron Burr, quickly narrow-eyed. "Don't tell me, Major—but yes, I did hear at the tavern, coming over, you'd had something of a quarrel."

"Quarrel!" Major Monroe seemed to heighten to nine feet. "Listen, Burr, this was more than a quarrel. It was a fight, sir—a monstrous attack. It was calumnious and unwarranted, a slap from ambush, a venomous assault. It scoffed at my intelligence and impugned my honor, and it wasn't the first time but it's the last time, for no man can long pick a quarrel with James Monroe."

"Tell me about it," said Aaron Burr, sitting down and leaning forward, interested. "I heard it was yesterday. What about?"

"What about?" The major was choking.

"The quarrel," said Aaron Burr.

Well, to tell the truth the major had forgotten what it was about. In his rage he couldn't remember the minor details. All he knew was that Hamilton had gotten into his hair, as Hamilton had got in his hair from the first. It wasn't so much what he said, but the way he said it; not so much what he did, but the way he did it.

He was a ruffian, that was all, and the major didn't like him.

"He's been crossing me ever since I met him!" the major roared. "If I vote one way, he deliberately votes the other. If I propose a bill to Congress, he proposes a bill against it. I don't care what side of the fence I'm on, he always takes the opposite. He's stubborn-headed and arbitrary and opinionated and one-sided, and I'm damned if he doesn't think he knows the right way to run the government."

"That's Hamilton all over," agreed Aaron Burr.

"HE WAS THAT way on George Washington's staff," James Monroe said. "He was that way at the Continental Congress. Now he's that way in Washington's Cabinet—stiff-chinned, never give an inch, contrary as a granite mule."

"Alec Hamilton's like that," Burr agreed.

"I'd swear he put James Madison to running against me in this state," the major glowered, hotter by the minute from reviewing the affair. "Then all these banking bills he's putting through. This attack of his on states' rights. These taxes he's proposing, and that high protective tariff!

"He's a Federalist and a central-government man. Wants a big national bank and his own system of money. I tell you, he's a politician."

"A politician," agreed Burr, who knew the breed perhaps better than he was willing to admit. "Yes, major, he's a politician."

"Now, by heaven, I've had enough of him," the major

concluded, gasping. "He's crossed my path in politics for the last time. Do you hear me, Burr? This last is too much!"

"Have another drink," said Burr leaning forward. "You hate him, don't you."

"Hate him?" roared Monroe. "No, I don't hate him. I don't hate anybody. But I can't bear the sight of him, do you understand? I can't abide his politics. He's a favor-currying, vote-getting, ornery umph-te-dumph! I don't like him. The world isn't big enough to hold us both."

"He's certainly been a danger to this country," said Burr. His eyes were fixed on something he'd found across the room; fixed in a sidewise stare. And what he was thinking didn't show on his face just then, for his glance was leveled on a case of long-handled dueling pistols, left on a table where the major, a week ago, had been cleaning them.

But the expression of Aaron Burr was one of friendly anxiety and surprise.

"Jehu!" exclaimed this Aaron Burr, looking sidewise at the pistols. "You'd better be careful, major!"

"Careful?" Monroe exploded, sitting up.

"They say Alexander Hamilton is a mighty good shot."

"Shot?" retorted James Monroe, turning in his chair.

"Well, if you've challenged him to a duel—I mean, you're saying the world wasn't big enough for you both—"

"And so it isn't!" thundered Major Monroe jumping up. He rounded at his pistols, glaring. "No, by George! Why didn't I think of it before? So he thinks he's a good shot, does he?"

The major wheeled at Burr. "I suppose he's been boasting about that, too. Now, b'Gad, I'll fix him. I'll show him some true marksmanship if he wishes. You can take him a message from me that I'll meet him any time he dares at his convenience. You're right about him being a danger to the country. This time I'll settle his hash for good and all."

But Aaron Burr's black cloak was already fluttering out of the doorway, and the answer from Alexander Hamilton wasn't long in coming.

Choose Your Own Weapons!

2

WELL, THEY TRIED to stop it. Jefferson signaled by wigwag from Monticello he was coming over; and he drove up, tall and anxious, concerned for the safety of his junior law-partner. All night they argued under the Virginia stars, Jefferson talking as father to son, for he was that fond of James Monroe.

"I don't like Hamilton's politics, myself," Jefferson pointed out. "But he's done a lot for the nation just the same, and there's no denying he's a brilliant man."

"His brilliance gets in my eye," the young major scoffed. "He talks too smartly for his own blessed good. You've said yourself, sir, that you couldn't listen to him argue, you had to run out of the room for fear of being persuaded. He's dangerous, that's what he is. And I aim to exterminate him, sir."

"But he's an expert shot," Jefferson groaned. "One of New York's finest marksmen."

"And I'm one of Virginia's finest," said James Monroe, drawing himself up. "Do you think a Virginia gentleman would be afraid to test anyone's marksmanship? It's no use, sir. I'm adamant."

Then came little James Madison from Montpelier— little Madison, grave and dignified. He could argue every bit as well as Jefferson, and he didn't try pacifism, but logic.

Dueling was really a French custom, argued Madison, and as such it didn't belong on the American scene.

But Major Monroe wouldn't budge for that. He didn't like Madison politically much better than he liked Alec Hamilton, and he took the occasion to point out the fact. Besides, he had an idea that Madison wanted to conciliate, fearing Hamilton might be killed, Madison favoring most of Hamilton's Federalist ideas.

"I'm going to duel him," the major declared. "I've made up my mind. I've had enough of him, sir. That's all,"

The Kortrights got wind of it—they didn't tell Betty, but they came over post haste, begging the major not to risk his life.

"I'm not risking it," Monroe assured his in-laws, "fighting Alexander Hamilton."

Lastly President Washington, all the way from Mount Vernon, tried to patch it up. He said the country couldn't afford to lose one (or two) of its best men.

But Major Monroe knew all about that—"That cur, Hamilton, has pulled the wool over Washington's eye for years!"—and he politely reminded Washington that it was impossible to back down from a duel; and Washington, being an army man, remained silent, knowing the code.

"I'm dueling Hamilton," James Monroe concluded to his friends. "There's no use trying to stop me. I've suffered from that rascal's opposition for years, and I've made up my mind to put an end to him. Even if I wanted to I couldn't back down after a formal challenge—and, by Godfrey, I don't want to."

SO THAT WAS that and preparations went ahead for the duel, Aaron Burr generously offering to take care of all the arrangements. A field was picked out, not far from Ash Lawn in Virginia, and a surgeon was arranged for—it might've been Dr. Benjamin Rush.

Word came to Major Monroe that Alec Hamilton was up at dawn every day on a pistol range, getting into mighty fine form. Aaron Burr brought a story that Hamilton said they ought to have an undertaker instead of a surgeon, and Hamilton had agreed to meeting in Virginia because he figured it was nicer for a man to die near his home.

James Monroe was fit to be tied when he heard that.

"I'll riddle him," he promised. "I'll have him so heavy with lead it'll take a tandem of seventy-five oxen to drag him back to New York. You can tell him for me, Burr, that I've sworn an oath to eradicate him. It's just as a favor to a condemned man that I let him draw his last breath in Virginia!"

And the major flung up a handful of playing cards, and, loading and firing like a madman, shot the spots out of all the hearts up to the nine before they fluttered to the ground.

That was pretty good shooting, but not good enough for Major Monroe. He said he wouldn't be satisfied till he could drill every heart in the deck; and Aaron Burr chuckled and rubbed his hands.

All that week the major never left the house without his pistols. See a hoptoad under the hedge, he'd shoot it. See a bottle floating in a creek, he'd blow it to pieces. He knocked the corks out of jugs at twenty paces, and picked crows out of cornfields across the road, and hit just about everything or anything that made a target.

Still, he wasn't satisfied. He knew he mustn't underestimate the enemy. Hamilton must be pretty confident to've accepted a mortal challenge; and along about the middle of the week came news from the Hamilton camp like to've scared anybody else but Major Monroe.

Hamilton was shooting the pine cones out of the tops of trees. Yes sir, and doing it with pistols from the ground. Pick out a particular cone, and he'd knock it down. Nobody had seen any better shooting at a stationary target, and Hamilton's seconds were laying bets of two to one.

"Stationary targets!" thundered Major Monroe. "I'm shooting at *moving* targets! I expect him to be running, d'ye see!"

That afternoon he went out to the woods, and things looked pretty dark for the 'possums, bobcats and coons. Only there weren't any 'possums, bobcats and coons around that afternoon, and the major began to wonder where all the moving targets could've gone.

He tramped a long way, hunting something to shoot at, and finally he drew a bead on a big old owl.

It was high in the tree, about a hundred yards perhaps, and the major, sniping fast—and the light being bad—missed the shot. Major Monroe made haste to load, and the owl made haste to depart, hooting around to the other side of the tree.

But it wasn't a very wise owl, for it peeked angrily from around behind the treetop. In the brush at James Monroe's back there was a spanking bang, and that hoot owl came plummeting down with a bullet in its eye.

"Ye gods and little fishes!" the major had to swear, for he'd never seen a shot like that. "What sharpshooter is this who can hit an owl as it peeks around a tree-top?"

"One of th' best shots in America, I reckon," drawled a voice behind him, and out of the underbrush sauntered a gangling figure with a squirrel rifle crotched in its arm—a moccasined figure, all muscle and whiskers and fringed buckskin.

WELL, MAJOR MONROE recognized the figure as a famous frontiersman—maybe it was Dan'l Boone, or it might've been George Rogers Clark. At any rate it was a pioneer scout who'd been revisiting civilization in Virginia for a spell, and the major saw why all the bobcats, coon and 'possum had left the neighborhood.

He'd heard of these famous hunters who could shoot, at half a mile, a running deer. But he'd never before met one, and his mouth stayed agape in admiration.

"That was a wonderful shot, sir." He had to applaud. "Is it true that you frontiersmen can kill a deer at half a mile?"

"Half a mile!" The woodsman chuckled. "At half a mile I c'n knock the eye from a squirrel that's peeking around a tree."

Squinting into the distance, he flung up his gun— *bang!*—and nailed a critter so far off in the forest the major hadn't been able to see it. Sure enough, it was a red squirrel, and Dan'l Boone or George Rogers Clark or whoever it was hit him right in the eye.

"Shades of Caesar!" exclaimed Major Monroe. "I wish I could shoot like that."

"Want to kill a deer at half a mile?" the other asked.

"A dog at ten paces!" the major declared. "Sir, maybe you can give me some pointers."

The buckskinned frontiersman allowed as maybe he could, although he didn't have much use for these near-to-the-target pistols. Monroe explained that the pistols were made for ten paces, and he displayed a few trick shots to show the frontiersman.

Then the frontiersman took the pistols and showed some trickier shots to Monroe. He asked Monroe to hold up a pinch of snuff, and he shot it right out from between his fingers without so much as scratching a finger-print. He drilled a bumblebee flying by; and then firing two pistols in a crossfire simultaneously, he made the bullets meet together in midair.

"Only trouble with these here pistols," he declared, "is that they haven't got the range for long-distance shots. Only a couple of men I ever heard of could nail an owl in a treetop with a pistol. One of them is Merriweather Lewis. But give me old Faithful." He slapped his long-barreled rifle.

Nevertheless he was good enough for Major Monroe with pistols, for the major wasn't out for any owl-shooting. He showed the major how to load and prime faster. How to squint a lot sharper through the sights. How to squeeze the trigger and not pull it. How to keep the recoil from throwing him off the mark.

Yes indeed, he gave the major the best coaching he'd ever had, and by the end of that afternoon James Monroe was twice as good a shot as he'd been before.

"Burr," he told his second, the night after, that target-shooting lesson, "you can go tell the undertaker to make a special floral horseshoe. A big Gates Ajar with *Rest In Peace* done in funeral flowers. And the ribbon to say, *From James Monroe in Memory of Alexander Hamilton.*"

Aaron Burr smiled, wrapping himself in his black cloak,

for he'd seen the major's latest shooting, and he was sure it could beat Hamilton's. Monroe was certain, too, after the marvelous coaching he'd had.

3

———

DAY BEFORE THE duel he was up at sunrise, out in the fields practicing. He'd never been in better fettle, and he wished he'd brought someone with him to witness his style. That frontiersman's pointers had worked a big improvement, and the major told himself he'd been a dashed good marksman to start with.

Bang! Bang! Bang! He sure was shooting now. He hit a field rat at sixty-five feet from the hip, and just before breakfast he shot down a bumblebee.

Then down in the lower thirty acres he saw a scarecrow. It kind of looked like Alexander Hamilton—"That straw-stuffed nincompoop!"—and he walked over to the scarecrow and bowed formally with, "At your service, Mr. Hamilton!", and strode back twenty paces and shot the scarecrow square in the heart, just as he was going to tomorrow.

Twenty times he paced off the distance, practiced spinning and firing, first right hand, then left hand, going through all the formality of the code. Each time he hit the scarecrow plunk in the heart.

That was pretty bull's-eye shooting, thought Major Monroe.

He was so engrossed with his practicing that he didn't see the Gypsy. Not until she was fair on top of him. She'd been coming across the field in a little two-wheeled cart, a foreign kind of cart with a queer round-topped roof, pulled by a melancholy foreign little donkey. There was a back door to the cart and a funny little step, and on each sidewall of the cart there was painted a huge brown hand.

The Gypsy was brown, too. Old and brown and all bent over with a face like a wrinkled walnut. Her hands were like twigs and she had three horsehair whiskers on her chin. But her earrings were big as brass hoops, and her patched dress was bright as autumn color.

She halted the funny cart on the path behind James Monroe, and she sat there watching him duel the scarecrow, nodding to herself, never making a sound. It gave him sort of a turn when he wheeled around and saw her there.

"What's this? What's this?" The major was uncomfortable under those beady black eyes. "You've been watching me shoot, old woman?"

"Aye," she answered in a voice at least familiar to the scarecrow. "I've been watching ye shoot, my master."

"And do you like it?" Major Monroe asked her, disturbed for some reason he couldn't explain.

"Aye, I like it fine," was the toneless answer. "Only I've been wondering, master. Wondering—"

"Wondering what?" demanded Major Monroe, not fancying the way her voice trailed off. It was still early in the morning, and he'd had no breakfast yet, and there was a stillness and mistiness on the field.

"Wondering if it was good enough," was the croaky answer. "Wondering if it was good enough for the moment in which you might need it, my master."

"Hey? Well, it's a whole lot better than I'll ever need,"

said Major Monroe, getting hot. "Where have you seen better pistoling than this in your travels? Certainly it's good enough, old woman, and better than I'll ever find necessary."

"As to that, there's only one way to tell," said the Gypsy. "There's only one way to find the answer to that, my master."

"In a contest," said the major hotly, "with something besides a scarecrow."

But the old woman shook her head. "By that time it may be too late."

"How then? demanded Major Monroe, not liking the Gypsy or her talk or anything else that might unsettle him at a time like this. "If not in actual contest, what's the only way to tell?"

For reply the old woman pointed to the painting on the side of the wagon, and the major found himself glaring at the big hand.

"Well, I'm demmed!" he said, inadvertently thrusting out his own, as if expecting to see something written there.

The old Gypsy woman looked down at his defiant palm. She hooked her finger over her nose and stared like an eagle with a talon hooked over its beak.

"You've an interesting palm, James Monroe," she whispered. "The most interesting palm and most revealing palm I've seen in all my many years as a fortune-teller."

"Is that so?" The major glared, surprised that she should know his name. "Tell me more."

"THE LINES ARE like those of a book."

The old Gypsy woman's black eyes glittered. "Like those of a book, James Monroe, and it's quite a story there. That line, now, under the heel of your thumb"—she traced it on his palm with a long, crooked fingernail—"I see you're going to fight a duel, James Monroe."

"What else can you see?" The major was pretty startled.

"The future I can see," the old Gypsy whispered, leaning down. "The future, and your future written there in the palm of your hand. There's history in your palm, James Monroe, American history. It all depends on tomorrow, and the answer to that is in your life-line."

Tomorrow. His life-line. James Monroe couldn't help but swallow. "Can you see the outcome of my duel with Hamilton?" he asked.

The old woman peered and peered and squinted her gimlet eyes. "I could see a lot better," she said hoarsely, "if I clutched a piece of silver in my own palm."

"Here's a sovereign," said Major Monroe. "You ought to see aplenty clutching gold."

The old Gypsy's eyes gleamed like a spirit's at that, and it seemed as if she could peer through the major's palm as if it were made of glass.

"Aye, I do see better. I see a great deal. I see you going to the dueling ground, James Monroe, with a dark handsome man as your second, I see your antagonist approaching, walking with confident step. You're an expert shot and so is he, James Monroe—by the saints, you are evenly matched.

"You bow. You choose your weapons from the case. You wheel and pace off. And then—"

"And then?" The major's voice was a little husky.

The Gypsy woman was tracing his lifeline with her fingernail. James Monroe could feel that light scratching go right down his spine.

"The umpire-calls, 'Ready!'" she whispered. "The umpire calls, 'Aim!' The umpire calls, 'Fire!'"

She broke off with an in-pulled breath, drew Monroe's palm within two inches of her eyes, then sent a swift stare across the field at the scarecrow.

"What's the matter?" Monroe jerked back his hand. "What in heaven's name do you see?"

"History," the old woman whispered, gazing at him like one in a trance. "A world-shaking event in American history. The fate and future of your nation may rest on the outcome of tomorrow's duel, James Monroe.

"But I can't believe my eyes—no, I can't be sure. I can't be sure of the outcome till I compare your palm with the mystic chart. Come into the wagon, James Monroe."

She held aside the door-flap, beckoning; "Come where we may compare by the mystic chart."

Well, he didn't believe in-such claptrap, but just the same it shook him a little. How would this old Gypsy woman know his name? How'd she know about the duel in the first place? She looked as if she'd come in her donkey-cart straight from Romany—maybe by an incantation, for she had that look about her—and he didn't like the strange stare she'd given that scarecrow.

More than reluctant, he climbed up into the cart, impelled by something he couldn't seem to control. Inside it was dark and smelly with a lot of strange smells he'd never experienced before—roots and herbs and musty blankets and things like that.

There was a stuffed mole on the table and a bottle of something that looked like cat's blood. A strange Aladdin-like lamp gave off a queerish dim light, and there was a big charted palm on the wall—an outlined hand all marked up with numerals and lines and Gypsy characters. "And now," said the old brown woman with the face like a walnut between huge brass earrings—and the glitter of her eyes like midnight witch-shine!—"I'll read your palm, Major James Monroe!"

Ten minutes later, when he left the wagon, he had the look on his face of a man in death, and he walked across the fields like a corpse on the way to its funeral. His hands were shaking and his forehead was mossy green and the sweat ran down his features like melting candle-wax.

"I've got to stop it!" he was moaning to himself. "They'll brand me as a coward. They'll say I was afraid. After all the things I've said—and me sending him the challenge! But somehow—somehow I've got to stop that duel."

NOW DUELS ARE like wars—it's a whole lot easier to start one than to stop one. They're all bound up with tradition and code, and to begin with they're a matter of high honor.

Of course they aren't today because we live in our modern world differently; but they were back then when America took its dueling seriously and men challenged each other at the drop of an insult or a hat.

Major Monroe was on the spot—on a terrible spot. If he went through with the duel he'd go to—well, he didn't like to think about it. But if he didn't go through with it, he'd arrive in something worse than Hell: loss of face, dishonor, the catcalls of his enemies, the scorn of his friends.

Jehu! He'd be blackballed. They'd drum him out of the regiment. And what a jeering smearing he'd get from Alexander Hamilton.

Locking himself in his house and telling, the servants

he'd see nobody, he paced the floor. Pacing, he groaned like a soul in travail. How could he find a way out?

He *had* to find a way out! Lord, he'd rather drink himself to death on Vermont vinegar than crawl before Alexander Hamilton. He'd rather go to that field and die—but he just couldn't die!

"And I've got to go on living," he groaned, walking up and down. "I've got to stop the duel and go on living. In every one of the Thirteen States I'll be branded for cowardice. Me! Major James Monroe!

"They'll say I was afraid to fight Hamilton. They'll say I was afraid to die." He put his face in his hands, and the tears came out through his fingers. "And I am afraid to die." He sobbed. "I can't die. I can't! Ah, why did I see that Gypsy woman? I want to die, and I can't."

That's a pretty bad position to be in—when you want to die and can't. Right then James Monroe wished he were dead and buried. He wished he had never lived to see that Gypsy fortune-teller. He wished a cannon-ball at White Plains or Trenton had taken off his hand.

Cursing blue oaths through a mist of anguish, he glared at his offending palm. He couldn't doubt the lines the old Gypsy woman had read there. His past she had told him in wizardish detail: intimate little episodes of his boyhood; things about his parents; his Scotch ancestry; how he was wounded at the Battle of Trenton; how he went to William and Mary College and studied law under Jefferson; the date of his birth, April 28, 1758; about his quarrels in the Senate with Hamilton.

When she read his past like that, he couldn't doubt her reading of his future! It was right there in his hand, she said—right there on the palm of his hand. Perspiration broke out all over again on his forehead as he thought of her scratchy fingernail, her beady clairvoyant eyes.

"Behold!" she had croaked. "There it is, my master. Compare it with the charted palm on the wall. You observe how the life-line—"

The life-line, yes. And that charted hand on the wall. James Monroe clenched his palm into a fist and walked up and down.

"I've got to stop the duel. Somehow I've got to stop the duel."

But he couldn't stop it. It was too late. The clock on the stair was ticking the time away. Besides, you couldn't call off a duel after you'd challenged. In the tight little society of early America it just wasn't done.

He'd be a laughing-stock. Dishonored. What would Aaron Burr say? And Franklin's *Saturday Evening Post?* Gad, they'd ride him out of the county on a rail.

Well, for a minute he thought of committing suicide, and he fetched out his pistols and cocked one at his head. But his hand was shaking so he'd probably have missed; and besides he couldn't do it, for if he wasn't able to face death on the dueling ground, neither was he able to commit suicide. No, that exit was closed to him, too. Only way out was to somehow stop the duel.

"God, if Hamilton would only back down. Hamilton—"

He pulled up short with a gasp. That would be an out. If Alexander Hamilton—

Major Monroe shook his head at the hopelessness. Not Hamilton. Not a chance. As well expect an apology from the Great Stone Face. As well expect a statue of Caesar to back down out of the Coliseum.

Hamilton was granite. Hamilton was a mule. Hamilton never backed down from anything. Ruffian he might be, but nobody ever suspected his nerve. The man was stubborn as a rock, and besides—besides, he was confident of winning.

No, Hamilton wouldn't back down.

Major Monroe, drowning, let go of that straw; but, going down for the third time, he grabbed it again. It was his only chance, and he was desperate. His only possible way out. The only answer that could keep him alive and at the same time save his honor. If Hamilton somehow would back down! If he only would....

In his desperation he thought for a moment of going to Hamilton, but that wouldn't do. He couldn't go to Hamilton. The man would think he was crawling—just wouldn't believe—

"I can't go to see him. I can't let him know. The offer must come from him. Somehow I must make *him* call it off. If he could be made to back down, somehow! If I could only scare him—"

The major shocked to a standstill. Scare Hamilton? He was made of iron. But there might be a chance—James Monroe clutched his forehead—one spider-thread thin chance.

"Sweet Land of Liberty! It might work. Lord, it would be enough to scare anybody. By Heaven, it's my only possible chance."

Grabbing up pistols and hat, he rushed out of the house and raced for the woods. Time was running like sand from an hourglass, and he had to find that frontiersman!

4

IT MIGHT'VE BEEN Daniel Boone and it might've been George Rogers Clark; but whoever it was, it was one of those pioneer sharpshooters passing a week-end in the neighborhood, and James Monroe found him because he had to find him.

All buckskin and whiskers and coon-skin cap, he was wrapped up in his deer-hide sleeping bag when the major came, on him at moonrise in the forest, and the major woke him up with a Choctaw yell.

It didn't take him five seconds to explain the situation; and that frontiersman, mighty impressed, said he sure understood.

"Helluva fix, all right," he agreed, plenty soberly, scratching in his backwoods whiskers. "Looks to me like yore twixt the devil an' the deep blue sea. But I'd do anything for my country, young feller, which means I'll do anything for you. Say the word, and I'll shore lend you a hand."

"It's your trigger-finger I want you to lend," said James Monroe, breathing hard. "I'd say it was about the best shot in the world. Am I right?"

"Possible exception of Merriwether Lewis an' maybe one or two others," was the modest answer. "I do aim to be something of a sharpshooter. But my specialty ain't white men," he added dubiously. "Injuns is my specialty. An' squirrels, an' b'ar, an' hoot owls."

"It's a hoot owl I want," said Major Monroe. "Do you think you could hit another hooter, say at five hundred paces? A big old hoot owl peeking around a high p'ine, especially if it was up there tied?"

"Five hundred paces? A-roostin' in a high pine? Tied?" The frontiersman laughed. "Young feller, if I had a shootin' iron powerful enough with sights that'd carry that far, I c'd hit such a bull's-eye at five hundred miles! But what's a tied ole hoot owl peekin' around a treetop to do with—"

"You're to be ambushed in the underbrush," said James Monroe, husky. "I'll be coming up the path. Other end of the path, there's swaggering Alec Hamilton. 'Look,' I'll say offhand to my second. 'Look, Burr, do you see that peekin' owl up there? Well, I don't want him witnessing the duel,' I'll say. And with that, I'll raise my pistol up and fire."

"Think ye can hit him?" the woodsman was anxious. "That's a mighty impossible kind of shot for a duelling pistol."

Major James Monroe shook his head. "When I fire, you're to fire, simultaneously," he said softly. "It'll be a snap of a shot for you, like hitting the broadside of a barn. But I want to make sure that bird is hit so's the bullet cuts the string around its collar and brings it tumbling down.

"That's where you come in," he said softly. "And if the gods are with me, that's where Hamilton goes out."

WELL, IT WAS beautifully arranged, and it seemed like a beautiful morning was part of the arrangement.

James Monroe had never seen a finer sunrise. The sky

was clean and cool azure all the way from the Potomac to the Blue Ridge Mountains; there was a tang and a ping to the atmosphere; the air was soft as silk, and way down some cornfield a black man was pickin' a banjo—the finest kind of morning in Virginia.

Major Monroe was up at cockcrow, and Aaron Burr was on hand with the rooster. The doctor rode up, somber with his bag of medications, and crack of dawn the party started off over the fields where the larks were swooping and the copses still dewy and dark and the hollows still filled with floating pools of mist.

Aaron Burr walked ahead, carrying the pistol case, a smile on his handsome features exactly like a gleam from dark mahogany, James Monroe walked last, hat-brim down, hands clenched at sides, wondering over and over again, "Will it work?"

Nearer they got to the dueling ground, the surer he was it wouldn't, and the sweat began to mingle with the dew on his forehead. His heart was pounding in his chest like a drum, and he whistled, off-key, but loud, *The Girl I Left Behind Me,* for fear the others would hear it.

"That's the spirit," Burr smiled back once. "You can't lose, Major. God's truth, I've wagered a hundred pounds at Fraunce's that Hamilton never walks back from this morning."

The major's whistle screeled off like a spittle-stuck fife, but he answered something or other, glad of a shadowy thicket where they couldn't see his forehead. It was the longest walk he'd ever made—to that dueling ground. Longer than the retreat-march with Washington to White Plains.

But they got there finally, just as his legs felt like giving out, and then he knew what it was like when a man finally saw the gallows. It was a beautiful field—a broad green square of grassy carpet, all hemmed in on four sides with locusts, laurel-brush and boskage; a willow grove at the far end where a man might lie down on moss; and overshadowing the smooth green lawn, a tall Virginia pine going straight up to the blue.

A path approached the green carpet from the south, and a path approached the green carpet from the north. Moving up the path from the south, in the silence of early morning with the mists rising, James Monroe thought it was like a curtain going up on the scene of a play.

His pulse was hammering like a blacksmith's maul, and he looked around, secretly fearful, hunting the frontiersman. Matter of fact, the fellow was practically on top of him before he appeared—those woodsmen could melt into ambush like that.

Out of the bushes came the sharpshooter's wink; and looking up, far ahead in the high pine tree, James Monroe finally spotted the owl.

Same time, at just that minute, he spied Alexander Hamilton coming. He was coming down the path out of the north. Even at that distance Major Monroe could see the confidence in Alexander Hamilton. Head up. Hat cocked. Shoulders jaunty.

The undergrowth along the path came as high as his shoulders, and he looked like a bust, proud and smiling—a granite-chinned bust on its way to the Hall of Fame. His seconds were a good distance behind him; and James

Monroe thought bitterly how it was like the man to show off by walking forward to the combat alone.

"Confound him," the major gritted. "He's certain he's going to win."

WATCHING THAT COCKY head and shoulders come jaunting toward him through the underbrush made the sweat-globes swell on the major's forehead. Jehu! his stomach felt like gelatine. He was glad his own path was high-hedged with elderberry, for his knees were shivering.

It wasn't fear that shivered them, though, so much as rage. Rage that he couldn't take his chances at ten paces. Rage that he didn't dare defy the fortune-telling of that old Gypsy; that he daren't go forward and risk his life against this adversary like a gentleman.

He had an impulse to carry on and duel, but it turned his marrow cold. He couldn't risk it. He couldn't take that chance with American history.

Everything now depended on the whim of a dice-throw. He was hanging on his life-line, and his life-line now was a mere wisp of thread.

"Burr," he called hoarsely, choking to get it out. "Look, Burr, do you see that peekin' owl up there?"

He made sure his voice carried through the misty stillness to that figure approaching on the opposite path, and he pointed at the pine to indicate the bird's-eye.

Aaron Burr halted just as James Monroe had wanted him to, shading his eyes with a hand and looking up.

"Well, I don't want him witnessing the duel!" James Monroe said, hoarse and loud, moving forward to take a pistol from the case, exaggerating nonchalance and off-hand.

Corner of his eye he could see Alec Hamilton had paused, way the other side of the tree, and Major Monroe jelled to stockstill, and raising the pistol to shoulder-height above the underbrush so Hamilton could see it, he aimed at the pine-top and drew a bead.

This was history's moment.

Both he and Hamilton were equidistant from the dueling ground, about five hundred yards from the tree.

The major pulled an icy breath. Glory! his hand was shaking so he couldn't have hit a haystack at three paces, and he knew right then that if the trick didn't work, that Gypsy's prophecy would surely come true.

Aaron Burr and the doctor were staring up at the pine-top. Hamilton was staring up at the pine-top. James Monroe's eyes blurred; when he pulled the trigger he couldn't even see the owl.

Bang!

In the stillness it was like a doom-crack; and the echoes went clapping and clapping, far off to the Blue Ridge foothills.

He heard Burr cry, "Jehu! what a shot!" and he opened his eyes just as the hoot owl started to fall. But he didn't look at the owl. He looked at Alexander Hamilton looking at the owl.

From the highest limb that hoot owl came down through the pine cones—*blippety-blip-blip-blip*—and Alexander Hamilton's upturned stare was following it down. And Hamilton's stare was just as owlish as the bird's.

Off the bottommost limb it gave an acrobatic little flip, and Hamilton's eyes watched it hit the ground. It seemed to James Monroe as if Alexander wasn't smiling any more, and he breathed a "Thank God the frontiersman didn't miss!"

That woodsman must've fired on the very simultaneous tick, for the squirrel-rifle hadn't missed by a split second on the echo, and it was a marvelous sharpshooting shot.

Now it all depended on Hamilton, and James Monroe didn't dare trust his eyeballs. For Hamilton, on that path over there, had halted. Halted and turned, waiting for the arrival of his seconds. His seconds came breasting through the undergrowth, and then James Monroe could see them gathered in consultation with their heads together.

HE HEARD A hissy exclamation from Aaron Burr. A mutter of surprise from the doctor. Scenery swam on his vision, and then, when his focus cleared again, there was Hamilton marching out across the dueling ground—marching forward alone.

Midway across the greensward, Alexander Hamilton stopped. In the shadow of the tall Virginia pine. Right beside the dead owl.

James Monroe could see the man's square Scotch jaw. His lips were fixed expressionless, and his face looked bleak and cold. Standing there on the field of honor, he faced James Monroe's stalled party. He swept off his hat, and bowed.

"Major Monroe!" and his voice sounded queerly tight. "Might I have words with you a moment, Major Monroe?"

Walking out to meet the man, James Monroe's legs felt stiff as wood.

"At your service, Alexander Hamilton."

"James Monroe," said Hamilton, chewing the words as if they tasted chalky, "I came here to give you satisfaction. But a duel with you, sir, would be just plain murder. Don't you think that such a murder would be downright un-American?"

"Perhaps it would, sir!" agreed James Monroe, trying not to blurt. He kept his eyes downfixed at the bird. "And what might you suggest?"

"I suggest an apology," said Alexander Hamilton, "and under the circumstances, knowing you as I do, I'm quite prepared to make it. Whatever I've said, James Monroe, I've never said you weren't American and a hero. You're a brave man, James Monroe, and you'll do a lot for this country."

But it was James Monroe's face that was flushing red, and it took an effort to raise his eyes. "Hamilton," he said thickly, "it's you that's owed the apology. For you're brave enough to have risked being called a coward, and it's the highest kind of courage that faces up to such a charge. You're an honest man and a brave man, too brave to fear being called afraid. Will you take my hand, Alexander Hamilton?"

And they were shaking hands in the sunshine when Aaron Burr in his black cloak, scowling, left the field.

5

THAT'S ALL THERE is to the story—except this. Back at the house, where he locked up the pistol-case, there was a tap at Major James Monroe's door. It might've been George Rogers Clark or it might've been Dan'l Boone, but whoever it was, the whiskery, buckskinned frontiersman with his long-barreled shooting iron was there.

"Man!" said the young major, grabbing the frontiersman by the shoulders, "that was a wonderful shot! Whatever I've got is yours, for I owe you my life, and it seems that American history should put up a monument to a hoot owl."

"But I didn't shoot him," the frontiersman drawled, spitting a ploop of tobacco juice that lit in James Monroe's fireplace like a wet bomb. "Naw sir, Major, you must've shot the critter yourself."

"I?" James Monroe gasped. "Why, my aim was shaking so I couldn't have hit a petrified elephant. What the devil can you mean, you didn't sharpshoot that bird!"

The frontiersman shook his head. " 'Twasn't me," he declared, "cuz my shootin' iron didn't fire. I had 'er all primed an' ready, waitin' since midnight out there in that bush-patch. Just afore daybreak, I left the gun a-lyin' in the blind, and walked over to the pine tree to make sure th' hoot owl was still up there where I'd tied him. Came back an' picked up old Faithful, lyin' where I'd left her, an'

230

waited for th' show to come along. But, by cracky, when I took aim an' fired, the trigger just clicked."

Mystified, the woodsman shook his head. "Naw sir, the gun wasn't loaded!"

So Major James Monroe stared blank-faced at the old frontiersman, and the old frontiersman stared blank-faced at Major James Monroe. And slowly a very strange look came on James Monroe's stunned face.

"Man!" he whispered. "You don't think—but the bushes were up to his shoulders; he might have had a pistol in his hand!", and James Monroe's eyes were staring blue. "You don't think Alexander Hamilton—"

And that's the story. That Hamilton, firing from the hip to display his own marksmanship—Hamilton, himself, killed the hoot owl. It would've been like Alexander Hamilton, say he noticed the shake in James Monroe's unsteady aim. Like Alexander Hamilton to snipe that target, himself—he was a pretty fine marksman, remember—and then, shocked by his own expert sharpshooting, to refuse to walk out and murder a fellow man.

And everybody knows how Alexander Hamilton shot in the air at duels. Everybody knows how he shot in the air that bloody dawn years later at Weehawken when Aaron Burr was his opponent—shot in the air just one second before dark Aaron's venomous bullet struck him to his death.

Who unloaded the old frontiersman's squirrel-rifle? Well, this is only a story and maybe he forgot to load it himself. But Burr had always hated Hamilton, and maybe, on his way to Major Monroe's house before cockcrow, passing the dueling ground and seeing the frontiersman and the tied owl—suspecting....

Yes, suspecting; and wanting Hamilton dead, not alive and scared....

Yet many of our patriot forefathers had tempers like to kill each other. They took their polities seriously in those days, and a fortune-teller, if there were such things, could've read some astounding histories in their palms. Take that future in the palm of James Monroe!

Four years in the Senate. American Minister to France. American envoy to England. Governor of Virginia. Secretary of State under Madison.

President of the United States—1817–'25.

AND THEN THE Monroe Doctrine—that *Keep Out!* sign to the lusting powers of Europe—that stay-away warning to the Holy Alliance that the Americas wanted no interference from the governments of Europe which were certainly in alliance but not holy.

Did the old Gypsy woman read that in his palm? How the European monarchies planned to break up the American republics? How they would join together with so-called heavenly blessings to stamp out liberalism and wipe Democracy from our Hemisphere?

All that was in the future for James Monroe's Presidency; his Doctrine was to save the Americas from that fate—and certainly he wouldn't dare to die before he composed that Doctrine!

It may be a fortune-teller could have seen all that, and the fact that a man was going to be killed if he fought a certain duel.

And for those who don't believe in palmistry, it might

be that an old Gypsy woman had been hired by James Monroe's far-seeing friends—hired by some man like Thomas Jefferson, who knew the young major's past and could well imagine the future—hired to prophesy to hot-headed James Monroe and convince him he must not fight that duel.

We know he didn't kill Hamilton, and we know Alexander Hamilton didn't kill him. And if an old Gypsy woman could be really clairvoyant, that palmist could have foretold another interesting fact to James Monroe. He was to be the third American founder, patriot and President to die on Independence Day, following Thomas Jefferson and John Adams.

James Monroe—July 4th, 1831.

SPEAK FOR YOURSELF, JOHN QUINCY

Do you know him, this somewhat testy gentleman who was our sixth President? Perhaps you've read of his unflagging industry, his granite integrity, his long public record. But you don't know how strange and perilous a road he followed for sixty years— for John Quincy didn't know himself

Boston, dear old Boston—
The Home of the Bean and the Cod—
Where the Lowells speak only to the Adamses,
And the Adamses only to God—
With apologies to E. St. V. Millay

1

HIS CRUSTY EXCELLENCY

NOW JOHN QUINCY Adams was a great man, the son of a great man, and the father of great men. For the past hundred and fifty years the name Adams has been "up there" in the United States. When the country wanted great lawyers, great teachers, great writers, great thinkers, great legislators it went to the Adamses to get them.

Those who believe in heredity say it's a matter of heredity—good blood, family tree, and all that.

Those who believe in environment say it's a matter of environment—New England, Boston, and whatnot.

Anyway and whatever, John Quincy was one of the greatest of his line—lawyer, writer, teacher, diplomat, statesman and sixth President of the United States all rolled into one. He could talk like a charm—Old Man Eloquent, they called him—and write most fascinatingly. He could play diplomatic poker without stacking a card, and win from the fastest, crookedest gamblers in Europe. In the White House and Congress afterward he was always a scholar and a gentleman. He was devoted to his family, and he loved and did a lot for his country.

Why, he had the longest service record of any man in American history, for at the age of nine he was cheering the militiamen at the Battle of Bunker Hill, and seventy-one years later he had a seat in the House not far from Abraham Lincoln's. He was the only one of our ex-Presidents to die on duty in the Capitol.

Naturally, with a name like that and a record like that, he was proud. Proud? Just look at the portrait photograph of him (the one featured in the Daguerretype exhibit at the New York Metropolitan Art Museum) if you want to see pride! Sitting there in his velvet-collared dress-coat with his hands folded and his knees crossed; bald headed; white feathers on his jaws; tight-lipped and frosty eyed; ready to stand right up, young man, and let you know he was still going strong and an Adams! He was eighty-one years old when that photograph was made, and it was made in 1848 just before he died with his boots on, there in the House.

So he wasn't at all surprised to see that picture of himself in the Passport being examined at the Frontier Station. **"YES, SIR, THAT'S** my tintype," he admitted a little crustily, for he was somewhat annoyed that a man of his position and prominence should be held up for a passport examination, instead of being put right through with a diplomat's immunity. The room was bare-walled and draughty and uncomfortable, like any frontier way station, and he felt grumpy and impatient, for he'd always chafed at red tape and niggling delays.

"That's me. John Quincy Adams." Then he couldn't help puffing his chest a trifle. "I'm the first American President ever to've had his picture taken."

The Emigration Official looked over his glasses and smiled.

"Quite a likeness. Quite a likeness, Mr. Adams. Some of these Passport photographs aren't apt to be so good." He turned to the next page of the document, nodding.

"Let's see. You were born Quincy, Massachusetts, 1767. English descent. Grandfather was a cobbler. Hmmm. Which Adams was your father?"

John Quincy scuffed an impatient boot under his chair. "John Adams, Second President of the United States, was my father. Samuel was a distant cousin. My mother's name: Abigail. Wife's name: Louisa. It's all down there in black and white."

"So it is," said the Emigration Official, smiling at the shaky handwriting and ignoring John Quincy's crustiness because he was such a venerable old customer. "So. Your sons were George and John and Charles Francis. One daughter—died in Petrograd. Grandsons: Henry Adams and—mmmm—hmmm—well, they certainly go on. Now that's quite a family, isn't it? Yes, sir, quite a family."

"One of the best in the United States of America,"

said John Quincy Adams, squaring up. "Or Europe, or anywhere else, for that matter."

"And you've got a mighty long service record down here, Mr. Adams. Well! Minister to almost every country in Europe; Senate; Secretary of State under James Monroe; President; then all those years afterward in Congress—hardly room to list all of it in the Passport."

"Longest record of anybody in American public life," John Quincy declared with emphasis. "You ought've heard the things they said about me on my last tour in the United States—that trip I made across upper New York. Why, at Buffalo and Rochester they cheered me for an hour. Sort of evened up some of the slanders I suffered when I was President."

"Don't know when a better record has come through," agreed the Emigration Official. "Distinguished career. Full, useful life. Fine wife—fine sons—celebrated family. Remarkable record!" His smile across the desk-top invited confidence. "Come, how would you account for your success, Mr. Adams? Heredity? Environment? Or what?"

"Well, I didn't know as I'd have to account for it," John Quincy Adams sat up a little defensively. He was never the one to blurt out a first-hand answer; he liked a minute or two to think things over, liked to size up a question and the man who asked it, and then frame an honest reply. Now he considered his questioner a trifle suspiciously, diplomatically on guard.

He'd been through customs offices before, and this Frontier Station didn't seem any different from the rest of them, only the circumstances were a little peculiar. He wasn't familiar with the country he was going to; in fact his

Into a roadside ditch careened the stagecoach,
and two figures atop were sent flying

destination was uncertain. He didn't know if he'd brought
the right clothes. Then the room was dim because there was
a thick, whitish fog outside; everything was sort of blurred
in an atmosphere he wasn't used to, and he couldn't make
out this Emigration Official very well.

BUT THE EYES regarding him were kindly; the smile reassuring. The Emigration Official's voice was friendly, explaining, "You Adamses are so famous in the States. Perhaps you don't realize you've become such an example to the savants. They point to your heritage and your long line of front-rank citizens to prove their theories of inheritance."

"Humph!" said John Quincy. "Well, I don't know that I hold with all these theories about heredity. Of course I believe in it as far as my sons are concerned, and I do come from good sound stock. But I don't hold with the English and their theories of blue blood and all, for our Democracy says every man's created free and equal, and I'm not forgetting my grandfather was a shoemaker," said John Quincy Adams.

"Then how about environment?" inquired the Emigration Official. "Do you attribute your success to that?"

"New England and Massachusetts may be the best environment in the world," said John Quincy Adams. "But last year there was a man alongside me in Congress who was raised on the dirt floor of a backwoods cabin, with no family tree but those in the surrounding forest, and what you'd think was no good environment at all. I'm speaking of Honest Abe Lincoln."

"Abraham Lincoln." The Emigration Official nodded. "It would seem as if he scotches these pat theories of environment and heredity."

"My father and mother were wonderful people," John Quincy Adams went on. "I had the best sort of home, educational chances. But there's that long backwoodsman with no home to speak of, and never within miles of a college, now in Congress. Last analysis, I'd say a man is just about what he makes of himself. Riches can be as big a handicap as poverty. Having a great man for a father can sometimes be a handicap. How many sons of great men do you know who turned out to be as great as their father?"

"Not many," said the Emigration Official.

"Being son of a President," John Quincy pointed out, "isn't easy. My father was a hard man to keep up with— almost gave me a case of inferiority—had to learn to stand on my own. Folks thought I was favored, being a President's son; several times I had to refuse appointments that I'd won by my own efforts."

"But you went ahead on your own, then, Mr. Adams?"

"Studied my schoolbooks, and was diligent." John Quincy nodded, square-jawed. "Kept my mind always occupied, and worked from dawn to dark. My father took me all around Europe when I was a boy, but I studied my lessons instead of gallivanting around like other lads."

"Saved your money and went to church, too?"

"Never was a spendthrift—wore this same hat I've got for ten years," said John Quincy. "And I used to read the Bible from cover to cover twice a year."

"And you didn't do things underhanded. Honest as rock, the record says."

"Honesty's the best policy," said John Quincy Adams firmly. "I guess everybody knew how I stood on an issue. You can see how I broke with the Federalist Party. Always ready to let politics go hang when they got in the way of my principles, sir."

"Boil it down, then, you'd say a man is the captain of his fate and the master of his soul?" was the question.

"That's what I'd say," said John Quincy Adams.

"That he shapes his own destiny? A self-made man?"

"Success or failure—I'd say it was up to the man himself."

"Then you're proud of what you achieved for yourself, is that it, Mr. Adams?"

"And who do you know could be prouder of his record?" John Quincy asked, ruffling and squinting. "And may I ask what these personal questions are leading up to?"

"Well, I'd like to show you something," said the Emigration Official, smiling quietly. "Look a moment, John Quincy Adams. Did you ever see one of these?"

2

THE PAST-CATCHER

ALL IN ALL it was queer, for John Quincy had seen a lot of strange things in his life, but he had to admit he'd never seen one of those. In America or Europe, in all his long career and travels he'd never seen such an object before.

The Emigration Official took it carefully out of a drawer, and placed it on the desktop in front of John Quincy; and John Quincy Adams stared, puzzled. One way, it resembled a microscope, and in another way it resembled a telescope, and again it bore resemblance to one of those stereoscopes your grandmother used to keep on her parlor table. At the same time it was a little like a magic lantern, and in another aspect it looked like a penny arcade peep-movie machine.

The Emigration Official fiddled with focus-screws and adjusted dials and injected a glass slide.

"You've never seen anything like this before," he told John Quincy, "because in America it hasn't been invented yet. You've seen some wonderful inventions in your lifetime, John Quincy—steam engines and oil lamps, paddle-wheel boats and photographic cameras, the first Iron Horse and David Bushnell's submarine. But there's a long way to go before they come to this. There's the Edison light and the X-ray, the gramophone and the telephone, the moving picture and the radio and television and a host of marvels before they arrive at this."

"What is it?" John Quincy squinted, interested. "I've never heard of those last things you mentioned. What is this contraption?"

The Emigration Official looked up and smiled. "It's a Past-catcher."

"A Past-catcher!" John Quincy scowled in incomprehension.

"Sort of a combination of those other things I mentioned," explained the Emigration Official. "Pretty complicated to go into the workings, but it has to do with the fourth dimension, and something they're going to call the time ray. You know, Mr. Adams, light and sound travel on waves through the atmosphere. Events travel much the same way. Something happens on earth—an event. The sound waves and vision waves of that event go traveling on and on out into space. To eternity."

"Like echoes and such." John Quincy gestured.

"Exactly. Say you're sitting on the North Star, then," the Emigration Official pointed out of the window, "looking at the Earth through a spy-glass. That old star is trillions of miles from the Earth. Quintrillions of miles. Now on the Earth it's the Fourth of July: someone fires off a gun. The echo and the flash of that event start traveling.

"But the North Star's so far away, it takes those light and sound waves years to get there. Maybe a century later that gun-flash and echo reaches you. Meantime on Earth a hundred years have gone by. But the North Star is behind time, so to speak. You'd be seeing an event that had happened on Earth in the past."

The Emigration Official pointed to a wall-map of the zodiac; drew out his watch. "Things that happened way back in Caesar's day haven't reached the North Star yet. On Polaris you'd be seeing them building the pyramids."

John Quincy cupped his hand to his ear. "And what's this machine here to do with the pyramids?"

"No more than with any other past events," said his instructor. "But it's a Past-catcher—captures all the past events that are traveling on and on out through space. You tune in, as we call it, to some event that's happened; and this machine, to put it simply, captures the sound waves and the light waves of that past time, and brings the event back into focus. Like this," said the Emigration Official, twisting a screw and putting his eye to an eye-piece. "Here. Take a look at this."

WELL, JOHN QUINCY Adams was pretty skeptical, as who wouldn't be? But he'd always taken an interest in scientific things, and he put his blue eye to the eyepiece. Then he got a shock. That machine was fizzing like one of old Ben Franklin's electrical experiments, only it wasn't an electrical jolt but an emotional one that shocked John Quincy Adams.

Looking into that eye-piece, or peep-hole, he saw a little scene on a film—such a scene as you might see today on a television screen. The picture had motion, and it was in technicolor, and the machine was wired for sound, too. And what John Quincy Adams saw was a boy in a room—a lad in quaint knee-breeches and old-fashioned ruffed shirt and buckled shoes, bent over and writing busily with a quill pen at an antique desk.

The room was strangely furnished with damask draperies, ikons and silver samovars. Candles guttered on the table, and snow fell like lace curtains at the windows. He could even see an onion-spired building silhouetted against wintry sky, and a frosty moon and the ice-sheen of a distant river.

"Why, that's me!" he cried, unable to believe his eye. "Me, when I was fourteen years old and secretary to the Russian Legation in Petrograd!"

"Interesting, isn't it?" asked the Emigration Official. "Yes sir, that's you back in 1781—just a boy in the foreign service in Russia. Can you hear the scratching of the pen?"

Listening astonished, John Quincy could not only hear the scratching of the quill; he could hear the log fire and the cry of wind at the panes and in some far-below quarter of the house voices singing. He saw himself there in the room alone; he was writing very fast, for the hour was late and the room was chilly and he should have been long abed. He saw himself in his hurry blot the writing paper.

"I didn't say that!" he protested to the Emigration Official.

"You did," the Official chuckled over his shoulder. "Everything you witness here is just as it happened in the past."

Old John Quincy marveled at that scene of himself recaptured from long ago, and then, as the novelty and wonderment of it wore off, he felt a considerable admiration for the boy in that picture. The lad was so tired he could scarcely keep awake. His eyelids and shoulders would droop, and he had to prop himself up with sips of black Russian coffee. Books and documents were strewn about, and a dozen candle-stubs attested to long working hours.

"I told you I was always industrious," old John Quincy observed pridefully. "See how I'm working while everyone else is having a party. Diligent. At my desk overtime. That's how I came to be Legation secretary when I was only fourteen."

The lad in the scene wrote furiously, then paused to pull at knuckles stiff from writer's cramp.

"That was a mighty hard job," old John Quincy recalled. "Had to apply myself every minute. See! I'm writing out a speech for the minister. Organizing his material. Why," his voice rose excitedly, "it's that important address to be given to the czar's councillors.

"We'd just won the Revolution in America and were hoping for recognition from Russia. If Russia recognized our government, the other European powers would follow suit. It all depended on that speech, and most of the preparation was left up to me. Can you see what an important job I was doing?" He stared into the Past-catcher admiringly. "America had to have Russia's recognition, and it was my work on that paper when I was only fourteen that put it over!"

"That was a delicate negotiation," the Emigration Official noted. "You might say the history of America depended on it?"

"At the time our whole foreign policy depended on it!"

"A pretty big load for a boy's shoulders to carry," the Emigration Official murmured.

"They trusted me!" Old John Quincy's eye gleamed at the eye-piece. "I was just a nipper, but I could handle international diplomacy with the best of them."

"And you did that job all by yourself, Mr. Adams?"

"If I do say so," old John Quincy said. "You can see how I'm working at my desk there alone."

"But you were not alone," the Emigration Official said softly. "Observe," he adjusted a focus-screw. "Watch the scene closely. Watch by that gabled back window."

THE WINDOW IN that scene was behind the lad's back. Fourteen-year-old John Quincy couldn't see it, but old John Quincy, glaring into the Past-catcher, could see it very well because Past-catchers are four-dimensional and show all sides of what went on. Old John Quincy watched the back window in that scene, sharp-eyed; then he pulled a quick, sharp breath.

"Why, there's someone out there!" he exclaimed. "Someone is standing on that balcony outside!"

"Was standing on that balcony," the Emigration Official corrected. "Remember, the event you're witnessing happened in the past. But soft. There are two prowlers. Listen, and you'll hear them talking."

Sure enough, there were two on that outside balcony— two furtive, shadowy figures. They wore long greatcoats and tall fur hats, and they were booted like Cossacks and creeping up to the casement like Russian bears. Standing at the window frame, they pawed the snow-curtains aside, and one rubbed at the frosty pane with his mitten and peered into the room. In the outwash of candlelight their faces came into view. One was thin with a drizzly black beard, and the other was fat with a tremendous red beard; and the eyes of the two men were curiously similar—a light, hard green, penetratingly sharp.

"Ah, Nishkin," said the black-beard to his companion,

"there he is! Bones of Saint Stanislaus of Zmeinogorsk! He is only a boy!"

The red-bearded one nodded, peering in. "And writing. Always writing."

Those guttural Russian voices made old John Quincy's hair go up, but the boy, engrossed at the writing desk, did not hear that pair outside the window. Young John Quincy heard only the quill and the wind and the firelog and the voices singing in a distant quarter of the house. He bit his pen thoughtfully; then bent to scribbling again, his boyish cue bobbing up and down on his necknape as he wrote.

"He cannot hear us," murmured the black-whiskered Russian, nudging his companion. "No one will hear us. There is a banquet downstairs, and they are singing. Now is our chance."

Red-beard chuckled. "I am ready when you give the word, Goranoff. This is easier than I expected."

Old John Quincy pulled back from the eye-piece, aghast. "My God, they're going to kill him," he cried to the Emigration Official. "I mean, they're going to kill *me!* That dirty red-whiskered scoundrel has a knife in his clutch. The gaunt black one is priming a horse-pistol!"

"Watch! Watch!" was the breathless reply. "Keep your eye on the scene and you'll see what happened."

Panting, squinting, horrified, old John Quincy pasted eye to eye-piece and watched in amazement and consternation. On that snowy balcony the red-whiskered one was grinning, his strange green eyes alight. The one called Goranoff, having cocked his horse-pistol, was crouched ready to spring.

"Ready, Nishkin?"

"Aye, Goranoff. Ready."

"I will throw wide the window. You leap in fast."

"Faster than he can cry out, Goranoff. Faster than the Devil."

"If he moves, I will shoot him through the head. If he doesn't, you will cut his throat. Understood?"

"It is understood."

"Then it is one-two-three, go!" snarled Goranoff, "One! Two—"

OLD JOHN QUINCY could hardly stand it. Young John Quincy at that writing desk didn't hear a thing. He was scribbling busily when that killer on the balcony whispered, "Three!" and grabbed for the windowlatch, and old John Quincy wanted to yell out wildly and warn the unsuspecting boy of the danger.

"Murder!" the old man gasped, grabbing at the box-shaped machine as if to catch the assassins envisioned on the screen. Then, peering, he couldn't help but shout. Just as Goranoff touched the window latch, it happened. A rumbling roar, like thunder in the winter's night. A basso tumult that came down from the roofs above that balcony; then *whoosh! crash!* under tons of wet snow and icicles the balcony and the foul pair on it were buried.

Old John Quincy saw young John Quincy leap up at the roar of the snow-slide. But he saw what young John Quincy hadn't seen—that booming white avalanche burst over the balcony like an explosion; two dark figures leaping for the icy balcony rail; the figures caught and enveloped as if in a down-tumbling glacier. That avalanche went over them as they went over the rail; engulfed, they fell forty feet into a courtyard and were buried under a hill of ice and snow.

The picture faded as young John Quincy shrugged and turned back to his writing desk. Old John Quincy didn't shrug. Mopping his forehead, he leaned back from the Past-catcher and glared at the Emigration Official as if the event he'd witnessed had just happened.

"I remember hearing that snow-slide," he said hoarsely. "But those murderers—I never knew they were out there! Great Glory! they might have slain me!"

"So they might," said the Emigration Official. "Very easily."

"They wanted the papers," old John Quincy panted. "That document I was working on! They were Anarchists, and they wanted to kill me and steal those papers and ruin our American negotiations with Russia. Why, thunderation! Our whole European policy might've been wrecked!"

"That was close," came the smiling answer. "But you'll recall this next incident even better, although I doubt if you realized at the time it was such a narrow escape. See it for yourself in the Past-catcher. Take a look at this."

3

BY COACH TO JEOPARDY

LOOKING INTO THAT machine was like looking at the scene of a play; when the view came into focus it was rather like a curtain going up. Act two: The scenery had changed. Old John Quincy found himself staring at an evening landscape, a turnpike winding through a peaceful countryside of fields and streams and woods. There was a woodcutter's cottage at one road-bend; a style at another, and a crossroads where a signpost pointed, *To London.*

"The London Post Road!" gasped John Quincy Adams.

He remembered that turnpike, remembered it well. He'd traveled it in 1795 when, as the young American minister of twenty-seven, he'd been ordered by George Washington to go to Holland by way of London where he was to deliver some important papers to John Jay at the Court of St. James.

"It was my first big mission," old John Quincy cried, glaring at that post-road scene. "Those papers were so important Washington wouldn't let anyone else carry them. The British were making trouble, and those secret instructions had to reach Jay or the United States would be in a dangerous mess. Washington told me to deliver them at all costs. Foreign agents wanted to steal them, but I got them to London, all right. I used my wits!"

"How was that?" the Emigration Official asked quietly.

"I left the boat ahead of time and went to London incognito by a roundabout way. That's the road I took to London."

He bent over the eye-piece excitedly; he had every reason to remember that London Post Road.

The scene blurred a little as the machine crackled and fizzed; then it came back clear as a painting, a brown road stretching through green woods in twilight.

"Look," said the Emigration Official, "do you see the coach, Mr. Adams? Do you see it coming?"

Yes, blinking hard into the eye-piece, John Quincy could see the stagecoach—far in the distance, a rolling cloud of dust advancing through the pastoral twilight. Pretty soon he could make out the vehicle; four horses, lathered and galloping; the top-hatted driver on the high, swaying seat; the guard on the tally-ho seat behind. Up hill and down dale came the careening stage, growing larger and larger on John Quincy's vision. He could hear it approaching, too: the whip-cracks, the creak of harness, the rattle of rolling wheels.

He stared hard at that picture on the television screen, and then he could see within the stagecoach—a close-up of the passengers. There were five men crowded together, beefy Englishmen in the costumes of the time, and a young man crowded into a corner, all hunched up with books and baggage and a pad on his knees. The young man was trying to write, but having a difficult time, for the coach was jolting like anything and his companions jostled him, and the coach was stuffy with dust and British conversation and pipe-smoke.

"Hi, Alf, an' when shall we get to London?" asked one of the passengers for the dozenth time.

The traveler at the young man's elbow made a great fuss at pulling out his watch. "'Arf hour late now, an' it's getting dark. Won't be there till well on midnight, I expect."

The young man, jostled, looked up annoyed.

The young man was John Quincy Adams, himself.

He bent to his scribbling, biting the pencil and trying to concentrate, and the close-up altered into a picture of the careening stagecoach. The driver swore and laid about with his whip as the horses pounded around a turn; then there was the screech of brakes, and "Whoa, Joe! Whoa!" as the stage pulled up before the woodcutter's cottage where there was a roadside trough for water.

Young John Quincy Adams looked out of the coach-window briefly, then returned to his jotting. Old John Quincy Adams, staring into the Past-catcher, muttered under his breath.

"I remember stopping at that watering trough. I was smart to pick a backcountry stage without a lot of crowded waystops."

"Listen to what's said," the Emigration Official touched old John Quincy's shoulder. "Then keep your eye on that woodcutter's cottage."

THE STAGECOACH DRIVER, draping the reins across his knees, looked around in the dusk, then turned to the guard on the perch behind. "Hey, Percy. Looks like the woodcutter ayn't at 'ome."

The guard, who sat with his arms folded carelessly and

his boots histed up, nodded and looked toward the cottage without interest. He was a tough-looking customer, the guard. With his tricorn hat pulled down, his brace of pistols in his belt and a black patch over one eye, he resembled a pirate on the lofty sterndeck of a ship. His one good eye was a queer shade of green.

"Ayn't no smoke from his chimney," remarked the driver. "Might be he's chopped off a toe, like he did last Easter. Might be he's sick."

"More likely he's gone to th' fair," said the guard, shrugging. "Why be a worry-wort? Th' blighter's off havin' a good time."

The cottage under the trees was dark, and the guard's good eye under his down-pulled hatbrim was darker. The driver didn't notice it, and turned his attention to the thirsty horses. Young John Quincy Adams, writing inside the stagecoach, didn't notice it. But old John Quincy watching breathlessly into the Past-catcher, noticed it and wondered what the devil. Then he saw exactly what happened.

With much gee-hawing, whip crackings and, "Giddap!" with the strain of harness and clatter of hoofs, the heavy stage got under way. Just as it started off, two shadowy figures raced from around behind the dark woodcutter's cottage, and, sprinting out to the road caught the tailboard of the lurching stage.

From the way they ran, low-bent, furtive, they looked like highwaymen, each clutching a pistol. The driver, busy with whip and reins, didn't see them. The passengers in the coach didn't see them. But the guard on his rear perch saw them—not only saw them, tut leaned down, reaching to give them a hand.

Yes, Percy with the eye-patch leaned down to help those two climb aboard; there was a dizzy minute with the dust and pebbles flying when it looked as if those road-runners weren't going to catch on; then each got a handhold and they hung for dear life on the back of the swaying coach. Only the guard knew they were riding back there, blind-baggage.

" 'Old on!" his thick voice was just audible above the clattertibang of the wheels. "Grab a-holt of that luggage. I'll fetch ye aloft soon as there's a chance."

Several cowhide trunks and some carpet bags were lashed to the luggage-rack on the coach's rear; the top was piled high with baggage, and the guard could converse with these riders without fear of the driver's detection. Sweating, tight-jawed, they clung to the luggage-rack, almost lost from view in the twilight and dust. It was extraordinary that the guard should let them steal a ride like that. What was more extraordinary, one of those riders was a thin, dark man very elegantly clad, his weskit covered with gold watchchains and earrings in his ears; and old John Quincy recognized him with a yell.

"Why, that's Falcon! The famous English gambler! Played on all the trans-Atlantic vessels! I met him on the ship coming over from America. Certainly that's the man!"

Old John Quincy recognized him, but young John Quincy, in the coach's dark interior, didn't even know he was back there. Squeezed back on the hard, jolting cushions, young John Quincy was trying to doze.

"I never dreamed he was on that coach!" old John Quincy gasped. And then he noticed something else: He had a full-view look at the gambler's face, and the man's eyes were a light, hard green and strangely piercing, very like Percy's one eye.

"Watch," said the Emigration Official. "See what they're doing now."

WHAT FALCON AND his companion were doing was at first hard to make out because the scene was veiled in gloaming, but it all came clear on the screen. Falcon had out a knife. His companion was struggling to untie the straps of a cowhide trunk. The guard leaned down to help.

"You're sure it's the right trunk?" the gambler panted up.

"Sure," from the guard. "There's 'is initials—J.Q.A."

"I wouldn't want to make a mistake," Falcon scowled. "We had to kill that woodchopper before he'd let us hide in his cottage. We've got to work fast now, and this is our last chance."

"That's the luggage he's carryin'." The guard kept a cautionary eye on the driver. He bent down. "It's the Yankee you're after, ayn't it? Bloke named Adams? Well, 'ee's right inside the coach."

Falcon nodded. "Good work, old chappie. Aboard ship it was too dangerous. This time we can't miss."

Knife in teeth, he began to climb to the top of the coach.

"Pass me the blade," called the one below. "I'll 'ave to cut these straps. 'Is luggage is locked an' hogtied."

"Don't lose that trunk," Falcon cursed, transferring the blade. "When you cut it loose, jump with it to the road. I'll come back and meet you. He's probably carrying what we want in his pocket, but we'll have his baggage, too." He swung himself lightly up beside the guard.

"Let me handle the driver," the guard advised. "If they

ever learn I'm in on this I'll be 'anged in Old Bailey before Whitsuntide. 'Ave we got to kill this 'ere Yankee?"

"Dead men don't call out the police," Falcon said coolly. "I'll take care of the American. You shoot the driver. Grab the reins and stop fast, understand? I'll swing down over the whiffletree, and it'll look like an ordinary holdup. I've got to call out the Yankee and search him, and he'll frisk a lot easier if I put a bullet in his head.

"Minute I shoot him, you whip up the horses and make off. Afterward you'll say you were trying to save the other passengers and the stage was held up by Irish highway-men. If you stop any chase, I'll double your commission."

"Better wait'll we're out of the open, then." The guard spat. "There's a likely spot—those woods up ahead. Just beyond that crossroad."

Rattle of wheels on a plank bridge drowned their plot-ting voices; the driver, unconscious of jeopardy behind his back, cracked his whip and swore at the horses; rocking and careening, the coach raced on through lavender dusk.

On behind, the robber was sawing desperately at the luggage straps. Percy the guard, pistol in hand, began to claw his way across the coach-top toward the driver. On hands and knees, clinging savagely, for the top of that stage was like the deck of a storm-tossed ship, Falcon followed.

"Great Jerusalem!" old John Quincy Adams blurted. "And me dozing inside there. Never once suspecting!"

"Look at the crossroads at the entrance to the woods," the Emigration Official murmured. "Look closely there in the road ahead. Do you see that pebble?"

The horses were almost on top of it when old John Quincy saw that pebble in the road. A big pebble it was,

almost the size of a rock, smooth-polished and brown
and possibly limestone or basalt. Maybe some child had
thrown it there, or maybe it had just come there by wind
and weather and the road's erosion. Where do pebbles
come from, anyway? Nobody cares. Who ever notices a
pebble, beyond giving it a kick?

Certainly the driver of that London stage didn't notice
it. And those devils creeping up behind the driver had
their minds on something else. As for the baggage-robber
behind, he couldn't have spied it there ahead; while those
within the coach didn't know about it either.

Then everybody concerned learned about it all at once.
Wham! That stage was going like sixty, and when one front
wheel hit that pebble the whole equipage sprang into the
air. *Whang-bang!* what a jolt that was. For full a minute
that coach was over on two wheels, swerving and careening
all over the road, defying all of Newton's laws of gravity.
Axles shrieked. There was a screech of iron springs. Into a
roadside ditch went that stagecoach, and out of the ditch
with a jounce to split the hubs, held upright only by its
runaway speed.

Inside, the passengers almost brained themselves on
the ceiling.

Outside, the hollering driver yanked the reins and
fought to hold his horses. Somehow the guard hung on.
But two dark figures went sailing off the stage—two wild
figures that soared through the air like a circus act, lit in
the highway like acrobats, and went rolling tail-over-tea-
cup in the dust. One of them got up and rabbited for the
woods, but Falcon, with a broken neck, lay still. When the

coach lurched around a dizzy turn and came at last on an even keel, the road to London was clear.

Some miles later the driver looked around at the guard.

"W'y, Perce," he remarked, "you're w'ite as a bloody sheet."

At midnight, when the London stage pulled finally into Charing Cross depot, the guard was still waxy around the gills.

"Gor'my, Mr. Adams," he blurted to the young American minister, "someone's gone an' sawed through two of yer luggage straps. Now when could some dirty thieves 'ave done a trick like that?"

4

GENTLEMEN, A TOAST

OLD JOHN QUINCY Adams sagged back from the machine, his own gills waxy. That attempt to steal his luggage was a historic incident, already in the history books; he'd always wondered who, on that London-bound stage, had cut those baggage straps.

But the trunk had been safe, all because of a pebble he'd never seen or known about.

"The papers for Jay were in that trunk," he said thickly. "So that trans-Atlantic gambler was a British spy! If the Tories had ever got hold of those instructions it would've meant war a whole lot quicker than in 1812. America wouldn't have been ready; we wouldn't have won as we did in 1812. Stars and Stripes! I remember that devilish bouncing, but I never imagined Falcon—and that pebble—!"

The Emigration Official smiled at the Past-catcher. "Many things of one's life are never imagined," he said gently. "Speaking of the War of 1812, aren't you, Mr. Adams, considered largely responsible for the peace in 1814—the Treaty of Ghent?"

Old John Quincy snorted. "Largely responsible! I consider myself wholly responsible. The English wanted to quit fighting, but they wanted their own terms, impossible terms! Henry Clay, on our side, wanted a long war. The British were pigheaded; Clay too hot tempered; no one in our Commission knew what to do. There'd never have been any Treaty of Ghent if it hadn't been for me!"

"Look in the Past-catcher," came the soft-voiced instruction. "Your diplomatic genius did much to save the treaty, Mr. Adams. And if that treaty had failed, the United States could not have survived. But look in the Past-catcher—"

GHENT—CHRISTMAS EVE, THE year 1814. The quaint old Flemish city wearing its holiday ermine of snow. Candles in windows and merrymakers in narrow streets. The low-roofed, historic house where the treaty was to be signed. Peace on Earth, good will toward men. The Past-catcher showed it all.

How well old John Quincy remembered that particular Yuletide. As the scene came into focus he saw himself as Mr. J.Q. Adams, American minister extraordinary; a scholarly, cosmopolitan gentleman of world affairs, seasoned by years of travel and long experience in European diplomacy. At forty-six he could point with pride to a reputation and service record equaled by few statesmen. The Continent had come to know Mr. J.Q. Adams.

As American minister to Prussia (where his entry to Berlin had been challenged by a stupid Prussian officer who had never heard of the United States) he had won wide respect and admiration from the German king.

His return to the United States during Jefferson's administration had been distinguished by a brilliant, if stormy, period in the Senate.

Appointed ambassador to Russia by James Madison, he

had achieved great success in St. Petersburg and become a close friend of Czar Alexander.

No diplomat was better fitted to handle America's foreign affairs, and America's foreign situation was never more ticklish than in 1814. The Napoleonic Wars had battered the Continent. Europe was a jungle of suspicions, jealousies, hates. In America the War of 1812 had muddled to a stalemate with both John Bull and Uncle Sam exhausted.

But, while fending off the United States with its left hand, Great Britain had suddenly knocked out Napoleon at Waterloo with its right. The Little Corporal was a ghost in exile, but Prussia loomed as a new specter, and London, anxious to recover prestige, might try to finish off the U.S.A. during the breathing spell.

The British were only half-heartedly suing for peace, and with Wellington's army released for action, the Tory government might change its mind. If a peace treaty was to be signed, it had to be signed fast. So Mr. J.Q. Adams had been ordered post-haste from St. Petersburg to Ghent to head the American peace commission. It was the high point of his diplomatic career, and he'd never had a tougher assignment.

TO BEGIN WITH, the British peace commissioners sent over from London were quarrelsome. They looked down on the Americans as their social inferiors. They were imperious and domineering. They made impossible demands. They demanded the right to fortify their side of the Canadian border, refusing to allow fortification of the American side. They demanded navigation control of the Mississippi. They proposed to erect an Indian buffer state between the U.S. and Canada. They demanded most of Michigan, Wisconsin and Illinois; refused to grant fishing concessions off Newfoundland; insisted America must assume responsibility for the war.

At which the American peace commissioners became even more quarrelsome. They not only quarreled with the British Commissioners; they quarreled among themselves. Mr. Gallatin, senior American commissioner, was ready to throw up his hands. Mr. Bayard argued sourly with Mr. Russell. Mr. Henry Clay wanted to punch the British and everybody else in the nose and go home.

Bitterness and spleen brought the conference to a deadlock. The commissioners haggled over the treaty like dogs over a bone. Time and again it looked as if the peace commission would break up into a first-class gang battle. Words flew across the conference table like fists, and the sound of fists banging the table frightened the good people of Ghent who thought they heard guns. For six months the negotiations dragged, everyone at loggerheads. The peace commission would have blown up like a powder keg if it hadn't been for Mr. J.Q. Adams.

He, himself, had a terrible time controlling his temper, for he was quick-triggered like his father, and he hated Tory snobbery, and the effort for self-control almost burst the muscles of his face.

But he could bargain like a Yankee, and he could talk like a mesmerist, and he knew the desperate position the United States was in. Now Napoleon was beaten, the British could throw their full sea-power across the Atlantic, and the hard-pressed American army wouldn't have a chance against the iron-hardened troops of Wellington.

Peace with England was the only answer, but it had to be an honorable peace, lasting and permanent. Mr. J.Q. Adams knew that.

He knew, too, that the British people were reasonable even if their government often wasn't. He knew how to handle his fellow Americans. He trusted the judgments of Mr. Gallatin and Mr. Bayard; he sized up Russell as incompetent; he knew explosive Henry Clay wanted the war to go on for personal reasons, for Clay in the Senate had been a war hawk and his reputation was at stake. And Mr. J.Q. Adams had some cards up his sleeve.

Stubbornly he argued for conciliation. He pacified Clay on one hand and the British commissioners on the other. Somehow he held the conference together. At last it was accomplished. The dove of peace was a pretty skinny looking bird and had lost a lot of its pinfeathers, but on Christmas Eve, 1814, the treaty lay on the table waiting to be signed.

THAT HISTORIC SCENE, revealed by the Past-catcher, brought a tight lump to old John Quincy's throat. He saw himself standing by the fireplace, his face seamed with fatigue. He saw his fellow American commissioners— Gallatin and Bayard and Russell and Clay—seated about in characteristic attitudes. He saw the massive Flemish table and the expectant inkwells and the treaty waiting there in the middle of the table like a Christmas gift.

Old John Quincy looked up from the Past-catcher, bright-eyed.

"We were waiting for the British commissioners to arrive! That treaty was one of my greatest accomplishments! It ended the War of 1812, and it looks as if England and America would never break that peace!"

"One of the strangest treaties ever made," the Emigration Official acknowledged. "It will last for a long, long time."

"It would never have been made," old John Quincy declared, "if I hadn't held my two trump cards Czar Alexander and the Prussian king! Great Britain was afraid of those powers and knew they were favoring America. If I hadn't made good friends with those rulers that treaty would never have been signed."

"Ah," said the voice at his shoulder. "But keep your eye on the Past-catcher, Mr. Adams. Observe how nearly that treaty wasn't signed."

"What?" Old John Quincy looked up aghast.

"Watch the scene," he was advised.

Well, even at the time he'd been anxious, and there on the screen his anxiety showed behind his smiles. The British commissioners were late. Could something at the last minute have miscarried? Gallatin was nervous, pacing up and down. Clay was drumming the table impatiently. It was like the Englishmen to be late; gave them a sense of superiority to keep the Americans waiting.

Mr. John Quincy Adams was on edge. Besides, he was a little blue. It was Christmas Eve. His wife, Louisa, and his young son Charles Francis were in St. Petersburg. He got to thinking about them away off there in Russia, and about his father and mother in far-away America, the old homestead in Massachusetts and Yankee plum puddings and Christmas trees. It was not the night for anything to go wrong. There just wouldn't be any Santa Claus if something stopped the signing of this treaty.

As if to calm his anxieties, then, the strains of a Christmas carol drifted into the room. Everyone listened. Outside in the snow the carolers were singing.

"Stille Nacht—Heilige Nacht—"

John Quincy Adams felt warmed, reassured. A mankind that could write such a song could hitch its wagon to a star. He walked to the window and looked down. There were three singers in the street below, all wrapped up in overcoats, tophats and mufflers—two men and a woman with lanthorns in their hands. Mr. John Quincy Adams threw down a grateful sovereign.

"Gentlemen." He wheeled about. "This is indeed a memorable Christmas. Come, let us celebrate the occasion. A bottle of something to toast the British when they arrive."

Even Henry Clay grinned, for John Quincy Adams, being Puritan by upbringing, was generally pretty sparing with the spirits. But all of them thought it a good idea to toast the British commissioners (although Clay added that Satan's grids might be more appropriate for such a toasting) and Mr. John Quincy rang at once for his servant.

OLD SCHRECHLIKEIT, THE servant, presently appeared; he was a melancholy old fellow with a horse-like face and faded blue eyes, very polite and always bowing in the manner of European servants. He had been hired to take charge of the American commissioners' household. (One of the most trying aspects of the business had been the necessity for the American diplomats to live together).

Commissioner Adams told the servant to fetch a bottle

of very old Chartreuse from his private stock in the wine cellar. Sadly the servant shook his head, replying in doleful Flemish that all the Chartreuse—the last choice bottle— had disappeared.

"You will recall that I spoke to you about it, Mynheer Adams. During the six months you have been quartered here, someone has been stealing your wine."

Mr. J.Q. Adams almost lost his temper about that. In the long fight with the peace commissioners, he hadn't been able to bother with petty thievery. Now this seemed as big an outrage as the British trying to steal Wisconsin.

"That rare Chartreuse has all been stolen? I'd like to get my hands on the thief!"

"I've been missing champagne right along," Gallatin put in.

"Not a drop of wine in the pantry," Henry Clay glowered. "I used up my last bottle last night. I thought you chaps would have a holiday supply. They don't deserve better, but we can't offer these Englishmen beer."

Mr. John Quincy Adams was choleric. No wine on Christmas Eve! But he couldn't blame poor Schrechlikeit if the scullery boy or someone was light-fingered.

"Here," he offered the servant a handful of bills. "Buy a bottle of the oldest Chartreuse you can find in Ghent. And get it back here in jig time."

"But there is no one to send to the wine shop, *mynheer*," the servant mourned. "The cook has gone to a Christmas mass. The stable boy is at a party. If I go there will be no one to attend the door. I can send one of the carolers in the street if—"

"No matter who you send." John Quincy Adams

gestured, impatient. "Have that Chartreuse fetched in a hurry."

Then the scene shifted to the street door where old Schrechlikeit was beckoning to the carolers, asking if they would run an errand. At promise of a tip all three were more than willing. Off they hustled down the street, heads bowed to the blowing snow.

Turning a corner, they hurried for a wine shop not far from the Hôtel des Pays-Bas. At the entry of the wine shop they paused together in confab. The scene showed a close-up of those Christmas carolers, and old John Quincy gasped when he saw in the Past-catcher the faces of that trio.

Their singing had been angelic, but those faces, unmuffled, rivaled anything in a rogues' gallery. Close-up of the tenor showed a hook-nosed, curly-haired dwarf, as ugly as the Hunchback of Notre Dame. No less hideous was the baritone, his features scarred by smallpox. As for the woman, she was beautiful; but it was the sinister, cold beauty of a leopardess. These were evil faces, and to old John Quincy they seemed inhuman and yet familiar, for the eyes of each were a piercing, unnatural green.

"It is up to Little François," the leopard woman was whispering in French. She gave the dwarf's hump an affectionate pat. "You are the leader, *mon petit*. The Tomcat and I will agree to anything you say."

"Ah, *oui*," agreed the Tomcat, he of the scarred face. "You are the brains of this party, Little François. Myself and Marie are but the arms and legs."

The humpback nodded appreciatively. "Leave it to me," he snarled. "I know you would like to use your garrote,

Tomcat, and Marie is such an expert at throwing darts that it is a shame not to use her talent. But Santa Claus has provided us with a better way. *Sacré Dieu!* No risk to us at all, and we can kill all those birds with one stone."

"Parbleu!" the Tomcat exclaimed. "All at once?"

"I told you," Marie declared. "Little François is a genius."

The humpbacked dwarf sneered. "Do you think I am the highest paid assassin of all France for nothing? Listen, then. I have thought it all out. Do you not see the possibilities in this bottle?"

"I see nothing but snow-flakes," the Tomcat blinked.

Frowning, the dwarf held up his lantern. "Attend, comedian! It is as simple as two times two. We will deliver this sacred bottle but when we deliver it there will be more than Chartreuse in the bottle."

The Tomcat let his mouth fall open. Marie gave a high, tinkling laugh. Little François pointed a finger. "That apothecary shop over yonder, that is our next stop. A little cyanide, perhaps. A pinch of laudanum. I have a recipe used in chocolates by Lucretia Borgia. After which," he looked up piously, "I think the heavenly choir can sing the carols to our happy peace commissioners."

OLD JOHN QUINCY Adams clenched his fists when he heard that speech in the Past-catcher. "Damnation!" he choked out. "They're putting poison in that bottle of Chartreuse—that bottle we were going to drink before signing the treaty!"

He saw the trio buy Chartreuse and then cross to the druggist's establishment. Saw them come smiling out of the drug shop and go down an unlighted alley where they doctored the fatal bottle. They were singing an anthem as they returned arm in arm up the snowy Flemish street—three jolly Christmas carolers handing a bottle of Chartreuse in at the American commissioners' door. Looking up at the lighted window, they caroled to the inmates in English.

"God rest ye merry, Gentlemen, let nothing you dismay—"

Perspiration broke like oyster-sweat on old John Quincy's forehead as he saw Schrechlikeit accept the deadly bottle. Schrechlikeit closed the door; and the three Christmas carolers drifted off down the street with the snowflakes, as the three British commissioners arrived.

Old John Quincy watched, horrified.

He saw Schrechlikeit admit the British commissioners—pompous Lord Gambier and that stuffy little doctor who wrote books and that exasperating popinjay, Mr. Goulburn.

He saw himself welcoming the Englishmen to the conference room.

"Gentlemen, this is a historic occasion."

"Quite. Quite. His Majesty's Government is prepared to sign—"

"May it be a lasting peace between our nations, gentlemen. Let us propose a toast to that effect. Mr. Clay, will you ring for Schrechlikeit?"

How could Commissioner John Quincy Adams have suspected? In that upstairs conference room, seated about the table with the others, he fingered his pen light-heartedly and chatted cheerfully to Lord Gambier and wondered why the servant didn't hurry. And presently he heard Schrechlikeit coming up the stairs. The footsteps were slow in coming; the old stairs creaked; the servant seemed to be taking an unconscionable long time.

"What," he wondered to himself, "is the matter with that man?"

Then the door at room's end opened, and Schrechlikeit was there. He was breathing heavily; in the candlelight his features were pale; he seemed to have difficulty balancing tray and glasses and uncorked Chartreuse bottle.

Commissioner Adams hurried to the servant, backed him out into the hall and closed the door. "Schrechlikeit," he snapped, peering into the man's yellowed face, "you're drunk."

"No," the servant answered. "Sick!" With that, in the hall's dimness, he staggered; fell flat across the stair-head. John Quincy Adams jumped too late. Crash went the tray and glasses. *Bumpety-bump-bump bump*—that was the Chartreuse bottle clattering down the stairs, emptying itself.

It had seemed a bad omen for the peace treaty at the time—too ominous to be mentioned in letters and notes. But just as the bottle broke to pieces on the bottom step, the cook entered the front door. It was that good Flemish lady who hurried off to fetch the doctor and returned by way of the wine shop to buy another bottle of Christmas cheer.

The scene faded when, having toasted their governments all around, the peace commissioners reached for their pens to sign the Treaty of Ghent.

5

MR. SECRETARY TAKES THE AIR

OLD JOHN QUINCY Adams felt ill at the fade-out of that scene. As ill as he'd ever felt in his life. He swung around from the Past-catcher and loosened his collar with a finger, and his lips were trembling.

"So that's what happened to that servant," he said huskily. "That's why he collapsed! I remember how he fell over that night. The doctor took him away and he never came back afterward, and I—I thought he was just sick. But he was poisoned! It was *he*—Schrechlikeit, himself— who'd been robbing the wine cellar. He took a nip of that poisoned Chartreuse! Good Godfrey! If he hadn't, it would have killed us all!"

"Yes," said the Emigration Official quietly. "You'd have died."

"And the peace treaty wouldn't have been signed," old John Quincy cried. "The war would have gone on. Wellington would have hurled his troops across the Atlantic. England and America might be at each other throats today! That's what those French agents wanted. They wanted to bring back Napoleon, wanted England and America to batter each other to exhaustion. Those assassins were hired to kill us and stop that treaty. I see it all now."

"The Past-catcher reveals everything," was the low-voiced response. "It shows what happened and what *nearly* happened. In every man's life there are things that nearly happened—things of which he never dreamed. Those three French killers were following you, Mr. Adams, every hour of the six months you were there in Ghent. From the moment peace was decided upon your life was in jeopardy."

Prickles crawled on old John Quincy's bald-spot. "By heaven!" he swore. "If I'd known!"

The Emigration Official shook his head. "Behind every happening in the life of a man are the unknown things that nearly happened. What man, as he turns a corner, knows what lies at that moment ahead or what goes on behind his back? He turns to the right and, all unaware, avoids the accident which might have happened at the left. Or, turning to the left, he side-steps, all unknown, some misfortunate pitfall at the right. The Past-catcher, being four dimensional, shows all. Let us see what nearly happened while you were Secretary of State."

"While I was Secretary of State?" old John Quincy cried.

"In the Cabinet of James Monroe," The Emigration Official nodded. "You had won high honors in Europe, Mr. Adams, and when you returned with your family to the United States you were President Monroe's first choice for the highest post in his Cabinet. Look, Mr. Adams." The official adjusted a dial. "The year is now 1820. You will see yourself in Washington, D.C."

WASHINGTON IN THE spring! Ah, softly as May itself it came into focus on the television-like screen—the town misty with a Sunday morning sunlight and decked in fresh

greenery that cloaked the rawness of unpainted buildings, the shabbiness of the negro quarter, the dirt and dust
of unpaved streets, the piles of lumber and masonry and
helterskelter aspect of a new boom town.

Burnt by the British during the War of 1812, Capitol and White House were still a-building. Everywhere
wooden frameworks were going up. The American capital
in 1820 was young, raw-boned, taking root. White boule-
vards, parks and national monuments were yet to come.
But magnolias and wild flowers blossomed everywhere,
and in the surrounding forests there were birds singing.

A carriage was coming down Pennsylvania Avenue;
Secretary of State John Quincy Adams with his wife and
young sons were to be seen enjoying their Sunday morning drive. It was seven o'clock and dewy in the morning,
but that wasn't early in an era when families breakfasted at
five-thirty and church began at half past seven.

But Secretary of State Adams wasn't going to church.
There was no Unitarian service in town; besides, although
he was a rigid man of principle, he was pretty much a free-
thinker like his father and preferred to say his own prayers.
A Sunday morning drive through the woods down to the
Potomac could be worshipful, too.

"What a lovely drive it is," Louisa was delighted. "I'm
so happy here in Washington."

Secretary of State Adams, jotting notes on the back of an
envelope, looked up. "No finer city anywhere in the spring,"
he assured his wife. "It's going to grow, Louisa. Just as the
United States is going to grow. Some day it'll be the most
important city in the world."

Mr. John Quincy Adams felt fine that morning. How

good it was to be in America with his wife and boys. Just to be an American citizen, out of the stale decaying atmosphere of Europe, made him want to expand. Europe was like an old and November-blighted forest; America was like a promise of spring. Democracy would grow strong and healthy and tall. To know he had an important part in building the great Republic filled him with a glow of pride.

And what American had more reason to be proud? Even his political enemies had to acknowledge his supremacy in the State Department. No one in Washington was doing a better job, and the State Department was a mighty tough job under James Monroe.

People were calling it the Era of Good Feeling, but if there was any good feeling around, John Quincy Adams wasn't aware of it. His job had been thorny as a briar patch. There'd been that squabble with Great Britain over the Columbia River, and that ticklish dicker with Russia over the Pacific Coast. Then he'd had to purchase Florida from Spain, and buying Florida real estate from a Spaniard was as risky as going blindfold to a horse trade.

He'd done a fine peace of work, buying Florida for the United States, and meantime he'd accomplished a lot of exacting little odd jobs like holding his temper in the Cabinet and establishing the Bureau of Weights and Measures. And now he was putting over the biggest job of statecraft so far in his career. He was dealing an all-time death blow to the ambitions of the Holy Alliance.

He told Louisa about it as the carriage promenaded under the shade trees.

THINGS HAD BEEN happening since he'd been Secretary of State. The natives of Central and South America, revolting against intolerable tyranny, had broken away from Spanish domination and set up republics of their own. The Spanish people themselves were fighting against the king. Italy, too, was in bloody revolution.

All over Europe the people were crying for democracy, striving to throw off the monarchs who held them down. The right to life, liberty and the pursuit of happiness—all over the world those ideals were on the march.

The kings were scared. They saw that democracy in America was a big success. They hugged their money-bags and clutched their tottering thrones and put their heads together. "Democracy," they decided, "must be smashed. If it is smashed in America it will die out forever. The first step is to reconquer for Spain the colonies in South and Central America."

So they said a lot of hypocritical prayers and formed a sanctimonious league called the Holy Alliance. Top dogs of this crew were the emperor of Austria, the emperor of Prussia and the czar of Russia, once friendly toward America but now inspired by Prince Metternich to seize world domination. Save for England and Turkey, all the other powers in Europe rushed to get on the bandwagon. They pledged to stand by the divine right of kings, to stamp out democracy in Europe and recapture South America for the king of Spain.

"Do you see what that would mean?" John Quincy Adams asked his wife. "Huge European armies in South America, the Caribbean, Mexico. The United States constantly threatened. Little by little our Republic would be undermined. It's an insidious plot to end all representative government."

"Goodness!" Louisa said breathlessly. "Isn't that terribly dangerous for our country?"

"Dangerous!" John Quincy Adams snapped. "It's the worst threat our nation ever had. Luckily the British people won't have anything to do with that gang. But they're powerful enough as it is. If they ever get a foothold in South America they'll be on top of us like a pack of wolves. James Monroe turned pale when he heard about it, I tell you."

"And what's President Monroe going to do about it?" Louisa asked.

"It's up to the State Department," John Quincy Adams explained, "and he's left most of it up to me."

"What are you going to do about it, Pop?" young Charles Francis asked.

"I'm going to do plenty," John Quincy Adams said, square-jawed. "I'm working on it now, and I'm almost finished. The President will get the credit for it, but I'm responsible for it, if I do say so. You'll hear about it when it goes through."

HE SMILED, THINKING it over, as the carriage trundled under the shade trees. He'd concocted a scheme to scotch that Holy Alliance, all right. A few days more and the plan would be made public. He must work on it later this morning.

He consulted his watch. "Better hurry it a little," he called to Antoine who was driving the landau. "We are twenty-one seconds behind time. I must be punctual today."

Antoine flicked his whip, promising to make the routine drive on the dot. So many minutes in the woods. So many to the Potomac Bridge. Across the river and back home on the very tick. John Quincy Adams did everything exactly to schedule. People in Washington often set their clocks by the comings and goings of John Quincy Adams.

And that very Sunday morning someone was setting a clock by Mr. John Quincy Adams. It wasn't a grandfather clock or a coo-coo clock, but a most extraordinary clock all fitted up with wires and gadgets and springs, and when it went off it said something a whole lot louder than coo-coo.

The youth who was setting it was extraordinary, too. Thin. Pasty-skinned. Black-browed, smooth black hair. In the close-up shown by the Past-catcher he had the face of a male Mona Lisa, the same inscrutable smile; and his dapper hands, setting the clock, were slim and white as a woman's. But his eyes were not Mona Lisa's; they were a light green, and somehow they made him seem the unreal creature of a dream.

As he came into focus on the television screen, he was crouched down behind a thicket of willows near the Potomac River bridge, watching the road with his beady eyes and fixing the strange-looking clock.

"*Bueno!*" he whispered, as Secretary of State Adam's carriage came in sight. "As usual! He is right on time."

Secretary of State Adams, crossing the bridge with his wife and sons in the carriage, didn't see that queer figure in the willows. But the Past-catcher showed him very clearly, and old John Quincy, riveted to the eye-piece, cried out in fear.

"What's he doing? What's that queer clock in his hand?"

The picture on the screen supplied the answer. As the carriage passed out of view, the lurking figure darted out of the willows, slipped stealthily down the river bank, and ducked under the wooden bridge.

"Five minutes," he murmured. "In exactly five minutes the carriage will be coming back. *Por Dios!* this is one Sunday he will not be home on time. As my name is El Bomba!"

Old John Quincy rocked back from the Past-catcher, horror-stricken. "El Bomba!" he gasped. "That's the notorious assassin who was deported from South America. He'd been hired by the Spanish king to murder Simon Bolivar the Liberator. I never knew he was in Washington!"

"Listen," murmured the Emigration Official.

OLD JOHN QUINCY listened. The youth was planting that funny-looking clock under the bridgehead. Then, quick as a ferret, he raced out from under the bridge and sped off Into the underbrush. The view on the screen was peaceful. Blue sky and puffy white clouds and the Potomac placid across the landscape. Only one sound disturbed the Maytime scene—a faint, thin *tick-tock* from under the wooden bridge.

"He's planted a bomb!" old John Quincy moaned. "An infernal machine!"

Tick-tock, tick-tock, he could hear it plainly, the ticking magnified by the early morning hush. Then a new sound came into the scene. The clop-clop-clop of horses' hoofs. The carriage was returning.

"Help!" old John Quincy cried out in spite of himself. "My wife and boys are with me in that carriage. We're going to be blown to pieces!"

He gripped the Past-catcher as if trying to shut off the picture, but there was no stopping the past. Closer and closer came the carriage to that ticking infernal-machine. Old John Quincy watched in a paralysis of fascination. What had happened? What could have happened?

Then all at once there was an explosion. It happened before the carriage returned into view, and it wasn't under the bridge but in the sky. *Slam-bang!* A crack of thunder! Then, *whoosh!* Like that. A rainstorm! A torrent! One of those springtime cloudbursts that rush from the blue without warning and ruin ladies' Sunday hats.

How it rained! Landscape, river and bridge were almost washed right out of the picture. The scene was inundated; the Potomac flooding its banks on the television screen.

Old John Quincy Adams yelled as the carriage came into view, and Secretary of State John Quincy Adams, in the carriage, was yelling too. He was shouting at the driver not to spare the horses. The open landau was like a chip in a deluge; poor Louisa had her shawl over her head, and the boys were huddled under the drenching, and Antoine was whipping the team.

"The bridge! The bridge!" Secretary of State Adams' yells were almost smothered by the downpour. "Hurry up, Antoine! The waters are rising—the span isn't safe."

"Not safe!" old John Quincy groaned, echoing his own cries from long ago. "My God! And I was in a hurry to get there. If I'd ever guessed!"

But he hadn't guessed. He'd spurred the driver to top speed. The bridge was shaky, low to the river, a temporary makeshift span to be replaced when the government had more time. Already the foaming flood was licking the understructure. Wavelets lapping up through the boards.

And the bridge was long. In the picture it seemed to stretch for miles.

In a cloud of water the carriage was coming across. The long span trembled under the hoofbeats and flying wheels. Just as the carriage reached the bridgehead the river poured across the span. Then, abruptly as it had started, the rainstorm was over. The flood stood level with the bridge. Sunshine broke through the sky. The carriage was safe on solid ground, vanishing in a shower of mud on its way back to town.

As the picture faded out in the Past-catcher there was only the sound of water lapping the bridge-boards and foliage dripping.

6

TWO SHADOWS UNSEEN

OLD JOHN QUINCY'S face at the eye-piece was ashen. He could barely manage to whisper. "It didn't go off! Flooded! The water rose under the bridge and the mechanism was flooded!"

The Emigration Official said nothing.

"And I was angry about that cloudburst," old John Quincy whispered. "I remember now. It ruined Louisa's new dress—soaked us all to the skin. I remember being furious at the time."

"Into each life some rain must fall," the Emigration Official reminded.

"But that bridge might've been blown to matchwood!" Old John Quincy's voice scaled up off-key. "My wife—my sons—that fiend El Bomba would have killed us all. He—great Lord!—he was an agent of the Holy Alliance!" The old man's features hardened fiercely at the realization. "If he was working for the king of Spain, he was hired by the Holy Alliance! A plot against our government! They were trying to stop me."

That job he was doing for James Monroe. To make the Western Hemisphere safe for democracy. Saved by a rainstorm! It made his blood run cold. And now, staring at the

Past-catcher, old John Quincy experienced a sensation of fear, a haunting uneasiness, a sudden anxiety about something that he couldn't put his finger on. Just what it was he couldn't explain, but it had to do with the Past-catcher—some episode in his past—some event not as yet revealed—something he couldn't remember.

Fascinated, he stared into that picture machine. That secretary of state episode wasn't quite over. Twice more El Bomba the Spaniard tried to assassinate him. The second time the bomb was planted under a watermelon in the Botanical Garden where he was making some of his famous horticultural experiments. The bomb was a dud.

The last attempt was on the night before he finished the last draft of his job for James Monroe. John Quincy Adams was an expert billiard player, and the night before that draft was completed, he dropped into the only Washington tavern that boasted a billiard table, arriving on customary schedule for an hour of relaxation.

There was quite a crowd and he was cueing brilliantly, but he wouldn't have cued as brilliantly had he known that El Bomba, the notorious Spanish assassin, was in the crowd. Old John Quincy groaned when the Past-catcher showed that vicious face among the spectators. Secretary of State John Quincy didn't even look up from the table. He was clicking off a run, maneuvering the little ivory balls with the dexterity of a professional. Applause burst, through the cigar smoke as he ran the score to ninety-nine.

Among the spectators was John C. Calhoun.

"Bet you five dollars, Mr. Adams," he called as the secretary of state paused to chalk his cue. "Five dollars you can't score a hundred."

"Done." Secretary of State Adams smiled confidently. He hadn't missed a shot all evening, and he was feeling in rare form. "I'll give you two to one, sir, and it's my last shot of the evening, after which I'll take your money and go home. The State Department's making a world-wide announcement tomorrow."

Instantly everyone was wagering; money changing hands. Secretary of State Adams took a long time chalking his cue, smiling around to make it impressive. Nobody noticed the youth with the Mona Lisa face. Everyone was staring at Calhoun and Mr. J.Q. Adams. So the Spaniard got away with it, quick an lightning with sleight-of-hand.

Leaning against the table, he substituted one white ball for another white ball so fast it was hardly visible in the Past-catcher. And there was dynamite in that substituted billiard ball. Enough high explosive to take off the roof. Kiss it, and that tavern would be blown to atoms.

And there was Secretary of State Adams aiming at it deliberately. Calculating the distance. Planning with all his skill to hit it with a carom shot. The Past-catcher showed everything. It showed what was in that ivory ball; it showed El Bomba sneaking quickly out of the crowd; it showed the onlookers watching breathless and John Quincy Adams letting fly with the cue.

Click—the cue ball raced across the green table. *Click*—it hit ball Number One. There was a second while the two caroming balls made geometric patterns on the cloth; then a cry from the secretary of state. Between the cue ball and that fatal third you couldn't have put a hair.

"Missed!"

Hanging up his cue, Secretary of State Adams stamped

out of the building; the proprietor turned off the lights; El Bomba sneaked back to salvage the unexploded high explosive; and next morning the powers of Europe were told to keep out of the Americas and stay out. That was the Monroe Doctrine.

SAVED BY A rainstorm—a dud—a faulty billiard shot! Well, the history books would never know that. But there are lots of angles history books don't know—the secrets that never came out—the happenings around the corners—the million things we don't know about which make up the million things we do.

Old John Quincy at the eye-piece of that Past-catcher, learned such things. That machine went on. Reel after reel it reviewed the past events of his life, and went on behind the scene, so to speak, of those past events. And what went on behind the scene was plenty.

Take that year of 1824. He was being followed. He never knew at the time he was being followed because those spies who trailed him were careful to keep it a secret. How can anyone know that they're being followed in secret? If the spy is caught it isn't a secret any more.

But lot of spies have never been caught. Think of all the people in history who must have been trailed by spies at one time or another but never knew it because those secret agents were never apprehended. Historians can't let such cats out of the bag; they don't know about them. But that Past-catcher showed a pair of spies trailing John Quincy Adams in 1824, and those two secret agents were so secretive they almost evaded the Past-catcher.

Their names were Commodore Breed and Mrs. Jammer. The Commodore was a gross, swaggering, red-faced Navy deserter, covered with tattooing and flogging scars. He had a drawl as soft as Georgia and the soul of a spider. Mrs. Jammer was a big blond German woman, built like a Percheron horse, and with fewer morals.

They lived in a secluded shack on the outskirts of Washington, and they had orders from certain parties not to let John Quincy Adams out of their sight. Mrs. Jammer would trail the quarry; then the Commodore would take up the job where the woman left off. Day and night they were on his heels, and, glaring into the Past-catcher, old John Quincy watched these shenanigans dumbfounded. Probably it was his outraged amazement that kept him from noticing the eyes of these two spies—the similar green eyes.

"Sweet Land of Liberty!" he exploded. "Those two hounding me in Washington like that! By thunder, if I'd ever known!"

Why, a dozen times he passed Mrs. Jammer on the street without so much as giving her a glance. Once, skidding on a muddy corner, his carriage almost ran over the Commodore on Pennsylvania Avenue.

"Great Godfrey! If I'd ever suspected that villain was after me—!"

But he hadn't suspected. No one in Washington suspected. The town, in 1824, was jammed with all manner of strange people. Taverns and boarding houses were filled to overflowing. Foreign diplomats rubbed elbows with uncouth frontiersmen. Soldiers, Indians, politicians, gamblers thronged the mud streets. Roustabouts, slave-traders, office seekers and Virginia gentlemen swarmed in the capital. There was no organized police force; no lights at night; no indoor plumbing. The town was wildly excited. No one thought of anything except the presidential election.

No one was more excited about it than John Quincy Adams. James Monroe was retiring to be the last of the so-called Virginia Dynasty, and John Quincy Adams was picked to run as Monroe's successor. It was a violent campaign, for Mr. Adams' opponents were Andrew Jackson and Henry Clay.

As Secretary of State, John Quincy Adams had defended Jackson's reckless invasion of Spanish Florida; now Jackson, tricked by politicians into believing the opposite, attacked John Quincy with stinging denouncements. Clay was no mean opponent, either. John Quincy Adams had his first real taste of bitter politics in the mud-slinging contest that followed. He was accused of blundering in Europe. Bungling the Treaty of Ghent. Southern papers called him a snob. Newspapers in Philadelphia said he was a public disgrace who never wore a cravat and went to church in his bare feet.

The race was close; the candidates coming down the home stretch neck and neck. Jackson got the most electoral votes; failed to gain the necessary majority. The vote went to the House, and John Quincy Adams was elected President. The nation, the capital and Andrew Jackson went wild. Months of uproar and excitement followed; in the hurlyburly of politics and argument, no one noticed the pair from that shack on the edge of town.

PRESIDENT OF THE United States, John Quincy Adams had too many open enemies to imagine a couple more. His inaugural speech wasn't out of his mouth before the politicians attacked him. He advocated a vast scheme of public and social improvements; said there ought to be colleges built as well as roads and canals; suggested the government ought to back free education, put up astronomical observatories, explore the West and do something about the darkening slave question.

"Impractical!" howled the politicians. "Dreamer!" shouted the editors. Jeers echoed from all over the country, especially the South; whatever he said or did thereafter, it seemed to President Adams as if the ten million people of America were after him.

His four years in the White House were as tough as any President's in history. His own party, his home state, members of his Cabinet turned against him. He was accused of fraud. Of conniving with Henry Clay. Of stirring up the slaves to near rebellion. Of bribing the House to elect him. Of going on benders. Of robbing the U.S. Treasury.

Stung to desperation, falsely maligned, he struck back at his traducers with mounting anger. He wrote of his Vice-President Calhoun as "stimulated to frenzy by success, flattery and premature advancement." He described Randolph of Virginia, one of his slanderers in the Senate, as a man of "besotted violence" who stood up in the House, drunk, "to revile the absent and the present, the living and the dead." He deplored the narrow-mindedness of New England and the hypocrisy of the slave-holding South.

The death of his aged father up in Massachusetts saddened him. He became depressed, tight-lipped, bitter-eyed. Deserted by friends, harried by unscrupulous foes, President John Quincy Adams was a lonely man.

But he wasn't as lonely as he thought he was. Two there were who remained always with him. He didn't know they were there, but there they were. Behind doors. Under windows. Around the corner. Back of the tree. They followed him to Cabinet meetings and official dinners, to political powwows and parades. They peeked over the wall of his Botanical garden and haunted his private life in the White House. Two unseen shadows.

It made old John Quincy shiver to know, see himself hounded like that. He swore, looking up from the Past-catcher.

"The whole town was full of rats! Those two were lost in the shuffle! Why, they walked right into a White House reception—no different from the rest of the crowd."

Yes, Mrs. Jammer and the Commodore were there at a White House reception; the Past-catcher showed them there. That was the reception where General Winfield Scott had his pocket picked of eight hundred dollars. John Quincy Adams had always wondered who had stolen the general's wallet.

"The Commodore!" old John Quincy, at the eye-piece, raged. "If Winfield Scott had only caught him! Ah, he would have sabered the cur!"

Then the Past-catcher showed another close-up of those spies. The kitchen of that shanty in the suburbs. Shutters closed and lights down. Mrs. Jammer and the Commodore, heads together over the table, plotting. Now they had new orders—the Past-catcher didn't show where those orders came from, but in that dim-lit kitchen they were plain enough—orders to kill President John Quincy Adams!

"It's dangerous," the Commodore kept muttering. "It's dangerous as hell."

"*Ja wohl!*" Mrs. Jammer conceded. "So I haff a plan—"

7

DIAMONDS IN HIS TEETH

HISTORY BOOKS RECORDED the burning of the Treasury Building. How John Quincy Adams organized a bucket brigade and himself took charge of fighting the fire. The President's courage was applauded, and spontaneous combustion was blamed. It took the Past-catcher, however, to tell the whole story. To show that the spontaneous combustion which started that blaze was in the brain of Mrs. Jammer.

That was her idea. Set fire to the Treasury and then, while all Washington rushed to the conflagration, to catch the President alone in the White House—and kill him. She never figured he'd rush out there in a fireman's hat with the Protectives, any more than she could imagine the Prussian kaiser swinging a bucket. That was when she got a lesson in American Democracy.

Historians, too, recorded the famous swimming exploits of President J. Q. Adams; but those historians (for historians don't know everything) should have looked into that Past-catcher. True, the President loved to swim and his skill was the talk of the town. But take that famous incident when his clothes were stolen. The Past-catcher's story was different from the record in the history books.

He liked to get up at 4:15 in the summer and ride from the White House down to the Potomac for a sunrise dip. Bathtubs were an unknown luxury in the Washington of those days—there wasn't a bathtub in the White House until Millard Fillmore installed one twenty-five years later—and John Quincy Adams preferred the river to a water pitcher and basin. Ordinarily his servant accompanied him swimming, but that morning Antoine stayed in bed.

Now the scene as shown in the Past-catcher was colored for old John Quincy with fond memories. A willow grove shrouded in morning mist. Sunrise, and the Potomac pink and blue. The President tethering his horse, stripping down at water's edge, soaring off the bank on a running dive. He made a perfect jackknife, hit the river in form and struck out for midstream like an athlete, churning the cool current with powerful strokes.

At this point the Past-catcher differed from the historians. Neither they nor the swimming President saw the sinister face of the Commodore, as shown on the television screen, peering from the riverbank underbrush.

Murder almost caught the President that time. Not daring to tackle the swimmer alone, the Commodore stole John Quincy Adams' clothes and raced off to fetch Mrs. Jammer, knowing the President of the United States couldn't ride back through Washington like Lady Godiva and would have to stay there in the water.

"I've got him." He burst in on Mrs. Jammer. "Stitchless! Down there in the river! His servant isn't with him, an' he can't get out. We're going in swimming with him. All we have to do is hold him under water—it'll look like he had a cramp an' was drowned. Come on!"

Goose pimples swelled on old John Quincy's skin as he saw that pair rushing cross-town through the early morning mists—to drown him. The Commodore was built like a gorilla, and Mrs. Jammer was a powerful woman.

"I remember now!" he cried, even before the final sequence. "I was stuck there in the water wondering how in Sam Hill I'd get home. I couldn't ride to the White House with nothing on—not the President! But a kid came down the river's bank. Just a freckled, barefoot boy with a fishpole—"

Yes, a boy—a ten-year-old kid, who raced to a nearby farmhouse to get the President of the United States a pair of pants. Saved by a nipper and a pair of pants!

"And I always thought a tramp stole my clothes," old John Quincy groaned. "If that lad hadn't chanced to come a-fishing I'd have been drowned like a dog!"

"Yes," said the grave voice at old John Quincy's shoulder. "Or if that farmer had not had an extra pair of pants."

NOW HE HAD two more close calls there in the Potomac—famous incidents for the schoolbooks, but chronicled a little differently by that Past-catcher. There was that time he was swept around a riverbend by the current, and two toughs came after him in a rowboat in the fog, and a Navy barge scared the toughs away. Well, Mrs. Jammer and the Commodore were the toughs in that rowboat.

And that narrow escape when he was paddling across the river with Antoine and their canoe sank suddenly under them without warning, nearly drowning them both in the channel far from shore. Old John Quincy cried aloud when the Past-catcher revealed that it was the Commodore who, the night before, had cut the seams of that canoe.

"And I thought those were accidents!" old John Quincy gasped. "Accidents!"

Those episodes as shown in that Past-catcher put a coat of ice around his soul. That succession of close calls froze him to the marrow. It was terrible to know how many assassins had been after him. Worse, to think he'd never known it at the time. And once more he was haunted by that other fear—something he couldn't identify—something that had happened and he couldn't remember. What was it? Was it coming up in the Past-catcher?

The Emigration Official touched his shoulder. "Are you beginning to understand, Mr. Adams? Are you beginning to see?"

Old John Quincy's eyes glared, bloodshot. "I see, all right. I was a marked man while I was in Europe, and slated for murder while I was Secretary of State. And they wanted to kill me while I was President. Jumping Jehoshaphat!"

He put a dilated eyeball to the eye-piece. The scene was Mrs. Jammer's kitchen. The Commodore was advising her to lay low for a while—give the President a chance to get over his fright—catch him off guard.

"But I was never frightened!" old John Quincy panted. "In all that time I was never *on* guard!"

Twice more the German woman and the Commodore tried to kill him. The Commodore had a plan to shanghai him on an African slaver, but the crew got drunk on the appointed night and shanghaied a Boston carpet-bag salesman by mistake. Then, during his second Presidential campaign, he was sniped at while making a speech.

Fourth of July. He was standing on an outdoors platform. Firecrackers were banging. No one heard Mrs. Jammer's pistol. A chance reach for a glass of water saved him. He never heard the bullet go by.

WHAT A CAMPAIGN that was! One of the foulest exhibitions of below-the-belt politics in American history. Both candidates were smeared. Soured by previous defeat, Andrew Jackson hated John Quincy Adams with all the venom of an Indian fighter for a man he considered a New England bluenose. Adams thought of Jackson as a swaggery, tobacco-chewing wildman, an unlettered demagogue and whoopla public hero.

Jackson's marriage was dragged in the mud; his wife's name publicly sullied; he was called a murderer. John Quincy Adams was called a drunkard, a grafter and a libertine. The story was passed around that while he was ambassador to Russia he had ruined a beautiful young girl and sold her to a Slavic nobleman.

Neither candidate was responsible for the dirt that was flung, but each blamed the other. The nation shook with passion and prejudice. Old John Quincy was glad when the Past-catcher finished with that unsavory chapter in American history. He saw Andy Jackson elected President; saw himself returning to Massachusetts in galling defeat.

He was glad when the scene went on to 1831 and he saw himself going back to Washington to take a seat in Congress. He was vindicating his honor. No other ex-President had returned to Washington after such a beating. His own father, defeated for a second term, had never set foot in the capital again. John Quincy Adams wanted to keep on serving his country.

He served it, too. Those scenes in Congress went so fast they blurred on old John Quincy's vision. Years fled swiftly through the Past-catcher. Events, episodes, incidents passed across the screen as a series of flashes. He saw himself once more in the Capitol, a solitary figure fighting for his principles. He fought for international security, for the establishment of the Smithsonian Institute, for a sounder democracy. But mostly he fought against slavery.

And that was the hardest fight of all. Harder than the work he'd done in Russia. Harder than carrying papers to Jay. Harder than the Treaty of Ghent. Than putting over the Monroe Doctrine. Than all the things he'd done as President.

For he hated slavery, but he loved the Union, and while fighting one he tried to hold together the other, and it was like trying to juggle fire and dynamite. The South—arrogant, rich, loafing along on the bondage of a million black men—hated him as one hates the rebuke of conscience. The North—his own New England—hated him as big business hates something that may interfere with money. Pacifists hated him as a trouble maker. Abolitionists hated him for compromise. The meanest issue in all American history was the slavery question, and John Quincy Adams was juggling it.

They tried to stop him. They shouted him down in Congress; shelved his petitions; at last tried to silence him by passing a law that slavery couldn't be mentioned in the House. That was the famous Gag Rule, but it didn't gag John Quincy Adams. He went right on talking, for the Constitution assured all Americans free speech. All through the 1830s he went right on talking, standing up alone to shake the House with his thunder-toned appeals for freedom. Single-handed, he carried on the fight. It was his proudest achievement—breaking the Gag Rule in that fight against slavery.

Finally they tried to gag him in another way; but John Quincy Adams never knew about it at the time. He didn't know until he saw it in the Past-catcher.

ONCE MORE MRS. Jammer and the Commodore were on the scene, and old John Quincy learned, then, who had hired that precious pair. They were agents for a vast ring of slave traders, a syndicate of slavers engaged in the outlawed African traffic. Importation of slaves had been made illegal, but the South was still hungry for black cargo, and that shack on the edge of Washington was a smuggler's outpost. A new face appeared in Mrs. Jammer's kitchen.

That was an evil countenance! It was icy. Blue-tinged. A nose like the beak of a bird of prey. Thin, curled moustachios, and diamonds glittering in the sharp, white teeth. And green eyes that were not human. When that portrait came into focus on the Past-catcher screen, old John Quincy cried out as if he were seeing the Devil himself.

Gaylord Rudolph the man's name was, and he was head of the secret slave syndicate, and not until that moment had old John Quincy heard of such a man. But Gaylord Rudolph had heard of John Quincy Adams. There in Mrs. Jammer's kitchen, picking his diamond-studded teeth with a gold toothpick, he was laying plans for the absolute destruction of John Quincy Adams.

"He must die!" the voice from the Past-catcher was like the whispering of a crow. "This time we must not fail. He is ruining the slave traffic, costing us millions. You will continue your bungling attempts to kill him; meantime I am hiring from an international spy-ring the most famous assassins of Europe. They will join us here in Washington, and we will band together in an assassination from which no man could possibly escape!"

So the Commodore and Mrs. Jammer were after him again, and that diamond-toothed devil with them—trailing him, shadowing his shadow, following his every move. In and out of doors they hounded him, waiting in ambush, hiding around corners, weaving through the warp and woof that made the pattern of his unsuspecting days. All through the latter 1830s they followed him, unbeknownst to Congressman Adams, unbeknownst to anyone but themselves.

Operating from their secret hide-out, they kept their secret well. Nor did they wait for the international assassins' league to gather. Five more times they struck at John Quincy Adams with death-plots invented in their kitchen. And each time something intervened—something unplanned, unexpected, uncalled for—like a snow slide, or a pebble, or missing a billiard shot, or reaching for a drink of water. Once it was when Congressman Adams stooped to pick a four-leaf clover, and again, when he accidentally missed a wreck-bound train.

"Do you see now," the voice at old John Quincy's shoulder murmured. "Now do you understand?"

Old John Quincy turned on the Emigration Official. "My life was hanging by a thread," he whispered. "Ever since I was fourteen years old, there in Petrograd, my life was hanging by a thread!"

It was terrible to see how close and unknown Death had

been. And it couldn't go on. Impossible for the thing to go on. Sooner or later those death-dealers must get him. Law of averages. Guns couldn't always miss; rainstorms couldn't always come along. What threads for his life to hang on!—a billiard play, a fireman's hat! Sooner or later Luck would run out of wine-bibbing servants and extra pairs of pants.

"To think my life depended on such things!" he groaned out.

The Emigration Official smiled gently. "Man's life is a journey through a myriad of unseen perils. The germ and the chance lightning bolt, the unknown heart-weakness and the shift of wind all lie in wait for the traveler, even as the ambushed animal or masked highwayman. Who knows when he is saved by a pebble or a flood? Past good and ill fortune alike the traveler walks blindfold."

"I was walking blindfold, all right!" old John Quincy cried. "Every minute there in Washington I was in jeopardy. And now—a whole gang of international assassins—they were bound to get me. How could they miss?"

He broke off with a gasp. All at once he realized what it was that had worried him, the source of that strange and growing inner fear. Something *had* happened to him there in Washington. Something—he couldn't find it in his memory—something he couldn't explain.

"Those fiends!" he whispered. "What happened? What?"

"Look into the Past-catcher," the Emigration Official said.

8

PASSPORT IN ORDER

HE HAD GROWN old so imperceptibly that when he saw himself there, standing up to speak in Congress, his bald head, white pinfeathers and feebleness came to him as a shock. The House of Representatives, the flag-hung gallery, the curved rows of Congressmen blurred on his failing vision.

He didn't like the way the great gathering went silent as he rose. Veneration for his white hairs? Bah! Maybe he was eighty-one, but he could still play a good game of billiards, write with a steady enough hand and think clearly enough to give these stupid politicians and Southern hypocrites a lambasting.

He didn't want heir respect; he knew them. Only a few weeks ago he had written to his son, who was entering politics, not to fear public life with its "opposition and defeats and slanders and treachery, and above all the fickleness of popular favor Your father and grandfather," he wrote, "have fought their way through the world against a host of adversaries, open and close, disguised and masked, with many lukewarm and more than one or two perfidious friends." That was in a letter to his son, and now he was standing up in Congress once more to speak his mind.

And how he was going to speak it! No one knew what he was going to say; they thought him just an old man. He'd been planning this speech for a long time, its content known only to himself. Now he was going to let loose with both guns, going to shoot the works, expose the whole matter of slavery. Slavery was ruining the country; the nation must be made to see the horrible lie of human bondage in a democracy. But worse, slavery was threatening the Union. Sooner or later it meant war. Half slave, half free, America could not stand. He must cry out the danger, warn the people while there was yet time.

Perfidious friends! Adversaries disguised and masked! Old John Quincy Adams, paralyzed at the Past-catcher, watching himself stand up in the House of Representatives, gave a wail of terror. "If I'd ever known!"

For the Past-catcher showed him something that a dim-eyed old Congressman hadn't been able to see. Two figures in the visitor's gallery: Goranoff—Goranoff, the Russian anarchist—and Mrs. Jammer. Two strollers in the outer lobby—Percy, the one-eyed stagecoach guard from London, and the hunchbacked Little François, the Terror of France. A lounger standing on the outside steps of the Capitol—the red-faced Commodore, and two figures hidden around the corner of the building—Gaylord Rudolph and El Bomba.

"Those killers!" Old John Quincy's throat was numb with fright. "Europe's most famous assassins! All there together!"

Seeing them close-up on that television screen was like looking into the private records of Hell. Satan, himself, couldn't have recruited as lurid a brood. Their reappearance in the Past-catcher shook old John Quincy to the core. They too had come a long way in their professions; they too were getting old. Goranoff the Russian, now shriveled, wearing glasses, his beard like dirty snow. Percy with the eye-patch, leering like an aged rat. Little François hunched over farther than ever. El Bomba with his Mona Lisa face gone stale. Incredible coincidence that those were the recruits Gaylord Rudolph had combed from Europe?

"Get ready!" In the gallery Mrs. Jammer had her lips to Goranoff's ear. "When he starts to speak we go out and give the signal in the lobby. Then the Frenchman and Percy signal to those outdoors."

The Russian nodded. "All is prepared. Our colleagues signal to the Commodore, who in turn signals to those around the corner to light the fuse. *Da, da!* One ton of dynamite—a year of tunneling to get it planted—it will blow this whole House of Representatives to fragments. He escaped me once, years ago. But no snow slide will save him this time!"

"*Sehr gut!* Nor a drink of water!"

OLD JOHN QUINCY, seeing that scene, was white-faced. A ton of dynamite under the floor of the House!—enough to blow the whole Capitol sky high. No pebble or fireman's hat or extra pair of pants could put a stop to that. Nothing was going to stop it. Gaylord Rudolph, around the corner of the building with El Bomba, was going to stop at nothing.

"At last," his diamond-studded teeth made a flash in the bushes as he whispered, "at last we have him. You did a fine job planting the dynamite. Seven of us and a ton of dynamite! His anti-slavery talk is ended. Nothing under heaven can save him now!"

The scene switched to a close-up of Congress; old John Quincy saw himself getting slowly to his feet. Terror knotted his heart as he watched, for the lives of his fellow Congressmen were at stake. The Union was at stake.

"They mustn't!" old John Quincy shrilled. "My speech— the nation must be warned! If slavery continues it will mean Civil War!" He broke off, choking.

Goranoff and Mrs. Jammer were getting up to go. In the lobby, the hunchback and Percy awaited the signal. On the Capitol steps the Commodore stood lookout. Around the corner, concealed in shrubbery, El Bomba and Gaylord Rudolph had matches ready. Standing up in the hushed auditorium, Congressman John Quincy Adams opened his lips to address the Speaker of the House.

"Lookout!" old John Quincy, at the eye-piece, cried. "Speak! Speak! Oh, my God!"

What happened there in the scene was not clear to old John Quincy even as he viewed it in the Past-catcher. He saw himself start to speak, then clutch out feebly, topple backward. He was falling. The House of Representatives spun around him. Congressmen's faces blurred in pin-wheel. Hands came jumping at him.

There were frightened shouts. "Stop! Stop!"… "Wait, Mr. Speaker!"… "Help him, somebody!"… "Mr. Adams! Mr. Adams!"

Everything went black.

Old John Quincy looked up from the Past-catcher, panic stricken. "The picture is gone!" he cried to the Emigration Official. "Great heaven! Did they blow up the House?"

"No," was the smiling answer. "They never set off the dynamite. It will be found under the building years later by workmen who will think it must have been planted there during Lincoln's Administration."

"But my speech?" old John Quincy Adams sobbed. "My speech to save the nation?"

"No speech could have saved the nation," was the quiet answer. "The Union will stand, but the stain of slavery can be wiped out only in blood."

"But what happened?" old John Quincy whispered. "Those assassins!"

The Emigration Official tuned up a dial. "Look now, Mr. Adams."

CLOSE-UP OF THAT shack on the edge of town. Blinds drawn, and tumult in the smoky, dim-lit kitchen. Gaylord Rudolph, pacing in rage among his hirelings. Goranoff the Russian drinking vodka in a corner. Percy slumped, cursing, at the table. Mrs. Jammer at the stove, swearing tremendous German oaths. El Bomba biting his thumbs in fury; Little François weeping like a hyena in a tantrum; the Commodore, red-eyed, guarding the door.

"So we don't get paid?" the Commodore's bloodshot glare brought the owner of the slave syndicate to a standstill. "After all our work—risking our necks time and again—we don't get a cent!"

Under the shiny tophat, the slaver's green eyes gleamed. "Not a cent!" His sneer swept the kitchen. "Not a penny or a centime! Your contracts called for an assassination. Was there any assassination?"

"No killing him now!" Goranoff spat. *"Da!* Cheated again!"

"*Tu Madre!*" El Bomba cursed. "Look how I got nothing for my efforts. Two bombs and a billiard ball! Now a ton of dynamite gone to waste!"

"Fools!" Little François was hysterical. "There in Ghent I took a thousand chances. But to come all the way to America—*Sacré Dieu!*"

"Me too!" Percy banged the table. "I risk a 'angin' in Old Bailey, an' now bein' blinked as a spy. What do I get?"

Mrs. Jammer swung around from the stove. "Me, I am just a poor woman. Not only do I cook and work my fingers to the bone for this gang, I also risk my neck to kill that old fool. Years I haff tried. What do I get? Nothing!"

"It ayn't fair!"

"To think that old baboon should cheat us after all!"

"He made his get-away."

That kitchen resembled a cage of jungle animals as Gaylord Rudolph announced, "Well, you can all go back to your ratholes. The show is over." He might have been a ringmaster, starting for the door with a tap for the tophat and a flirt of the moustaches; even as the Commodore, red-faced, growling, squaring up to bar the threshold, might have been an unruly lion.

"Just a minute, Rudolph! Maybe the show isn't over."

The slaver stopped. "What the devil do you mean."

"That old fool Adams—I seen him writin' in it many times—he kept a diary!"

"A what?"

"Mrs. Jammer and these others can tell you. He kept a diary!"

"Well, I'm damned!"

"Yeah." The Commodore nodded. "You sure are, if there's anything in it about you."

"I, too," Mrs. Jammer gave a squawk. "I never thought—"

Little François cried, "I remember seeing him writing!"

"Why, he had it with him in England!" Percy exclaimed.

Goranoff and El Bomba, popeyed, were out of their chairs.

"*Por Dios!* A day-to-day record!"

"His memoirs! If he had them in Russia—"

Gaylord Rudolph's eyes glowed in fear. "We must get these records! Now! At once!"

"Leave it to me." The Commodore grabbed the doorknob. "He won't be home at his lodgings, yet. Before anyone gets there, I'll get 'em."

"I will get them," Mrs. Jammer jumped forward. "Let me!"

"*Jamais!*" Little François' voice was shrill. "I must and shall have this diary."

Percy the Cockney cried, "It belongs as much to me!"

"I am more concerned!" El Bomba squalled. "I was here longer."

Goranoff thrust himself forward. "But I was first. Years ago in Russia—"

"But I'm involved with the American government," Gaylord Rudolph lashed out, "and I've more to lose than any of you. Out of my way! It's mine!" Leaping, he struck the Commodore to one side. "If you think you're going to blackmail me—"

The picture that followed almost tore the television screen. In his wildest nightmare, old John Quincy had never dreamed of such a fight. One rush, and that kitchen was a bloody, whirligig shambles. Little François knifed the Commodore from behind. El Bomba drove a dagger into Little François' back. Quick with a gun, Percy shot the Spaniard through the head.

Goranoff flung a kitchen fork into Percy's good eye, and in turn, Mrs. Jammer brought a meat cleaver down on Goranoff's head. Dying on the floor, the Commodore reached around behind himself to pull the knife from his shoulderblades and hurl it at Mrs. Jammer. When the smoke and blood finally drained away, there was only Gaylord Rudolph the slave master, upright, unharmed and grinning, like Mephistopholes posing among the fumes.

"And now," he whispered, "to get John Quincy Adams' diary!"

He didn't get it. Reaching for the doorknob, he slipped on the blood-soaked floor and fell throat-down on the upturned meat cleaver.

OLD JOHN QUINCY leaned back from the Past-catcher, exhausted. "Murder," he whispered. "All that murder—over my diary!"

The Emigration Official nodded. "Perhaps you don't realize you wrote the most famous diary of any great man in American history."

"What did they want it for? Why?"

"They were afraid that some day it might be published. International politics—public life—a diary can be pretty revealing. And they didn't know how much you knew, Mr. Adams."

"But there was nothing about them in it," old John Quincy said. "In all those years they were after me I never knew they were there." Old John Quincy, who'd never had a guilty conscience in his life, didn't understand people with guilty consciences. There were a lot of things old John Quincy Adams didn't understand.

He was silent a moment, pondering over something that had been troubling him. "Those spies," he said at last. "Somehow they did not look as real as the other people on the screen. And there was something alike about them— every one of them had those strange green eyes."

The Emigration Official nodded and spoke gravely. "What you saw in the Past-catcher did actually happen; but Goronoff, Little François and the rest were more than spies. They were symbols, you see; they were the agents of an evil fate that never befell you. That's why they did not seem quite human, and why a feature repeated in all of them. In a sense they were one and the same."

Old John Quincy was digesting that when another, more significant thought struck him. He turned to stare at the Emigration Official. "What happened to me there when I stood up in Congress?" he asked in a whisper. "They said I made a get-away. How? There in the Capitol—what happened to me?"

But the Emigration Official only smiled. And then, looking around the Frontier Station, at the misty room, at the Past-catcher, at that pleasant but inscrutable smile, John Quincy Adams caught sight of a calendar on the wall—February 21, 1848. And he understood.

"Well! "he exclaimed.

The fog was clearing outside; he could see blue sky and sunshine and a black-striped Frontier gate, and a country beyond that he couldn't describe because the colors were unlike any he'd seen before.

"Now do you understand?" the Official asked.

"I know why I'm here," John Quincy Adams said.

"And do you still think you were a self-made man—captain of your fate—that you forged your own destiny?"

Well, John Quincy Adams wasn't the man to back down on any point like that. Maybe his legal entry to this country depended on it, but he stuck to his guns. He allowed that his life had hung by a lot of unknown threads. Maybe he had been saved by a snow-slide and a pebble, an underhand theft of wine, unseasonable rainstorm.

Agreed that life was a matter of chance turnings and twistings, a contrivance of being at the right place at the right time. You might never suspect when a fireman's job saved you from falling downstairs and breaking your neck at home. Or that when you missed a train you missed a murderer hidden on that train. Or when a ton of dynamite was under the floor.

But John Quincy Adams was logical. If his own life had always been in the balance, wasn't it so with every man's? Weren't there millions of unknown factors in every man's life—things going on around him that he never dreamed of—circumstances behind the scenes, so to speak, of which he had no knowledge and no control. All lives were maneuvered by secret springs; the hidden wires of destiny ran under every house on earth. If it was so with him, it was so with every man, John Quincy Adams argued. So in the last analysis everybody got an even break. And starting from there, that even break, every man was on his own.

"Then at the point where every man goes on his own, some men fall down and some succeed," argued John Quincy Adams. "It's still up to the man, himself. I don't mean to be arrogant, but I'm proud of what I accomplished in my life, proud of what I did for America. If I hadn't been ambitious and industrious I wouldn't have been in Russia to be saved by a snow-slide; I wouldn't have been there at Ghent; I wouldn't have been risking my life even unknowingly as President of the United States—"

He could talk, John Quincy Adams. Not for nothing had they called him Old Man Eloquent. No man in American History ever spoke more brilliantly, and he wouldn't give up an argument to save his soul.

He didn't have to.

After a while, from the corner of his eye, he saw the Frontier gate was going up.

"But I'm not entering under false pretenses," he concluded, looking the Emigration Official in the eye. "I still believe I'm a self-made man, by God!"

The Emigration Official smiled. These Americans might be asked where America came from in the first place. Even so, aspiration was preferable to hypocritical humility.

"Yes, you are," he agreed gently. "By God."

SHAKE HANDS WITH OLD HICKORY

Now they give dinners in his honor at twenty-five dollars a plate. But at his biggest party the White House was overrun with hobnail boots, and the entrée was a huge cheese. Here's the incredible history, and the wholly credible legend, of our brawlingest President, who kept himself going on a bottle of water—Andy Jackson!

1

ACROSS THE GREAT SMOKIES

THIS IS AN American legend; it is not a fairy tale. The difference between a legend and a fairy tale is this: A fairy tale is pure moon-stuff—like a promise from Hitler, or the story of Puss in Boots—whereas a legend is based on historical fact and might have a lot of truth in it.

The hero of this legend is one of the goldarndest, high-spiritedest, quickest-triggered characters ever nephew to Uncle Sam, and just about the fightin'est man in the world. Nothing ever stood in his way he didn't want there. Nothing!

Only he wasn't any phoney superman. He was human and he was real. He liked to smoke a pipe and sink a glass of brandy; he had his faults like any American; and when he bet on the wrong horse, or when a bullet hit him, it hurt. That makes the enemies he beat and the things he accomplished all the more amazing.

There was just one thing he couldn't beat, and *that's* legendary. And this legend tells what it was, and how he beat it in the end, anyway. It concerns a bottle of water—the strangest, most valuable water in all creation—and even though it's legendary, it has its source in historical fact. Explorers crossed unknown oceans to find that water; discoverers, searching it, lost their lives in unmapped jungles; men cut each other's throats just hoping for a drink of it.

So even the legend may be true; it's the historical *facts* in this particular legend that seem a whole lot more incredible than the fiction.

For example, historically this legend begins in a place called the Garden of the Waxhaws, which wasn't a garden at all, but a howling wilderness full of wild animals, Indians and other hardships in the southwest corner of North Carolina, or, maybe, the northwest corner of South Carolina—the Carolinans bicker about it to this day.

Anyway, it was howling wilderness back in 1767. The inhabitants lived in log cabins that weren't anywhere near as fancy as the ones you see pictured in maple sugar advertisements. The cabin floors were muddy; the fireplaces were smoky; winter wind whistled rigadoons through the cracks. No radios or electric lights or davenports or doorbells or all those things we think we can't exist without today.

Well-dressed women went barefoot in summer; and every well-dressed man carried a gun. You never could tell. On your way to church you might meet up with a bear, and on your way home you might bump into an Indian and lose all your hair. The Garden of the Waxhaws was a crude, tough spot, but our fellow countrymen who lived in America back then could take it. At least when they died they didn't die of boredom or nervous trouble or heart failure from watching the stock market. They were just as tough as their garden was; and that crude spot was born a great American gentleman.

He didn't look great when he was born. He didn't look

*Andy looked at the bottle. "Try it," said
the stranger. "Make you feel fine"*

like a gentleman. His parents were poor Scotch-Irish
immigrants—which means they were poor only in worldly
possessions when they came from the North of Ireland
to America. Yes, his father was an Orangeman; and it's
another historical fact that these Orangemen from the
North of Ireland played a big, proud share in the founding of our country. Democracy was the faith that brought
them to America, and the U.S.A. has had six presidents of
Scotch-Irish descent.

But in 1767 the colonies belonged to England, and
nobody knew anything about Presidents. These Scotch-
Irish settlers were so glad to be clear of Europe with its
tyrants, race-prejudice and religious persecution that
they called a wilderness a garden. Indians and varmints
were a nuisance, but over here they could think what they
wanted, speak what they wanted, go to whatever church
they wanted, or not go to church at all if they were so

a-mind. They thanked God every day for Freedom, these free-thinking, hard-working Scotch-Irish Americans.

So that's the kind of man our hero's father was, only he died before our hero was born. The lad never knew his father. His mother had to work her fingers raw to keep things going in the little cabin—wasn't anyone around to hand him nickles or buy him lollipops, or later pay his expenses through college.

But a Scotch-Irishman never dies without leaving his son something. This father left his son a couple of things. A flaming head of orange hair. Bright blue-green eyes. And a name that was going to make history—Andrew Jackson.

NOW LET'S NOT mix him up with Stonewall Jackson— Stonewall Jackson made plenty of history, too, but he made it during the Civil War. Andy Jackson was a boy during the Revolutionary War; he enlisted in the fight for American Independence when he was just under fourteen years old.

It wasn't his first fight, either. With that head of orange hair and those snapping blue-green eyes he'd been fighting from the word go. His mother was poor, and that was an obstacle. The tough neighborhood kids were obstacles. The wilderness, itself, was an obstacle; he was hardly able to toddle when someone put an axe in his hand and he had to go out and chop down trees.

Seemed as if all around him there were obstacles, barriers and handicaps to stop him from going places and keep him from being somebody. As a small boy he'd had some defect that made his mouth leaky, and the blunt frontiersmen called him a "slobberer." Time he got over that, he'd developed a terrific temper. Wow! Andy Jackson had about the wildest zam-blang temper in American history. It blinded him, deafened him, made him like to strangle.

Like the time some of the frontier boys loaded a musket, double charge, and handed it to Andy to fire, hoping to see the recoil knock him flat. It knocked him flat, all right, but the gun's explosion was nothing to little Andy's. Hopping up from the dust, he aimed the musket at his playfellows. "By Glory!" he cried, "if anyone laughs, I'll *kill* him!"

Nobody laughed. There was a weird light like candle-shine in Andy's eyes, and from then on no one ever laughed when he faced them with a gun. But the incident scared Andy's mother, and it scared Andy. A temper like that was a fierce thing to control, and it was going to be another obstacle.

Well, plenty of fellows with all these handicaps to over-come would have just sat down and said, "I give up!"—but not Andy. He was Scotch-Irish-American, remember, and he hated things that got in his way. Seeing his mother scrubbing on her hands and knees infuriated him, and he vowed to lick Old Man Poverty with one hand tied behind him. He licked the tough neighborhood kids the same way. He determined he'd never let the wilderness trees hem him in; and he set right out to bridle his wild temper like a man sets out to bridle a wild horse.

Then he ran into the British.

Now the British back in colonial times weren't as democratic as the British today. King George III was part German and all reactionary. But everyone knows the reasons for the Revolutionary War. Young Andy knew them, too. Why, ever since he was born he'd been fighting to be independent; so a War for Independence was right up his alley.

Terrible Tarleton and the Redcoats started raiding through the Carolinas; and Andy enlisted with his older brother, Robert, to stop him. Betrayed by a Tory sympathizer, the Americans were ambushed, and Andy and his brother were taken prisoner. To young Andy's fury the British Redcoat captain refused to treat him as a soldier (in which case, in due fairness to the officer, young Andy would've been shot) but treated Andy and Robert as boys. What was worse, the officer ordered Andy to shine his boots.

Wham! Off went Andy in a whopping rage! He called the British officer names that aren't quoted in our history books, and kicked the officer in the shins.

The Britisher lost his own self-control, and struck Andy across the head with his saber. Andy didn't die. He bled like an uncorked wine bottle, and he gave that officer one of his blue-green glares, and went reeling on his way to a prison camp surrounded by a whole new slew of handicaps and obstacles.

Among other things he caught a bad case of smallpox. His brother died of exposure. That prison camp was enough to kill an ordinary boy, but Andy set his teeth and survived. His mother appealed to the British General Staff and had him released, but he wasn't back home long before his mother died.

She'd gone on to Charleston—traveled over a hundred and fifty miles on foot, the records say—to volunteer as a nurse on a prison ship. Within two months she died of what the doctors in those days called "ship fever." She was buried in an unmarked grave somewhere near Charleston. That was a mighty big loss to young Andy Jackson.

AND ON TOP of that he'd discovered another handicap. Ignorance. Men who didn't know anything never got anywhere. If you wanted to beat such obstacles as poverty and Redcoat officers, you had to have an education. Andy Jackson determined he'd get himself an education.

He got one, too. The Revolution having ended, he went to Charleston to earn money for books; then he taught school for a while to brush himself up; then he went to Salisbury to study law. You can read how he became a lawyer in one sentence, but the effort took Andy a number of years, and it wasn't easy.

He learned of some other obstacles while he was studying law at Salisbury. Salisbury being a small town, it was apt to look down on people from smaller towns and folks from the backwoods. That made Andy mad. He hated hypocrisy worse than poison ivy, and snobbery was the worst kind of hypocrisy. Snobs are always hypocrites because they pretend to be Americans, and American Democracy is the very opposite of snobbery. Andy, being a real gentleman, never snooted or bootlicked anybody. Hypocrisy was another thing he set out to wallop.

At twenty-one he was lean as a whip and looked as if he was made of rawhide. He had a long, sharp nose and a chin like a blacksmith's anvil and a pompadour like the crest of an angry eagle. Folks thought him pretty homespun when he first came to town, but they stopped calling him that when they caught that candle-shine look in his eyes. He could out-wrestle, out-ride, out-drink and out-shoot any other man in sight.

Now he'd set his mind to it, he out-distanced all the other law students; and at the end of his course a Federal judge appointed him district attorney to America's wildest frontier town. At last he was started places. On horseback, across the Great Smoky Mountains to Nashville.

2

SCANDAL-SHOOTER

WE HAVEN'T COME to the legend yet—we're still in the American history part of it that you can read in your biographies and history books. It was 1788 when Andy landed in Nashville, Tennessee, and he wasn't just an equestrian statue or a face on a postage stamp; he was a long, brick-haired, emotional American with a passion for liberty and justice and a gusto for conquering obstacles.

He found plenty of obstacles in Nashville. Main Street was crowded with swarms of bearded Indian-fighters, trappers in coonskin, woodchoppers, explorers, surveyors, soldiers, bushwhackers. They were a mighty tough crowd. They married squaws and chewed black tobacco and drank corn that would burn the lining out of a brass pipe. There wasn't any Law until Andy Jackson got there, and they didn't particularly want any after he arrived.

Andy allowed they were going to get some whether they wanted it or not.

"The district courts in this territory are going to be respected!" he made public announcement. "If the local sheriff can't enforce the law, I will."

Nashville Court House was nothing but a log shanty,

but the Federal Judge was a good one, and Andy rolled up his sleeves to go to work.

"Take it easy, Jackson," a Nashville citizen warned. "Some of the gentry around yere are right mean customers. Better go slow, or y'all might get a knife in yore back."

"Blankety-blank-blank-blank!" said Andy. "We'll see."

He wasn't any tenderfoot when he lit into Tennessee, but one of his first mornings in court when a big, strapping bushwhacker deliberately brought a brogan down on his foot, Andy couldn't help a yell. The bushwhacker opened his beard to laugh. *Crack!* Quick as a catamount, Andy'd snatched up a slab of firewood and beaned the culprit. The court didn't even convene.

Frontier towns in those days always had their champion bullies, and the champion bully of Nashville was a six-foot-six gorilla who liked to load up with hydrophobia in the Red Heifer tavern and then go out and bite an ear off the first man in sight.

Andy thought to dignify himself by buying a walking stick such as gentlemen carried in the East; and it's an indication of his nerve that he'd carry such an article on Main Street, Nashville. Imagine Mr. Bully's eyes when they spied the young D.A. carrying a cane. Whoops, boys—a sissy!

Howling with joy, this gorilla minced up to Andy, mimicked a nancy bow and slammed a fist at Andy's lean stomach. Some reports say he merely jostled Andy. No matter, the outcome was the same. Andy'd been waiting for this, and with the whole town as audience, that made it better.

Whack! Like it was a rapier, the cane drove into Mr. Bully's bread-basket. On Mr. Bully's face there formed a look of acute indigestion. Bellowing with stomach ache, he hurled three hundred pounds of reprisal at Andy. *Slash! Slash! Slash!* went the cane.

Then Andy treated Nashville to a bully-fight that rivaled anything similar in Old Spain. Dancing, dodging, side-stepping around his foe, he gave that six-foot-sixer a lesson in law that made Nashville feel law-abiding for years after. The crowd roared. Nobody could see the cane. Dust boiled up to hide the combatants from view. When it cleared away, there was Andy with his hands in his pockets, cool; and Mr. Bully on the ground with his head as full of splinters as a toothpick holder. No man ever equaled Andy Jackson when it came to handling a cane.

Moonshiners, drunken Indians and other frontier bad boys got out of town rather than face that stick of Andy's. It had a way of cracking down on the outlaws who tried to block the Federal Government in Tennessee.

AFTER A COUPLE of years of that exercise he felt fit as a bull fiddle and ready for love. That's how he felt when he met up with Rachel Robards. Rachel lived in the big log house where Andy boarded; she was a pioneer woman, no question about that. She was as red-cheeked and healthy as all outdoors, with beautiful black hair and fine dark eyes, hardy and graceful as a deer.

She could swing an axe or ride a horse as well as hemstitch a hanky; her smile was friendly and American as one of her wide apple pies; but when she was baking bread she mussed her hair, and when she chopped wood she didn't wear gloves. Wasn't any lipstick in those days, and the only kind of powder she'd ever seen was gunpowder.

What's more, she went barefoot a lot, and sometimes on

a cold winter evening she liked to sit in front of the fire-place and smoke a pipe.

Andy liked that. Shoes were enough to cripple anybody in those days, and Rachel's foot was beautiful. And if you like tobacco Andy thought a pipe a lot better than taking snuff. Most of the so-called society ladies at that time took snuff, which simply means they stuffed dry tobacco up their nose. Then they sneezed. It was supposed to be elegant and healthy. Andy thought Rachel was six times as elegant and healthy as any society dame he'd ever seen.

Well, she'd known all the hardships of the frontier, but she was still full of fun and sweet and gentle; she could understand a man who'd spent his life knocking down obstacles, and she liked Andy. Trouble was, she was married to Lew Robards, a scowling, moody ne'er-do-well who figured himself too good for Rachel because he was a Virginian. He was always brow-beating poor Rachel and threatening to leave her.

Andy Jackson, who was always chivalrous and kindly to women, thought Robards was a heel. One night he criticized Robards for the way he talked to Rachel, and Robards blew up in a jealous fit, accusing Rachel and Andy of being sweet on each other. Poor Rachel wept, and Andy, who couldn't stand seeing a woman cry, blew up himself like a powder factory.

"Rat!" he thundered at Robards (or words to that effect). "You say anything mean about Rachel and me, and I'll cut off your head with a butcher-knife!"

"All right!" Robards taunted back (or something mean like that); "I never loved Rachel, anyway, and I'm going right up to Virginia and get myself divorced."

With that he saddled up and galloped away, and Andrew Jackson felt terrible. He thought he'd brought Rachel's life down in ruins until Rachel assured him that Robards had always been a scoundrel. Then Andy felt better. He told Rachel that he, Andy Jackson, would be mighty honored to have her for a wife, and he asked her to marry him soon as everything was settled with Robards.

Now in those days divorce had to be granted by State Legislature in the State where you were married. Virginia was a wilderness away from Tennessee; for weeks there wasn't any news from Robards; but a traveler finally brought back word that Robards's divorce had been granted. So Andy and Rachel were married in the frontier church, and no newly-wedded couple were ever happier.

Andy started right in to clear a plantation and build the home later famous as the Hermitage. His law office was booming; he was saving money, and he bought himself some fine-blooded horses. Rachel managed the Negroes and planted a garden and ran the big, wide log house.

Nashville was booming, too, and Andy was busy as a bee. Besides D.A., he was captain of the first fire brigade and an officer in the militia. Seemed like all the obstacles were just about cleared. He worshiped Rachel and she worshiped him, and they both loved Tennessee and thought America the finest country in the world.

Then *bang!* came the bombshell. Official notice from Virginia that Robards hadn't obtained any divorce!

NOW THIS IS all as much a part of American history as the Declaration of Independence, and it's told here because it's a main part of the life of Andrew Jackson. Try to figure his feelings when he heard that news from Virginia! They say

Andy was infuriated, but rage seems hardly the word. All the rainbow crashed in a twinkling; overnight there were obstacles bigger and blacker than any he'd ever seen. For Robards had made Rachel a bigamist, and she and Andy weren't legally married.

Some say Robards did it on purpose, and some say it was an accident common in a day of legal tangles when there weren't any telephones and letters often went astray. Anyhow, Rachel's heart was broken, and a first streak of gray showed up in Andy's orange hair. As for his temper— the effort to hold it almost threw him flat on the floor.

Robards hadn't been legally entitled to a divorce before; but he got one now, charging bigamy. The story got around Nashville—Andy had made himself some enemies as district attorney—and it seemed like all Tennessee was whispering.

Andy put his arm, protective, around Rachel and took her back to the church, and this time they were married tight as the sinews in Andy's grip. But that night at home, after Rachel went to bed, Andy crept downstairs and got out his dueling pistols. He cleaned them and oiled them and tested the locks until they were hair-trigger. Then he went to the window and for a long time stood looking out. His hair stood up like an eagle's crest, and there was a light in his eye like candle-shine; and the obstacle in front of him now was a slimy, grass-hidden, snake-like creature with hooded eyes and a whispering, green tongue—half reptile, half human—named Scandal.

THEY SAY THE shooting started so fast that the Governor of Tennessee almost had the words shot out of his mouth.

The Governor's name was Sevier. He was a grouchy old

politician with more blab than sense. Tennessee had been admitted to the Union and Sevier elected Governor as the loudest talker in the State. At the same time an orange-headed young lawyer named Andrew Jackson had been elected to Congress.

The orange-headed young lawyer had quite a record. He'd kicked the stuffing out of the criminal element in Nashville. He'd made the law respected in Tennessee. He'd organized the State militia and thrown the fear of God into hostile frontier Indians. His reputation for honesty, democracy and reckless stop-at-nothing courage—like his racing stables—couldn't be beat.

But Sevier didn't like Andy, and he told him so one morning when they chanced to meet on the main street of Nashville. That was all right with Andy and he calmly exchanged the compliment. But he added that he had more to do than wrangle politics on a street corner as he was too busy giving his services to his country.

"Services!" sneered the blab-mouthed Governor. "I know of no greater service you have rendered the country than running off with another man's wife."

Bang! the two shots came so fast they sounded like one explosion. Sevier reeled back howling, clutching a bleeding ear. Flinging down empty pistols, Andy hurled himself like a cyclone atop the Governor. He'd have torn Sevier to pieces like a strawstack if bystanders hadn't interfered. Then with ten men holding him, he challenged Sevier to a duel in a voice that rang across the Great Smoky Mountains like a thunderstorm.

Blabby Sevier's blood froze. He knew Jackson's record

as district attorney, and he suspected he was hearing his own death-sentence.

Duels were the code on the American frontier, those days, and Sevier couldn't back down. Arrangements were made for a meeting on the Kentucky border before Sevier could think up an excuse. Historians don't seem to know exactly what happened on that field of honor, but they do know Andy Jackson was there at the crack of dawn. Sevier was slower in arriving. Finally, two hours late, he got there looking as if he hadn't slept a wink in three years.

Andy's eyes were like hells frozen over, and Sevier was so terrified he shook like a big bag of crabapple jelly. Some say the Governor was so scared he fell off his horse and the animal bolted with his pistols. Others say that as he walked to meet Jackson he tripped over his own sword and flopped in a faint. Anyway, his hand was shaking so he couldn't have held a pistol made out of sticking plaster.

Andy threw down his gun in disgust and accepted a public apology. A man used to fighting obstacles wouldn't waste his time in busting an old windbag.

But Andy vowed to slay the next green-tongued scandal-monger who mentioned Rachel's name, and it got around Tennessee that Andy was a challenging demon. Charles Dickinson heard about it and laughed. Charles Dickinson was another fool.

This Dickinson, in the slang of the day, was a sporting gentleman—which meant he played cards at Nashville Tavern, bet on the races, wore a swallow-tail coat and an imitation diamond and a big, cocky coachman-like hat. In his cups he had a scurrilous loud tongue and was apt to boast what a wonderful shot he was. Unlike most braggarts he had something to back it up with, for everyone conceded he was the best pistol-marksman in Tennessee. Everyone, that is, except Andrew Jackson.

Andy exchanged compliments with Dickinson in an argument over a race horse. The year being 1806, a lot of water had run under the bridge since Andy first came to Nashville. He'd been to Congress and back; risen to be major general of militia; made the Hermitage into a fine plantation, climbing over obstacles all the way. Rachel was happy once more, and Andy was taking Saturday afternoons off to race his thoroughbreds on the Nashville track.

An argument over a thoroughbred was part of the game, only Dickinson made some remarks insinuating that Andy's horse, Truxton, had won a fixed race. Andy made public denial, denouncing Dickinson as a falsifier. Dickinson challenged, calling Andy a poltroon. Andy refused the challenge, saying he wouldn't duel over a horse. Dickinson openly called him a coward. Andy said his record could easily disprove that.

Then Dickinson published a statement that Andy was a "worthless scoundrel" and, rumming in a tavern, let fly some remarks about Andy's marriage. Once more the green-tongued Gorgon whispered around the Jackson homestead. Andy's challenge went to Dickinson, special delivery.

"**BUT YOU CAN'T** fight that cur!" Andy's friend, Overton, cautioned him in alarm. "My God, Andy, he's the best shot in the West!"

"Don't care if he's the best in creation!" Andy's eyes were terrible. "No man living can malign my honor or my wife's."

"He'll kill you, Andy! It's a plot. Your enemies have hired him to get you out of politics."

"Let him be a hireling of Satan! I'll kill the scandal-mongering snake if it's my last mortal act."

They met at sunrise over the Kentucky line, in a poplar grove by a little mountain stream. Dickinson smirking, venomous, murderously confident. Andy gaunt and flame-haired with molten eyes.

Grim-jawed, Overton gave the word to fire.

Like a flash Dickinson shot, quick as magic, aiming to kill. Overton, horrified, saw dust flick from the lapel of Andy's greatcoat; saw Andy wince, pale, then stiffen up, the candle-shine brightening in his glare.

Dickinson recoiled in terror from that unearthly gaze. "Good God!" he gasped. "Have I missed him?"

"Back to the mark, sir!" Overton threatened with his umpire's pistol. "Back to the mark. It's Jackson's turn."

Sweating, Dickinson took his stance, staring in fascination at Andy's gun. Slowly, deliberately the gun came up to aim. *Crack!*—the explosion was like one sharp, clear drum-tap in the dawn. Morning coat, plug hat and diamonds, the gambler fell a-heap. Andrew Jackson stood.

"Mortally wounded," Overton reported after a quick look at the fallen figure. "He won't want anything more of you, General." Then, noticing blood on Jackson's weskit—"Thunderation! Andy, you're wounded, too!"

"In the ribs," Andy nodded. "He only pinked me. But, by God, if he'd shot me through the brain I'd have stood up long enough to kill him!"

Mounting his horse, unaided, he rode back to Nashville in the sunlight, teeth clenched, gritting groans. He knew what the gossips, what the politicians would say. More obstacles than ever—such terrible obstacles! So little time, and so much to do!

3

OLD HICKORY

NOW WE'VE GOT the historical background pretty well established, and we're getting close to the legend. Andy's fight against Poverty and the Redcoats and Wilderness Hardship and Himself, his battle against Ignorance and Hypocrisy, Snobbery and Scandal—that's all down, black and white, in the records.

Take the War of 1812.

We think World War II is a crazy rumpus, but the War of 1812 was the prize screwball war of creation. In the White House little James Madison didn't know what to do. The war began at sea, while in Washington Clay and Calhoun, neither of them sailors, thundered for action.

Half the States didn't want to fight; they called it Mr. Madison's War. The inland States, rarin' to go, called it the Second War of American Independence. While everyone was bickering over what to call it, the New England maritime States, which had the most to gain from a victory, threatened to secede from the Union.

Meantime the American Navy, outnumbered hundreds to one, began to chase the British all over the sea. The American Army, with strategic and numerical advantage, was being chased all over the land. Slugabed Armstrong,

Secretary of War, dozed over maps and forgot where to send supplies.

A Quaker named Jacob Brown with a handful of militia saved New York State from invasion while the regular army ran away. Flustered old General-in-Chief Wilkinson wrung his hands, which didn't do a thing to stop the Redcoats from capturing Maine, Niagara Falls, Fort Dearborn, Detroit, most of Michigan, Illinois and Wisconsin.

To cap this military fiasco, the Redcoats landed in Maryland and attacked Washington, D.C. In the battle for the capital they ran low on ammunition and started firing skyrockets. The American militia, who'd never seen squibs and Roman candles before, ran pellmell. Little Madison escaped the city just in time, and the Redcoat commander sat down in the White House and ate Madison's untouched dinner before he scornfully set fire to the executive mansion.

Poor old General Wilkinson ran around in circles like a rooster with its head cut off. No one in the Army seemed to know how to fight this war—no one, that was, except Andrew Jackson.

Imagine Andy's feelings when he heard the Redcoats were back again! In 1812 there wasn't any telegraph; the news was late in reaching Tennessee, but when Andy heard it he practically hit the ceiling.

The Redcoats! *Blankety-blank-blank-blank!* Clutching an old scar under his hair, he swore like he'd been scalped. Hadn't he put an end to those obstacles to Democracy? No, there they were, up in Maine and Niagara Falls and Wisconsin. Maine, Niagara Falls and Wisconsin were a long way off from Tennessee, but quick as lightning Andy saw the danger.

Suffering catfish! With the Redcoats invading from the North and the British Navy on the Atlantic Coast, the last free port in America would be New Orleans. If the British ever laid hold of New Orleans they could plug up the whole Mississippi. Already His Majesty's frigates were probably crowding into the Gulf of Mexico. Wow! Once they captured New Orleans, the whole American nation might fall.

Andy didn't wait for orders. He was a major general of Tennessee Militia, and he called for volunteers. Although he had rheumatism in his right hand at the time, and he'd never quite learned how to spell, he wrote out this summons which echoed across Tennessee like a bugle call:

> CITIZENS! YOUR GOVERNMENT HAS YIELDED TO THE IMPULSE OF THE NATION.... WAR IS BREAKING OUT BETWEEN THE UNITED STATES AND GREAT BRITAIN.... A SIMPLE INVITATION IS GIVEN FOR 50,000 VOLUNTEERS!
>
> ARE WE THE TITLED SLAVES OF GEORGE THE THIRD? THE MILITARY CONSCRIPTS OF NAPOLEON? OR THE FROZEN PEASANTS OF THE RUSSIAN CZAR? NO—WE ARE THE FREE BORN SONS OF THE ONLY REPUBLICK NOW EXISTING IN THE WORLD! ARE WE GOING TO FIGHT TO SATISFY THE REVENGE OR AMBITION OF A CORRUPT MINISTRY?... NO—WE ARE GOING TO FIGHT FOR THE REESTABLISHMENT OF OUR NATIONAL CHARACTER... FOR THE PROTEC-

TION OF OUR MARITIME CITIZENS...TO VINDI-
CATE OUR RIGHT FOR FREE TRADE....

MANY TENNESSEE FRONTIERSMEN had never heard of
Napoleon or the Russian Czar, but they'd heard of Andy
Jackson and they volunteered in droves. Once more Nashville was a-jam with bearded men in buckskins carrying
squirrel rifles. Coffee's Cavalry showed up in dark blue
homespun, and there was a batch of friendly Indians and
half-breed scouts.

Andy didn't fuss around with fancy uniforms and parade
drill. These frontiersmen were fighters from scratch, the
way he was, and he dispatched a letter to President Madison in Washington offering to march down to New Orleans by way of Canada and capture Quebec in the short-cut.

He can most certainly do so, Governor Blount of Tennessee wrote in agreement, backing Andy's plan. *He delights
in peace, but he has a peculiar pleasure in treating his enemies
as such.*

Andy's letter confused James Madison, and he gave it
to the War Department. Secretary-of-War Armstrong was
annoyed. Who was this frontier general, anyway? Some
wild, red-headed Tennessean with a reputation for a terrible temper and fighting duels. The man's only military
experience was with a lot of Indians. There were plenty
of school-trained generals to handle the situation; the
Regular Army would resent the intrusion of this harum-
scarum hill billy. Furthermore, General-in-Chief Wilkinson had already gone waddling down to Louisiana to take
command of New Orleans.

Andy's letter wasn't even acknowledged, but Andy hadn't

waited for that. No time to wait around for engraved invi-
tations from the War Department with things going like
they were. Any minute the Indians were liable to uprise,
and the redskins could be worse than the Redcoats. The
whole Mississippi River was ready to break loose.

Florida was a powder-keg, too. Florida, in 1812,
belonged to Spain; there was a Spanish army hanging
around Pensacola, and His Catholic Majesty of Spain had
no more use for the American Republic than George III.

"You've got to commission me to take my troops into
war!" Andy pounded the desk in front of Governor Blount's
nose. "I've got to get down there to the Gulf of Mexico!"

"But Andy, that's over three thousand miles almost.
Solid wilderness between here and New Orleans. Hostile
Indians. Besides, you've no orders from Washington."

"Confound the sleepy-heads in Washington! Damnation on the wilderness! The British are coming! I'm going!"

He was out of the door with the Governor's permission
before Blount even realized he'd signed it. But what about
provisions for the men? The State of Tennessee didn't
have the extra cash, and the War Department seemed to
be deaf. Swearing like an iron cannon, Andy thundered
into a frightened banker's office and on his personal note
borrowed sixteen hundred dollars.

Next day with two regiments of militia and Coffee's
Cavalry, Andy stood on the edge of Nashville for the take-
off. Somehow everything was ready. The cavalry was to go
overland by way of the old Natchez Trace, and the infantry
was to go down the Mississippi on flatboats. Assembling
the boats, the horses, the supplies had been the hardest kind of job for Andy—almost as hard as holding his

temper; and hardest of all was leaving the Hermitage and Rachel.

Under the breast pocket of his uniform he carried a little miniature of Rachel; and in his belt, as though to protect that picture, he carried his dueling pistols.

So there was a lump in Major General Jackson's throat that morning, and just at the last minute he lost his temper. For forty-eight hours he'd been working sleepless to get the expedition ready; now some Nashville politician, who'd spend a comfortable night in bed, criticized the shabby apparel of the volunteers.

"Why, you damned infernal scoundrel!" Andy caught the man by the collar. "Any more of that talk and I'll ram a red-hot poker down your throat!"

But at last the infantry was embarked and the cavalry was started off. Straight-away everything in the world seemed to conspire against Andy. The month was December; the weather, unusual for Tennessee, turned zero. The river froze, filling up with great chunks of ice. On their clumsy flatboats the infantry had the devil of a time. They ran out of firewood; provisions froze solid; three scouts were drowned.

Coffee's Cavalry regiment, following down the old Natchez Trace, had it every bit as bad. Snow impeded the horses and blanketed the unmapped woods off which the soldiers had intended to forage.

OBSTACLES, OBSTACLES, OBSTACLES! Andy Jackson tore his orange hair. Unseen Indians began to snipe at the troops the minute they entered the wilderness. Woodsmen who'd been weaned on icicles fell sick of pneumonia. Andy didn't feel so chipper, himself. He had rheumatics in his right hand; the old wound Dickinson had dealt him started to ache; he caught a painful case of dysentery.

Even the Mississippi River raised hell. The worst kind of an obstacle at best, it staged an earthquake just for Andy's benefit—a big earthquake under the channel that threw up sand-bars and pulled down banks and changed the river's course. If you don't believe it, you can read in your history books how the Mississippi River raised cain.

But snow and sickness, Old Man River and earthquakes couldn't stop Andy Jackson. Raging, cursing, kicking the men forward, staying up nights to tend the fires so some exhausted guard could sleep, he took those handicaps in his stride. He got down to Natchez, too, just as John Coffee's Cavalry came staggering in.

Half the volunteers were crippled, the other half were out of rations; the cavalry was on its last legs and it was still a long way to New Orleans—but Andy'd brought the expedition a thousand miles from Nashville, and he'd have taken it the rest of the way if the War Department hadn't stopped him.

That was an obstacle Andy Jackson hadn't counted on. The Government order was handed him by a dispatch rider when he limped ashore at Natchez. Try to figure Andy's feelings when he read this historic message:

> *The causes for embodying the Corps under your command having ceased to exist, you will on receipt of this consider it dismissed from public service and deliver to General Wilkinson all articles of public property. Accept for yourself and the Corps the thanks of the President of the United States. I have the honor to be.... Sec'y-of-War Armstrong.*

Reading that message from the Secretary of War, Andy Jackson saw red, turned white and swore blue. He wouldn't have disbanded in this limberlost if the war had been over. Public property! Why, he'd paid for most of this equipment himself! Thanks from the President? He'd bet a race horse James Madison didn't have any part in this. As for the war being over, the Redcoats were winning everywhere!

It was a plot, that was what—a confounded political machination—a trick of crooked politicians and squabbling, jealous generals to keep Andy Jackson from getting anywhere.

"Come on!" he thundered at John Coffee. "It seems those damned fools, Armstrong and Wilkinson, have turned me around. If they think they've stopped me from going to New Orleans to save the day, they're crazy, but it looks like we'll have to detour. I brought these volunteers down here on my own means and responsibility. Now, on my own means and responsibility, I'll take them home!"

Sick with dysentery, his duel-wound and fury, he swung into saddle. Doleful drums lined up the discouraged men.

"We're going back to Nashville!" Andy roared. "I'll pay you out of my own pocket, and I'll get you there if we have to eat crow, and I'll wager you a million we'll be down this way again before long." Then he dismounted with an oath. "By heaven I'll march on foot with you boys. Some ailing man will ride my horse."

"He's a tough one," a soldier admired from the ranks. "Tough as hickory!"

Someone set up a cheer. "Three cheers for Old Hickory!"

Stumping off at the column's head in the snow, Andy stiffened up at the cheer. It's not, in the record, but a couple of nights later Andy might've been sitting with John Coffee in the cavalry leader's tent.

"What's this nickname the men are calling me?" he asks.

"You mean Old Hickory?"

"Don't know as I like it."

"But they don't mean it uncomplimentary, General. Hickory's just about the toughest thing they know."

"That's all right," Andy nods, glaring into the campfire. "And I suppose they mean the adjective for affection. It's just that I don't like being called old...."

4

—

OUT OF THE FRYING PAN

NOW THE LEGEND has it that Andy Jackson was down-right upset about that nickname. Old Hickory. All that bitter march back to Nashville it preyed on his mind. He couldn't stop the men from calling him that—he was glad they thought enough of him to call him that instead of the other things soldiers sometimes call a general—but secretly it worried him worse than anything so far in his career.

Minute he got back to Nashville he galloped to the Hermitage and threw his arms about Rachel.

"Rachel!" he cried. "How do I look?"

"Why, Andy"—she kissed him—"you look just fine."

"I feel fine!" he roared, swinging her up by the elbows in a sort of dance. "By Glory! I feel great. The trip's done me good! Look!" he thumped his chest. "In spite of some triflin' hardships and those fatheaded arm-chair generals in Washington, I'm fresher right now than a daisy."

To prove it, he bounded upstairs five at a time; but when he got to his room with the door shut behind him he sort of sagged there against a bed-post, panting. Rheumatism twinged through his fingers as he sat down to pull off his boots. Frostbite stung in his toes. When he straightened up, his backbone cracked and the pain of his never-healed duel wound almost bent him double again.

He sat there for a long time, clutching his ribs and chewing molten oaths. His breath was thick in his teeth when he stood up and strode over to a wall-mirror. Mad? He was so mad he couldn't swear. Whatever he saw in that portrait-reflection of himself he didn't like. He glared at it for an hour, maybe two, standing feet apart, hands clutching the butts of his dueling pistols, chin down like an anvil on the tarnished buttons of his chest.

"Old Hickory!" he glared. "*Old* Hickory!"

Yes, his cheeks were lined and weathered like saddle-leather—the knuckles were swollen in his leathery hands—he was bent a little where Dickinson's bullet had nicked him—he was over forty—tell-tale streaks in his hair. For a moment he had an impulse to rush down to the kitchen and dye his hair with henna tea.

"By Godfrey, I can't be! I *can't!*"

But he was, and he knew he was. There's a moment in every man's life when he suddenly realizes he's getting along. Up to now Andy'd been so busy conquering obstacles he hadn't thought about it; but that nickname the army'd given him made him conscious of the fact, and the realization hit him harder than Dickinson's bullet.

"Great thundering Jehosophat!" he bellowed at himself in the mirror. "There's too gol-danged much left to do! There isn't *time!*"

Only there was time. Time with a capital T. Over the mantelpiece, in a china clock. Ticking merrily away as if it had all the hours in the world. Old Hickory—*Old* Hickory! What the devil could you do about Time?

"Beelzebub's britches!" Andy clutched his hair, glaring at the ticking clock. "Nothing's ever stopped me before, and I'll beat that, too. I'll run it a race like Truxton against Ploughboy in the derby! Damnation!" He yanked himself together. "Already five minutes have gone by, and I'm standing here talking—"

Well, he'd never been the type to stand around talking, and now he went into action faster than he'd once pulled his guns on Blab-mouth Sevier. History tells how he went into a whirlwind of activity after that first expedition to New Orleans was scotched, but it takes the legend to maybe explain why. Anyhow, it happened after he got that name of Old Hickory.

FROM THEN ON there wasn't a busier man in America; day and night he was on the job. Talk about an eight-hour day! Talk about a five-day week! Andy Jackson's days lasted twenty-four hours, and his weeks included Sunday, and he made more history in a month than your average man makes in a lifetime.

For instance, that month of September, 1813. He was writing letters to the War Department—sending fierce dispatches to Madison, Armstrong, Wilkinson—writing to the politicians, to the papers, to Governor Blount—moving Heaven and earth to get his Tennessee Army back into the war.

He was recruiting volunteers and training infantry. He was managing his plantation and grooming his thoroughbreds and studying law, geography and military maps. He was sending scouts down to Mississippi Territory and Florida; laying out a battle campaign to have it ready; struggling—once more with Poverty—there was a Depression on; juggling his account books to keep out of debt. With all that to do that month, Old Hickory sandwiched in the wildest gun-roarin' duel in American history.

Tom Benton had been a good friend of Andy's, but Tom's brother, Jesse, got into a scrape with Billy Carroll, one of Andy's best volunteer officers. Jesse challenged Billy, and Billy asked Andy to be his second. The code being what it was, Andy Jackson could hardly refuse.

Standing witness at this contest, he saw Billy plump a bullet into the seat of Jesse Benton's pants: it seems Jesse, after firing and missing, turned around and bent double like he'd eaten green apples, unable to face his opponent's gun.

Anyhow, Jesse Benton couldn't sit down in Nashville Tavern after that without the whole town laughing; and Tom Benton came raging to Andy, saying Andy had let Bill Carroll make a fool out of Jesse. Andy reminded Tom it was none of his affair, and Tom said anyone called Old Hickory ought to have more sense. Andy roared he didn't have time for any argument, warning Tom to shut up before he lost his confounded temper. Tom kept on giving hot-headed insults, and Andy's temper threw him again.

"I told you I didn't have time to argue!" he exploded. "Now get out of town, Tom Benton, and give me a chance to cool down, or the next time I see you, sir, I'll horsewhip you!"

Tom was a Tennessean and darned near as fierce-tempered as Andy, so he didn't take Andy's advice. Still, nothing likely would've happened if Jesse Benton had kept his own mouth shut. Jesse had to go into a barroom and rattle

Charles Dickinson's skeleton with some ugly cracks about Old Hickory's "double wedding."

Shades of Dickinson and Sevier! Andy heard about the cracks, and there was that slimy, green-tongued Scandal-monster hovering over the Hermitage again.

Pressed for time like he was, Andy didn't lose a minute in starting out after Jesse Benton. Jesse and Tom were lodging at the City Hotel, a ramshackle place on Public Square backed up against the river. Old Hickory thought they were living at the Nashville Inn across the square, and he rode into town hell-for-leather and dismounted before the Inn, teeth breathing oaths of fire and green sparks coming out of his eyes.

Big John Coffee and Stockley Hays were standing on the curb; minute they saw Andy they knew something resembling dynamite was up. Like a mountain lion upright, Andy stalked at them, both pistols cocked in his belt, a long horsewhip in his hand.

"Where is the varmint? Where's Jesse Benton?"

Then before either friend could answer, Andy spied Tom Benton in the doorway of the hotel across the square. Tom had two pistols in his belt, too; he was pale as plaster, but no one could ever say he was yellow. Not like Jesse, for instance, who, seeing Andy arrive, ducked into a back hall and hid behind a door.

Tom clutched his belted pistols and stood his ground, while Old Hickory, followed by Coffee and Hays, came marching across the cobblestones. He roared at Tom Benton to get out of his way so he could go into the hotel and challenge Jesse; Tom only spread his legs and tightened the grip on his pistols.

"Holy calliope!" Fury elevated Andy's crest. "I told you to clear out, you interfering rascal! Now I'll give you such a horsewhipping you won't be able to sit down any better than your brother!" He swung the long whip.

Tom's answer was to try to yank his pistols, but the muzzles stuck in his belt, giving Andy time to drop the whip and draw for his own. Then Nashville never saw such a scene. Tom Benton drew his pistols. Andy Jackson drew his pistols. Big John Coffee drew *his* pistols. Stockley Hays drew a sword-cane. And behind an inner door Jesse Benton drew his pistols. Seemed as if the whole town had drawn its weapons when Andy started into that doorway after Tom.

NOT WANTING TO kill a man who'd been his friend, he drove his pistol into Tom's midriff, and shouting, "Drop those guns! Drop those guns!" Jabbing paralyzing punches into Tom's solar plexus, he drove Tom Benton backwards, step by step, down the dark inner hall. End of the corridor a door stood open on a rickety porch and a long flight of steps going down to the river; but before Andy got there, Jesse Benton sprang from ambush, firing from an alcove at the side.

Gun-flame seared the gloom, the blast taking Andy Jackson unawares, tearing a great raw hole in his left shoulder. Andy staggered and whirled, firing. Tom fired. Jesse, unhurt, dropped to save himself while Andy, thinking he'd felled his enemy, reeled around to shoot at Tom.

Then everybody was shouting and shooting: Andy and Tom at each other, Jesse leaping up to fire a second shot at Andy, Coffee and Hays rushing forward to save Old Hickory—the din as loud as any War of 1812 battle.

Andy's shot only burned Tom Benton's sleeve. Tom's two

shots missed Andy by a miracle. Jesse's second bullet tore into Andy's smashed shoulder, and brought Old Hickory down like a chopped tree. Blood flowed in the shadows as Big John Coffee jumped Andy's body to charge Tom Benton with guns a-blaze, and Stockley Hays rushed Jesse Benton with his sword. The slim blade broke against a brass button on Jesse's coat just as Tom Benton, dodging Coffee's bullets, jumped backwards onto the outside porch, crashed through a railing and fell down a hundred steps to the river, uttering a hundred wild yells.

Tom and Jesse got out of town plenty quick after that historic experience, but Andy went across to the Nashville Inn on a stretcher, cursing red, white and blue, and close to dead. His shoulder was a wreck; the ball-and-socket were well nigh shattered, and there was a bullet embedded in an upper arm-bone that didn't feel any too good, either.

Historians say he soaked two mattresses with blood; every doctor in Nashville tried to save him from gangrene (since he wouldn't let them cut off his arm) and every doctor in Nashville and everybody else thought he was going to die. In fact, a local type-setter went so far as to set up type saying Old Hickory was already a goner.

A goner? They were beforehand with that obituary. News he'd been half assassinated was hardly out when a dispatch rider came walloping into Nashville: the Indians were on the rampage, the garrison at Fort Mims had been massacred, and all of Mississippi Territory was under fire.

Andy Jackson sat up in bed with a shout. He didn't have time to pass out like this; like the blood from his shoulder, Time was leaking away. "By the Eternal!" he bellowed at astonished doctors. "Our country has got to be saved!"

"But General Jackson, your shoulder—"

"I haven't got time! Tell Coffee to assemble the cavalry! Tell the townsfolk General Jackson is restored! I want twenty-five hundred volunteers—I'm going to lead them in person, by thunder!—and I want them ready to march with me in nine days!"

5

STRANGER WITH A BOTTLE

HISTORY IS FULL of famous marches; but historians who
know about it have to agree that Old Hickory's march to
the relief of Fort Mims beat those other parades all hollow.

Thirty-two miles in nine hours! That's the all-time
record of Andy's first day. Infantry moving that fast today
would die of corns, bunions and exhaustion; it would be
marching on paved highway, too, and not on an Indian trail
through early-American wilderness.

And that was only the first lap. After that he had to slash
a road across the unmapped Raccoon Mountains beyond
Fort Deposit, and march down through the whole savage
Mississippi Territory, all the hundreds of miles down to
where the eagles fly so high in Mobile. That was Andy's
plan, and he wasn't waiting for the Federal Government to
authorize it, either. The war had reached the frontier as he'd
feared it would; the Indians weren't waiting for anybody,
and neither was Old Hickory.

Well, if his first march south had been tough, this march
was ten thousand times tougher. Multiply all the handicaps
of that first expedition by ten thousand burning, murdering, war-whooping redskins. The Creeks—fiercest tribe in
the South! Armed by Redcoat gun-runners; roused to fury

by the propagandists of Tecumseh; led by that homicidal maniac, William Weatherford.

Andy had heard about Bill Weatherford before. Seven parts white man, one part Indian, the renegade combined all the seven sins of the white race with the cunning, craft and barbarity of the red. Voted chief of the Creeks—called Red Eagle—he'd vowed to wipe out every American settler in Mississippi Territory and deliver to the British the orange scalp of Andy Jackson.

That was a foe for any man's contest, and the game was to be played on Weatherford's home field; but Andy Jackson, All-American Indian fighter, didn't care. Odds ten thousand to twenty-five hundred, his smashed shoulder in a sling, he set out to tackle Weatherford like hell on wheels.

Stockades massacred. Cabins burning. Arrows flying out of ambush. Tomahawks whistling through the dark. Scalped corpses rotting in pillaged corn-plots. Frontier women crucified on cabin doors. All the horrors of Indian warfare confronted Andy and his Tennesseans; but mile after mile, fighting Time as well as Redskins, Old Hickory pushed on.

Skirmishes. Surprise attacks. Pitched battles. Midnight assaults. Battle after battle, Andy drove his army down through the wilderness. Behind him he left a trail of dead redskins, demolished wigwams and burning Indian towns.

Weatherford began to realize he'd picked a scrap with the wrong man; the Creeks gave Andy the title of Sharp Knife, and their moccasins grew thin from running. A crimson haze hung over the Mississippi forests. Weatherford and his painted braves fled like weasels pursued by hounds.

Nothing could stop Andy Jackson. Ambushes, barricades, earthworks, man-traps—all the crafty obstacles Weatherford threw across his path. Old Hickory battered down.

WINTER JOINED THE Indians as an ally. So did Famine. In the lower Mississippi Territory, the swamps and mud holes and fever-bogs were terrible. Big Chief Weatherford thought Andy would slow up, but Andy only went faster.

Napoleon claimed an army marched on its stomach, meaning the troops had to eat once in a while. Well, Andy and his army marched on its feet. Halfway down to Mobile the supply wagons were as bare as Mother Hubbard's cupboard. The soldiers chewed the fringes of their buckskin shirts for breakfast; lunched on their fingernails, and feasted at night on acorns.

Flu and dysentery joined Andy's column. Ammunition ran low. Sick men moaned all night on litters. A detachment of volunteers deserted. Governor Blount, up in Nashville, answered a hurry call for supplies and money with an unhappy letter suggesting Andy throw up the sponge.

"What? Retrograde?" Andy shouted. "I'll perish first!"

Kicking his starving, weary riflemen to their feet—with a ferocious threat to shoot the next deserter—he hitched his smashed shoulder in its sling, pulled out his pistols, and hurled the column forward to hit Weatherford by surprise at Horseshoe Bend.

Bad Bill Weatherford never knew what hit him. Old Hickory smashed into that Indian encampment like a cyclone going through a chicken yard, leaving in its wake a great swirl of weathers. The savages fought like fiends, but they couldn't stop Andy Jackson. Not when he was making history. That Battle of Horseshoe Bend was one of the few American victories in the War of 1812 as far as the army was concerned.

Of course Andy had some good men in his company—Big John Coffee was a scrapper, and there were a couple of wild young frontiersmen named Davy Crockett and Sam Houston—but it was Andy who inspired the boys.

Close to eight hundred redskins bit the dust that day, and Weatherford's moccasins never stopped running until they reached the neighborhood of Pensacola, Florida. Neither did Andy Jackson's military boots. Just as he'd suspected, the Redcoats and the Creeks had a tie-up with the Spaniards in Florida; and when he saw which way the Indians were retiring, Andy decided to investigate Florida real estate.

He investigated it, too. Another general might've been satisfied with a victory like Horseshoe Bend; might've taken time out for medals and mint juleps and military reviews. Not Old Hickory! Straight down through the country of the Creeks he slammed—driving his men; driving himself; driving the Redskins in front of him like stampeding cattle.

How he chased those savages off the map; how Weatherford came in and surrendered; how he surprised and walloped a treacherous Spanish army at Pensacola—all that you can read in the history books where the historians seem as surprised at Andy's accomplishments as anybody.

But the historians don't know about the legend. For the legend has it that Andy was racing against Time, racing against a shadow, racing against that nickname of Old Hickory.

Yes, all the way to Pensacola it was there in the back of his head, haunting his thoughts around the campfire, keeping him wakeful at night. Seems like it almost gave him a complex; wouldn't let him waste a single minute. Why, even the historians agree that about the only timeout he took out on that campaign was when he was doubled up so bad with dysentery that he had to go and hang himself groaning over a log.

Sick? He was sicker than a ptomaine-poisoned dog. Then he'd yank himself upright with an oath, snatch out his pistols, shout, "Forward march! Double-quick!" to the column, and rush on.

Spain was supposed to be neutral, but there were Redcoat frigates in the harbor at Pensacola and the Spanish fort was supplying the Creek Indians with guns. Andy hit the fort at sunrise and at sundown it was smashed as though it had been made of A-B-C blocks. The Redcoat warships fled as the Spanish Governor ran up a white flag against the Florida sunset and sent a buttery message of surrender requesting the privilege of kissing Andy's hand.

THE GOVERNOR DIDN'T get the privilege. It's no legend that Andy was all in after that Pensacola fight. No double-crossing Spaniard would've kissed his hand, anyway, but that night Andy was cooked. Hundreds of miles of forced march had worn him to the nub. Acorns had left his stomach an agonized wreck. Weak from dysentery, haggard from lack of sleep, his shoulder a mess, one lung giving out, he was just about used up. He knew the fumbling diplomats in Washington would criticize him; he missed Rachel's companionship; he wished to God he'd never left the Hermitage.

Up in the captured fort they were giving three cheers for Old Hickory. Andy stumbled out of his tent; crept off by himself under the palm trees. Nobody saw him go, and maybe that's why this episode isn't in the history books. The legend has it he sneaked off, deliberate, wanting to be alone.

Lord, he was tired! Downright fagged. It was cool in the twilight under the Florida palms, and he was glad to get away from the smell of gun-powder, the campfires, the scene of battle. Bats flittered in the dusk; strange birds called; lizards ran underfoot; the perfume of tropical flowers, and a big yellow moon coming up made it all like a dream.

It was wonderful country, but Andy wished he was home. His boots moved, dejected; he walked hang-dog, chin on chest, not at all like the victor of Horseshoe Bend, the general who'd just won a great battle.

When he came at last to a clear, moon-lit pool and sat down all by himself on the mossy bank, he glared at himself in the pool like a woebegone tramp.

Old Hickory! he was thinking. It's true.

His features, he saw, were as worn-out as his uniform; his eyes were like burned-out candles; he felt at least a thousand and three.

"I'm superannuated! I'm a gaffer! I've licked the Indians and the Spaniards, but I've still got to go to New Orleans and lick the Redcoats, and then this whole darned country has got to be set on its feet. All that I've got left to do, and here I've gone and passed forty. *Old* Hickory! I can't beat the calendar. I'm licked."

A paroxysm grabbed his stomach, worse than any he'd

had on the march, and he doubled over, groaning and cussing. His shoulder burned as if the bullet in it were a branding iron; his lung, damaged by Dickinson's bullet, pained in his chest; sweat blistered his forehead; he'd never felt as sick and old and ready to retire in his life.

"What's the matter, General?" a voice asked. "You look kind of poorly."

Andy stiffened up with a grunt. Was he hearing things? In this palm-glade by the pool he'd thought he was alone.

"You seem kinda done up, General. Anything wrong?"

Wrong? Well, there was something uncanny in the way this stranger came moving up out of the shadows, Indian-like, without disturbing a branch or a leaf. At first, staring right at him, Andy hadn't been able to make him out. He sort of blended with the moony foliage like camouflage; then he stepped toward Andy and stood squinting, still half-melted in shadow.

Hands to pistols, Andy hopped to his feet. "How do you know who I am, sir?" The stranger appeared all right, but he might be an enemy spy.

Only his eyes were friendly and sympathetic as he moved out into full moonlight; his drawl was easy-going and kindly. Although he wore the fringed buckskin of a woodsman, he wasn't armed. His hair was long and thick and silvery about his ears; he wore a chin-beard; on his back he carried a big pack, so that he appeared to Andy like some traveler who'd lost his way, some missionary maybe, or vagrant, a little like Santy Claus.

"Why, everyone knows you, General," he drawled. "Everybody knows Old Hickory."

ANDY WINCED LIKE he'd exposed a raw tooth. "Don't say

that name to me! And who are you, anyway, sneaking up on me like this? What do you want?"

He was in no mood for trickiness.

"Me, I don't hanker for anything." The stranger smiled. Then he gave Andy his name— Funny! Maybe it was Doctor Somebody or Brother Somebody or Uncle Somebody—afterwards, for the life of him, Andy couldn't recollect it, although it somehow impressed him at the time.

The stranger had an impressive way about him, too: genial, but somehow dignified; homespun, yet genteel— the air of a man who'd traveled widely and lived widely and wasn't at all abashed in the presence of famous generals. A man who'd been somebody or was going to be somebody—that sort of air. But whatever it was, it was hundred percent American.

"Nossir, I don't want a thing," he said in his smooth, easy way. "Kind of looks to me, General, like you're the one that wants something."

"Something!" Andy glared. "I want time! Time to lick the Redcoats and serve the United States and run my plantation and look after my wife. Time to do all the things I've got to do. Time! I thought I could beat it"—he shook his fist at his reflection in the pool—"and look at me! Crippled! Getting gray! Over forty! They call me Old Hickory. Why, a man my age—the way time flies—is soon in his dotage. Won't be long before I'm fit for nothing but a rocking chair."

A spasm of gripes doubled him, and he clutched his stomach, groaning.

For a minute the stranger regarded him from one squinted eye, head cocked, sympathetic, like a doctor diagnosing. Then he lowered his pack and after considerable rummaging fetched out a fine quart bottle.

"Got just the thing you want," he promised Andy. "Here. Try a swig of this."

Andy eyed the bottle, suspicious. It was shaped like a wine bottle; the liquor was clear as crystal. "What is it? Gin?"

"Try it," the stranger urged. "Make you feel fine."

Andy pulled the cork and sniffed. It didn't have any smell. He didn't favor patent medicine, but he was sick enough to try anything, and somehow the stranger wasn't to be refused. Andy took a quick gulp.

"Well!" he exclaimed.

"Feel better, don't you?" the stranger smiled.

Queerly enough, Andy did. In fact, he felt revived. "But"—he stared at the bottle in his hand—"it hasn't any taste. It's only water."

He glared at the bottle and then he glared at the stranger, who still smiled.

"So it is," the stranger nodded, sitting down on his pack and eyeing Andy through the Florida moonlight. "But it's probably the most wonderful water in the world. Notice how it settled your stomach? Cleared your eye? Gave you a lift?"

Funnier than ever—when the stranger said those things, Andy did notice marked improvement. The gripes went away and his shoulder eased up and all over he sort of limbered. He was even able to grin, because of the relief.

"Say!" he exclaimed. "What spring or well did you get this from? I did hear there was water in Florida with curative properties."

"Curative properties?" The stranger smiled in his easy way. "There's more than that in that water, my friend. It's Adam's ale of the purest vint. It's better than the nectar of the gods. It's what Ponce de Leon was lookin' for when he landed with his conquistadors at St. Augustine.

"That water, my friend"—and the stranger pointed impressively in the moonlight—"is from the Fountain of Youth!"

6

THE COLT BREAKS LOOSE

THE FOUNTAIN OF Youth! Andy Jackson darn near dropped the crystal bottle. He wasn't a great hand at reading, but every schoolboy knew how old Ponce de Leon came over from Spain in 1521 and explored all over Florida, looking for the marvelous Fountain.

"But I thought he never found it!" Andy cried. "I thought the Fountain of Youth was just a myth!"

"That's what historians tell you." The stranger nodded his shaggy head. "Old Ponce sailed off to Cuba and died in disappointment. Trouble was, like all those Spanish explorers he was more anxious to find gold. And gold and youth don't mix."

Andy's stare widened in astonishment at this strange, friendly-eyed man with the poetic locks and Yankee chin-beard and Southernish drawl, who sat there in the tropical moonlight, like a traveler on his pack, and talked so convincingly of this magic Fountain.

"But it's supposed to be magical." Andy stared. "A secret spring that you drink from, and it keeps you young. No historian would believe in that; it's not scientific! I thought it was only a fable."

"The historians don't know everything," the stranger

said. "Old Ponce was smarter than he realized, for he believed in the fountain, and only the blindness of gold-lust kept him from making the discovery. It's a fabulous fountain, all right—mighty secret and hard to find. But if you think it's only a fable, look at yourself, now, in the pool."

Well, Andy Jackson looked in the pool, and once more he was startled into almost dropping the bottle. Where he'd been haggard as a scarecrow before, sick and ready to give up, now fatigue was gone from his face, the blue fire was back in his eye. His orange hair crested up, fierce again; even his uniform looked better, as if the starch were back in his high military collar.

"Now I'm damned!" He jolted upright, squaring his lamed shoulder. "Why, I believe I *do* feel younger!"

From his reflection in the pool, he stared to the bottle in his hand, delighted. Then, as the miracle grew on him, he raised the bottle as if to drain it at a gulp; only the stranger's calm voice delayed him.

"Tut, tut, General! Take it easy. A little sip now and then, and only when you're in a tight fix; otherwise it's like an over-dose of medicine and it doesn't work. And I've only the one quart, you know."

Andy stared over the bottle a little shame-faced; in his excitement he'd forgotten his manners. "Sir, accept my apology. I'm acting like no gentleman." He corked the bottle with trembling fingers; then couldn't help holding it up in the moonlight and regarding its crystal contents with shining eyes. "But this wonderful fluid, and your hospitality in offering me a drink—it's all so confounded breath-taking and unexpected "

"Please." The stranger waved his hand. "Delighted to be of service to you, my friend. Don't thank me for the Fountain of Youth. It was just by luck I found it where so many other seekers missed."

"And it's here in Florida?" Andy couldn't believe his eyes, his ears, any of his senses. That rejuvenation from one little drink from the bottle had him emotionally dazed.

The stranger smiled gently at Andy's excitement. "There might be others in other places. I've got an idea there are. But they must've pretty near dried up in Europe and Asia—I reckon that's why Ponce de Leon came lookin' over here in America—and this particular one is down here 'mongst the Florida palms."

WAY THE STRANGER described it to Andy it was sort of a cross between a waterfall, a bubbling spring and an artesian well, hidden in a glade where you had to look sharp to see it—a beautiful palm-glade full of oleander and nightingales and trumpet flowers and hibiscus, like the Garden of Eden, American variety.

"Minute I drank some of that water I knew what it was. I'm not a boy, my friend, but when I quaffed from that fountain the years fell away. You won't believe me when I tell you how long ago that was." The stranger's eyes beamed at Andy, and he lounged back, folding his arms. "Do I look as if I'd come over on the *Mayflower?*"

Andy Jackson stared spellbound. "On the *Mayflower?*" he gasped. "With the *Pilgrims?*"

"That's right. Landed on Plymouth Rock, 1620. One of the original hundred and two. Of course I don't recall the landing none too well. You'll remember a child was born on that voyage—first real American, you might say. I was that child."

Andy's eyes were like moons in his head. "But that was almost two hundred years ago!"

"Since this is 1814," the stranger calculated, "it's a hundred and ninety-four, to be exact. Yessir, I knew John Carver and Billy Bradford and the Alden family and all of 'em. Remarkable, when you come to think of it."

Remarkable wasn't the word. Andy Jackson stared at the stranger, numb-struck. In the moon-drugged hush of that Florida palm grove the night air was saturated with mystery. If you're incredulous, think of Andy's sensations. He was Scotch-Irish descent, remember, and the Scotch-Irish are a hard-headed, skeptical race. He gaped at the stranger; at the crystal bottle clutched in his own hand. It seems he couldn't speak above a whisper.

"You're a hundred and ninety-four years old! And it's this water from the Fountain of Youth—"

"And you don't need much of it," the stranger interrupted. "As I said, an over-dose don't work. My first drink kept me going for a long while. Just swallow now and then when you feel kind of run down and petered out. A quart ought to last a generation."

And two quarts, *two* generations! Three quarts, *three* generations! Why, with this precious liquor a man could go on forever! No more worries about the calendar. With a swallow of this under your belt you'd have time to accomplish everything, overcome all the obstacles!

Andy's eyes blazed and his hand shook with excitement. He could beat the Redcoats now if it took years. He could do all those things he'd wanted to do. He could hardly wait to get started. And just a moment ago he'd been cooked, fagged out, ready for a fireside rocker, *Old* Hickory—!

A whole host of possibilities struck him. "This water! Is it good for race horses? And—and could you give it to your wife?"

"Afraid not. There's a special Fountain of Youth for women, and they say there's one up at Saratoga, New York, for thoroughbreds. This here is particular for men."

A shade of disappointment crossed Andy's face, but he couldn't help shouting, feeling younger by the minute.

"By Juniper!" he blurted. "And it's right here in America. Why, man, it's the greatest discovery in the universe! The Fountain of Youth! What anyone wouldn't pay for just this one bottle!"

The stranger pulled his chin-whisker, thoughtful, then stood up and shouldered his pack, beaming. "Sorry I only brung the one with me," he said lazy-toned. "But you follow my prescriptions and that quart should keep you young a lifetime. Seeing it's you, I'll sell it to you, General. It's a gift at five dollars."

Well, Andy had the money out of his pants quicker

than he'd ever made a wager on Truxton, and he slapped the five Continentals into the stranger's hand. He heard the stranger thank him, but he never heard the stranger go. His heart was pounding like a new-covered drum under his military buttons, and he stood there, half mesmerized, admiring the water in the crystal bottle.

Then when he looked up he was alone in the palm grove, and the buckskinned stranger with the Yankee chin-whiskers, Southernish drawl and traveler's pack was gone.

YESSIR, HE WAS gone like he'd come—without a sound, like a shadow that had been absorbed in the moonlight. Andy yelled a startled, "Hey!" but not even an echo came back through the Florida undergrowth. For a second Andy thought he'd been dreaming, but there was that bottle in his clutch and that feeling as if he'd shed twenty years. His wounded shoulder was spry. His rheumatics were gone. He felt heady as a cricket, as chipper as a stripling. It was marvelous how he'd recuperated after a swig of that wonderful water.

Andy stood there smiling to himself and thinking about what he could get done, now with a swig of this marvelous water every little while. He could go slam-bang straight ahead—and keep on going indefinitely.

Only there was just this quart in his hand—already he'd drunk a little from the bottle—and all at once it came to him he'd neglected to ask the exact location of the Fountain. In Florida, the stranger'd said. But Florida was a vast peninsula of everglades and wilderness; in 1814 much of it was still unexplored.

"Holy thumping Calliope! He didn't say where it was, and now I can't even remember his name!"

Andy stared about him in the moonlight in dismay. Had that fellow called himself Doctor Foster? Or had he given his name as Samuel? Was it one of those early Pilgrim names? Or was it Johnny Appleseed? For the life of him Andy couldn't remember, and now he came to think about it there'd been something mighty odd about that character with his Yankee chin-beard and traveler's pack, his buckskin clothing and Southern drawl.

Of course he could've been a Pilgrim in 1814 dress; but harking back to his schoolbooks, Andy was certain that child born aboard the *Mayflower* had been a girl. Had the stranger been ribbing him, or had he meant to imply that the child born on the *Mayflower* was the spirit of Democracy or something—like the Spirit of '76?

"Sweet Land of Liberty!" Andy breathed. "If there's such a thing as the Fountain of Youth, anything is possible. Now I wonder...."

But Andy Jackson didn't stand around wondering in Florida very long. The legend has it that he raced back to his headquarters with that bottle under his coat, as full of git and gol-dammit as a colt inspired by an electric battery.

There wasn't any holding him after that Battle of Pensacola. You can think it was that bottle of tonic, or you can think it was that victory filled him with fresh confidence, but it's historical fact how he set out from Pensacola like a whirlwind to catch the Redcoats at New Orleans.

7

PARADE OF FORSAKEN SOLDIERS

THE GERMANS TALK about a *blitzkrieg*. Well, the Germans moved like snails compared to Andy Jackson. Look at the facts. Bad enough today, the Gulf Coast roads of 1814 were sloughs of red glue. Andy's army wasn't mechanized. Cannon had to be pulled by horses and hand. Some places the men sank to their armpits, and like as not there wasn't any road at all.

Mud wasn't the only obstacle. December rains had turned the whole countryide to a bog. What's more, the whole nation was bogged that winter. From Wisconsin to Georgia the Redcoats had been victorious; enemy frigates, despite desperate naval resistance, fenced the Atlantic seaboard; sugar sold in Philadelphia at twenty-four dollars a pound; in New York a cup of coffee was worth its weight in quicksilver; New England wanted to secede from the Union.

In Washington the Treasury was almost bankrupt; poor James Madison was on the verge of a nervous breakdown in the charred ruins of the White House; the War Department was at its wits' end.

The War Department hadn't had many wits to get to the end of, and now it had good reason to despair. The

Redcoats were going to blockade and attack New Orleans with such an army as they'd never gathered before. Wow! what a force that was. There were ten thousand seamen, fifteen hundred horse marines, and nine thousand six hundred Redcoats all trimmed and polished up for battle.

Like an armada on a holiday, they sailed into the Mississippi delta. Soldiers and officers brought their wives with them, and new parade uniforms, and bands to play for dancing, not neglecting dozens of brass cannon and shiploads of ammunition.

In charge of the armada was General Sir Edward Pakenham, supposedly a genius. The Redcoats under his command were the best in the world. There were four regiments of that infantry that had chased the Americans out of Washington. And there was a brigade of Wellington's veterans all covered with medals—the veterans of Wellington, mind you, who'd beaten Napoleon Bonaparte.

Troops that had beaten Napoleon! You'd think Andy Jackson would've had a nightmare. He was riding through Mobile when he heard about it, and where anyone else would've run the other way, he headed for New Orleans like a limited express. All along he'd known the danger, and now it had arrived.

Scouts kept rushing up with reports that enemy ships were crowding into the mouth of the Mississippi, and dispatch riders brought frantic calls for help from the Governor of Louisiana. Everyone wanted Old Hickory. Even the War Department woke up to the fact that Jackson was their only hope, and promised him some Government supplies and a couple of measly regiments from the Regular Army.

Things looked mighty black when Andy unsaddled in New Orleans. Enemy frigates, brigs, gunboats and barkentines were picketing the river mouth thick as teeth in the mouth of a shark. The whole town was trembling. Creole ladies locked themselves in at night; planters huddled behind bolted doors; about the only ready defense was a swaggering, outlaw pirate named Lafitte, who'd offered to protect the harbor.

Andy Jackson, who'd been a Federal Judge, thought that was a fine state of affairs; he didn't trust the buccaneer at first. But when the fellow came to headquarters for an interview, waving a cutlass and swearing in French accents that he wanted to fight, Andy took him on. Parsons or pirates, he was in a bad way for recruits.

Working like fury, he could muster some five thousand men. There were his own Tennesseans, worn to rags by months of fierce campaigning. There were wood-choppers and trappers, some local soldiery with antique muskets, fishermen from the Louisiana bayous. Pirates and clerks, rivermen, halfbreeds, Negroes and wharf rats and Cajans from the swamps added to the militia. Big John Coffee was on hand as always, but his handful of cavalry and the few Regulars were lost in the shuffle like patches on Joseph's coat.

That was all Andy had to throw against that army corps of trained Redcoats and crack veterans who'd beaten Napoleon. First off, Andy put the port under martial law. No people or boats could leave town; street lamps out at nine;

anyone roaming the alleys after dark would be strung up as spies—but the citizens were scared indoors, anyhow.

TO SPUNK THEM up, Andy collected a fife and drum corps and marched his militia along the levee daytimes to the tune of *Yankee Doodle,* the *Marseillaise* and *The Girl I Left Behind Me.* Pirates, backwoodsmen, Indian fighters, ragtag and bobtail paraded out of step roaring songs at the top of their lungs, and the citizens pretty soon joined in. Supply wagons failed to come, but Andy had those Americans singing. *General Jackson,* wrote one witness at the time, *electrified all hearts.* Maybe our legend explains why. Anyway, it's a fact he had the whole town going like a Mardi Gras.

Through their telescopes off-shore, the Redcoat admirals and generals watched amused. There was that gangling backwoods general with his arm in a sling, riding up and down the waterfront like a madman. His troops were nothing but squirrel-hunters, by Jove! They were digging ditches along the mud flats—to drain the Mississippi, you'd think—and piling up absurd bales of cotton.

Now what were the jolly fellows doing that for? Soldiers digging ditches! It was all ridiculous like everything else in the War of 1812, and Sir Edward Pakenham had to laugh. Sir Edward didn't know about what happened to people who laughed at Andy Jackson. He didn't know Andy's record for demolishing such obstacles as blockades, and he'd never heard of such a thing as trench warfare.

Some preliminary skirmishing with Andy's sharpshooters around the swamps and bayous of the delta should have taught him better, for most of Andy's Tennesseans could put a bullet through the eye of a gnat at four hundred yards. Americans were weaned on cartridges in that frontier country. For all its scarecrow appearance, Andy's army could shoot.

But perhaps General Pakenham was too old to learn. Professional soldiers get sot in their ways. After a couple of minor landing parties had been rebuffed, Sir Edward became impatient. It was January, 1815, and Sir Edward was annoyed with further delay. His transport admirals were kidding him, declaring they could sail right up to the docks and capture the city with a thousand sailors.

Not wanting the navy to steal his thunder, Pakenham decided to attack. Frontal assault, by George! Ten thousand Redcoats and Wellington's veterans. March 'em across those mud flats in full regimentals—flags, bugles and ten thousand bayonets—and you'd scare that backwoods general and his rabble galley west.

Andy heard they were coming, and his eyes flamed like torches in his head. From Christmas to New Years he'd been on the go, combing the town for recruits and muskets, kicking sentries awake, riding between outposts and planning his reception for Sir Edward. He lacked cannon and munitions; he was living on handfuls of rice. But his receiving line was ready: between the mud flats and the city there was an old canal bed screened by cotton bales.

History says when Andy heard the Redcoats were landing, he clutched an old scar under his hair and cried, "I'll smash them, so help me God!"

The legend has it that he rushed out to his saddle-bags and took a nip from a crystal bottle.

All night he waited on the ramparts where the mud flats were blurred with winter fog. About dawn, like in the *Star Spangled Banner,* a rocket went off. Muffled drum-rolls seemed to clear the mist. Pale sunrise lifted the fog like a theater curtain, and to Andy and the watching Americans it seemed as if the beach was swarming with flocks of scarlet tanagers.

Like bright birds the Redcoats wheeled and maneuvered on the flats. Bugle-calls organized parade lines. Flags spread out on the breeze. Bayonets flashed. A ringmaster on a fine horse rode to the fore. General Pakenham and his mighty ten thousand came a-marching.

Andy exclaimed, "By God! that's beautiful!" unable to withhold his admiration. It was the 8th of January, 1815, and Old Hickory'd never felt younger in his life.

BUT THERE'S NOTHING legendary about the Battle of New Orleans. The historians pretty much agree that it was the gol-blamedest *blitzkrieg* in history. Some say Pakenham's battle-plans went wrong, and some say he just didn't know what lay behind those heaped-up bales of cotton. In any case he missed the guess. He was hit in the head before the battle was five minutes old. Was *his* face red!

Because what lay behind those bales of cotton were some of the best marksmen in America, plus the toughest, fightin'est general in the U.S.A. He waited till he could see the buckles on the Redcoats' belts, then his yell echoed out like a blast from Gabriel's trumpet.

"Fire!"

Wham! The Redcoats found out what was behind those cotton bales, then. Two thousand muskets sent a sheet of flame across the American ramparts, and the whole front line of that circus parade went down. Pakenham dropped from his horse like he'd been shot, which he had. His aide-de-camp was thrown to the ground. The parade jarred to a halt, gaped in consternation, then reformed its disciplined lines and came on.

At three hundred yards it caught a second jolt. *Wham!* This time it ran into cannon balls, chain-shot, pistol bullets and such a screaming volley of lead as swept aside the front rank like toy soldiers swept from a table. No one could say that Wellington's veterans weren't brave. Stubbornly they reformed their broken ranks; advanced again through the smoke-pall at a dog trot, bayonets fixed to charge.

Wham! Two hundred yards from the rampart they were hit by a blast like the crack of Doom. Then volley after volley the Americans fired; row after row the Redcoats went down. A splatter of musket-balls hit the bales of cotton with about as much effect as a spatter of rain; Andy's Tennesseans answered with a whistling hurricane that knocked down the Redcoats as if they were stalks of wheat.

At one hundred and fifty yards the carnage was awful. Redcoat General Keane was wounded in the neck. Redcoat Colonels Dale and Rennie fell like chopped trees. Panic overwhelmed the remaining officers. Corporals spanked their men with angry swords to drive them on, and found themselves spanking corpses. Advancing columns stumbled over hills of dead and wounded. Horses went down in droves. Grenadiers piled up like cord-wood.

Behind the cotton-bales the gun-smoke was thicker than a forest fire, so dense the riflemen could hardly see. Andy ordered the cannons to quit firing so's the snipers could have a chance. History admits there was something miraculous about Old Hickory in that battle—rushing up and down the ramparts, lively as a nipper on the Fourth of July. "Give 'em hell, boys!... Let 'em have a blast of grape!...

How you doin', Joe?… Hey, Pierre, keep your head down!… Hold your hats, boys, here they come again!"

He didn't keep *his* head down, you can bet. Eyes blazing, sword aloft, shouting orders, oaths and encouragement, he raced along the American line like fury unleashed. Imagine that energy after all those months of wilderness campaigning and starvation.

If the Fountain of Youth didn't keep him going, what did? And he must've been exposed to enemy fire a hundred times, yet not a bullet grazed him. But for that matter, there was something miraculous about that entire battle.

Those Tennessee Dirty Shirts and Louisiana squirrel-hunters were having a field day. All their lives they'd been practicing on redskins; what targets those scarlet tunics made! Even the local boys made good, and Lafitte's buccaneers were in their element. Crouching behind the cotton bales, they loaded, aimed and fired so fast that the shooting made one continuous, drawn-out roar.

In the teeth of that leaden tempest the army of Redcoats just withered away. Flags fell, shot to ribbons on their staffs. Bugles, knapsacks, canteens and the soldiers who carried them were riddled. A haze of crimson disaster hung over the mud flats.

One bayonet charge after another fell a-heap. Colonels pitched dead into the arms of astonished majors, who toppled, in turn, into the arms of dying captains. Exactly twenty Redcoats reached the American ramparts where the cutlass-wielding pirates of Lafitte choped them down to a man.

They say generals die in bed. Not General Sir Edward Pakenham. In that battle he died like a gentleman in front of his troops with more bullet holes in his uniform than anyone could count. General Gibbs died heroically in the same tradition. Seemed as if every general in sight was going to die in that battle. Excepting General Andrew Jackson.

Posed like a statue in a shooting gallery, he stood on a cotton bale scanning a scene which bore close resemblance to sunrise in Hell. Far as his eagle eye could see, the cane-bottoms and mud flats fronting New Orleans were strewn with enemy dead. Never had he beheld such a massacre. Any sportsman would've stopped it; and Andy, sporting to his jack-boots, gave the signal to cease fire.

As the Dirty Shirt guns went silent, brass bugles were tootling like off-key fishhorns in the dawn; what was left of ten thousand white-faced Redcoats retreated helter-skelter from the battle field.

"Providence!" Andy murmured. The legend says his own hand was in his overcoat pocket where a bullet had left two neat little holes but had missed the bottle.

Anyhow, he'd won the battle of New Orleans.

Time: 20 minutes.

Score: Redcoat losses—1,971. American losses—13.

8

FIRST OF THE FLORIDA TOURISTS

NOW SOMEONE MAY think this is anti-British propaganda: it is not. The British Government of 1812 was not the democratic British Government of today; neither was the American Government as democratic. The War of 1812 was a muddle: Many Britons favored the American cause, while in Washington, D.C. early in the war, Wellington's great victory over Napoleon had been publicly celebrated. As for Democracy, Andy had almost as many enemies in Washington as he had on the battlefield; and this account of New Orleans is a proof that historic facts can out-fantasy any legend.

But do you think the local big-wigs gave Old Hickory any credit for that victory? Well, the Louisiana Legislature voted to give him a new sword. The vote was vetoed by jealous politicians, and Andy didn't get so much as peanuts. They were sore he'd put the city under martial law and their saloons had lost some business. And if that wasn't gratitude, a long list of citations was read off to Andy's army—Andy's name wasn't even mentioned.

His name turned up, though. Where? In court where he was hailed for arresting a politician while the city was under martial law! He was accused of violating the Loui-

siana Constitution by putting New Orleans under martial
law to begin with. He was accused of consorting with
Lafitte. Andy was so mad he couldn't answer the prose-
cuting attorney, and the judge ended the case by fining him
a thousand dollars for contempt of court.

No one knows how Andy kept his temper then—he
must've been ready to blow up like an arsenal—but he
made a cool-headed speech and said he respected the Law,
and he paid the fine.

Even the captured Redcoat officers were better treated
than Andy. Generous as always, he returned to General
Keane his surrendered sword, and he saw to it that Sir
Edward Pakenham was pickled in a casket of alcohol and
shipped off with full honors to London.

Then while Andy was defending himself for the way he'd
defended New Orleans, why, word came from Washington, D.C. that peace had been signed in Europe between
Great Britain and America two weeks *before* the Battle of
New Orleans!

That tied it!

"So I lost those thirteen soldiers for nothing!" you can
imagine Andy roaring. "Here I've gone and run myself
ragged and lost a thousand-dollar fine to win a battle after
the war's already over!"

But the truth is, he'd won a couple of great battles
anyway. He'd beaten the Redcoats all hollow, and, what's
more, he'd conquered his temper. And despite the jealousy
of picayune politicians, the people of New Orleans gave
Old Hickory a great hand. Flags, bouquets and lady-fin-
gers waved at him from every balcony in town. Citizens
saw him coming and cheered.

News of Andy's victory reached Washington, and New England heard about him and decided it better not try to secede from the Union. Andy Jackson! Like a gale the name swept the country, waving all the flags from the Gulf to the Great Lakes. President Madison wrote letters of congratulation, and the War Department voted Andy a gold medal.

BEST OF ALL, Rachel wrote she was coming to New Orleans, and the whole town turned out to give Andy and his wife a Mardi Gras. The Louisiana politicians decided they better get on the bandwagon before they were lynched. Andy and his Dirty Shirts were showered with honors.

Parades, speeches and dinners astonished Rachel when she arrived. A great ball was whooped up in her husband's honor; Rachel was wide-eyed at the elegant Creole ladies, the magnificent ballroom, the brilliant assemblage. Such wines! Such wonderful cooking! Why, in the center of the table there was even a gold ham. If you don't believe it, look it up on the menu of that ball.

Andy, in a brand new uniform, sat opposite the gold ham, shining like Aladdin in front of his lamp. Rachel thought she'd never seen him as handsome. Everybody remarked how young he looked. The legend says that Andy heard the remarks and had to chuckle to himself. All the obstacles seemed to have melted away in front of him; the world was his oyster, that night of the Victory Ball, and Rachel was his pearl.

So if he was seen to slip a bottle out from under his coat-tails and sneak a few drops into his wine glass, it doesn't mean he was spiking his champagne. No wonder he danced that night in a way that's astonished the historians. After that dinner of gold ham, the fiddles struck up. "Come on!" Andy caught up Rachel with his good arm, and whirled her to the middle of the floor. Before or since in New Orleans there's never been seen such a dance.

Then out there in the middle of the dance floor with Rachel, something spoiled that party for Old Hickory. A Creole lady staring over her fan. Another laughing behind her jeweled fingers. Rachel didn't see 'em, thank God, but Andy knew. They were like those women in Salisbury who'd once looked down their noses at his homespun; only this time they were looking at Rachel.

Those who thought Andy looked suddenly played out from the dancing, didn't know. If lines came back into his face and his shoulders sagged a little, it wasn't from a ruined digestion and a duel-wrecked arm. Wilder and wilder Andy danced with Rachel, stopping polkas and gavottes and polite minuets to show New Orleans a frontier jig.

Maybe Andy spied the snob-faced young European dandy who was standing in a corner of that ball room. Maybe he wanted to show that particular young highbrow a thing or two.

Anyway, Vincent Nolte was there. Here's what he wrote in his famous *Memoirs* about the ball:

> *After supper we were treated to a most delicious pas de deux by the conqueror and his spouse, an emigrant from the lower classes.... To see these two figures, the general, a long haggard man with limbs like a skeleton, and madame la generale, a short fat dumpling, bobbing opposite each other like half-drunken Indians to the wild melody of* Possum Up a Gum Tree... *was very*

remarkable and far more edifying a spectacle than any European ballet.

Lucky Andy never saw those comments or there'd been one more fatality to the Battle of New Orleans.

You understand, after all, it wasn't Andrew Jackson who was old and haggard. It was snooty young Mr. Nolte—does anyone give *him* dinner parties today?—who was on his way to history's boneyard.

FOR THE WAR of 1812 was over, but Old Hickory was just beginning to fight. Fountain of Youth? Well, an ordinary human might've collapsed from what Andy'd been through—might've retired with his laurels and a veteran's pension to a hearthside of memories and security. It's true, when Andy got back to Nashville with Rachel he laid low for a spell. But even the historians admit he was only giving his shoulder and stomach a chance to recuperate.

Andy Jackson rested up by running the Hermitage plantation and racing his thoroughbreds on the Nashville track and writing military reports for the Government and answering hundreds of letters of fan mail.

Some of his fan mail needled him, for James Monroe had been elected President and the country was run by a whole new set of politicians. "Era of Good Feeling" it was called. That was a laugh. With Calhoun and Clay and Dan'l Webster in Washington, and Congress arguing the Protective Tariff, if there was much good feeling, why, not many people noticed it.

Andy kept pretty well out of this political pie, except for his little squabble with Winfield Scott. Seems that General Scott, U.S. Army, was outraged at Andy's refusal to put his

Tennessee Riflemen under command of the War Department. Scott spoke up in Washington and called Andy a "mutineer."

Andy didn't let that one pass. He let out a roar you could hear across the Great Smoky Mountains, and published a paper calling Winfield Scott a "hectoring bully" and one of the "intermeddling pimps and spies of the War Department." On top of that, just to keep in practice, he challenged General Scott to a duel.

Winfield Scott saved himself a premature funeral by ducking the challenge, allowing he'd rather die on a battlefield. Since he already had a duel on the schedule—some Kentucky editor who'd criticized his tactics at New Orleans—Andy scratched General Scott and loaded his pistols for Louisville. His friends argued like anything to get him to cancel that fight. Rachel was worried half to death. It just seemed like there was no holding Old Hickory.

Fact is, he was feeling livelier all the time there at the Hermitage; six months of peace and quiet, and he was ready to blow up from sheer spontaneous combustion.

"My goodness, Andy," the legend says Rachel said to him one night. "I can't understand what's come over you these days. Pacing up and down every minute you're in the house. And getting into that fracas with Winfield Scott—a man of your age!"

"Man of my age?" Andy snorted. "Why, a man ain't in his prime until he's fifty!"

"I know." Rachel put down her knitting and looked at him across her glasses. "Andrew Jackson, you've been drinking."

"Drinking, ma'am?"

"You can't fool me, General Jackson. I know you like a book. Ever since you come back from the South, I've known you was up to something. Way you look at your hair in the mirror, then pull down your lip, like you was a colt, and examine your teeth. Way you been doing your morning exercises lately. Man your age, trying to stand on his hands!"

"Now, Rachel—"

"You been bringing me flowers every morning, too; so first off I thought it was a woman—one of those Creole ladies, maybe, at New Orleans. Humph!" Rachel pointed her knitting needle. "I might've guessed you'd been tippling on the sly. Mandy Lou saw you in the stable only yesterday, and so did I, the night before you wrote that awful blast at Winfield Scott."

"Rachel!"

"I saw you!" She bobbed her head. "I opened one eye. Got up out of bed, you did, and snuck one from that bottle you've got hid behind the chimney corner. It's that prize applejack you brought back with you from the South. My land! you been mighty secretive about it, I must say. It must be pure corn alcohol, way you take on after you've had a swallow."

Andy scrooched his neck, uncomfortable. "Honest, Rachel. There's nothing in that bottle. It's only water."

"That's what I can't understand." She looked at him, puzzled. "That's what it tasted like to me."

"You drank some?" Andy wailed. "Some of that water?"

"I put the bottle back, you goose. If a wife hasn't a right to know what her husband's up to when he goes sneaking around like a boy with a key to some wine cellar—Heavens to Betsy!"

IF SHE HADN'T known Andy, she might've been scared. Andy was off like a pistol bullet, ricocheting up the stairs. Stubbing his toe on the top step, he swore like a cannonade, and the door-slam as he went into the bedroom almost brought the ceiling plaster down.

The bottle was there behind the chimney, and he fetched it out, shaky-handed. Not that he minded Rachel taking some. Never! If that magic liquor only worked with women, Rachel could've had it all. It was that black wench Mandy Lou that worried Andy. She'd been acting kind of young lately, too, according to reports around the plantation. Mandy Lou had a way of swallowing anything she could get her hands on, especially if it looked like gin.

Then, holding up the bottle in the candlelight, Andy Jackson breathed a sigh of relief. He'd been nursing it along like that stranger in Florida had instructed; the precious bottle was still three-quarters full.

"Good!" Andy measured it against the candle. "It's only a quarter gone."

Funny. Minute he said, "It's only a quarter gone!" why, it didn't seem to have as much in it as when he'd thought it was "still three-quarters full." He regarded the crystal bottle in sudden dismay. A quarter gone! He hadn't realized he'd used up so much. Maybe he'd been drinking it too fast. Why, at this rate, it would all be gone in about six years.

"And I haven't hardly done anything yet!" Andy exclaimed. "Sweet Land of Liberty! I've licked Poverty and the Redcoats, and I've done a fair job on my temper, considering. But there's still all that Scandal and Snobbery to be hammered down, and the U.S.A. to be put on its feet, and—Holy mackerel! If I had just one more quart of this Fountain—"

Just one more quart! The idea hit Andy like a bombshell. Why hadn't he thought of it before? A quart? Why not the whole Fountain?

Ten minutes later, his arms full of military maps, he thundered downstairs like a cavalry charge.

"Rachel!" His eyes were stars of excitement. "Can you fix me some lunch? And pack my uniform? I've decided to spend the winter in Florida."

"Andy Jackson, you've been drinking again. You know as well as I do, Florida doesn't belong to the United States."

"Mebbe it doesn't." Andy swung her up and hugged her, dancing. "But them Seminole Indians are raiding in Georgia—it's those crooked Spaniards in Florida who's sicking them on—an' President Monroe's been askin' me to campaign. I've just made up my mind. You take care of the Hermitage, Rachel. I'm going to add another State to the Union!"

9

ANDY CHOSE TO RUN

NOW NOBODY'S SAYING that Old Hickory conquered Florida on account of the Fountain of Youth. According to the legend, that Fountain had plenty to do with it; but the Spaniards had it coming to them, and if Andy hadn't done it, some other American would.

The records seem mighty confused about the issue; even President Monroe and the 1817 State Department officials were confused. President Monroe had told Andy to go ahead, but he hadn't expected Andy to go quite as fast.

The Creek Indians rose again. The Seminoles raised hell. Spain threatened to declare war on the United States. Everybody in Washington washed their hands of the affair, and everybody blamed Andy Jackson.

Obstacles, obstacles, obstacles! Andy, never confused about anything when he made up his mind, had gone down to Florida like a bullet. Now he found himself tangled up in red tape worse than the Florida swamps. First the Government would order him forward; then the Government would order him back. As usual supplies didn't come.

Not knowing how to march backward and forward at the same time, Andy marched forward. Quagmires. Diplomats. Jungles, Spaniards. Everything, including wild tribes of Seminoles, got in his way the minute he set foot in Florida.

Just take the weather. Well, if anyone was used to weather as an obstacle, Old Hickory was. Old Man River had staged an earthquake for his special benefit; all he had to do was set out on a march, and it would rain. So he was prepared for mud and earthquakes when he set out for Pensacola this time, but naturally, since he was going to Florida, Rachel had packed his summer underwear.

What happened? Why, the worst Florida season in history. Snow! Ice! Cold waves! Blizzards! Sneezing, coughing, waving their arms to keep warm, the Dirty Shirts limped after the Seminoles on chilblained feet. Red-nosed, shivering and fit to be tied, Old Hickory sat hunched in saddle, glaring at the spectacle of icicles on orange trees.

All that winter the cold wave went on. Then, stubborn as Old Hickory, himself, it went right on into the summer. There's never been the equal of it in the Almanac, and if you don't believe it, ask the historians and the weather bureau. For that was the year that *America didn't have any summer!*

Nossir, that's not any legend; it's Gospel truth. There wasn't any summer at all that year Old Hickory set out to mop up Florida. In New York, Fourth of July, the thermometer dropped to twenty. New England, middle of August, experienced hail-storms and zero. Snow blanketed some of the West, year 'round; crops didn't grow; robins went down to Rio to recover from pneumonia; they called it the Year of Eighteen-Hundred-and-Froze-to-Death.

But the legend has it that all that time he was mopping up Florida, Andy had his eye peeled for the Fountain of Youth. Around Pensacola he hoped to find some trace of that stranger who'd sold him that wonderful bottle three years before. Nights he'd ride off by himself through the icy swamps. Every scout he'd capture, he'd ask questions. Spanish renegades shook their heads about it; Seminole prisoners said they'd never heard of such a fellow.

"I've got to find it!" Andy swore to himself.

To keep himself in trim, now and then he'd sneak a pull from his precious bottle. With that bracer under his belt, he'd go out and knock down another obstacle. You didn't know it was Old Hickory who brought Florida into the Union? Well, he hanged two renegades and four Indian chiefs before the Spaniards knew they were at the end of their rope. He knocked the tar out of Pensacola for a second time, and he chased the Seminoles down into the Everglades where they've been paddling their canoes and selling souvenirs to tourists to this day.

Realizing it was up against a mighty tough customer, Spain decided to sell its Florida real estate for five million dollars. Figuring it was worth five million to get Andy home, President Monroe picked up a bargain. Andy was ordered to retire by the War Department; eyes bleak, fists clenched, he marched his Dirty Shirts back to Nashville.

Retire? And let those dopes in Washington run the country? Like hell! There was still a pint left in that crystal bottle, even if he hadn't found the Fountain.

The legend says he didn't find the Fountain because, that year, it was frozen over!

ALL RIGHT, HE thought he'd go back and look for it the next summer, but somehow he didn't get around to it. He didn't get around to it the following year, either. What with his race track and the Hermitage, he couldn't get away, and things kept happening that got in his orange hair—things that would've driven a brunette red-headed.

John Quincy Adams was one, and John C. Calhoun was another. Old Hickory conceived a dislike for those statesmen that was close to his aversion to poison ivy. It was New Orleans all over again, only worse. Instead of thanking him for running the Spanish out of Florida, the Washington politicians talked about having him arrested. The Cabinet held a meeting in which Calhoun proposed to have Old Hickory tried by a court-martial.

As a matter of fact, it was John Quincy Adams quashed the court-martial proceedings, but Andy didn't know that; choking with a fury he couldn't suppress, he blamed the Secretary of State, and hurled some molten epithets that John Quincy never forgot. That scared Calhoun into sending Andy a War Department citation. For a long time Andy thought it was Calhoun who'd befriended him; when he found out different, he was mad enough to burn.

Truth was, all the big men in the country were scared of Andy Jackson. Scared stiff. Open your mouth at him and he'd challenge you to a duel. Get in his way and he'd knock you flatter than a puddle. What kind of a man was it, anyway, who frightened rivers into earthquakes and overturned the seasons when he set out to campaign?

The legend explains some of it by that crystal bottle, doesn't it?

Well, Andy needed that bottle around 1824. He'd kept it well hid where the servants couldn't find it, you can bet. Like it was liquid gold, he'd cherished that dwindling quart; the legend has it that he took a few drops in a spoon, once a year, on his birthday. He hadn't found time to go back to Florida and look for more, and what goes swifter than youth? In 1823 he'd been all packed up to go to Pensacola, but Tennessee had sent him to the Senate. That's where he met Martin Van Buren.

"Andy." Martin caught him out in the lobby one day. "Andy, what you doing next year?"

"Taking a vacation," Andy said, thinking of the bottle. "Going to Florida. They're naming a town after me, down there, and I thought I'd go down and make a speech."

"Ah?" Van Buren's voice was soft as a kitten's paw. "If you like to make speeches, stick around. There's a Presidential election next year."

"Not interested," Andy said, short. "To hell with Presidential elections."

"Your opponent," said Van Buren, velvet on the emphasis, "your opponent would be John Quincy Adams."

Andy's eyes flared, blue-green. *"My—* John Quincy Adams?"

"Come on over to my hotel, Andy, and have a drink."

"Thanks, I got a bottle in my room. Anyway, I'm not drinking anything but water."

Snoopers, seeing Andy's shadow on the blind that night, probably thought Old Hickory was a toper. Editors said so afterwards, as they've said about every Presidential candidate before and since. Crack of dawn next morning, though, Andy met Van Buren, and Andy's eye was bright.

"Marty, I'll run. Huh! John Quincy Adams! Rachel's always been First Lady of the land, anyway, and it's time she was in the White House."

10

THE DARKEST HOUR

YOU DON'T RECALL Martin Van Buren, the Fox? Van
Buren, the Little Magician? He was nicknamed the Little
Magician because nobody in America had his talent for
pulling votes out of a hat; there wasn't a slicker campaign
manager in American politics.

Ever since he'd met Andy in the Senate he'd figured
Old Hickory would be a crackerjack Chief Executive. And
what's more fitting than Andy with his bottle of miracle
pop should tie up with the Little Magician?

John Quincy Adams beat Andy on that first time
around, sure. But the race was so close it had to be left up
to a judge's decision in the Senate. Then four years passed
so fast that John Quincy hardly had time to get his breath.
Eighteen-hundred-twenty-eight, and there was Old Hickory fresh as a daisy and stronger than ever, rearing, snorting
and champing at the post, ready to run again.

Andy wasn't the man to take a beating lying down. For
four years he'd been waiting for another crack at old John
Quincy. Training himself like he'd trained his thoroughbreds at the Hermitage—groomed by Van Buren, and
fortified by a swig from that crystal bottle—he was off like
a streak of lightning, first crack from the campaign gun.

Whack! He wasn't away from the post before he ran into mud. A great big blob of mud that hit him full and foul in the face.

In this case it was a political poster: a handbill printed in Philadelphia and pasted up on a Philadelphia brick wall.

SOME ACCOUNT OF THE BLOODY DEEDS
OF GENERAL JACKSON!

Like a funeral announcement, the poster was framed in black. Sixteen black coffins were pictured standing upright in two rows. The "bloody deeds" were listed: the men he'd challenged to duels, the two renegades he'd hanged in Florida, deserters and mutineers he'd ordered executed on the March to New Orleans. The poster accused him of lying, cursing, cruelty to the Indians. At the bottom of the handbill there was a gory account of his Nashville gun-fight with the Benton Brothers.

"Holy thundering cock-eyed Moses!" Andy's bellow, echoing across the city, like to put another crack in the Liberty Bell. "It's printed by some devil named Binns and it's signed by that viper, Tom Benton! Now, so help me Hanna!"—he whirled on his campaign committee—"you can cancel my speech tonight, Marty. I'm going to find those two blankety-blanks and lay them out in lavender."

Van Buren shied in alarm. "Take it easy, Andy. It's only a campaign poster."

"Then Adams is behind this! By heaven, I'll go down there to the capitol and put a bullet in him, too."

Only the Little Magician could've kept Old Hickory from boiling down to Washington with cocked dueling pistols; you can believe Van Buren had to use all his gray-gloved diplomacy to argue Andy out of it, too.

"John Q. Adams is a fuddy-duddy," you can imagine Van Buren soothing. "But he's a gentleman of sorts, and this mud-slinging is more likely the work of Henry Clay."

"Clay? His name'll be mud if I ever get my hands on him! I'll show him some bloody deeds!"

"No, no, Andy! Heavens! You can't shoot all your political opponents; it's not done, you know. Way to finish 'em is to swamp 'em in November. Go back to Nashville and leave 'em to me."

WHAT A JOB of temper-holding poor Andy had to do then! That coffin-decorated handbill was nothing to what followed in that muddy Presidential race. Whispered calumnies. Gossip columns. Public denouncements. Forged misstatements. For scum and muck-rakes that campaign reached an all-time low.

"Atheist!" the narrow-minded screamed. *"Never goes to church!"*—A lie.

"Friend of Aaron Burr!" howled enemy Congressmen. *"Plotted treason against the United States!"*—A lie.

"Ignorant frontier bumpkin!" jeered the uppercrust. *"Consort of the Dirty Shirts! Wants to start a class war! He'll turn Washington into a pig-sty! His father was a half-breed Indian!"*—A lie.

"Wants to devalue our money!" squalled the banks. *"Plans to bring on inflation! Schemes to build up his own investments!"*—Lies, lies, lies!

In the Hermitage under the shadow of the Great Smokies Andy Jackson foamed, gnashed his teeth and fought down his temper. Twice he wrote challenges to Henry

Clay; tore them up at the advice of persuasive Van Buren. Libeled and hounded and traduced, he groaned as in a torture chamber, his way to the White House blocked by such obstacles as he'd never confronted before.

He knew what was coming. He smelled the creature on its way. Tears stung, vitriolic in his eyes, when he read the newspaper account which called his mother a woman of the streets. Now, he thought, they've reached the final low. But they hadn't, and he knew they hadn't.

For just before election, there it was: the final infamy—that insidious, snake-tongued ghost which had hovered about the Hermitage since the day of his marriage, creeping and crawling to poison the heart of the Rachel Jackson.

In New York City an editorial: DO WE WANT A WIFE-STEALER IN THE PRESIDENTIAL CHAIR?

In Tennessee an underground handbill: *Andrew Jackson Is An Adulterer!*

In Washington an evil pamphlet: *Ought a convicted bigamist and her illegal husband to be placed in the highest offices of this free and Christian land?*

Big John Coffee held him. Martin Van Buren held him. Strong men pinned him to his Hermitage chair; took away his dueling pistols.

"Rachel!" Andy whispered. "They're talking about Rachel—my poor wife!"

"Soft, soft!" Van Buren counseled. "You can't kill them all."

"Sit tight," big John Coffee advised, pleading. "They're *trying* to get you into a duel, Andy. There's a thousand hired pistolmen in this country asking only to get a shot at you."

"You're going to win," Van Buren assured. "The scandal-mongers have only muddied themselves. You'll see. They're through."

History absolves John Quincy Adams from any part of that wicked mud-slinging; John Quincy Adams was a gentleman always, says history, and he wasn't aware of what was going on. Seems only just to mention that the infuriated Jacksonians did some mud-throwing on their own hook, although Martin Van Buren denied inventing the specious tale that John Quincy once sold a beautiful white slave to a cruel Russian nobleman and was a drug addict. John Quincy Adams? When Andy Jackson heard that white slave yarn he ordered his campaign manager to put a stop to it.

"I don't fight women like they do," he groaned. "God pity them if Rachel ever hears their scandal-mongering. She doesn't want to go to the White House, anyway. It would break her heart."

THEN WHERE DID Rachel hear the scandal? Historians don't quite know. Some say she had an idea of what was going on all along, although Andy kept the papers out of sight as if they were infected with leprosy. Others say the scandal came to her as a demon voice whispering under the Hermitage window. Maybe she heard it at the dressmaker's—gossips murdering her character in the next room, perhaps—at the dressmaker's where she'd gone to have a dress made for the Election Ball.

For Andy won by a landslide, a victory that should have put an end to political mud-slinging for all time. Nashville, cheering at the triumph of its famous citizen, decked itself in flags and planned a tremendous banquet. Bands played in the streets. Rooftops streamed banners and red-white-

and-blues. Dirty Shirt veterans paraded on re-review, while Andy, at the Hermitage, listened to astonishing last returns from Pennsylvania.

Perhaps Rachel, at the dressmaker's was listening to something else.

"*Her* in the White House! Why, she smokes a pipe!"

"That's nothing, Mayzie. They say as a girl she never *seen* a pair of shoes."

"First Lady! That's rich? Dumpy Rachel Jackson!"

Heart-broken, Rachel went home. No, she'd never wanted to go to the White House. She'd wanted Andy and the Hermitage, and declining, peaceful years on the old plantation. Historians tell you that as she climbed the stairs painfully to her room, she suffered a heart attack. Others might tell of a slimy, snake-tongued monster, invisible and malign, who reached through the walls to grip her by the throat.

She never left her room. Until the funeral. On the day before the Election Ball, she died. Nashville, mourning as few communities will ever mourn again, draped itself in black. Old Hickory stood at the death-bed, stricken.

Big John Coffee stood with him, and gallant Sam Houston, and other great Americans and long-true friends. They helped him bury Rachel at the bottom of the Hermitage garden where she lies to this day, mute victim of savage gossip-columns and the cruel, forked tongue of Slander.

"The righteous shall be in everlasting remembrance," preached the minister. "The widow and the orphan will long lament the death of Mrs. Jackson...."

Deaf with agony, Old Hickory stood as a blighted tree.

"May God Almighty forgive her murderers," he whispered afterwards. "I never can."

This part of our story is no legend.

11

THE STRANGER DIDN'T COME

SLOWLY, PAINFULLY THE old soldier picked himself up.
Old Hickory. The storm that had felled the only woman
he'd ever loved had left him bent-limbed, bowed, withered
inwardly, gray. Deep grooves furrowed his cheek. His eyes
stared through mist. As if overnight, his orange crest had
faded to gray salt.

But he was on his feet, upright, starting for Washington.
Legend or no legend, he had too much fierce vitality to stay
down, even when the heart in him was gone. He wanted
to lie down there in the Hermitage garden beside Rachel.
But the country demanded him; he was too good a soldier
not to answer the national call; too fierce a duelist to forego
the challenge of obstacles, to forget unpunished enemies.

So gaunt, broken-shouldered, haggard in his uniform
of mourning, he left the lonely Hermitage for the lone-
lier field of honor of the White House. His last day at the
Hermitage (according to the legend) as he wandered about
the empty rooms and gathered his spare belongings, he
came on the crystal bottle.

It was there behind the chimney corner, gleaming in a
nest of cobwebs—half full. He picked it up and stared at

the contents dully; then wheeled toward the fireplace in a sudden, violent impulse to smash it.

"Youth!" he snarled. "What do I want with it now?"

Then it occurred to him he might need it more than ever. He had still far to go and much to overcome: hosts of obstacles, hordes of unconquered foes. Did he down a swallow of that Fountain-water before starting? Nobody knows. But on the journey to Washington his shoulders began to square; color returned to his cheekbones; his iron jaw came up; once more the gleam of candleshine out of midnight returned to his deep-sunk eye.

Dan'l Webster, apprehensive, wrote a letter to a friend, advising that Jackson was coming to the capital: *My opinion is that when he comes he will bring a breeze with him. Which way it will blow I cannot tell.*

No wonder the District of Columbia was scared. Anti-Jackson politicians felt the breeze on its way and shivered in their boots. The breeze grew to a wind that went down the neck of Henry Clay who sold his furniture and got out of town for his health. One Congressman after another left town with the chills. John Quincy Adams' Cabinet members suffered palsy, nervous breakdown and vertigo. The breeze mounted to an icy gale; old John Quincy, himself, gave up his clock-like strolls on the White House lawn and nervously waited indoors.

It's historic fact that the gale attained almost cyclone proportions. Washington society locked its doors and shuttered its windows, hid the family plate and blew out of the city.

Listen to a society columnist who wrote a fashionable tittle-tattle at the time:

Never before did the city seem so gloomy... so many changes in
Society... so many families broken up, and those of first distinc-
tion. Drawing rooms in which I have so often mixed with gay
crowds, distinguished by rank, fashion, beauty and talent, now
empty, silent, dark, dismantled. 'Tis melancholy.

Just in case you're weeping for all this fashion, beauty
and talent, remember the gaunt, black-garbed President
entering the city for his Inaugural. Did he go, then, through
Washington with horsewhip and pistols as they'd expected?
Did he thrash, as he'd ought, through the hotels and drawing rooms, shooting down poison-pen politicians and flay-
ing to crumbs those members of the gossipy uppercrust?

Like a soldier and like a President he rode on horseback
down Pennsylvania Avenue. A vast throng, unhatted, stood
in awe as he took the oath of office and made the speech
of a great President and statesman. There'd been enough
death in that election for Andrew Jackson. It was life that
counted now—life for the United States, for American
Democracy.

They say he paused in his speech several times and
refreshed himself with a sip of water. He must have had
that crystal bottle with him, all right. Only a young man
could have done what Old Hickory did after his inaugural address. He invited all his friends to the White House
and threw a party.

STARS AND STRIPES, what a party that was! Never previously or afterwards did Washington see the like. Old Hickory had friends; he never knew he'd had so many friends.
For days they'd been gathering in the city, coming afoot, by

boat and on horseback from all the corners of the United States, it seemed—especially the frontier.

Why, there were men he hadn't seen since he'd studied Law in Salisbury, men he'd seen last when he crossed the Great Smokies as a D.A. on his way to Nashville. Pioneers were there in coonskins. Indian fighters with long beards and long rifles. Trappers and scouts, river-men and teamsters, hunters, wood-cutters, traders—all the buckskinned, homespun early Americans who'd been able to ride or hike east from America's back woods.

On the march to the White House the Dirty Shirts led the parade—veteran militiamen who'd been with Old Hickory at Horseshoe Bend, Pensacola, New Orleans. Friendly Indians capered with Mississippi settlers, whooping it up for Big Chief Andy. Bog-trotters, bayou Cajans, fishermen, half breeds, anybody and everybody who'd swung an axe, skinned a cougar and blazed a trail piled into the White House and fought to shake Andy's hand.

"Hoo-ray for the President! Hoo-ray for Old Hickory!"

Shouting, cheering, waving their battered caps, they snake-danced through the reception halls, whooped and jigged in the parlors, swarmed around Andy in the ballroom. Doormen were thrust aside by elbows that could knock the teeth from a panther. Office-seekers, tophatted politicians, lame-duck Congressmen and silk-stockinged flunkies were jostled out of the way.

"Let 'em in!" Old Hickory cried. "Open house. There it is, boys." He pointed at the loaded banquet tables.

Can you picture that rush of hungry frontiersmen attacking those banquet tables like they'd charged at Horseshoe Bend? Woodsmen in buckskin and shaggy-whiskered pioneers sashaying around the ballroom, yelling like the Wild West?

Cakes and pastries disappeared as if at a single gulp. Kegs or rum and whiskey were drained quicker than they could be replaced. On the White House lawn the Dirty Shirts pellmelled with the horseplay of a rodeo. Such socialites and gentry as had dared appear at the reception were shocked to their elegant bootstraps by the sight of an Indian scout eating ice cream with a gold spoon, and the East Room racketing to *Turkey in the Straw, Yankee Doodle (unabridged edition)* and the *Chicken Reel.*

Sure, there were some fights. Sure, some gilt chairs were smashed. What's a rough-and-tumble between high-spirited trail blazers and lumberjacks? What's a gilt chair-leg to a soldier who's risked his own hairy ones on the battle field?

Yes, they squirted tobacco juice on the carpets; leaned sweaty shoulders on the wallpaper; tracked their muddy clodhoppers, moccasins and cavalry boots across waxed floors. They hooked their spurs, accidental, on damask draperies; fell over footstools, sofas and escritoires; smashed about ten thousand dollars' worth of china and glassware, and raised holy hob.

It was their day. It was their house. Andy was their President. Not very often those frontiersmen had a holiday, and when they did they sure went to town.

And élite? Well, perhaps those frontiersmen didn't know how to enter a drawing room, but they knew how to grip a great man's hand. If they were short on table manners they were long on courage and kindness. They were the lifeblood and sinew of the nation, the aristocrats of the West, the "first families" of the Republic. Maybe they brought some civilization to Washington, those frontiersmen.

Suppose the East Room did have to be redecorated, gilt chairs repaired, every carpet in the White House beaten for a week? What's smashing a set of dishes—a thousand sets!—to smashing the reputation of innocent people?

NO ONE KNOWS a man's innermost thoughts, but Andrew Jackson, seventh President of the United States, that night might've been thinking some of those things. Crippled from hours of hand-shaking, deafened by the cheering, tired from the strain of his inaugural speech, he was weary to the point of exhaustion.

But he'd won a tremendous victory against an enemy of Democracy that evening, a victory as decisive as the Battle of New Orleans. Under the clodhoppers, cavalry boots and moccasins of his White House guests, Snobbery was pulverized. Planned or not, he was even with that hypocrite for all time.

Some say Old Hickory retired early, fagged out by the festivities. They don't know he was the youngest frontiersman of them all. They say that, exhausted in his lonely bedroom, he groped into his luggage for a bottle of medicine They don't know this legend about Old Hickory.

For the legend has it that one reason he invited those frontiersmen to the White House was in hopes of seeing that stranger he'd met long ago in Florida. And the bottle wasn't medicine, but crystal water from the Fountain of Youth.

He was going to need it now, more than he ever had before....

12

THUNDER ON CAPITOL HILL

TWO TERMS OLD Hickory served as President. Eight years of conflict and obstacles. If he didn't have that Fountain-of-Youth bottle with him, what accounts for the drive that kept him going?

Few Presidents of the United States had more problems than Andrew Jackson. His own party split into a hundred angry factions, for the slavery problem was growing and the South was snarling at the free North. In his famous Kitchen Cabinet the members were at loggerheads; states rights and tariff were bones of furious contention; and it was about this time that Old Hickory discovered it wasn't John Quincy Adams who'd tried to railroad him on the Florida real-estate matter, but his own Vice President, John C. Calhoun.

Lucky for Calhoun that laws had been introduced against dueling. Andy was wild at learning of Calhoun's treachery, and if kid-gloved Martin Van Buren hadn't stepped between, there'd have been a knock-down and drag-out fight.

The Little Magician was Andy's Secretary of State and there were times when he had his hands full. Still and all, the country didn't fall to pieces under Andy's Presidency as his opponents had sworn it would.

Dapper Van Buren, as deft and quick-thinking as any man in the government, had to marvel at Old Hickory's drive and ability. They were a pair, Andy Jackson and his Secretary of State. Coming to the White House in a varnished carriage, Van Buren, the picture of fashion in tall hat, buff morning coat and snuff-colored breeches, would find Old Hickory flat on his back, smoking his pipe in his shirtsleeves on the White House lawn.

"Ah, Mr. President, you're looking fine this morning. After that ruction in Congress yesterday, I don't know how you stand it."

"Huh! I'm learning how to stand a lot of things, Van. These office-seekers swarming around here! Pressure groups and delegations. Everybody wanting something *from* the government, but no one willing to *give* it anything! Damned selfish louts! One got mad at me yesterday and pulled my nose."

"What?" Van Buren gaped in consternation. "Really?"

"I sat there in my chair and took it," Andy growled. "Ten years ago I'd have caned him out of the house. I think at last I've got control over my infernal temper."

That was another handicap conquered; Old Hickory had put up a long, hard fight to curb that dynamite temper of his.

IF THAT CRYSTAL bottle lasted long enough, Andy reflected, he'd be able to conquer all the obstacles in the world while he was President. Not just his own, but all those hampering the nation, then he could turn the country over to his successors and America would be able to run

itself. Dreaming of the nation's future brought him back to the present; he couldn't lie here on the White House lawn and smoke all day.

"Now that new Treasury Building," he sat up and asked Van Buren. "Is it finished yet?"

Van Buren fussed with his gloves. "That's one of the things I came to see you about, Andy. You see, they haven't yet started to build it."

"Haven't started to build it?" Andy whipped to his feet, bellowing. "I authorized that Treasury Building months ago! Great thundering golden Jehoshaphat! Doesn't anyone ever do any *work* for this government? What's the matter with those architects? Must I put up the bricks myself?"

Not waiting for Van Buren's answer to smooth him down, he darted to get his hat, coat and stick, and went hiking down Pennsylvania Avenue, pipe smoke chugging from his teeth like one of those new-fangled steam engines. Pennsylvania Avenue was straight as an arrow in those days, but it wasn't when Old Hickory got through with it that morning. Glaring down its mud-rutted vista, he could see a group of government architects standing under a shade tree, chewing their pencils, bewildered, over blueprints. Straight down the middle of the avenue Andy hiked; then he pulled up before the building contractors, mad as a hatter.

"What's all this gold-bricking going on around here?" he roared. "Where's the Treasury Building? Why the devil is there all this delay?"

"We're suh-sorry, Mr. President. We don't know where—uh—you see, we can't decide where to lay the corner stone."

"Why," Andy thundered, stabbing his walking stick down whack into the middle of Pennsylvania Avenue. "Lay it here!"

Brother, that's where the corner stone of the Treasury Building was laid; if you don't believe it, go to Washington and look. They had to uproot the boulevard and make traffic take a detour. That's how Old Hickory did things, though.

Lazy Federal employees and Governmental time-wasters weren't enjoying holidays under President Jackson. Pennsylvania Avenue wasn't the only thing in Washington he put a crimp in, either. One of the strangest wars in American history broke loose while Andy was President—if he hadn't been a veteran in just that kind of warfare he might've been thrown for a loss.

John Henry Eaton, handsome as any man from Tennessee, was an old friend of Andy's who'd worked hard to see Andy elected. Major Eaton was a soldier and a gentleman, and not long after the election Andy sent for him.

"Major," said Andy, "I've been talking it over with Van.

I'd like some young blood in my administration, and I want
you in my Cabinet."

As what patriot wouldn't be, Eaton was delighted. Then
he sobered gravely, thinking it over. "Don't know as I can
accept the honor, Andy. You see, I—I—I'm intending to
get married."

"And why not?" Andy held out his hand. "Congratulations! Do you think that would unfit you for a Cabinet appointment? All the other Cabinet members are
henpecked husbands!"

"That's just the point." The dashing major's eyes were
gloomy. "You—you know how some women are. I'm going
to marry Peggy O'Neale. She—well, she's not exactly
accepted in society."

Now you can imagine how much difference that made
to Andy Jackson! He'd heard the gossip about Peggy
O'Neale—that her father ran a tavern; that she danced on
Sunday; that she'd been married to a naval officer who'd
supposedly committed suicide because he was jealous of
her popularity. Why, Peggy's story compared almost with
Rachel's. After the hell he, himself, had been through,
thinking of the tortures Rachel had suffered, it took Old
Hickory about half of a split second to advise his young
friend about Peggy.

"If you love her, Major, marry her at once. In case there's
any gossip, she'll be the wife of my Secretary of War. That
ought to shut their tabby-cat mouths!"

JUST LIKE ANDY to make Eaton his Secretary of War as
a wedding present. Eaton and Peggy were married by the
Senate chaplain, and, excluding Rachel, Andy thought
he'd never seen a prettier bride. Whole trouble was, Peggy

O'Neale was the gayest, liveliest, best-looking woman in Washington.

Bang! The wedding march should've been played by a military band. Every Mrs. Grundy in Washington let loose at Peggy with both guns. The battle of the drawing rooms was on. The explosion went off like dynamite under every rocking chair in the city. A terrific conflict broke loose around Old Hickory and the wife of his Secretary of War.

Poor Peggy. The wives of the Cabinet members snubbed her. She was snooted, black-listed, insulted, piously scorned. Ladies gave her the business at garden parties; failed to recognize her on the street; forgot to invite her to the sewing circle; left her wall-flowered at official dinners and receptions.

"Go to tea with that hussy?" Mrs. Calhoun was heard to scoff. "A notorious female whose father runs a tavern? La!"

"*I'm* not going to call on her!" agreed Mrs. Navy-commander Patterson. "Just let me catch my husband conversing with that bold minx, either."

"What else could we've expected with Andrew Jackson as President. I'm not even going to the White House reception."

Peggy fought back, deft and game, meeting every attack with feminine skill. New hats. Smart Paris frocks. The latest thing in parasols and shoes. When snub-nosed ladies didn't call on her, she called on them, bravely counter-attacking the rocking-chair brigade.

"Hell'n high water!" Old Hickory hopped out of his presidential chair when Van Buren worriedly reported this state of affairs. "So these grimalkins have got their claws in Peggy! Well, she's a fine, courageous, good-figured woman, and I won't have these hypocritical old cats maltreating her! By Glory! I showed the men of this country what I thought of their high society; now it's time I showed the women. Van," his fist crashed on the presidential desk, "I'll escort Peggy Eaton to the White House reception myself."

The Little Magician looked startled. Then he beamed.

"And to think the Red Coats only brought ten thousand troops to New Orleans! Andy, you beat the Dutch! My own compliments to Peggy Eaton when she visits the White House. I'll make immediate arrangements to sit beside her at our first ambassadorial dinner."

But the Red Coats were one thing, and the red faces of society women were another. Staunch allies though they were, President Jackson and the Little Magician couldn't save the day for Peggy. Washington rocked with the din of whispering tongues. The row had repercussions in foreign embassies and the Kitchen Cabinet.

Old Hickory raged. This was what would've happened to Rachel. Cheated of their prey, the scandal-mongers were venting their fury on innocent Peggy Eaton.

In a battle with guns and troops Andy could slap down the champion generals of Europe, but a war of tea parties, upturned noses and hairpins had him outskirmished from the first. All his life he'd been at a loss surrounded by a lot of women. An Amazon war had him baffled. The viragos stormed the White House. Petitions! Delegations from such and such a church. Letters from sewing societies! To top it all, his own niece Mrs. Donelson, who'd come to Washington to act as his official hostess, joined forces against Peggy.

History doesn't record Andy's exact words to his niece

on the subject, but you can bet that when Andy found out she'd been snubbing Peggy with the rest, he said plenty. Packed her up and sent her back to Nashville special delivery. What a tea-pot tempest that raised! And it wasn't just a tempest in a tea-pot, either. There were a lot of underground strings being pulled in Washington at the time—a fight with the banking system was brewing, and worst of all there was a rumble in the South, talk of Civil War. It was a long way off in Andy Jackson's time; but there were men back then who knew it was coming.

"Damnation!" Old Hickory swore to Martin Van Buren. "All this Peggy Eaton trouble is driving me to a temper. You can horsewhip a man for slander—I'd prefer to shoot him!—but how the devil can you silence a lot of interfering, scandal-mongerin' women?"

"It's a conspiracy," Van Buren declared. "A plot cooked up by your political enemies. They think Peggy's snubbing will ruin Major Eaton's prestige, wreck your Cabinet and undermine your administration. Have you noticed Mrs. Calhoun is behind a lot of it?"

"What? Mrs. Calhoun? So it's Calhoun, hiding behind his wife's skirts—" Old Hickory broke off in a cannonade of oaths, then struck the desk. "It's a threat to the nation, Van. That's what it is! By heaven, we've got to do something about it."

"Major Eaton's the answer, Andy. He'll have to resign."

"Never!" Old Hickory whipped to his feet. "Let Peggy and her husband bear the brunt of this scandal? I'll hang the whole Kitchen Cabinet before I'll demand Major Eaton's resignation!"

The Little Magician smiled softly, fussing with his

gloves. "I'll hang 'em for you, Andy, myself included. I'm Secretary of State and I'd like Major Eaton as our minister to Spain—that'll take care of him and Peggy, honorable as can be. As for me, I'll accept the ambassadorship to Great Britain. You won't have to ask for Major Eaton to leave the Cabinet. *I'll* resign as Secretary of State; then the rest of the Cabinet will automatically resign."

No, they didn't call Van Buren the Little Magician for nothing. What Calhoun called him isn't on record, but what Old Hickory thought of him is. In Spain, Peggy Eaton and her husband became great friends of the queen—Peggy's daughter ended up by marrying a Spanish duke. Van Buren put himself in line for the Presidency, and Old Hickory wondered if at last he couldn't take that vacation to Florida.

SOMEHOW HE NEVER got around to it. Somehow there was always some new obstacle in the way. Legend aside, Old Hickory didn't get any chance to explore the Everglades and Lake Okechobee territory for the Fountain of Youth while he was President.

The legend claims he'd come to depend a lot on that crystal bottle, too. In the White House he had it hidden under his desk, and every now and then when he felt low in spirits or slowing down, he'd refresh himself with a drop. There's plenty of evidence to support that legendary claim.

There were obstacles to knock down while Andy was President—obstacles to American Democracy. Only that wonderful Fountain-water could've kept him going. He fought to knock out railroad speculators, stock-market gamblers, jugglers in national real estate. Steam cars had come chugging across the American scene; the West was booming; thousands of phoney bond salesmen and flashy promoters mushroomed across the country; Old Hickory went after these wildcats with both guns.

He needed that crystal bottle for refreshment in 1830. Dark clouds over the South, black as slavery. Wind stirring the cotton fields, whispering, "Secession!" Low thunder echoing in Washington, rumbling in Andy's hearing as: "Calhoun! Calhoun!"

They were attending a great banquet given in memory of Thomas Jefferson—Old Hickory and his shadowy Vice-President. Calhoun, called on to give a toast, spoke soft in his insinuating Southern drawl.

"The Union," he raised his glass. "Next to our liberty, most dear."

Old Hickory was on his feet like a thunderbolt—something more than wine in *his* glass. Blue-green lightning flashed from his eye, fixed hard and deadly on Calhoun.

"*Our* Union!" his voice cut the hush like a sword. "*It must be preserved!*"

So there was the opening skirmish—the sly, subversive dagger-thrust countered by the flashing, army sabre—the opening skirmish in the worst, deadliest war of all Old Hickory's fighting career.

The Union, human rights, American Democracy—or dis-union, states rights, slavery! Well, Old Hickory never had to stop one second to ask himself which side he was on. Above all, the American Republic must be saved, and those who threatened it now were more dangerous than the Red Coats, redskins and red-faced scandal-mongers ever were.

WHAT A FIGHT Old Hickory put up, then! The struggle raged through Congress; shook the ground under Capitol

Hill. Unexpected allies joined him: Daniel Webster, and his former enemy, Tom Benton. Old animosities, private duels, the petticoat war were forgotten as Andy called for unity and rallied all true patriots to save the Republic. Rising in the Senate, Dan'l Webster made a great, ringing speech for the Union, and the northern states cheered for freedom and liberty.

But the South remained sullen and gathered forces against Old Hickory. Brilliant, impassioned men bent on preserving an easy way of life and holding on to an outworn institution. Don't think they weren't dangerous fighters—Robert Hayne, Tyler, Randolph and the Southerners. Every obstacle they could think of to throw they threw across Old Hickory's path. Calhoun was their man, and Clay the Compromiser. In the 1832 election when Old Hickory's second landslide turned Clay's name to mud, the Southerners were fighting desperately for Henry Clay.

In 1833, Calhoun, finished as Old Hickory's Vice President, tried a death blow at the Union. Masking the slavery question behind a protest against the tariff, South Carolina voted openly to secede. Charleston was aflame with talk of rebellion. Bonfires burned in the streets. Wild young horsemen, handsome with pistols and sideburns, jeered the United States flag. On the shirt fronts of slave-holders, plantation overseers and tall-hatted politicians there appeared a sinister medal. *John C. Calhoun—For First President of the Southern Confederacy.*

To Old Hickory that meant just one thing. In the White House, he unpacked an old, threadbare uniform; then he went to his desk and picked up his official, eagle-feathered pen. As President of the United States, he was Command-

er-in-Chief of the Army—Calhoun nor no other South-
erner could have faced the candleshine in his eyes as he
wrote out that historic message.

> *Should Congress fail to act… and South Carolina oppose the*
> *execution of the revenue laws… I will, in ten or fifteen days at*
> *farthest, have in Charleston ten to fifteen thousand troops… and*
> *twenty thousand, or thirty, more in the interior. I have a tender of*
> *volunteers from every state in the Union. I can if need be, which*
> *God forbid, march two hundred thousand men in forty days to*
> *quell any and every insurrection that might arise. I repeat to the*
> *Union men, fear not. The Union will be preserved!*

He didn't need to march two hundred thousand men in
forty days. He didn't need to march them at all. Did you
know Andrew Jackson won the first battle of the Civil
War? No, the history books start the Civil War in 1861,
but Old Hickory was the reason why. Just the thought of
him marching at the head of two hundred thousand Union
troops stopped the southern secessionists for thirty years;
Calhoun was never the first president of the Confederacy
or anything else. March 15, 1833, South Carolina voted
to remain in the Union. Queer, when you think about the
legend. March 15, 1833, was Old Hickory's sixty-sixth
birthday.

13

HE SHOOK THEIR HANDS

SIXTY-SIX? HE PUT down the spoon and straightened his shoulders and (according to the legend) hid the crystal bottle in its accustomed drawer. He felt as rambunctious as a boy. Clay—Biddle—Mrs. Grundy—Calhoun—all beaten. One after another he'd smashed the obstacles, his enemies were whipped; the Union was saved.

By thunder, if he kept on long enough he might even learn to spell. Wasn't anything he couldn't accomplish with that crystal bottle to give him time. By using it mighty sparingly, a drop on special occasions and a spoonful every birthday, what was to stop him from going on and on and on?

Outside on the White House lawn the bands were playing; crowds thronged and cheered on Pennsylvania Avenue; all over the nation they were toasting his name; he was the greatest man of the country. Matter of fact, he could have a third term, a fourth, a fifth. What was to stop him from being President as long as that bottle lasted? Should he be candidate in the next election, or shouldn't he?

It was a problem that hadn't quite occurred to him before, and pretty soon he was on his feet, pacing. If the scene isn't recorded in history, it's because he was all by himself; he'd shut himself in his office to have his birthday spoonful of tonic, and he was always careful, as the legend points out, not to let anybody see that priceless bottle.

You can bet he kept it under lock and key, and securely corked, for it had a way of evaporating. Anyhow, there was still a half pint left of the sparkling water, and he got to calculating how long and how far it could carry him. It was wonderful, when he came to think of it. Why, when this half pint was gone, he could hustle down there to Florida and find the Fountain itself. He could go on forever, then, couldn't he? Right on, brisk, to eternity.

"Eternity!" he breathed. "There isn't anything I couldn't lick in that length of time—nothing I couldn't do!"

He'd go on getting wiser and more capable year by year. He'd have the wisdom of Moses backed by the experience of Methuselah and the nerve and dash of a young Alexander to put that wisdom and experience into action. That would be a wonderful combination. America would need such a leader, too. America was growing by leaps and bounds; its problems getting more and more complicated.

A tap the door. Old Hickory, jarred into the present, wheeled impatiently. "Who's there?"

"Martin Van Buren to see you, Mr. President."

"Please have him wait."

Van Buren—should he tell him about all this? A decision to go on as President? He'd planned to turn over the office to Van, but would Van be able to handle the job? He'd showed gray at the temples since his ambassadorship to England; the Little Magician wasn't as young as he'd use to be. Would it be safe to leave the nation in his gloved hands?

"I think," Old Hickory thought, "I'd better stay." And then, buttoning his collar to receive his more formal guest, his fingers touched something he always wore there under his throat. Never, since the day she'd given it to him, it hadn't been there. A little miniature of Rachel.

As always it misted his eye to look at her picture. And in that mist the visions of grandeur faded; the future altered; it was as though suddenly a tinsel veil had been torn away, and he was looking at something he hadn't admitted before.

For there, dark in front of him, was one obstacle he'd never be able to surmount; not if he lived to be ten thousand, not if he lived to a millenium. The obstacle of his loneliness—the emptiness of his life without Rachel. He couldn't bring her back; all the wisdom, power and experience of the world couldn't bring her back; and then and there Andy Jackson knew that to go on and on without Rachel would be intolerable.

His other friends, too, would pass. Big John Coffee. Sam Houston. Van. His adopted children, his nieces and nephews all would be gone. Familiar faces would disappear, and as they disappeared, he'd be dealing with a new generation, new people who would want to handle their new problems for themselves. In this endless, changing world of continual conflict and eternal, youthful endeavor, only his love for Rachel and his loneliness would remain permanent, and he'd be hanging on like some unnatural season, going on like a river that never reached its destination.

"Rachel," he whispered, only loud enough for the miniature to hear, "I've been a fool. Any man's a fool who wants to live beyond his time."

Crossing square-shouldered to the desk, he took out the

crystal bottle and slipped it into his pocket. His mulatto servant answered the bell-pull.

"George, start packing my heavy luggage; I intend to leave Washington this spring and go on tour. Meantime bring two glasses of wine. And then send in Mr. Van Buren."

WELL, ANY HISTORY book can tell you about Andy Jackson's presidential tour. Like Old Hickory, himself, it was a national triumph, and like Old Hickory it was full of slapdash, hair-trigger surprises.

First off, on a river-boat in Virginia some crazy young galoot of a dismissed naval officer stepped up as if to shake hands, then tried to punch the President in the nose. Cane flailing, Old Hickory chased the rascal around the deck, roaring to high heaven that he'd slay him. The fellow jumped overside, and Old Hickory leaned on the ship's rail, panting fire and brimstone and fighting down his temper. He fought it down, too. Friends rushed up to help, but Old Hickory wouldn't let them chase after his assailant and kill him.

That set the pace for the triumphal journey; as one of the Cabinet members said afterward, the incident seemed to have set Andy's "blood in motion." It was certainly in motion in Philadelphia where the Quaker City gave him a tremendous hand. On a white horse he rode past the Liberty Bell, doffing his cocked hat so often his forehead got badly sunburned; for five hours he paraded through the cheering crowds.

In New York the mobs were so dense they broked down the bridge from Battery Park to Castle Garden, half drowning the presidential party. For hours the parading and celebrating lasted; Old Hickory wrote to a relative he'd bowed to more than two hundred thousand people that day.

Up in New England where he journeyed, the ovations were immense—Providence, Hartford, Boston turned out to welcome him, calling him the hero of New Orleans and the savior of the Union. Every hamlet, village and town saluted him with twenty-one presidential guns. He was swamped with hospitality; besieged with honors.

Meeting governors, mayors, farmers, workmen, everybody, Old Hickory traveled right on. Equally democratic, he chatted with celebrities and blacksmiths, poets and plumbers, rich and poor, ready to give any American a handclasp. He visited Bunker Hill and heard the great orator, Edward Everett; he stood to attention at a vast military review on Boston Common.

Everybody noticed he was showing his age, then. His crest of hair seemed to've whitened overnight; his voice had cracked a little from speech-making; his step had slowed.

"You can't go on with it." Van Buren was worried. "All this round of dinners and functions would finish any man."

"Shan't I cancel that Harvard dinner?" young Aide-de-camp Quincy asked.

Stubborn as ever in his life, Andy Jackson refused to cancel anything. Not that he cared about some honorary degree, but if the college boys expected him, he'd go.

So at last (it must've seemed to him ironic) he'd conquered Ignorance, for Harvard was making him a Doctor of Laws. The greatest professors in the country, all the big personages in New England would be at the ceremony—all except sour old John Quincy Adams who sulked at home in Braintree and wrote in his diary he couldn't bear to see Harvard's "disgrace in conferring her highest literary honor upon a barbarian who could hardly spell his own name."

Spell his own name? Well, the name of Andrew Jackson was spelled clear across the American sky. All the Harvard scholars lined up to applaud him, and he stood in the college yard, straight and keen-eyed, to shake hands with the whole student body.

Then somebody realized that the President's grip was faltering; lines deepened in his face as the celebration wore on; he winced at each handshake as though the old duel wound had begun to bother his shoulder. Word was passed to stop the handshaking, but Old Hickory wouldn't leave his post until he'd spoken a word to every student and member of the faculty.

That afternoon he had to lie down, but he wouldn't cancel an evening celebration at Salem. As Van Buren and young Quincy had feared, that night Old Hickory's strength gave out, and all at once the President caved in. He forced himself to go on as far as Concord and then, on the old Yankee battle-ground, he collapsed. The doctors said it was from that lung scar Dickinson had given him; they were all afraid he was dying.

Dying? They didn't know Old Hickory, and they didn't know about the crystal bottle. It wasn't empty yet, that bottle. And he was still the President of the United States. His term wasn't over, and there was something mighty important he had to do, and that's the reason, according to the legend, he went on.

14

ONLY A CUP OF MAGIC LEFT

NOW IT'S HISTORIC fact how he rallied his health there at Concord and went back to Washington and kept going. Friends remarked how much older he looked, but the flash remained bright in his eye, and he could still look any man square in the face. In fact, the keen stare he gave to strangers, you might have thought he was looking for somebody.

Nothing could stop him, and it seemed like nothing could kill him. You don't have to take the legend's word for that. While he was resting up back in Washington he went every day to the races, and one afternoon a runaway broke from its jockey and threatened to jump the fence.

Pellmell the crowd fled forty ways as the horse came galloping headlong. Little Van Buren at Andy's elbow was almost knocked flat. Cane upraised, Old Hickory held his ground.

"Get behind me, Van Buren, or that hoss will run you down!"

No horse could run over Old Hickory, and his shout drove that runaway rearing back on its haunches. It saw that look in Old Hickory's eye; it knew if it ran a step farther, Old Hickory would've knocked it dead.

Yes sir, he went right on scrapping like a gladiator, even

though the last months of his administration were comparatively quiet, and he could've taken it easy, maybe gone to Florida. Autumn of 1834 he took another trip across the country. He didn't go to Florida, though.

His coach traveled westward over the jolting Appalachian roads, and this trip he took his time. Some days when he felt extra chipper he'd leave the coach and ride on ahead a ways, moseying by himself along the mountain trails. You can see a long ways from the Blue Ridge, especially in the autumn when the air is high and clean as the smell of pine needles, and where the trail would come out on some aerial panorama, Old Hickory would halt and look off across America, like an equestrian statue.

Far to the north he could see, and miles and miles to the west, but hardly ever he looked south. Pretty soon the coach would come up and he'd ride on again.

It wasn't any triumphal tour, so there isn't much in the history books about it. Officially he was on a vacation. So the legend doesn't make much of it, either; only to say he had that crystal bottle with him in his saddle-bags. And anywhere he'd meet a mountaineer or woodsman on the trail, he'd stop to shake hands with the man, or maybe dismount for a little chat. How's the crops? Getting any deer this season? Things all right in this part of the country?

But he'd look at each man, keen, with those eyes that could see so sharp. Whenever the coach would halt at some cross-roads or settlement or tavern, Old Hickory would scan the impromptu little crowd as if—well, as if he hoped to recognize somebody.

The mountain air braced him; it was doctoring enough

just to be back in this old, familiar country. He didn't need any presidential party to lay out his route for him here. Right quietly and unofficially he crossed the Great Smoky Mountains; no aide-de-camp had to map his road to Nashville, Tennessee.

Anybody'd have said he'd come to the Hermitage to get it ready for his retirement from the White House, for it was pretty well known that he was planning to retire. He didn't stop long at the Hermitage, though. He talked with old Nashville friends, and hobnobbed around the neighborhood, and evenings at twilight he'd stand bareheaded by the mound in the Hermitage garden, communing, just himself with Rachel. Then, quiet as he'd come, he set out on the road going back to Washington.

EVEN THE LEGEND kind of loses track of him on this journey, for the roads were bad and there were detours; his route ambled and took it easy and went roundabout. Seems like he kept to the mountains and woods off the main roads. Reporters didn't hound him; he was traveling almost incognito; only fair for a President to have some liberty and freedom once in a while.

So the legend doesn't follow him too closely, so to speak, but catches up with him one afternoon—you might say, almost unintentionally—where he's stopped to water his horse at a woodsy cross-roads. He was tired and dusty, Old Hickory, and he'd ridden on ahead to do some thinking, but he was pretty near all in; it was one of his bad days.

The rheumatics had him bad, and he dismounted stiffly, swearing at the pain in his joints. Dam-blast that shoulder! Stomach, too. When he coughed it seemed as if a sword was going through him. He had to catch hold of the saddle and support himself by clinging to the horse.

Leaning there, he saw his reflection in the wayside trough: face wrenched and shriveled—hair white as snow. He hadn't licked Time.

"I can't go on!" he groaned to himself. "I can't keep up with it! I'm too confounded sick and old to go on!"

Old? The remedy was there in his saddle-bag, right under his nose. Well, why not? Just one spoonful from the bottle. Just a few crystal drops.

Old Hickory pulled himself upright with a curse. No, by Jerusalem! There wasn't much left in that bottle now, and if he kept using it every time he felt like a nip, it would pretty soon all be gone.

It was pretty tempting, though. A spasm of cramps seized his knees, painful as Indian torture. He could hear his joints cracking as he tried to stiffen up. That bottle had become a habit; it would do him a lot of good right now. Desire for a drink of it seized him like a drug.

"I won't touch it," he swore to himself. "Not a drop!" But then he got to thinking of all the work he had yet to do—a year left in the White House—how a nip from the bottle would make it so much easier.

"One more," he muttered, bending over to massage his knee. "Damnation! I'll always want one more. That's the trouble with this blasted bottled stuff!"

He vowed he wouldn't use it if he aged to a hundred in his tracks. Minute he set his jaw, determined, the desire increased tenfold. All sorts of arguments presented themselves; sweat-beads came out on his forehead; his mouth seemed dryer than the autumn leaves; thirst came over him so powerful his hands were shaking.

He thought of how the doctors had told him to lay off his tobacco. Of how people lately had been helping him by the arm. Of how his son's little girl at the Hermitage had called him grandfather. Grandfather! Hell's tinkling bells, he wasn't ready to be called grandfather! He wasn't ready for any of this!

Well, almost without knowing it, his hand groped into the saddle-bag, for the bottle. He just wanted to look at it, that was all. Only, looking at it made it harder. Sight of that crystal liquor quivered his lips; holding the bottle infected his fingers with palsy.

Old Hickory looked around. Why not? Who'd ever criticize the President? Help him with his work. Give him a chance to finish that last important job he had to do. Be a good thing for the nation. Besides, nobody'd have to know. The cross-roads was deserted in the drowsy afternoon. Across the dusty wagon-ruts, shaded by roadside trees, there was a little, rustic building—a crude, back-country store.

Didn't appear to be anyone around, and the store looked as if its stock didn't consist of much more than corn liquor and a cracker barrel. Old Hickory fairly tusseled with his will. This backwoods storekeeper wouldn't know him. Easy as anything to walk in there and slip just one little drop from his bottle into a good cup of mountain corn.

No, it's not an easy thing to give up your youth, and there in the mountains full of blue sky, squirrels and laurel, even Old Hickory's iron will-power had to bend. Ducking the crystal bottle under his coat, left-hand, so as not to let his right hand know what he was doing, he stumped across to the little backwoods store.

FIRST THING HE noticed was a shabby, long, black, homespun coat on a wall-hook under a shabby, flat-brimmed, backwoods hat. Next thing he noticed was the storekeeper, lounging boots up on the counter, even shabbier. Old Hickory thought if there'd ever been a young man as homespun-looking, it was himself as a lad in Salisbury. Only this feller looked so homespun he might've been spun right out of a spinning wheel.

He was reading a book as Old Hickory walked in, and he was so absorbed in it he went right on reading. Wasn't anybody else in the store, Old Hickory noticed, and this hillbilly didn't seem to care if there was. Old Hickory cleared his throat, annoyed. Then he rapped on the counter, impatient.

"This a store or a library? What you reading young feller, there, that's more important than a customer?"

"Blackstone," without looking up.

"Humph!" snapped Old Hickory, irritated to his boots. "What's a backwoods clodhopper know about Blackstone!"

"Nothing yet," said the young feller amiably, looking up with a pleasant smile. "If I knew about it, I wouldn't have to be studying it."

Well, it was extraordinary to Old Hickory. Rheumatic and impatient to be waited on, he was on the point of telling this lazy yokel off; then irritation stuck in his throat and he found himself looking sharp at this young man.

Not that he was prepossessing in any way. He was lank and over-bony with long wrists and big countrified hands. His hair was long about his ears, and he had a big Adam's apple. But there was something in his homely face—something grave, yet humorous and kindly. Intelligence showed in his forehead, and Old Hickory thought he'd never seen such luminous eyes.

Meeting Old Hickory's glare, the young man's eyes were quickly sympathetic; he swung down his cow boots and dropped the book and stood up in solicitude.

"Sorry, sir—I'm not much of a storekeeper, I reckon. Anything I can do for you? If you ain't feeling well," noticing Andy's wince, "just rest yourself over there on the cracker barrel."

"I'm well enough." Old Hickory jerked back as the youth would've steadied his arm. "It's just I'm a little tuckered from long ridin'. How far would you say it was from here to Washington?"

"I don't right know the exact mileage, but it's a good long ways." The young storekeeper sighed. "Farther than I'd ever get, I expect."

Old Hickory squinted, sharp. "So you'd like to see the capital, would you?"

"Kind of dream of mine," the storekeeper said. "Ever see it?"

"Spend lots of time there," Old Hickory said.

"Jehu!" the storekeeper leaned across the counter, eyes shining. "Ever see the President?"

Old Hickory grunted, "On a number of occasions."

"Hear he's a darned old fool," the young man said. "Stubborn as a mule and hot-headed as a shaker of pepper. But I think he's a great man even if he is a Democrat. I think he's great because he saved the Union."

"Is that so?" Old Hickory glared, ruffed and at the same

time mollified. "So you think the Union's worth saving, do you?"

"Worth saving!" the young storekeeper exclaimed. "What's more worth saving? Money? A bonded life? Money's soon spent, and life is, too, but the United States of America and the liberty and justice it stands for, that'll go on! If I'd been President, I'd done the same as Andy Jackson."

"And what about slavery?" Old Hickory demanded, looking the young storekeeper square in the eye. "You were President, what'd you do about the slavery question?"

Never had Old Hickory seen eyes as luminous; there was a shine as deep and clear in them as the glow in Old Hickory's own.

"Slavery? If I were President I'd try to do away with it! But if I were President, the Union would come first. If I could save the Union without freeing the slaves, I'd have to do it. If I could save it by freeing some and leaving others, I'd have to do that. But if I could save it by freeing all the slaves, that would be best of all. For I agree with the Bible that a house divided against itself cannot stand; and a country divided into free states and slave states cannot long endure."

His voice rang out the words. To Old Hickory, bored by years of speechifying, there seemed to be deep music in the air; the light in the young man's eyes was reflected by the old man's face.

"Son," he put his hand on the homespun shoulder, "did you ever think of going into politics?"

Sobering, the homespun face went rueful. "Talk my head off every time I get a chance, I reckon. Politics? Well,

I'm local post-master. And," his expression clouded apol-
ogetically, "I swan, I've forgot to peddle the mail. Just help
yourself to anything you want in the store, will you? Set
as long as you want. I don't know how long I'll be gone—"

Catching up a mail-pouch, he jogged, long-legged,
out of the door. Old Hickory moved idly about the store,
touching this and that, musing; then he sat smiling to
himself on the cracker barrel. After a while the coach came
along the road and picked him up.

The escort noticed him moving stiffly from rheumatism.

"Do you think we ought to drive throughout the evening,
Mr. President? Don't you want to stay here and rest up?"

"Go on! Go on!" Old Hickory waved his hand, and his
voice was spry and brisk, despite his movements weren't.
"It's all right. I'm through tourin' and vacationing. I've
found what I been lookin' for. Ho! You can drive me right
through to Washington."

The legend has it, he was over his last obstacle.

NOW THAT SCENE with the young backwoods storekeeper is legendary, like the stranger in Florida and the
Fountain of Youth and the wonderful crystal bottle. Ask a
history professor about it, he'd say it was just a yarn because
there's no record to prove that it happened. Well, lots of
things happen in men's lives that aren't recorded. Millions
of things. If historians can't prove they happened, neither
can they prove they didn't.

Old Hickory *did* take that vacation to the Hermitage
while he was President; he *did* mosey over the mountains;
there were plenty of young backwoods storekeepers loll-
ing with their boots up on the counters of little backwoods
stores.

Back in Washington friends observed Old Hickory had aged a lot in recent months. His crest was grandfatherly; the grooves in his cheeks were deep as chop-cuts left by an ax; there were times when he was almost feeble. But the trip West seemed to have done him a lot of good. A sort of confident contentment had come to him. Always soldierly, in his general's uniform with its proud, high collar he appeared at military functions like the veteran of all the wars of the U.S.A. Always gallant, in his courtly black—top hat, stick and trousers that fastened under the instep—he made the picture of a courteous and kindly old aristocrat, President of the United States, America's First Gentleman.

He had mellowed like a bottle of rare old wine. He'd made friends with Tom Benton and other enemies; now he even offered his hand to Winfield Scott. Don't believe he was doddering and senile, though. Personal enemies he forgave, but never a cur who'd maligned Rachel. Nor any traitor who'd threatened the Union. Long as he lived he'd regret he hadn't shot Henry Clay. Until he died he'd regret he hadn't hanged John C. Calhoun.

But things were pretty quiet his last year in the White House; the administration ran pretty smoothly. Aside from coaching Van Buren to take over the office, and a Seminole uprising in the Everglades, and putting the finishing touches on Banker Nicholas Biddle, and settling an inconsequential squabble with the King of France, there wasn't much for Old Hickory to do. Time ran swiftly now, like sand running out of a glass.

No faster than that, though. You couldn't push Old Hickory before his time. A big, black-whiskered lunatic tried. Having attended a state funeral, Andy was crossing the Capitol rotunda, head bowed in memory of his friend, feeling low in his mind. He never expected the heir to the throne of England was around. The man with the black whiskers looked the part, too. Leaping out of the crowd with a wild yell, he fired two pistols at the President, point blank.

Clickety-clack!

Like that.

Old duelist that he was, Old Hickory never flinched. Straight at the whiskered assassin he threw himself, shattering his cane across the man's crazy head. The stick was half in splinters before Old Hickory realized both guns, right under his nose, had misfired. Both guns! No sir, there wasn't any killing of Old Hickory.

Protesting that President Jackson had robbed him of the British crown, the maniac was led off to an asylum. Gunsmiths later testified that the madman's pistols were in perfect condition and there was no earthly reason why they should've squibbed. No earthly reason? But there it is, black and white, in the record. A lot of things happened in Andrew Jackson's life you'd hardly call "earthly." Check with any historian who might call this Fountain-of-Youth legend improbable.

AS WHEN OLD Hickory had stepped into the White House with a blaze of fury, he went out with a blaze of glory; and right at the end he gave another White House party. It wasn't quite as wild as his inaugural ball, but as a President's farewell party it was unique in American History. You can see Old Hickory hadn't lost his prankish sense of humor. You can imagine him chuckling like a boy. Maybe, too, there was more than mischief behind the twinkle in his eye—he was giving America a final lesson in Democracy.

Anyway the public was invited, high and low, and hundreds of people came. White House attendants opened the doors; diplomats and draymen, dowagers and dressmakers, people who rode in varnished carriages and people who drove mule teams jostled in. There at the head of the banquet table, erect as a ramrod, stood the black-coated, white-crested old warrior, Andrew Jackson, retiring President of the United States, his eyes bright as blue chuckles. And there, monumental on the banquet table, golden and glorious, the only edible thing in sight, towered a huge, round, staggering half-ton cheese!

Shouting in hilarity, the crowd fell to like a swarm of mice, digging in with knives, forks, spoons, fingers. Yes sir, that was Old Hickory's historic farewell party. No matter how you sliced it, it was still a piece of cheese; no matter how dignified you nibbled or how loud you gobbled, it was a piece of cheese still. Nobody could snoot anybody at that party. Cheese is a great leveler.

A few days later, when the atmosphere was cleared, Old Hickory turned the White House over to its new President, Martin Van Buren.

Then, bent with medals and years, he went home to the Hermitage to wait.

15

HOME TO THE HERMITAGE

IN A HEARTH-SIDE rocker? Not Old Hickory. He got home with exactly ninety dollars in his pocket, and there were bills to pay. His plantation had gone seedy in his absence; his racing stable needed attention; everything wanted doing, for the year after his vacation visit the Hermitage had suffered a bad fire.

Busy as he was, the years passed, swifter than days, and now that he was *Old* Hickory the time didn't seem long. Time goes fast when you're over seventy. All at once you're seventy-eight.

The calendar said 1845, and Old Hickory was seventy-eight, and the doctors that spring said he was dying, but Old Hickory didn't mind. They'd said he was dying when he was a boy with smallpox back in that Revolutionary War prison camp. They'd said he was dying when he was wounded by Charles Dickinson; when he was shot up by the Benton Brothers; when he was doubled up on the march to New Orleans; when his legs gave out at Concord.

This time it looked like the real thing—eyesight, lungs, legs, everything giving out, as if all those strenuous gun-fights and forced marches were catching up with him at last. But he'd faced death too often on the battlefield and field of honor to fear it now. Besides, that's what he'd come home for.

He'd made out his will; he'd left the nation in good hands; he'd done his best about all the obstacles. So one Sunday in June when it tapped him on the shoulder, he said goodbye to the family at his bedside, and was ready to go.

All his friends had been there to wish him bon voyage— Peggy and John Eaton, Ike Hill, Major Lewis and a host of others. Good neighbors thronged the Hermitage yard; as the word passed of Old Hickory's going, people came from near and far. Way down the cornfield, Darkies sang that mournful song; stable boys and household servants wept on the veranda; folks stood at the gate with their hats off, eyes on the old soldier's window, waiting for the flag to float half-mast.

Gen'l Sam Houston, coming all the way from the Lone Star State with his son to see his old commander, broke down and sobbed, thinking he'd arrived late. Son by the hand, he tiptoed up to Old Hickory's room, and told the little boy never to forget he'd seen the face of Andrew Jackson. The little boy thought Andrew Jackson was asleep.

So history tells us that Old Hickory died June 8, 1845 at six o'clock of the evening. But the legend has it a little differently.

Who knows at what exact moment a man dies? Doctors don't know, and historians don't know. To begin with, death is a stickler of a word to define; so we say it's the passing of the soul from the body. But who knows when that takes place? who ever saw it pass? *Death does not take place suddenly and sharply, but more or less gradually,* writes a modern scientist on the subject. *By the very nature of the phenomenon there can be no exact moment at which death can be said to occur.* No, there's a borderline of seconds, perhaps minutes; the heart may have stopped, but the soul or will or personality or whatever you may call it, is still there.

History forgot about that.

WELL, THEN, THE legend has it that after the blinds were drawn and the last member of the family had tiptoed out, Old Hickory, so to speak, was still there. Being an old frontiersman, he'd naturally pause a moment to scan the prospect before going over an unknown border, especially when he might be rushing into a place where angels feared to tread.

It was pretty misty over that border, too, and he was too good a fighter to go scouting off before he got some bearings. And being a fighting man, his will wasn't quite ready to go. A little flare of stubbornness rose up in him, and he sort of held back just to show he was Scotch-Irish and American and not doing anything abjectly or meekly.

He was glad they'd left him alone by himself for a moment. It was kind of pleasant to lie there in the dusk-quiet room with the darkies singing outside and voices coming up from the veranda; gave him a chance for a last look around. His boots and stick and old cocked hat—he was sorry he couldn't take them with him.

Then while he was lying there wondering whether he'd walk or ride or there'd be guides on hand to meet him, he realized there was someone there in the room. Some visitor who'd tiptoed in for a look at him. Old Hickory glared across the bedstead, resentful of the intrusion.

It was dusky in the room with the blinds down and evening outside; Old Hickory's squint couldn't make out the visitor very well, except it was a man in fringed buckskin with long hair and a Yankee chin-beard and a wide-brimmed frontiersman's hat and the look of a fellow who'd been places and traveled far. First glance, Old Hickory thought it was Sam Houston; but no, Sam Houston hadn't arrived at the Hermitage yet.

"General Jackson! General Jackson!" says the figure, soft, as though not wanting to disturb someone who may not be awake.

Old Hickory sat bolt upright with an exclamation. "So it's you! The stranger I met in Florida! By gum, I always thought I'd see you again some time!"

Yes sir, it was the stranger Andy'd met years ago in the Florida wilderness, the traveler who'd given his name as Brother Somebody or Doctor Somebody or Uncle Somebody, the fellow who'd told Andy about the Fountain of Youth and given him that crystal bottle. Old Hickory had never forgotten the man's voice; right off, he recognized that strange air of distinction.

"Heard you was dying," the shadowy figure said quietly. "Didn't believe it. Thought I'd drop in and see."

"Kind of you," Old Hickory acknowledged, though not without a trace of asperity at having his last moments disturbed, particularly by a stranger. Still, he had to admit he owed this stranger a lot, for that bottle of Fountain water had had a big influence on his life; and he started to thank the man. NOW AT THIS point there's two versions to the legend. There're different versions to legends same as there's different versions to history; generally speaking, you accept the one that favors your viewpoint or whichever side you're on.

Anyway, the first version has it that the man at Old Hickory's death-bed wouldn't accept Old Hickory's thanks.

"Please, General Jackson," says he, taking off his hat to wheel it in his fingers. "Don't thank me, please. I—there's something I got to tell you. That's why," he looked around uneasily, "I waited till the others had gone, an' sneaked up here so I could have a word with you alone."

"Eh? Something to tell me?" Old Hickory peered.

"Well, it's this way," says the stranger, lowering his eyes. "I—I couldn't have it on my conscience—after you'd gone. You been such a great man and such a great President— saving the Union an' all. I just couldn't keep that five dollars you gave me."

"Five dollars?" Old Hickory snapped. "Five dollars?"

"Honest, General Jackson, ever since that day I've felt bad. An' lately, since I've heard the Hermitage was nearly bankrupt and your friends been subscribing money. I read in the paper how the government revoked that fine you once had to pay in New Orleans and how James K. Polk sent you the money back with interest. I—I didn't know you was almost broke. So I've come to return that money you gave me for that—that fake bottle of Florida water."

"Fake?" Old Hickory stared. "What's that you say?"

Eyes down, the stranger fiddled with his hat. " 'Twan't nothin' but well water, really. Well water with a dash of fermented juniper juice. Y'see, I—" the man was shame-faced, "I'm nothin' but a medicine doctor, that's all. Travel all about the country sellin' that bottled water. That Fountain of Youth story—that's just a sales talk I give. Of course, the juniper juice gives you a little pick-up. But it wasn't from any fountain. When I met you down there in Florida, I—I was lookin' for an Indian to hire for a medicine show."

"Now," says Old Hickory, "I'll be horn-swoggled!" (only he didn't say horn-swoggled.)

"Yes," says the stranger, nodding. "When I come on you there near Pensacola, sick like you were, I couldn't resist making a sale." Then he raised his head hopefully, meeting Old Hickory's fierce glance. "But it *did* seem to pick you up at the time. You never know about medicine. Why, sometimes, people I've told tall stories to, it actually seems to work. They believe me—they've got faith enough—and, well, they *are* younger. After all, ain't it the truth? A man's only as old as he *thinks* he is!"

And that's one version of the legend: that the buck-skinned traveler Old Hickory met in Florida was nothing but a vagabond medicine doctor, and that crystal bottle was nothing but juice-spiked well water.

You can imagine, too, Old Hickory must've been sore. Like as not he'd make a grab for his stick to give that sharpster a good, sound caning. Then he'd remember the circumstances and where he was, and how the fellow had come all this way to return the money. Nothing Old Hickory admired so much as an honest man.

And while his temper cooled down, he'd recall how that crystal bottle had bucked him up, how it had made him feel younger, a man was only as old as he believed himself to be. In the end, Old Hickory must've laughed.

Mind you, all this is only legendary, but it's a version that appeals to realists who want explanations for things and like their mysteries solved. As a legend it *could* have happened.

Then there's the second version. Maybe you'll like it better....

16

FINAL ORDERS, GENERAL

THE SECOND VERSION has it that the stranger at Old
Hickory's death-bed waved his thanks away. "Don't thank
me, General Jackson. Thank God for the chance that put
the Fountain of Youth in America. But why'd you stop
using it?" Peering across the bed to the table littered with
medicine bottles. "Why didn't you follow the instructions
I gave you, and keep going?"

"Keep going?" says Old Hickory, rearing up. "A man's
a fool who wants to keep going longer than his regular
appointed years. There's a time for spring and there's a time
for harvest, so's the next crop can have its chance to come
along. I didn't see any reason to hang around beyond my
time, and right now I'm on my way."

"The bottle! The crystal bottle!" The stranger rummaged,
excited as a doctor, on the littered medicine table. "Don't
tell me you lost the taste."

"Lost it when Rachel died," Old Hickory nodded flatly.
"Kept using it afterward out of duty, because I still had a
lot to do. There were a lot of obstacles around, and I figured
youth is the thing that gets you out conquering obstacles. Humph!" he paused, nettled at the thought. "That's
all I wanted it for—give me time and vim to finish off

those obstacles. But I found out something about obstacles, doctor—brother—what'd you say your name was?"

The stranger looked up to speak.

"No matter," Old Hickory went on impatiently. "As I was saying, I found out something. What? Why, there'd always be obstacles—always and all the time. You can't get rid of them; you can't do away with them; you can't demolish them if you live to be ten thousand."

"Interesting observation." The stranger's manner was calm and soothing, a little like a father talking down to a child.

"It's true!" Old Hickory flared, nettled by the other's bedside manner, yet somehow compelled to talk. He'd been wanting to get this off his chest for a considerable time, for it was a conviction that had been growing in him.

"Take poverty." He waved his hand. "When I was a lad it was the first thing I wanted to conquer. Eh? Well, in middle life I thought I had it licked. Just when I did, I signed a note for a friend. The note went blooey—took all my money to pay it of! Up pops poverty again."

Old Hickory shook his head. "But I don't mean only that. I mean, suppose you did get all the money you wanted. Then what? Why, you'd just feel bad about all the other people who were poor. Rich enough, you'd give all your money away. Wouldn't be enough to go around, though.

"And then ignorance, for example. I thought I'd conquered an education. Rats! I even got one of these college degrees from Harvard. And I still can't spell."

Old Hickory scratched his white crest angrily. "Then there's temper. I can feel mine bilin' up in me now. Just that I got one makes me mad. Thought I'd conquered it a dozen times; up it would come again—bang! I got so I could keep it, but I *had* it just the same. Bound to break out one way or another, like that fool time I challenged Winfield Scott.

"And that was the way with all those obstacles," Old Hickory went on, hot under the collar thinking about it. "Do you think you can ever lick such things as scandal and hypocrisy and snobbery? Look at the South right now. Supposed to be genteel and civilized, church people and all. Hypocrites!

"Loafin' along on the labor of a couple of million sweating blacks, yet singin' hymns on Sunday and callin' themselves Christian. Some of the Yankees ain't much better—skinflints grindin' the workers in their factories fourteen hours a day, but right up in the front pew every Sabbath, like camels trying to go to Heaven through the needle's eye.

"And snobbery," Old Hickory shook his fist, warmed up. "This country supposed to be a Democracy—there's as much snobbery in some of these people as in the Court of St. James. Holler about the Tories and they're Tories themselves, except their fathers likely were farmers an' shirt-sleeved woodsmen an' workmen."

OLD HICKORY GLARED fiercely at the buckskinned stranger with the poetic hair and Yankee chin-whisker. "Scandal? Try to lick *that* some time! Me, I've caned it and shot at it and dueled it for fifty years. I reckon there's folks who'll believe the worst of me so long as I'm remembered—yes, and about Rachel!"

Old Hickory broke off, choking, enraged by the memory. Then, as the stranger started to speak, he burst out, "As for obstacles to Democracy, the traitors in this country right now are a dime a dozen. Snakes underground. Snakes in the grass. I don't mean foreign agents—they're to be expected always. I mean people who call themselves American and don't give a damn for this country.

"Hell!" Old Hickory rose up on the bed. "You'll always have to fight for liberty and freedom. There'll always be those obstacles to Democracy and the Union. Slavery'll be put down, and something else will come up."

Shadows were gathering in the darkened room, but somehow he could see more clearly all the time. The stranger at the bedside, quietly sympathetic, waiting for him to finish, was smiling. There was something odd about this stranger who had a pilgrim name—or had he called himself Johnny Appleseed, or was it Samuel?

Despite his travel-stained buckskin, he had a dignity about him, the look of a man who knew a lot and was going places; but his expression, combining understanding and a humorous twinkle, puzzled Old Hickory. Old Hickory felt he was talking to someone with a lot of prestige. He didn't bother to puzzle about it, though.

Warmed up to his subject, he concluded irritably, "So what's the use thinking you can put an end to obstacles, I'd like to know—except you do all you can in a lifetime and let it go at that? That's what I learned about 'em, see? You can't put an end to them. Knock one down and another pops up in its place. Anyway, that's why I gave away the crystal bottle."

"Gave it away?" exclaimed the stranger. "Who to?"

"Backwoods post-master runnin' some country store. Don't even know his name. But the minute I saw him I could tell he was the man to pass it on to. Huh!" Old

Hickory gestured. "I slipped a little to Martin Van Buren, succeeding me in the White House, but I wasn't sure he should stay there too long, and the Little Magician had plenty of his own in him, anyway.

"Then I set out lookin'—Philadelphia, New York, New England—up that way. Talked to big-wigs and celebrities and everybody including the Harvard boys. They didn't seem quite what I wanted, so I thought I'd try the western part of the country. This post-master had the look, so I gave the bottle to him. Slipped it into the pocket of his coat when he stepped out."

Old Hickory chuckled. "Wrote instructions how he should use it. Hope he understands. He won't be storekeepin' long there in Sangamon County. The Union'll need a man like him, and I only wish there'd been more in the bottle."

"YOU DID THAT?" asked the stranger, sweeping off his hat. "You gave that bottle from the Fountain of Youth away?"

"Got old quick enough afterward," Old Hickory snapped. "It was hard work goin' on without Rachel. Besides, I'd lived long enough to find out someone else ought to have a chance."

"Andy," says the stranger, "you never got old at all. Right now you're seventy-eight years young. Don't you see?" He looked at Andy with shining eyes. "It's hurdling obstacles that develops great men. That's what obstacles are for. And only a young man would be as gallant about obstacles as you. Only a young man would love so bravely and long. Only a young man would give away his youth for his country. Why, you've licked everything—even Time!"

"You aren't dying, Andy," the stranger reached out his

hand. "You're not old enough. You're just getting started. Long as there's a United States of America, you'll be there around the White House, in the Army, in the Department of State. Long as there's a United States of America folks will give you birthday parties and talk of you on Election Day. As long as there's a U.S.A. you'll live, and as long as there's Democracy, you'll never die."

His hand clasped Andy's in a mighty shake. "Let's go, boy. You're comin' along with me. There's a welcoming dinner all set up. You'll find most of the Dirty Shirts on hand with Rachel at the head of the table. It'll be a zimblinger of a party. Sam Adams and John Hancock and Long Tom Jefferson and Jimmie Madison—all the boys will be there. George Washington's staging a big military review."

"Any races?" Old Hickory said, dazzled. "I always did regret I never owned a horse that could beat Jesse Haynie's favorite, Maria."

"Races all day," was the promise. "Fancy dress ball at night. Ben Franklin's head of the entertainment committee."

Andy Jackson couldn't resist that. Hand in the stranger's, he jumped up, ready to go. But the stranger in buckskin still baffled him—the Southern voice and the Yankee chin-whisker, the frontier boots and the Pilgrim-cut hair.

"But who are you?" he asked. "I—I didn't get the name."

The other's eyes twinkled. "You'll know me in my full dress costume tonight. Striped trousers. Blue coat. Vest all covered with stars. Sure," he linked arms with Andy Jackson as Andy's eyes widened. "I'm your Uncle Samuel."

A LEGEND? IT was said at the start that's what this story was. Something based on historical fact, and, unlike a fairy tale, apt to have a lot of truth in it. If you can't believe Andy Jackson drank water from the Fountain of Youth, that's up to you. But if you can't believe he never died, go to Washington his next birthday and attend the Jackson Day Dinner.

They always have a portrait of him at the head of the table, and some say that when the formal speeches get started and five-dollar cigars get smoking up the banquet table, if you look close enough you can see that portrait give a one-eyed wink. Those who've seen it don't know if it's a scoffish wink or a skeptical wink or a wink of plain amusement.

Anyway, as long as there's Democracy, Andrew Jackson will live.

And *that's* no legend.